Daddy's
Girl

Daddy's Girl

SHARON MULROONEY

POOLBEG

Published 2003
Poolbeg Press Ltd.
123 Grange Hill, Baldoyle,
Dublin 13, Ireland
Email: poolbeg@poolbeg.com

1 3 5 7 9 10 8 6 4 2

A catalogue record for this book is available from the British Library.

ISBN 1-84223-124-3

Typeset by Patricia Hope in Palatino 10/14
Printed by
Litografia Rosés S.A., Spain

www.poolbeg.com

About the Author

Sharon Mulrooney was born in Galway, and moved to London when she graduated in 1987.

'If you want to do Hotel Management because you're interested in people, go and get a job as a bus driver,' one of her lecturers said on her first day at college.

Without a driving licence, Human Resources was the next best thing. After ten years of working in hotels, the music business and the drinks industry, Sharon left corporate life, and now juggles working part-time with writing and looking after her two children.

Acknowledgements

I would like to thank Colin for sharing my big dream as well as my little ones, and working hard to make them come true.

Thanks to Mom and Dad for lots of things, but especially for making me look up words in the dictionary, and giving me the confidence to use them.

Ros Edwards, thank you for believing in me, for wielding your pencil with impunity and for offering your shoulder when it was needed.

To Louise Voss and Claire Harcup, thanks for your advice, encouragement, ideas and, most of all, for being 'my writing friends'.

To Paul Somers,
for giving me the freedom to succeed.

Chapter One

They were already laughing when the condom fell off. Somehow, when it did, the wrinkled piece of soggy rubber seemed to be hilarious, and Maria giggled helplessly. She snuggled up to Joe and they fell asleep. They were woken at eleven o'clock by the strident ringing of the doorbell. They looked at each other in a half-awake state, curious about who was at the door, but not inclined to get up and answer it. Suddenly the letterbox flapped, and a voice yodelled, 'Yoohoo, Joe darling, are you not up yet?'

'Oh my God!' he shot upright in the bed. 'It's Mum! Quick, you've got to hide!'

Before Maria knew it, she was standing in the bath, hidden behind the shower curtain, her beautiful green velvet dress and sexy black underwear bundled in her arms, and her feet in a puddle of water.

Joe yelled, 'Just a minute, Mum!' and pulling on his

tracksuit bottoms he opened the front door of the flat.

'Hello, love.' His mother kissed his cheek and wrinkled her nose at the pungent garlic odour mixed with stale cigarette smoke and alcohol on his breath.

'You were out late last night, I gather,' she said with slight distaste, making her way into the kitchen.

'It was the Medical School Ball,' he muttered.

'Oh, was it any good? Any nice girls there?' she asked coyly.

'It was a great night, but I went with a gang of the lads.' He flicked the switch on the electric kettle, and avoided looking at her.

'Where's Mike this morning? I suppose he's already up and in the library, studying?' Mrs Shaw enquired. She liked Mike. He seemed like a nice lad, and a good influence on Joe.

'I haven't seen him this morning.' They had struck a deal that Mike would steer clear last night, and stay at Michelle's place.

His mother raided the breadbin, was disappointed with the sad crust of wholemeal bread, and then delved into one of her shopping bags.

'I brought some doughnuts. I'm down in Galway for the day with Rita Duffy. I said I'd help her to find an outfit for her daughter's wedding.'

'That's nice.' Joe scratched his head and tried to shake it clear.

'Then I thought I'd pop in here for elevenses with you.'

'Mmm.' He sipped his coffee gratefully.

'Although it looks more like breakfast for you.'

Joe sank his teeth into the jam doughnut, and his salivary glands leapt into action as the tart flavour of the raspberry jam hit his tongue. He stood up and filled a stolen Guinness pint-glass with water from the tap and drank it in one go.

'Did you have a lot to drink?' His mother looked up at him doubtfully. He was a bit pale. Was that a trace of a lipstick-mark on his neck?

'A fair bit. It is the big social event of the year, you know.'

'I'm not disapproving, Joe. You're a student. You have to have a social life. But at the same time, I'd hate if it affected your studying. The exams are coming up soon . . .'

'I know, Mum. Don't worry. I'll be fine,' he said absently. Why did she have to pick this morning, of all days, to 'pop in'?

She looked at her watch. 'I must use your loo, and then I'm off. I said I'd meet Rita for lunch'.

She missed Joe's look of alarm as she bustled off to the bathroom.

Maria heard the bathroom door opening, and froze. She had managed to manoeuvre herself into her underwear, but she needed help for the dress. Standing in a black Wonderbra, G-string and sheer black pull-ups, she wondered whether it would be better for Mrs. Shaw to swish back the curtain and discover her naked,

3

rather than kitted out like a playgirl. Her face burned. She had to cross her legs when she heard the tinkling sound of pee, and she exhaled gratefully and took another deep breath concealed by the sound of the toilet flushing. She started to shiver uncontrollably and inched away from the shower curtain so that she wouldn't make it rustle. Joe's mother hummed as she washed her hands, touched up her lipstick and patted her hair.

The door closed and Maria nearly collapsed to her knees in the bath. The bottom of her dress was trailing in the pool of water and some bizarre capillary action in the fabric had made a dark stain soak right up the length of the dress. At last, she heard the front door opening again and had one leg over the side of the bath when she heard Mrs Shaw's parting comment.

'I'm glad you're not involved with anyone, Joe. You have a lot of work to do, and there's plenty of time for girls when you're qualified.'

Joe's murmured response was lost in the rustling of the shower curtain. Maria sat on the loo, her first doubts about Joe creeping into her mind.

Joe yelled, 'She's gone,' through the bathroom door. 'Do you want a coffee?'

'Yes, please,' she said, carrying the dress over her arm. It was soaking wet. 'Joe, can I borrow some clothes off you? My dress is soaked.'

'Sure, help yourself.'

She splashed her face with cold water and looked

4

closely at her bloodshot eyes. What a night! She had drunk three cocktails before the meal, then wine, champagne and had finished off with Baileys. She patted her face dry with loo-roll. She wouldn't touch the towels that were hanging on the back of the door. They looked like they hadn't been washed since the beginning of the term.

When Maria came into the kitchen in Joe's Gap khakis, cinched at the waist with his brown belt, and a big white shirt with the sleeves rolled up, he thought she had never looked so gorgeous.

'You should always wear guy's clothes – you look great.' He took her in his arms and kissed the top of her head.

'Thanks.' She smiled up at him. 'Where's that coffee?'

'Sorry about Mum coming.' Joe was gulping down another pint of water with two Solpadeine tablets.

'It's OK. How is she?' Maria didn't know why she asked. She had never met the woman, and was unlikely to, judging by what she had overheard.

'Fine. She's down shopping for the day.' He sounded a bit sheepish, but she couldn't be sure. Was he ashamed of her? Was she not good enough for his mother?

Joe looked across the table at Maria. He would have loved to tell his mother about her, but he couldn't face the interrogation. What did her father do? Where did she come from? What were her ambitions? For that, read, 'Would she distract him from his study? Would she appreciate what kind of family she would be marrying into? Would she be a good doctor's wife?' Maria would hate being questioned, and it was a bit too soon for all that anyway, so it was easier to pretend that Maria didn't exist.

Maria looked into his hazel eyes, then at his sandy tousled hair sticking up, full of wax from last night, a little blotch of red jam smeared on his cheek, and she thought, if I can find him attractive with bad breath, morning stubble and a hangover, this must be the real thing. She smiled at him, and he smiled back, relieved. She obviously hadn't heard his mother's comment.

Pauline laughed like mad when Maria told her the story.

'But wouldn't it bother you if your man didn't tell his mother that he was seeing you?' Maria asked, wringing out her hand-washing in the kitchen sink.

Pauline snorted. 'Chance would be a fine thing. I have to find a man first, and then I'll worry about whether he tells his mam. I wouldn't worry about it, seriously, Maria.'

'But it's been a year.' That was ages. More than long enough to know whether she met the mother's criteria. 'I love him, Pauline, and I can't imagine being with anyone else. What if I'm never going to be good enough for his mam?'

Pauline sighed, and Maria wanted to kick herself. She'd done it again. Pauline didn't even have a man, and here she was, wittering on about her insecurities.

'He's a lovely guy, Maria. The good ones are always real Mammy's boys. He'll introduce you when he's good and ready. Just live for the moment, as they say.'

'You're dead right. Did I tell you he gave me an orchid last night, as a buttonhole? It reminded me of our Debs. Do you remember that?'

'Yeah, I took Larry, who went off to be a priest. Trust me to pick that one! Do you remember the party back at Geraldine's house afterwards?'

Maria laughed. 'Her mam was on patrol, so me and Martin O'Dowd went out the back and had a good snog on the garden bench.'

'There was a queue for that bench, wasn't there? Even I got a snog that night!'

Pauline was always putting herself down, and sometimes Maria found that frustrating. Ever since school, Pauline had lacked the confidence to make herself look really nice. Maria was always lending her things and showing her hairstyles in magazines. If Pauline would only do something with her hair, and lose some weight, she would be really attractive. She had a great smile, huge eyes and fantastic skin. But Maria didn't want to push it too far and hurt Pauline's feelings. She sloshed her woollen jumpers and silky underwear into a bucket and nudged open the back door with her bum.

Pauline watched Maria hanging the clothes on the line and sighed. Maria had a great figure and even with a hangover and her hair all frizzy, she looked fantastic.

What other students hand-washed their clothes, not because they were too lazy to go down to the laundrette at the bottom of the hill, but because the clothes were wool and silk? Maria had always had style, since she was about nine years old. She had a feather-cut hairstyle and French polo necks long before anyone else in her class. Pauline buttered another piece of toast and sipped her tea. It didn't matter, she told herself. She was going to be a successful lawyer with no time to waste on men.

Chapter Two

Maria looked around at all the people in the huge chemist's shop, and then at the girl behind the counter. Relieved that she didn't recognise anyone, she went to pay. Her heart was pounding. She had a flashback to the first time she had bought tampons, when she was thirteen. Why her mother couldn't just get an extra packet with the weekly shopping, she did not know. She must have thought there was some rite of passage to be completed by being totally mortified in the village shop.

'That's late,' she could see Mrs Mahoney thinking, as she put them in a brown-paper bag. 'It's a wonder she didn't come on earlier, like her big sister Aileen.'

She had smiled meaningfully at Maria, as if to welcome her into the secret world of womanhood. Maria could still remember the musty mothball smell of the shop.

Now she wilted under the raised eyebrow of the white-coated assistant with the pancake make-up, who had automatically checked her wedding finger and found it lacking. She looked Maria up and down, as if trying to memorise her face, so she could tell someone.

The Thought Police. The Sex Police, more like. Honestly, it was like being in Saudi Arabia or somewhere, waiting for the Mukhabarat to come swirling in to haul her away at the point of a sword. Sex was still the worst sin, for some people. Probably the ones who weren't getting any. No, getting pregnant was worse. That meant you were stupid as well as a slag.

She stuffed the see-through plastic bag into her rucksack with the free Clarins gift for spending more than ten pounds, and walked up the hill towards Tirellan Heights. The estate of three-bedroom semi-detached houses was populated by hundreds of students and young families. Tricycles abandoned on front lawns, the smell of fish fingers and chips cooking, and the screeching of children from upstairs windows made Maria shudder.

They said you could miss your period from stress. The exams were coming up, so maybe that was it.

She sneaked upstairs to her bedroom. She could hear Pauline humming in the kitchen. Orla was probably studying manically in the library and wouldn't be back for hours. Maria sat on the bed, her head throbbing.

Maybe she should wait another few days? She looked again at the Wallace and Gromit calendar on the wall over her desk. Her feeble effort at a revision plan was scribbled over the last six weeks, but no capital 'P' intruded amongst the history and politics study sessions. She sighed. She had to do it now. With a towel draped over her arm, she raced into the bathroom, clutching the blue and white packet.

Joe was feeling guilty. He was kayaking down the river with Mike when he should be studying. He tried reciting the symptoms and treatment of all the diseases he could remember. But he could only think of the really gross ones that he and Mike had joked about when they were in first year. Like furunculosis, where black bread mould grows in the ear, and eyeworm, where this African worm migrates out through the eyeball. It was like playing a video of Friday the Thirteenth in his head. Really likely to come up as an exam question. It was no good – the guilt wouldn't go away.

Finally, he signalled to his flatmate that he wanted to go ashore. They paddled back to the university boathouse, as a light drizzle began to fall. No one else was around, and the racks of shabby upturned kayaks and buoyancy aids already looked resigned to being abandoned for another summer.

'So much for exam weather,' said Mike. 'Do you remember studying for the Leaving Cert? It was always roasting, and everyone else would be off outside, having a great time for themselves?'

11

'Yeah,' said Joe, miserably, 'but they probably weren't trying to get the points to study medicine.'

Mike laughed. 'Lucky them. Another three years is an awful long time to be stuck at it.'

He pulled off his wetsuit and stretched. His long legs were always cramped after a paddle.

'Still, it'll be worth it,' said Joe, 'when we're consultants. We can do a few hours in our rooms, a bit of surgery and then go off home in our big cars. All the women will be chasing after us.'

'What are you on about? If I had Maria, I wouldn't be worrying about any other women.'

Mike could never understand what the women saw in Joe, who was a skinny-looking fella with freckles and mousy hair. Mike himself was tall, broad-shouldered and dark-haired – supposed to be the classic tall-dark-and-handsome, but he rarely got past the first date.

'Well, you never know, we've only been going out this year – it might not last.'

Mike snorted, 'If I was you, I'd make damn sure it lasted.'

The truth was, Joe was surprised that Maria hadn't broken it off already, with all the fellas after her. Sometimes when they were out together on a Thursday night in Salthill, he wanted to just tell her to dance with them, to go with them. He couldn't stand the tension of wondering when she would find someone else and break it off with him. He loved Maria's long dark hair, and her big brown eyes with the curling lashes. Most of

12

all, he loved her body; slim and sensuous. She walked like a model, even in the baggy jeans and shirt that she had on the morning his mother came around. And she smelled so good. He got a hard-on just thinking about her, and he quickly turned his back and pulled on his jeans so that Mike wouldn't see.

The double blue line stared back at Maria as she sat on the toilet, not blinking. Her eyes stung and filled up with tears. A spider was making a web on the skirting-board beside her foot, and she didn't even feel the urge to jump off the loo and scream for Pauline to come and get rid of it.

How would she tell Joe? She couldn't. She had to. It was his as well.

It.

It was growing inside her now, probably the size of a pea. How could something the size of a pea be so scary?

Pauline rattled the handle of the bathroom door.

'Are you nearly finished, Maria? You've been in there for ages. I want to wash my hair for tonight.'

'Sorry,' said Maria, trying to sound cheerful. 'I'll be two secs.'

Secs. Sex. A few secs of sex, she thought as she washed her hands and looked in the mirror. She splashed her blotchy face and looked again at the blue line on the plastic stick, winking at her, mocking her.

'Well, that's another nice mess you've got me into,' she said in her best Oliver Hardy voice. She scratched her head in the mirror. 'And just what do you propose to do about it, Laurel?'

'Maria?'

'Sorry.'

She unlocked the door, and Pauline saw her puffy eyes.

'Are you OK? Sorry, I didn't mean to rush you.'

'Fine,' Maria said as she closed her bedroom door and threw her towel on the bed.

Pauline washed her hair, wondering if Maria had had another argument with Joe. He was always getting insecure and uptight when other men looked at her. No matter what Maria said, he didn't believe she wasn't interested in the other guys. Pauline couldn't see Joe's attraction anyway – too short, and a little bit too much of the strong silent type. Although he was very intelligent and interesting to talk to. Now Mike was a different story. She wouldn't kick him out of bed for eating crisps. Not that she had any chance. He had only been going out with Michelle, who was the complete opposite of Pauline in every way, for a few weeks. She looked at her pudgy face and lank brown hair in the mirror.

It was one of those mirrors that make you look fat, even on the days when you feel a bit thinner. She sighed and wrapped a towel around her hair, tight enough to give her a temporary face-lift. She felt a bit better, until she turned her head sideways. The double chin was undiminished. She must do a bit of dieting or something, she told herself for the umpteenth time.

14

With the towel still wrapped around her head, Pauline knocked on Maria's door and opened it. 'Are you all right?'

When Maria turned around, her face was red, and a tear was running down her cheek. 'No, Pauline. Jesus, I don't know what to do.'

She reached behind Pauline and pushed the door closed. All she needed was for Miss Pious Knickers to overhear her. She had to tell someone, and Pauline was her best friend. Orla would only look down her nose and wonder how anyone could be so stupid.

'What is it?' Then Pauline saw the blue packet clenched in Maria's hand. 'You're not!'

'I am.'

'Oh, no. God, Maria, how did it happen?' Drunken snogging was as far as she had ever got. Even when they were drunk, guys didn't exactly queue up to get her into bed.

'How do you think?' Maria couldn't help giggling.

'When? I mean, how far gone are you?' Pauline ran her eye down Maria's slim figure.

'I think about six weeks. I'm not sure how you work it out, exactly.'

Pauline sat on the edge of the bed, wringing her hands like a turbaned medium.

'What are you going to do?' .

'I'm going to talk to Joe tonight, but I'll probably have to go to England . . .'

'You would not!' Pauline's mouth hung open.

15

'I would – seriously, Pauline. Don't be so naïve. Loads of girls do it. I'm not ready for a kid.'

'I know, but an abortion . . .'

'It's not really a baby yet,' said Maria. 'Not for ages yet.'

'That's not the point . . .'

'Aileen will help me find a clinic in London. No one over here will be any the wiser.'

'What about Joe?'

'I'm not sure what he'll think.'

'I don't think he'll let you get an abortion.'

'Pauline, I'm the one who has to have the baby. He could dump me any time he likes. And he's terrified of his mam. One sure thing is, I don't want to have it if I'll be on my own.'

'But he wouldn't dump you – he's not that type,' said Pauline, her earnest face looking up at Maria, who was pacing around the room. Pauline was desperately trying to think of more persuasive arguments. 'What if you do damage to yourself, you know, and you can never have children afterwards?'

'They have proper clinics. It's all on the national health system over there. It's not like some gruesome Victorian thing with coat hangers and gin in a grotty backroom. There are leaflets in the Students' Union. I'll pick one up tomorrow.'

'Maria, stop!' Pauline wailed.

Maria trembled all over whenever she stopped moving. She had to keep walking up and down to keep her brain working.

'I can't have a baby on my own, Pauline. Mam would die of shame. Daddy would throw me out of the house. Honest to God, he told me and Aileen that often enough.'

'What?'

'That if we got pregnant 'out of wedlock' as he puts it, we shouldn't darken his doorstep ever again.'

'Yes, but it's different when it actually happens. My mother said the very same thing to me, but I know she'd never really throw me out. Look at my cousin. She had that gorgeous little boy, and they ended up getting married, her and Donal, and they're as happy as anything.

Pauline's mother was in the choir with Maria's father, and they were out of the same mould.

Maria shook her head. 'No, they wouldn't tolerate it.'

'I think you're exaggerating, Maria, honestly,' Pauline said emphatically. 'They only used to threaten us when we were younger, to put the fear of God in us. They don't mean it, really.'

'Mam would be all right after a while. But not Daddy. He couldn't handle it.'

'So you'll kill a baby to please your dad?' Pauline couldn't believe this was Maria the softy, who got stressed out if a dog was knocked down by a car.

'I'd never tell him, so he wouldn't know. He definitely wouldn't want me to get an abortion!'

'Exactly.' Pauline was often overwhelmed by the

power of her argument. She would make a great lawyer.

'Listen, I can't bring up a kid. I have another two years of college. Isn't it worse to bring them into the world and then not provide for them?'

Pauline looked at her friend. ' You know well you'd find a way, if you wanted to. Anyway, you don't even know what Joe will say, yet.'

She was only trying to play devil's advocate, but she couldn't bear it when Maria dissolved into tears again. She stood up and hugged her.

'I'll tell Joe tonight, and we'll take it from there,' Maria said, her voice muffled against Pauline's shoulder.

'That's right, one step at a time. Just take it easy and it will all work out. Come on downstairs, before Orla notices anything funny.'

She pulled out a tissue from her sleeve. 'Here, blow your nose. We can tell her you have bad hay fever.'

Chapter Three

Ryan's bar was even busier than usual on a Thursday night. Everyone was checking out the new wall-size video screen. Joe pushed his way through the crowd, looking for Maria. There she was, surrounded by three guys, all trying to chat her up.

She seemed to be enjoying herself, the way she was flicking her hair around and smiling at them. Her face didn't light up when she saw Joe. He thought he knew then. She was going to break it off so she'd be free for the summer. Well, he'd get in there first.

'Hiya.' She reached forward to kiss him, and said, 'Excuse us,' to the three admirers, who shuffled off.

'How's it going?' Her voice was falsely bright. She sipped her drink and avoided his eyes.

'What?' Joe was still feeling guilty that he hadn't done any studying. The exams were starting in three days. He had told Maria he couldn't see her because he had so much work to do. She had to beg him to come out tonight. Maybe that had annoyed her, and she had finally decided to finish with him.

'Life in general. I haven't seen you for a few days. Studying hard?' Maria looked across at the video screen. Liam Gallagher was leaping across the wall. She was building up for something, Joe could tell. There was no point in making a meal of it. He should help her to get it over with, and they could both get on with studying for the exams and then go home for the summer. 'Look,' he said, taking her arm and moving her to one side of the bar, where it was a bit quieter, 'I think I know what you're going to say, and it's OK.'

He figured that it wouldn't hurt him so much if he was the one to break it off first.

Maria's face broke into a huge smile, her eyes shining. 'How did you know?'

'I just know by looking at you that you're nervous about telling me something, and that's the only thing I can think of,' he said sullenly. Why did she have to look so relieved?

'Jesus, you must be brilliant at medicine! You'll make a great doctor!'

Maria was suddenly excited. If they were in it together, everything would be fine.

Joe looked at her. Was she being sarcastic? But her voice, and the way she was smiling at him? He didn't get it.

'Are you sure it's OK?' she asked. 'What about your

mother? Will she mind? She probably thinks you could do a lot better than me. Another medical student, at least.'

'Maria, what are you on about?'

'Well, you know, when you say it's OK, you mean it's OK to have it, don't you?'

'Have what?'

'The baby . . .'

'The baby? What baby?' Joe looked around, as if expecting to see one materialising on the bar.

The penny dropped and reverberated around Maria's head.

'*Our* baby . . . oh, you *didn't* know, did you?'

Maria saw the shock register on his face. She could feel a flush climbing up from her neck. She dropped her head so that her hair fell forward to hide her face in an automatic reaction from her childhood. Then she looked wildly around the bar, to make sure no one had overheard. They were all too busy getting pissed and singing along with 'Stand by Me,' on the Oasis video. How could she have been so stupid?

'Are you telling me you're pregnant?' It sounded like someone else's voice; metallic, controlled.

'You said . . . you knew what I was going to say,' she sobbed. Now she had ruined her chance to put it to him like she had rehearsed it, giving him a chance for it to sink in, and then talking about it properly.

'Come on, let's get outside – we can't talk about it standing here.'

Joe's face was hard now but he gently took her arm and steered her out, through the sweating bodies and waving pints, into the carpark. The cool air hit them. In the yellow streetlight, Maria's face was pale and drawn tight like a mask. Her lips seemed thinner and had lost their colour. Joe led her to the low wall in front of the pub and sat her down. Absently, he noted the symptoms of shock in himself mirrored in the shivering girl in front of him. He could feel his heart pounding, and his stomach felt like it was shrinking. Maria was shaking, and he took off his jacket and put it around her shoulders.

She didn't want to break it off. She wanted to tie him down, make him give up college, be damned by his mother as a stupid fool. Anger took over from the shock.

Maria took a deep breath and looked up at him. 'Sorry, Joe. I just got confused in there for a second when you said it was OK. I want to discuss the options with you.' These were the safe words she had rehearsed. Her distant, formal tone brought him back from his thoughts.

'Jesus, Maria. This is a really big thing.'

'I know, but don't worry. We'll sort it out.'

She reached up and stroked his arm. Something was wrong here. Surely *he* should be reassuring *her*?

'How can I not worry? How far gone are you? Not long, surely?'

'About six weeks.'

He took a deep gulp of the night air. 'Not too late, then.' He felt like his breathing was no longer an involuntary activity, but each breath needed to be consciously taken and exhaled, or he would collapse.

Was that a sigh of relief, Maria wondered? Had he already worked out that she could safely have an abortion? She read the panic in his eyes. She went on with the next line of her rehearsed speech. 'I'm going to England. I'll get rid of it.'

Joe looked at her. Funny how his pupils expanded and made his light eyes look dark. There was probably some medical explanation, she thought idly.

'Have you already decided, or are we really discussing options?'

'You don't want it, do you?' asked Maria, surprised.

'No, of course not, but we need to talk about it properly.'

'We are talking about it, aren't we?' Maria waved her hands around, as if there was an audience. 'What else is there to say?'

She had daydreamed as she put on her make-up before coming out tonight, about what would happen if they kept the baby. Joe could still finish University, and she could work. Her mother could baby-sit. Joe would make a lovely dad, and he'd be earning enough after he qualified to support them. They could get a house in Knocknacarra, in one of those new estates, and have a small garden out the back for a tricycle and space to kick a ball.

Joe sat down on the wall beside her and hugged her with one arm. A brotherly, bracing, 'We're in this together,' kind of hug. Maria sat there, rigid. The concrete was cold. You could get a kidney infection from sitting on cold concrete. Or piles, whatever they were. She would ring Aileen tomorrow, and ask if she could stay with her in London.

'I think I'll head off home now,' she said, standing up.

'I'll walk you.'

They walked in silence, and at Maria's front door, she turned and kissed him on the cheek. An impersonal kiss that felt hard on his skin, like the peck of a dutiful maiden aunt.

'Goodbye,' she said, stepping inside and closing the door. She knew she was pushing him away, testing him. What she really wanted was for him to hammer on the door, demand to be let in, say he wanted to spend the rest of his life with her and they could keep the baby.

Joe stood on the step staring at the peeling red paint on the cheap plywood door. He saw Maria's bedroom light coming on. It shone on the front lawn and then dimmed when she pulled the curtains. Was it goodbye for now, or forever? Was she shutting him out?

He hardly had the energy to drag himself home. He trudged down the hill. On the bridge, he stood for a while, staring down at the shallow jaundiced water reflecting the sodium streetlamps. He was glad that

Mike was out tonight. He wouldn't have to face any questions about being home so early. He made a cup of tea and sat on the floor in the living-room, leaning against the side of the sofa. He rubbed the palms of his hands, fingers spread, across the blue nylon carpet, pushing the pile one way and then the other, creating static. He stared at the blank television screen, imagining it playing out future scenes in his life. Telling his mother that Maria was pregnant. Leaving university and getting a crappy job to pay the bills, the three of them crammed into a tiny council flat. The baby crying all night, and Maria transformed into a tearful and needy wife, leaning on him for everything. He wasn't ready for all that. It just didn't feature in his plans. He was going to be a successful doctor. Maybe he would get married, but only when the time was right. Then he stopped himself. Why was he studying medicine at all? At first, he had just wanted to prove to his mother that he could get enough points in his Leaving Certificate to follow in his father's footsteps. Now his ambition was to make lots of money and maybe even be famous. Somewhere along the way he had lost the point of the whole thing. Curing people and saving lives. And now at the first real hurdle, he was prepared to kill his own child to stop it from interfering with his plans. He would go and see Maria tomorrow and they would talk about it properly, and make a rational decision that was best for both of them. He felt better and went up to bed with a vague feeling that everything would work out.

Chapter Four

Even Orla would soon notice the sound of puking from the bathroom in the mornings, thought Maria as she hung on to the cold ceramic edge of the toilet-bowl at seven o'clock on Sunday morning. Orla slept like a log because she studied all day and then went for a workout in the evening to 'maintain her balance'.

She would be up any minute now, making her herbal tea and brown-bread breakfast. How could anyone be that healthy? Maria had never seen her drunk. On a big night out, Orla would have two glasses of Guinness and then go on to the Ballygowan. She never let her hair down, that girl.

Maria showered quickly, resigned to being up this early on a Sunday. As she left the bathroom, Orla was waiting, towel in hand, to go in. Her pale-blue silk pyjamas didn't even look wrinkled, and Maria pulled down her baggy T-shirt to cover her bum as she went past.

'Morning,' she muttered.

Orla smiled. 'You're up early. Are you feeling all right?'

'Yeah, fine.'

Orla would think it was a hangover. She probably didn't even know how babies were made.

Joe had called on Friday, and they agreed to have a few days to think about things. He was coming around this afternoon to talk. In the kitchen, the smell of instant coffee assaulted Maria's nostrils as the hot water dissolved the granules, and her stomach heaved. She raided Orla's cupboard for a peppermint tea bag and threw the coffee down the drain. She made some toast and went back upstairs, wafting the peppermint fumes away from Orla's door as she passed. Maria settled at her desk to read the notes from her last seminar, and couldn't remember any of it. Her hand must have been taking notes on automatic pilot. And it was the session Professor Alexander had hinted that everyone should go to, because it might come in useful for the exams. Suddenly it all seemed so irrelevant. Who gives a toss what you get in your first-year exams, as long as you pass? Anyway, she had good results in the mid-term assignments, so she would have a bit of leeway.

Maria chewed her pencil top until the flakes of paint came off in her mouth, and she tasted the cool lead against her tongue.

Yeuch! She hadn't done that for years. What was happening to her?

She was used to being in control. She studied

enough to get by, had a great social life, and was always the one to break it off first with boyfriends. Ever since she was thirteen and the boys used to come to the Gaeltacht Summer School in Carraroe. It was great. Every three weeks, she would say goodbye to one boy, and a new lot would arrive, desperately trying not to get sent home for speaking English. Maria and Pauline used to hang around outside the school gates, talking in Irish.

'Look at him. He's a bit spotty.'

'I like him. He's nice and tall.'

The boys would gravitate towards Maria, who looked 'like a castaway from the Spanish Armada,' as her Daddy used to say. Aileen and their brother Hugh had ordinary brown hair and green eyes, inherited from their father. Aileen was jealous that her younger sister pulled the boys and she never did. She pretended to Maria that she was above it all. Hugh never pulled the girls either, but only because he couldn't hang around outside the school gates with his dad being the headmaster.

Maria's alarm clock went off at nine o'clock, jolting her from her reverie.

'Focus, focus, come on,' she said to herself. 'You were up two hours early and you haven't done anything yet.'

The dates swam around on the page in front of her eyes, as if they had a life of their own. Her notes were incomprehensible. She looked down at her tummy, still flat under her T-shirt. Her boobs were definitely bigger, though. And they ached.

It must have happened that night after the Med Ball,

when they'd both been really drunk. The condom had slipped off, and they had just laughed and fallen asleep. How stupid. She hadn't even bothered to work out the dates and get a morning-after pill. No, Miss In-Control Maria had decided to take a chance. Or had she even consciously done that? It was more of a vague belief that everything would be all right. And Joe had been too busy the next morning panicking about his mother finding Maria in the bed to think about anything else.

Maria looked at her watch. Half nine. Not too early to ring Aileen. She needed to do something, to take some control of the situation.

Aileen sounded groggy. 'What time is it?'

'Sorry, Aileen. I thought you'd be up by now. It's me.'

'Hiya. We were at a brilliant party last night, at Ken and Sandy's, and we didn't get in until three o'clock. Hang on 'til I put the kettle on.'

Maria heard her rattling around in the kitchen.

'Hi, I'm back. What has you on the phone at this hour anyway? Are you going to ten o'clock Mass?' Aileen laughed.

They had talked about sex and Mass and sins and everything when Aileen was home for Christmas. Maria thought Aileen was a real goody-goody, and would give her a hard time for sleeping with Joe only a month after she met him. Instead, Aileen surprised her by telling her that she had been living with Paul for the last year. Now they were co-conspirators.

'No, I'm up studying. The exams are starting next week.'

'Oh, I forgot to send you a good-luck card,' said Aileen sheepishly. 'They seem to have come around very quickly?'

'Don't worry. It feels quick to me as well, and I'm the one studying for them. Listen, I just wanted to see if it would still be OK for me to come over for the summer?'

'Yeah, sure,' said Aileen. 'I'll talk to Paul, but he'll be fine. He's out a lot of the time anyway, between working late and playing cricket.'

'Would the end of June be all right?'

'Sounds great. We'll get the spare room cleared out for you. What made you finally decide you could leave the gorgeous Joe behind?'

'It's a long story, Aileen, but I'll tell you when I see you.'

'Is something wrong?'

'Not at all, I'm fine. I'll talk to you beforehand to let you know the exact date, but thanks, that's a relief to have it organised.'

'What about Joe? Will you not miss him? Or is he coming in your suitcase?' she laughed.

'No, he's not. I'll give you the low-down when I see you.'

Aileen recognised the abrupt tone in her sister's voice, so she didn't dig any further. As she hung up, she knew there was more to this than met the eye. No doubt

30

she would winkle the whole story out as soon as she had Maria sitting in front of her.

Back in her room, Maria heard Pauline getting up and went downstairs to have a cup of tea with her. Any excuse to get away from the books. Pauline was standing in her bulky man-size dressing-gown and woolly slippers, looking out at a magpie on the lawn. 'One for sorrow, two for joy . . .' She turned around and smiled at Maria. 'Did I ever tell you that when I was small, I got upset that there was only one magpie, and my mam told me that his friend was hiding in the bushes? I always remember that when I see a single one.'

'Your mother is a great optimist, isn't she?' said Maria. 'Mine is more of a realist, I think. I wonder if I'll ever be able to tell her about this?' She didn't need to explain any further. Pauline made two mugs of tea and put one down in front of Maria, looking sympathetically across the table at her best friend.

'Is it today you're seeing Joe?'

'Yeah. I've really missed him, and it's only been three days. How am I going to survive the summer without him, never mind the rest of my life?'

'Why has he not been around? Isn't now the time when you need him the most?'

'He said he wanted a few days to think about things.'

'You don't think he's going to ask you to marry him, is he?' said Pauline, excitedly.

Maria tried to hold back a smile, but she couldn't.

'No, not really.' she said, but Pauline wasn't convinced. Maria had an air of suppressed excitement about her. 'I've got plan A and plan B. If he does ask me, I'll say yes. He's definitely Mister Right. He's so brilliant, and I know you don't think he's good-looking, but he has a really nice body, and he's kind, and intelligent, and he'd make a really lovely daddy . . .' Maria was gabbling.

Pauline had to do the best-friend thing and take her down off the cloud where she was floating. Just in case. 'And what's plan B?' she asked, smiling to soften her implied disbelief of plan A.

'I rang Aileen this morning and she said I can stay for the summer. I'll get an abortion and come back in September. If Joe still wants to be with me, we'll take it from there.'

Pauline knew the matter-of-fact tone hid a multitude of fears and she reached across and touched Maria's hand. 'Whatever happens, I'm still your best friend, and I'll be there for you.'

'Is that you angling to be my bridesmaid?' Maria laughed. But it was a short, brittle laugh that died quickly.

When Joe rang the doorbell, Maria already had her jacket on, and was ready to go out. 'Let's go for a walk down by the river,' she said. 'I've been in studying all morning and I need a bit of fresh air.' She had put on lipstick and eyeliner for the first time since Thursday, and had washed her hair and tied it back in a high ponytail that was supposed to be jaunty.

Joe thought she looked pale and her smile was a bit false. He took her hand and pushed it into his jacket pocket as they walked along the towpath. She loved it when he did that. It was protective, somehow.

'How are you feeling?' he asked.

'Fine. A bit sicky, but that's only first thing in the morning. Did you have time to think about things?' She couldn't wait for him to build up to whatever he was going to say. The rest of her life was hanging on his decision.

'Yes. Did you?' He looked at her, hoping that she had reached the same conclusion. They couldn't have this baby.

It would mess up both of their lives, and they would regret it forever. He loved Maria, and maybe they would stay together, and even one day get married, but he wasn't ready for it yet. The selfish red devil on his left shoulder had well and truly beaten his haloed counterpart on the right.

'Yes.' She could see in his eyes that he wasn't about to pop the question. There was no point in making it difficult for him. 'I rang Aileen. I'll go over and stay with her and get rid of it.'

She couldn't believe how sad she felt. Just for a little while, the pregnancy hadn't been scary at all; while she had that little hope inside that Joe might want her to keep the baby and make a go of it.

Joe stopped on the path, turned to her and hugged her, kissing her hair, and then lifted her hands and kissed them. He looked into her eyes.

'I love you, Maria, and I don't want to lose you, but I'm not ready to be a father yet. Both of us have plans. We've got to finish college and get good jobs and then maybe settle down. It's too soon to do it now.'

'I know,' said Maria, nodding, but her eyes filled with tears and they streamed down her cheeks. 'I'm scared.'

'I know. Do you want me to come over with you?' He hugged her again, looking over her head at the still water, with the mayflies gently landing, barely disturbing the surface.

Maria shook her head against his shoulder. 'I'll have Aileen and Paul there. I'll be fine. Your mother would wonder why you were suddenly going to England.'

'That's the least of my worries,' he said, but secretly breathed a sigh of relief. His mother would interrogate him, even if he said he was going on holiday, about who else was going, where they were staying, and why England.

Maria couldn't concentrate on the examination questions. The room was too hot, with the sun streaming through the high windows of the hall. A bluebottle dive-bombed her head and then tried to escape through the window above her desk. The question of how society in Britain was affected by the deaths of three-quarters of a million men in the First World War seemed remote and irrelevant. She tackled it, trying to take an unusual angle, and then got bogged down in the trenches and moved on to the next one.

Her mind wouldn't focus. She just wanted the three hours to pass so she could escape. This was the last exam and she was going home for the weekend. At last, the invigilator rang the bell.

Maria handed in her papers and rushed outside to the fresh air. Pauline appeared magically beside her.

'Maria, you're very pale. Are you all right?'

'I just felt a bit faint in there. It was really hot.'

'I came to say goodbye, in case I don't see you before you head off to Eng– to Aileen's on Monday.'

'Oh, thanks, Pauline. That's really nice.' Maria dragged her bag out of her locker, panting.

'Let me carry that – you shouldn't be lifting things.'

Maria gave her a withering look. 'It would save me a lot of hassle.'

'I'll walk you to the bus with it anyway.' Pauline took one handle of the bag. 'When is your dad coming to pick up your other stuff?'

'Next weekend. It's all packed in the room, so you can just let him in.'

'No problem. I can't wait to get my exams finished next week.'

At the bus stop, they hugged, and Pauline's eyes filled with tears. 'Good luck, Maria. I hope it goes all right. Ring me, will you?'

'Of course I will. Light a candle for me, will you?' It was a joke from their schooldays when their mothers lit a candle in the church at the slightest provocation. The girls calculated they had melted enough wax to supply

Madame Tussaud's for years. Maria climbed onto the bus. She smiled through the window and waved. Everything would be different the next time she saw Pauline.

On the bus, she kept going over and over in her mind the last conversation with Joe. He had offered again to come to England with her, but she didn't want him to. If they ever did go travelling somewhere together she wanted it to be a happy, exciting time. Maybe next summer they could go to a kibbutz or something and have an adventure that would cancel out this horror. Now, it was better to just get on with things by herself. Joe said he would phone her, and maybe he could come over for a week at the end of the summer. She would be recovered by then and they could explore London together.

Maria couldn't decide how much of this was just his way of making it easier to say good-bye. Pauline reckoned they could just get back together in September and put it all behind them. Maria wasn't so sure. The seeds of doubt that were planted while she stood shivering behind the shower curtain hiding from his mother had well and truly sprouted. Joe was probably showing his true colours, and she didn't really like what she saw.

Chapter Five

Maria's mother greeted her at the kitchen door. 'Hello, love. You're looking a bit peaky. Are you tired after all those exams?'

Maria nodded and smiled, dropping her bag on the floor.

'And I only have the weekend to feed you up before you go off on me again.'

Maureen filled the kettle and put it on the stove. 'Dinner will be ready for seven. Your dad has a choir practice at six.'

'What are we having?' Maria sniffed. A delicious smell was coming from the big old black Aga stove.

'Irish stew. I know the weather's a bit hot for it, but I have to give you some decent food before you go.'

'Smells yummy.'

'I suppose you have a big load of washing to do? Put

on the machine there, and we can have one load drying overnight in the back kitchen.'

Maria's mother never stopped. She was always juggling six things at once. Maria just wanted to sit in the cosy kitchen and soak up the feeling of being home. It was all so familiar – the waxed tablecloth with the fruit pattern, Snoopy the black and white cat curled up as close as he could to the stove, and the smell of baking brown bread. She obediently loaded the washing machine and turned it on. They chatted about the exams, Pauline's lack of men, and the end-of-year party in the house.

'So, are you looking forward to going to England?'

'Sort of. I hope all the good jobs aren't gone by the time I get there.'

'Will you not miss Joe?' Maureen had noticed that Maria hadn't mentioned him once since she got home.

'I miss him already,' Maria said wistfully, looking down at her hands, promising herself to grow her nails for the summer.

'He's a nice fella. Is he staying at home in Westport for the summer?'

'Yes. His mother has lots of jobs lined up for him.'

'Well, three months will pass in no time and you'll be back together again. Maybe we can even meet him before you go back to college?'

Her mother gave her shoulders a quick squeeze as she passed, putting floury hand-prints on the yellow jumper Joe had given her as an early birthday present.

Maria nodded but she couldn't summon any more enthusiasm for the subject. Joe might not even want her back.

'Here's Dad now,' Maureen said briskly, as they heard the car turning in front of the house.

She took the casserole dish out of the oven, laid the warm plates on the table, and was ready to serve up the dinner as her husband walked in the door.

'Well, well, she's home again to us!'

Maria stood up and hugged her father tightly, and he kissed her cheek.

'How's Daddy's Girl?'

Maureen tut-tutted at the sink. She didn't like Sean having favourites, but he had always doted on the youngest and the prettiest in the family. They sat down and said the grace before meals in Irish. After a year away, Maria had only just got out of the habit of saying it automatically. Over dinner, the gossip about the neighbours didn't tax Maria's brain too much. As she was reassuring her mother that she was eating properly, listing off sample breakfast, lunch and dinner menus, Maria was thinking about the new little life inside her with no maternal feelings at all. Just bitter resentment.

On Saturday morning, Sean knocked at Maria's bedroom door. 'Your breakfast is cooked, love. Do you want to go for a little walk afterwards?'

Maria pulled her head out from under the pillow, resisted the urge to throw a shoe at the door, and muttered thickly, 'OK, thanks, Dad. I'll be down in a minute.'

The thought of a cooked breakfast made her retch, and she gulped down some water from the dusty glass on her bedside table, and counted to ten. She sat on the edge of her old sagging bed, every lump moulded to the shape of her body, and looked around her childhood room. The walls were the same pink she had chosen when she was fourteen, trying to create a pretty, feminine effect in Hugh's cold north-facing room after he had left home. She had put up lots of posters and bought big bright cushions to pile casually on the bed, so that when Pauline came around they could pretend it was their studio flat in Dublin and they were working in cool, high-powered jobs. They used to paint their toenails all different colours. The nuns didn't allow nail varnish with the school uniform, so their bright toes were hidden under thick green kneesocks except on PE days, when the girls had to be nifty out of the showers and have their socks on before Sister Angela noticed anything. They used to call her Strangela, because she was skinny and had a very high-pitched strangled kind of screech when she was coaching on the hockey pitch. Maria and Pauline used to lie on the big cushions, eating chocolate and wondering what sex was like. It said, in one of the women's magazines that Pauline got from her cousin, that chocolate and sex released the same hormones in the body, and that's why women love chocolate – as a sex substitute. Once, Maria dared

Pauline to eat three Easter eggs and a large Cadbury's Dairy Milk bar at once, to see if she felt horny. Pauline said she just felt sick. Now, Maria could tell Pauline what sex was like. What pregnancy was like, as well. Give her chocolate any day. She pulled on her clothes and stumbled downstairs, yawning.

Sean was sitting in his usual place, his plate laden with sausages, eggs, rashers and black pudding. He poured her a cup of tea.

'Sit down there, love, and dig in,' said her mother. 'You need to build yourself up – you're gone a bit skinny since you went to college.'

Maureen put a plate of breakfast in front of her and Maria heaved. Visions of fat smelly pigs with bristly skin and wrinkly dirty snouts revisited her from a documentary she had seen the week before. She coughed to disguise the retching in her throat.

'Are you all right, love?' Maureen asked, passing her the toast-rack.

'Fine, thanks, Mam. I think I'll just have toast and tea, thanks. I'm out of the habit of a cooked breakfast.' She pushed the offending plate away.

Later, as they walked down to the sea, Sean seemed satisfied with her explanation that the documentary about organic pig-farming and 'humane' abbatoirs was still too fresh in her mind to think about eating anything vaguely pig-like.

They walked, as they always had done on Saturday mornings, separated by the grass and dandelions

41

sprouting down the centre of the little boreen. A skylark darted across the boggy field to their right. It ascended until it was a tiny dot, its trilling song a delicate counterpoint to the thundering of the waves as they crested the hill.

They stood on the brow, inhaling the fresh ozone and seaweed smell. The churning in Maria's stomach receded. Even in Galway, only twenty miles away, the sea wasn't the same as here. There in the sheltered bay, you didn't get the sensation of the open Atlantic ocean, stretching all the way to America. Except for the Aran islands, of course, looming mistily on the horizon.

Maria's hair flew in a tangled mass around her head like the seaweed under the waves. As they sat on their favourite rock, Sean savoured the ritual they had shared since Maria was about eight years old.

'I've missed our little walks since you've been away, Maria,' he said, looking out across the water.

'Me too, Dad.' Somehow, she knew this would be the last time, and tears welled up in her eyes. She absently rubbed the heel of her trainer against the crusty coating of barnacles on the rock.

'You'll be careful in London, won't you?' Sean said tentatively. Maria was so independent, she would probably take him amiss.

'Of course I will. I'll mind my bag, I won't be out too late, and I'll be careful who I mix with.' She parroted the parting speech he had made when she went to Galway. And that was only down the road.

'Ah, no, London is a different kettle of fish altogether. You'll meet a different kind of person over there.'

'What do you mean, Dad?' She thought she'd better humour him. What planet did he think she was on?

'Cities like London attract people who are looking for victims. Whether it's to pick your pocket, or mug you, or take advantage in a different way. Just be careful, that's all I'm saying.'

'Thanks, Dad. I'll be fine, honestly. Isn't Aileen over there to look after me, anyway?'

Sean looked sideways at his beautiful daughter and had a fierce urge to protect her from all the badness in the world.

'Do you think you'll get back together with Joe when you come home in the autumn?' he asked. There was a chance she'd take up with some English fella, unless she was still holding a candle for Joe.

'I hope so. But if I don't, there's plenty more fish in the sea. I'm too young to be settling for one fella at this stage.' She managed to sound flippant, but the smile she gave him felt taut and false, and she swallowed and looked away.

Sean could see right through her. It must be love that had her off her food. A few months away from young Joe would be the best thing for her. Get things in perspective.

She was a bit young to be so serious about one lad, suitable as he might be.

'You're dead right – you can take your pick of them,'

he said cheerfully, putting his arm around her shoulders.

It reminded her of the time Joe had held her, sitting on the wall of the pub, and she shivered. Her tentative dream of a definite future with Joe had been shattered since then.

'Let's go back. I've all my packing to do.'

They turned away from the sea and walked home arm in arm.

Chapter Six

The National Express bus was full of students going to London for the summer. There was an air of excitement as rucksacks were loaded on, and the window seats were quickly taken. Maria was glad she didn't know anyone else. She didn't want to hear them chattering about jobs and the craic they would have in London. She put her earphones on and tried to sleep.

For twenty hours she drifted between daydreams and nightmares as the road flashed past her window. She saw herself dragging a pushchair up the concrete steps in the Council flats on the outskirts of Galway. Joe would maybe come to visit sometimes, and she would make him a cup of tea in the cockroach-ridden galley kitchen of the damp flat. He looked like a visiting angel in her dreams, with a golden aura around him, dispelling the gloominess of the rest of her imaginary life. He would smile, and kiss her on the cheek in a chaste, angel-like way. Her dreams didn't stretch as far as the new house in Knocknacarra with a tiny garden out the back. Those dreams needed Joe as a real person, coming back from a hard day saving lives to kiss his wife and child. The baby didn't have a face in her imaginings – it just lurked in the background, androgynous and vaguely menacing. She couldn't have it. But what if something went wrong with the abortion? Then her mam and dad would definitely find out, and they'd hate her. The chance was worth taking, she thought as she dozed off.

All the passengers had to get off the coach for the ferry crossing, and she found a Pullman seat in the lounge of the boat and settled down to watch a movie. Jim Carey was leaping around in a green mask and everyone else was in fits of laughter, but somehow the slapstick humour of it just didn't work for her. Usually she loved movies like that, and she and Joe would mess around, trying to do the jokes, but without him she couldn't summon the energy to laugh. She drifted off to sleep again, and then an hour later, shot awake from a horrible blood-soaked dream. It reminded her of that Roman Polanski scene when all the dead children come back to haunt Macbeth. She sat up, wiping the dribble from her chin, and pressed the play button on her personal stereo, escaping into the rhythm of her Fugees CD.

Getting back on the coach was a distraction, and it seemed to take forever for the bus to disembark. It was pitch black so she couldn't get any idea of what Holyhead was like, apart from the acres of concrete and tall sodium lamps lighting the pool of cars waiting to board the returning ferry.

She watched the cosy cottage lights of the North Wales villages gliding serenely past, and was surprised how similar it looked to home. There were more two-storey houses than bungalows, but the architecture was similar and the villages looked somehow familiar.

The coach stopped at a motorway service station and Maria was tempted to just stay on the bus, when everyone else got off. The driver soon dispelled that notion. 'Come on, love – I'm going in for a cup of tea, and the insurance doesn't cover you to be out here on your own. You look like you need a bit of grub yourself, anyway,' he said, and his gruff, sympathetic voice made her want to cry as she stepped stiffly down on to the tarmac and followed the others into the self-service restaurant. The smell of fried food and wet shoes assaulted her as the door swung closed behind her.

Everyone else seemed to have either travelled with a friend, or made new ones on the journey, and she felt completely alone. She went to the loo first, and it was nice to sit on a full-size one, with room for her knees, after her frequent visits to the cramped chemical toilet on the coach. She took her time, put on a bit of make-up and brushed out her hair, delaying the moment when she would have to go into the restaurant and either sit self-consciously on her own, or make the effort to smile, and ask someone else if she could join them. She looked in the mirror, and realised that her mother was right – she had lost weight. Over the last few weeks she had completely lost interest in eating anything, and the exams had given her diarrhoea, as usual. She looked at her pale face and the dark shadows under her eyes and decided she looked about thirty, already worn out and unattractive. The sooner she could get rid of the thing inside her body that was draining her energy and making her miserable, the sooner she could get back to normal. She would do a bit of swimming at Aileen's gym, and eat healthy food over the summer, and get back in control. Just the minor hurdle of getting an abortion first. It seemed really straightforward on the leaflets she had picked up, and supposedly you got over it really quickly – which had surprised her.

She picked up her bag and strode into the restaurant – being miserable wasn't going to help, so she might as well just get on with things. She grabbed a plain bread roll and put a large glass of milk and an apple on her tray, paid, and walked up to the first table with familiar faces from the coach.

'Is it OK if I sit here?' she asked, and one of the guys shuffled on to the next seat to make room for her. A gang of them were moving into his brother's flat for the summer, and they were all excited about getting waiters' jobs in an Italian restaurant in North London somewhere.

'So, what are you doing?' one of the girls asked

Maria, leaning proprietorially against the guy who had started talking to her, and giving Maria all the warning signals.

'I have a sister in Brixton and she has a spare room, so I'm staying with her, and hopefully I'll get a job, even if it's only in a shop or something,' Maria said, flicking her hair back off her face, and sipping her milk.

The boy was watching her and she knew the signs. Now the girl would get all bitchy, or possessive, or just exclude Maria from the conversation. So she took control.

'My boyfriend couldn't come over, unfortunately, but sure the summer is short, and I'll see him again in September,' she said brightly, and the girl visibly relaxed, as her boyfriend's eyes left Maria and the conversation moved on to the best clubs in the West End.

'You have a bit of milk around your mouth,' the guy beside her whispered, pointing to his own lips, and licking them. Maria blushed. Why could she not just be left alone? She should have just sat with her book at another table. There was always some guy trying to hit on her, sometimes even when she was out with Joe. Pauline said she was mad jealous, but she had no idea what it was like. Maria couldn't just have a normal conversation with a guy, as a friend, like Pauline could. There was always this underlying sexual innuendo, and she had to either flirt with the guy, or ignore him completely – she didn't know how to just make them talk to her like a person.

Finally it was time to get back on the coach, and Maria could escape back to solitude of her own seat.

The lonely ache inside her was getting stronger as the miles passed. She wondered what Joe was doing now. Was he thinking about her, or writing a letter to her, or was he just tied up doing things for his mother?

Maria spotted Aileen's pale tired face in the crowd at Victoria Coach Station as she dragged her rucksack from the hold in the side of the coach.

They hugged and Maria said, 'You must have had to get up really early, did you?'

'Don't worry. It would have been fine, except I kept waking up thinking I'd missed the alarm. I was driving Paul mad, leaning across him to see the clock radio.'

The digital station clock said 7.34 as they emerged from the Underground at Brixton. Amongst the commuters shuffling their way down to the escalator, a tall hairy man was selling a magazine, waving it around and singing 'Big, big, biggie, get your Big Issue here!'

A Bible-thumper with a microphone was declaring the imminent end of the world, and an exotic-looking Rastafarian with a brightly coloured crocheted hat was selling incense, which filled the air with its sticky scent. It was like a seedier version of the Galway street market on a Saturday, with the Travellers selling garlicky olives and hand-painted glass.

'God, what's it like later on, when it gets busy?' said Maria, fighting her way up the steps with her rucksack.

'Oh, this is quiet. There's usually a woman who sings

on a comb, and a huge flower-stall. And there's all the dodgy guys trying to get your one-day travel card off you, so they can sell it again, Come on, quick, there's our bus.'

Twenty minutes and three flights of stairs later, Maria was relieved to put down her rucksack in the high-ceilinged hall of the flat.

'This is great,' she said, impressed with the Mediterranean colour scheme and the framed prints hanging in the living-room.

She was surprised by her sister's taste, or was it Paul's? The kitchen was full of shiny stainless-steel gadgets and blue glassware. Aileen had put a vase of freesias in Maria's bedroom, and a stack of magazines on the bedside table.

'This is lovely,' Maria breathed. 'It's like a hotel, after living in student houses.'

'Well, we *are* both working,' said Aileen.

She had always felt inferior to her sister, who had been more popular and intelligent at school. And now she was so cool, with her chunky silver jewellery and her trendy bootleg trousers. Aileen had started in the NatWest bank when she was nineteen, and already felt totally untrendy at twenty-four.

After a shower and a change of clothes, Maria was greeted by the smell of newly ground coffee. They sat in the bay window of the kitchen, eating warm croissants and sipping freshly squeezed orange juice. As she looked out at the terracotta pots of herbs in the tiny roof-garden, Maria couldn't remember when she had last enjoyed breakfast so much; she was so afraid of getting sick all the time.

'So, tell me about you and Joe, then,' said Aileen. 'How did he let you come over here for three months on your own, knowing that all the English guys would be after you?'

'It's a bit complicated. . .'

'I thought there was something up. Come on, let's go for a walk down to the market, and you can tell me all about it on the way.'

Maria talked about everything else, as they strolled through the stalls piled with richly embroidered African fabrics, sweet potatoes, strange bulbous vegetables and big red fish she had never seen before. Aileen told her they were called tilapia, and tasted delicious. Rap music blared from record stalls. They walked around high piles of woven baskets and the huge brass-studded trunks sold for family trips home to Jamaica or Barbados. Aileen had to remind her to hold on tight to her bag. Maria revelled in the buzzing, shouting, colourful assault on her senses. She inhaled deeply, and smelt mixed spices, and fresh fish, and the sweat of four men unloading carpets into a railway arch, mixed with the fumes of traffic and rotting fruit. Aileen dragged her past the jewellery stalls and into the coffee shop by the station.

'Tell me,' said Aileen as soon as they were sitting. 'You can't keep me in suspense any longer. What's happening?'

Maria stirred her tea and bit into a jam doughnut.

'I've never seen you eating so much,' said Aileen. 'Sorry, I sounded like Mammy there. You're on your holidays – you can eat whatever you want!'

'I don't know how I'm going to tell you this, so I'm just going to say it.' Maria looked at her defiantly. 'I need to get an abortion.'

Aileen gasped and went pale. 'God Almighty! No wonder it took a while to get it out of you. Mam and Dad don't know?'

'Are you mad?'

'And Joe?'

'Of course he knows. We decided together. Sort of. He said he wasn't ready to be a father yet.'

'Did you break it off with him?'

'No. We said we'd see what happens after the summer. We're going to keep in touch.' Aileen ignored the slight sarcastic edge to Maria's last words. She was obviously hurt.

'How far gone are you? You're not showing.' She leaned sideways to look under the table.

'I think about eleven weeks. I have to get rid of it. Joe doesn't want it, I don't want it . . . I can't bring up a child on my own.'

'Well, people in situations far worse than yours have kids. Two of the girls at work are single mums, and they cope all right.'

'It's different for them. They probably didn't go to . . .'

Aileen looked at her. 'Didn't go to college, so they

have lower expectations, and nothing to lose? Maria, what planet are you on? I can't believe you said that.'

'I'm not saying anything bad about not going to college. You know I'm not. Look at you, how well you're doing . . .'

'Maria, stop now before you dig yourself into a huge hole. You haven't got a clue what it's like over here. It's much more tolerant, and in a city nobody cares what you do – you just get on with your life, and there's nobody looking through the net curtains, judging you.'

Maria felt like a naughty little sister being rapped on the knuckles.

'Actually, one of the girls at work is Irish, and her husband left her when she fell pregnant. He didn't want to have kids,' Aileen went on.

'And she went ahead and had it?'

'She did. A gorgeous little boy called Aaron. She brought him into work once. She said it was the best thing she ever did and the husband was wrong for her anyway. She's met someone else now. An English guy, and he's really into being a family man.'

'But, Aileen, how can I have a baby? At least your friend is working. I can't go home to Mam and Dad and expect them to support me!'

'You could get a job. You don't have to finish college – it's not the be-all and end-all of everything, you know.' Aileen knew she was starting to sound a bit resentful, but sometimes Maria could be so blinkered.

'What would I do, live in the Rahoon flats?'

'I thought they were knocking them down?'

Maria took a deep breath. Sometimes Aileen could be so literal she drove her mad.

'You know what I mean.' Maria traced her finger around the white circular mug-stains on the red Formica-topped table.

'You could get a job over here. You can stay with us until you find work and get settled.'

'Sounds scary.'

'Having an abortion is scary too, Maria. It's killing a little baby,' Aileen whispered fiercely, noticing the interest of an old lady at the next table. Maria was surprised. Aileen was reacting very strangely. After all, she had been in England for five or six years. She must know loads of people who had got abortions.

'It's not a baby yet. It's an embryo – it's not the same,' she said, 'and anyway, people do it all the time.'

Aileen was being so harsh. Maria had expected more sympathy from her sister. Her face started to crumple but she managed to hold back the tears.

Aileen looked as if she was about to cry herself, but she patted Maria on the shoulder. 'You need to think about this some more. If you're going to go through with it, you have to be a hundred per cent sure you're doing the right thing.' She paid the bill. 'Come on. Let's go home now. You have a few more weeks to think about it, I'd say.'

Maria followed Aileen back through the cacophony of sound in the market. Now the colours were garish and the smells made her stomach heave. Aileen was right.

She wasn't completely sure. But she couldn't go through this for another few weeks. She had to make a decision.

When they got back, Maria unpacked while Aileen sat on the bed.

'Do you remember what Daddy used to say to us when we were younger?' Maria said, hanging her clothes in the wardrobe in the space that Aileen had made by pushing her winter clothes over to one side.

'About what?'

'You know, that we should never darken the doorstep at home if we got pregnant.'

'Ah, but it's different now that we're adults.'

'But I'm only nineteen. He still thinks I'm his little girl.'

'Well, it's about time he realised that you're old enough to vote, and get married, and lots of other things. This is your decision and nobody else's.'

Maria was really seeing a new side to Aileen. She was usually frustratingly non-committal and easy-going about everything.

'But what if Daddy does tell me never to come home again?'

'He wouldn't. Mammy wouldn't let him do that.'

'So how come you haven't told him yet that you're living with Paul?' Maria was not going to let Aileen get away with all this stuff about being adults, when she was being just as bad herself.

'OK, point taken. But it's still your decision. You have to take control of your own life at some point.'

'So when are you going to tell them about Paul?' Maria persisted.

'When I go home in August.'

Maria was suddenly struck with curiosity. 'What did you do last year, when they came over?'

Aileen laughed. 'That was hilarious. Poor Paul had to move out to his friend Andy's for the week. He took all his stuff with him, out of the wardrobe and the bathroom and everything. Dad was very impressed with my stereo and all the Habitat furniture! He said I had great taste.'

'Did Paul not mind? He must have thought he was back in the Middle Ages and Dad would come out with the key of your chastity belt or something.'

'He was great. He said it's up to me when I tell them.'

'But you didn't think you could tell them then, did you?'

Maria put her underwear away in a drawer and put a smiling picture of her parents on the dressing-table. They wouldn't be smiling if they knew what she was about to do.

'There's no point in stressing them out. It will be much easier for them to hear it when Paul's not around. I don't want Dad to give him a hard time for corrupting me or something.'

'I suppose you're right.' Maria yawned. 'At least I'm

not the only one who's scared of what Daddy thinks. Listen, do you mind if I have a little snooze to catch up after the journey? Then I can be on good form when Paul gets home.'

Aileen left her to sleep and went into the living-room. As the strains of Beverley Craven reached her room, Maria was stroking the picture from the Med Ball. She wouldn't put it out on the dressing-table. That would be like saying she and Joe were still definitely together, and she wasn't sure if they were. The picture was for her secret moments. She hid it among her knickers and went to sleep, her head throbbing.

Chapter Seven

Maria woke up from her afternoon sleep to a delicious smell wafting from the kitchen. Looking at her watch, she realised she had slept for five hours with no horrible dreams.

A deep voice was singing in the kitchen, and she had a nervous twinge about meeting the famous Paul for the first time. She put on some lipstick and eyeliner, and went into the kitchen. There was no sign of Aileen.

'Hi. Maria, I presume?' Paul said, standing at the cooker holding a wok, enveloped by the steam rising from a rice-cooker.

'Yes. Hiya, Paul. At least, I hope you're Paul, or else there's a strange man in my sister's kitchen!'

He strode across the room and kissed her on both cheeks. 'Welcome to London!'

'Thanks.' She blushed.

Paul was back at the wok, vigorously stirring in

spoonfuls of sauce from various jars at his side. 'Help yourself to wine, or beer from the fridge.'

He gulped a mouthful of chilled Chablis from a clear goblet that was standing beside the cooker. Droplets of condensation ran down the side of the glass.

Maria hesitated.

'Or would you prefer a gin and tonic?'

'I'll just have some water, thanks,' she said, reaching for the tap with a glass in her hand.

'No, no. Filtered in the fridge,' he said, opening the huge stainless-steel fridge door with a flourish.

'Oh, right, thanks.'

What was wrong with the water in the tap? Mind you, she had read somewhere that the water was recycled forty times between the reservoir in Reading and coming out of the tap in London.

She couldn't think what to say to Paul, and she was relieved when the front door opened, and Aileen shouted, 'Maria, you lazy-bones, are you out of bed yet?'

'Yes, I'm in here.'

'Oh, you're alive then. And you've introduced yourselves?' Aileen dumped three cartons of Häagen Dazs ice cream on the counter. 'What flavour? We'll leave one out to get soft while we're eating.'

'What is there?' Maria asked.

'Malibu, Baileys, or strawberry.'

'Wow! Beats the watery stuff that Mam gets. Malibu flavour would be nice.'

60

'Is that OK with you, Paul?' Aileen said, hugging him from behind as he drained the rice.

'Yeah, great.' He turned and kissed her forehead.

'Will I set the table?' Maria asked, tentatively pulling open drawers to find the cutlery.

'We'll use these,' said Aileen, putting out fine blue Chinese patterned bowls, and balancing chopsticks on little dragon-shaped china stands.

Maria had only ever eaten Chinese food with a fork, out of aluminium cartons – but she wasn't going to admit that she didn't know how to use chopsticks.

The food was delicious, and during dinner they chatted about Paul's job working for a record company. Maria didn't recognise the names of any of the bands, but Paul assured her that they were small now, on the indie London scene, but one day they would be household names.

'So they don't get chauffeur-driven limousines laid on for them?' Maria teased.

She had recovered from the embarrassment of asking for a fork and spoon.

'No, they're lucky if they have a van to take their kit to the gigs.' Paul smiled. 'We'll take you to a gig one night. It's good fun, isn't it, Aileen?'

'Yeah, the craic behind the stage is great, even if the music isn't always!' Aileen said, laughing.

At eleven o' clock, Paul and Aileen went to bed. Now Maria wasn't tired at all. She sat watching a late-night movie, eating tortilla chips and salsa, and drifting into fantasies of Joe. The night of the Med Ball had been really magical. The build-up had been incredible. All the girls were stressed out about what they were going to wear, spending huge chunks of their grant money on dresses, and buying new make-up and bags and shoes. The guys just had to hire dinner jackets, so that was easy, but they were nervous about who to ask, and how much the whole thing was going to cost them. Joe was so cool, and he wore an antique dinner jacket that had been his dad's, which gave him a real air of sophistication. He turned up in a taxi for Maria and Pauline answered the door, and yelled up the stairs, 'Ms Hardy, your escort awaits you!'

Maria knew when she came to the top of the stairs that Joe was impressed. She was wearing the full-length dark green velvet sheath-dress and glittery stiletto mules that were very dangerous and very glamorous. Her hair hung loose over her shoulders, emphasizing her long slender neck. When Maria looked down and saw Joe's expression of awe, she melted inside. He jumped up the stairs and kissed her hard.

'You look fantastic,' he said, sweeping his arm out from behind his back and presenting a delicate pink and white orchid. 'If it wasn't in a box, I'd have put it in between my teeth,' he said, laughing. His lips were red with her lipstick.

'Yes, you'd look like Mutley in that cartoon, with a box in your mouth,' said Pauline, who couldn't resist watching the Romeo act on the stairs.

'I like the jacket,' said Maria, fingering the rich old fabric. 'You look pretty good yourself,'

She kissed him, and it was nice to be standing one step higher than him, pressing down on his lips from above. 'So this is what it's like to be a man,' she said.

'Or a tall woman,' Pauline interjected, knowing exactly what Maria was thinking. Maria and Joe both resisted the urge to tell her to shut up and ran out to the cab, hand in hand.

'Have a lovely time,' Pauline shouted after them, like an anxious mother hen sending her chick off to her first dance.

They had cocktails when they arrived at the hotel and Maria felt like a queen, gliding around in her long dress, knowing that every other girl was looking at her jealously. She held onto Joe's arm, and imagined that they were at a medical conference, where he was the main speaker, acclaimed as a famous surgeon and she was his accomplished wife, intelligent, successful and graceful in any social situation.

She found herself nodding almost condescendingly at the other people who came up to talk to them, as the third Singapore Sling took hold and her fantasy world became more real. Luckily they sat down to eat before she did any damage, and the meal passed in a pleasant haze of laughter and conversation about nothing in particular. Joe occasionally put his hand down to touch her thigh and stroke the velvet, looking sideways at her and smiling wickedly. By the end of the meal, she was desperate to dance with him so that he could hold her tight, and she could close her eyes and inhale his musky aftershave. The DJ didn't put any slow songs on for ages and Maria had a Baileys on ice while they waited. Finally, Joe took her hand and led her to the dance floor.

She was so lucky. Loads of the guys had just piled straight over to the bar and their girlfriends were sitting looking wistfully at the other dancers, or resigning themselves to getting pissed as well. Joe was a great dancer and he held her close, nuzzling her hair, and singing the lyrics of the songs in her ear. It was like there was no one else in the whole world, just them and the music and the glittering lights of the dance floor, like stars above their heads. She knew she was out of her head, but it was great to surrender to the warm and gooey feelings inside, with Joe's arms holding her tight.

Maria didn't want to remember the rest, getting home and making love and . . . the rest. That night would always be special as long as she stopped the memory-video at the right place. At three o' clock in the morning, she crawled to bed in Aileen's spare room, leaving the remnants of her midnight feast on the coffee table.

Chapter Eight

Joe's mother was delighted to have him home for a few months. She had a list of jobs for him to do around the house.

'You inherited your father's practical turn of hand, as well as his brains,' she said from the bottom of the ladder, as Joe cleared the front guttering.

Sometimes Joe wished he hadn't. Then he wouldn't have to live up to his father's memory all the time. He couldn't even remember what his father looked like. He had died when Joe was only six, and he had worked so hard as the local GP that Joe hardly ever saw him.

The smell of tobacco still brought back distant memories of being tucked into bed by his daddy, hoping for a bedtime story. Otherwise, his father had faded completely. He had just become the icon that his mother painted, full of saintly virtue, intellect and good humour, whom Joe was supposed to emulate.

He was dreading the rest of the summer. His mother had become so clingy. She wanted to spend every minute with him when he was home, even to the point of coming into town with him to buy new jeans. He drew the line at coming out of the dressing-room for her approval, and she was quiet on the way home.

'So how do you think the exams went?' she had asked over dinner on his first night back.

'Not bad. I put in the work, so I should be all right.'

Next summer he would get a job. And it wouldn't be in Westport. He needed to get a life, like everyone else had. Loads of people got J1 visas and went off to New York and Boston. Mike was on a kibbutz in Israel, despite his own mother begging him not to go, and Maria was in London . . . suddenly he couldn't eat any more.

'Joe, you're very quiet, love. Have you something on your mind?' his mother said, her head cocked to one side.

'No, I'm just tired after the exams. I'll be fine in a couple of days.'

He sat in his room that night, thinking about Maria.

Had she done it yet? No, she would only have got to London that morning. It felt like much longer. She would probably have to book into a clinic in advance. Vague memories of the female gynaecological system came back from his first-year anatomy classes, but he didn't want to think about what was happening to Maria. He missed her dreadfully. They had spent nearly every night together for the last six months. Lying in his hard narrow bed with the fuzzy cotton sheets, he remembered the feel of her smooth soft skin, and the smell of her hair, and the perfumed nape of her neck where he kissed away the beads of sweat after they made love. He wondered why she hadn't called to say she had arrived safely. Joe sat up in the dark. Of course she hadn't called. She was afraid his mother would answer. He looked at his watch. Pity it was so late.

He'd have to wait until tomorrow to ring Mrs Hardy and get Aileen's number. It had been so weird saying goodbye to Maria that he hadn't thought of asking her for it.

He fell asleep listening to Meatloaf with his earphones on 'Love . . . happy forever . . . wife.' The words echoed in his dreams.

When Noreen got up to go to the bathroom in the middle of the night, she looked in on Joe. She still liked to do that when he was home. Gently, she took off the earphones and looked down at him, thinking how like Derek their son was, with his sandy eyelashes and his tousled hair.

She loved him so much. She dreaded the day when some girl would come along and take him away. Tip-toeing back to her room, she sent up a little prayer that he would always stay with her.

Chapter Nine

The telephone woke Maria from a deep sleep. She looked around the unfamiliar room and only remembered where she was when she saw the photograph of her parents looking benignly down from the dressing-table.

Where was the phone? It was still ringing insistently when she tracked it down to the kitchen.

'Hello?' she said breathlessly.

'Oh, thank God you're all right, love!' Her mother's voice sounded frantic.

'Oh, Mam, I'm sorry I didn't ring you yesterday.'

Maria couldn't believe she had forgotten. Already, Carraroe seemed a million miles away.

'No, you didn't. I was worried sick, but I didn't want to ring in case you thought I was fussing. You're a big girl now, but all the same –'

'I know, I should have rung. Sorry, Mam,' Maria said sheepishly. 'The journey was so long, I lost track of the time, and I was exhausted when I got here. But Aileen or Paul would have called you if there was any problem.'

'Paul? And why would Paul be ringing me? Anyway, I'm glad you're all right. Was the journey very tiring, so? Would you have been better to fly?'

Maria winced. She would have to be careful. It would be just typical if she gave her sister's secret away now, just when Aileen was planning to tell them.

'It was fine, Mam. It was a lot cheaper than flying.'

'You sound very distant, love.'

'It's only eight o'clock in the morning!'

'Well, if you're job-hunting, you need to be up early looking in the papers. The early bird, and all that, although I know you were never a great one in the mornings –'

'Tell you what, Mammy,' Maria interjected, 'I'll give you a ring at the weekend and let you know how I'm getting on. That'll give me a few days to get my bearings.'

'Grand, so. How's Aileen? Did she enjoy her day off with you?'

'She did, I think, except she had to be up so early to meet the bus. We had a great chat though. So that was good.' Suddenly she couldn't think of anything to say. The biggest thing that was happening in her life was the only thing she couldn't talk about.

'Give Aileen my love. I'll talk to you at the weekend. Good luck with the job-hunting. I'll tell your dad you sent your love.'

As Maria hung up, she saw a Yellow Pages on the shelf under the telephone. What would it be under? A? T?

She couldn't find any entries and stopped to think again. That was it: the leaflet said she had to get a referral from a doctor. As the kettle boiled, she flicked through the sections. Outside, a magpie landed on the roof of the shed next door.

'One for sorrow, two for joy,' she said out loud, automatically looking for the second one.

There wasn't another one. She looked at the plump magpie and noticed the iridescence of his blue-tinged wings, and his bright beady eyes looking down curiously at the empty bird-table in the garden. 'What's the time, Mr Magpie?' she said, and then felt silly. They had always said it as children to ward off the bad luck of a single magpie. Beate at college told her that in Holland, they say, 'Hello, Mr Magpie, how are your wife and children?' She had learned the Dutch saying off by heart, and loved the guttural sounds as they rolled off her tongue. Now she couldn't remember them. She'd have to rely on Pauline's mother's theory about the one hiding in the bushes.

She really needed to be in control again. Aileen had thrown her off track, saying she should think about it for a while. She had to do something now. Aileen's doctor. That made sense. She would get herself signed up and fill in the forms, or whatever she had to do. It would probably take a while for the appointment to come through.

On the wall over the telephone, Aileen had stuck a list of emergency numbers. Maria dialled the doctor's surgery before she had any more time to think.

'Morning. Surgery, can I help you?'

The cockney voice surprised her for a moment.

'Yes, I need to make an appointment as soon as possible.'

'What's your name?'

Maria hesitated. Should she use a false name? No, too complicated. It would never get back home anyway.

'Em, Maria Hardy.'

'One moment.'

Maria could hear computer keys clicking.

'You're not registered with this practice, are you?' The voice came back, accusing.

'No, do I need to be?'

'Yes. Where do you live?'

'What, do you mean in London?'

'Yes, where else?'

'Em . . .' Maria froze. She couldn't remember Aileen's address. 'Herne Hill. Yes, that's it – 389 Herne Hill. Flat 2,' she stammered.

'Are you sure?' the impatient voice asked.

'Yes, I am.'

'Right, you're in the catchment area then. There's been a cancellation for 10.30 this morning. Do you want that one?'

'Yes, that would be great, thanks. I'll see you then,' Maria effused.

'Get here five minutes early to fill in the forms,' was the final command from the voice.

Maria turned on the television to get some Breakfast TV news. The first item was about the Prime Minister visiting single mothers in a Council block somewhere in London. Great. She flicked the channels, but could only find Mr Motivator doing his morning exercise routine for fat housewives, and an old *Lassie* film.

She'd better get ready and make sure not to be late for the precious appointment.

In the shower, she wondered how long it would take to get to the surgery, and then realised she didn't even know where it was.

She wasn't going to phone that old bat again to ask for directions. It wasn't easy, like at home. You'd just ask someone, and they'd know. Maria sensed the emptiness of the whole block of flats. Everyone else was out at work, and here she was in her own little bubble, sitting thinking about the biggest decision of her life, and no one knew.

She could ring Aileen at work and ask for directions, but she would make Maria think about it for another few weeks, while this thing was growing bigger and bigger inside her. Her stomach clenched, and she gagged over the bathroom sink.

'Come on. Get a grip,' she muttered.

The doctor's address was probably in that local directory thing.

Wrapped in Aileen's fluffy robe, she sat on the edge of the sofa with her mug of cold coffee and flicked through the doctors' entries until she found the one that matched the telephone number on Aileen's pad.

'Right,' she said, and scanned the bookshelves for that A to Z map Aileen had told her would be invaluable.

There it was. Three minutes later, she had scrawled the address and directions on a Post-it note and was putting on her make-up in the bedroom.

Aileen was right; this was her decision and no one else's. She had her life to lead. She tied up her hair and put on some extra eye-shadow to look older and more responsible. Clutching the map and note, she locked the flat door and remembered to carefully double-lock the street door, as Aileen had instructed.

After a brisk fifteen-minute walk, she reached the crumbling steps of a red-brick Victorian building with a mildewy brass 'Surgery' plaque beside the door. Dickensian images of creaking doors and squinting windows came to mind as she climbed the steps and rang the doorbell.

She gave her name to the metallic voice on the intercom, and the door buzzed loudly. A minute later, no one had come to open the imposing black door. She pushed, but it didn't budge. She rang again.

'Hello? I can't get in.'

'Push the door,' the voice said.

Maria pushed tentatively when the buzzer went, and then harder. Finally it clicked and swung open. She stepped into a narrow tiled hall with a strong smell of antiseptic.

A tatty sign pointed to Reception, where three women sat on tall stools surrounded by brown patients' files.

'Can I help you?'

Maria recognised the snotty telephone voice. 'I have an appointment at half ten.'

'Name?'

'Maria.'

'Maria what?'

'Hardy, sorry.' She blushed.

'Fill in these forms and take a seat upstairs.'

She climbed the wide stairs to a huge waiting-room with five doors leading off it, each with a doctor's name in a slot. *Dr Van, Dr Ramprakash, Dr Batteshara, Dr Ringsangpore, Dr Ryan.*

The last one was comforting to see. She hoped that one of them was a woman. No chance though. They would probably all be really creepy. Not like old Doctor Sweeney, who had seen her since she got her first polio vaccination as a baby. But then, she couldn't imagine telling Doctor Sweeney what she was just about to do. Or have him rummaging around in her private parts.

She sat down and picked up a magazine, trying not to stare at the other occupants of the hard red plastic chairs. She filled in her forms. Opposite, a black lady was breast-feeding a tiny baby, its head nestled in the crook of her arm. She was wearing one of those voluminous brightly coloured dresses from the market, and she had a towel discreetly draped across her breast. She was smiling down at her baby, crooning softly to it.

Maria couldn't help looking at her. She wanted to touch the little baby's head, to feel the soft downy hair that was curly even as it came out of his head. The mother caught her eye and smiled. Maria looked down. Pauline was always giving out to her for staring at people. Finally, with the sound of a bullet sliding into a chamber, the door of Doctor Van's room clicked open.

He called out, 'Maria Hardy?'

Maria jumped up and followed him inside. The room was much more clinical than Doctor Sweeney's surgery at the back of his house. This one had green lino on the floor, and a stainless-steel and glass desk with a big computer screen.

'What can I do for you?'

He was looking at the forms she handed him. He sat down.

Maria was disconcerted. He was only about thirty, and was quite attractive, with black hair, dark skin and beautiful long-fingered hands with manicured nails. She hoped he wouldn't have to examine her *intimately*.

She looked sideways at the examination couch shrouded in its layer of hygienic green tissue paper.

'I came because I –' Maria stopped.

'Is that an Irish accent I hear?' the doctor asked, trying to put her at ease. Another student in London for a wild summer, wanting to have the pill prescribed. It always started like this. The Irish girls got so embarrassed. Why didn't they just buy condoms and not put themselves through the stress?

'Yes. I'm here for the summer, staying with my sister in Herne Hill.'

'So, what can I do for you?' His voice was soft and kind.

Maria's eyes filled with tears.

'Oh, it's not as bad as all that, is it?'

'I want to get an abortion. I mean, a termination, or whatever you call it over here,' she gabbled.

'I see.'

He swivelled his chair to the desk and made a note, gathering his thoughts.

'I'm not sure exactly how it works, how to get one, so that's why I came here. To get a referral, I think.'

'Yes, we can help you but let me ask you a few questions first, all right?'

He handed her a tissue. Maria nodded and blew her nose. The worst was over.

'First things first. Are you absolutely sure you're pregnant? You've done a test?'

'Yes, three tests, and they were all positive.'

'And when was your last period?' He rummaged in a drawer.

'The first of April.'

He pulled out a cardboard wheel printed with dates, spun it and said, 'So that makes you about twelve weeks pregnant then.'

'Eleven and a half.'

'And why do you want a termination?'

Maria thought it was fairly obvious. 'I'm only

nineteen, and I'm still at university, and my boyfriend doesn't want this baby, and neither do . . .' She paused.

'Neither do you?'

'No, I don't. I mean, I don't know how I'd cope. I'd have to give up university and my dad would throw me out of the house. My boyfriend isn't ready to settle down. I'd be on my own.'

'Are you absolutely certain you don't want to have this baby?' Doctor Van had had enough of these conversations to detect indecision when he saw it. He looked at Maria intently.

He had beautiful dark-brown eyes. Mesmerising. Like Kaa the snake in *Jungle Book*.

'Yes, I think so.' She looked down. Her trainers were in desperate need of a good clean.

'It is possible to continue living a normal life after a baby comes. Everything doesn't have to come to an end. Do you have any family members who would be supportive if you had the baby?'

'My sister. She's trying to persuade me to keep it.'

'It sounds to me like you are not totally sure yourself what you want. Is that fair?'

'I suppose so.' Maria refused to meet his eyes. She didn't want to be hypnotised by their dark depths. 'My boyfriend said he's not ready to be a father, and I suppose I'm not ready to be a mother. I'm too young.'

'Many girls younger than you have chosen to keep their babies. Maria, you are old enough to make this decision, and you are the only one who can make it. Let me explain the process to you, and then you can decide what to do next.'

'OK.' Maria sniffed and finally looked up at him.

The doctor reached for a bundle of forms and leaflets on the shelf above his desk. 'The law in this country says that every woman has the right to abortion, but it must be authorised by two doctors, and you must go through some counselling to make sure you have thought through all your options.'

'Right.' There didn't seem to be anything else to say.

'I would feel happier making a referral to the clinic for you if I was sure that you had really thought everything through, using all the information available. You are still relatively early in your pregnancy so you have some more time to think.' He handed Maria the papers. 'I would suggest that you read all this information and book an appointment to see me again next week. If you are sure you want to go ahead, I will make the referral. They can do the procedure within a couple of days, so don't worry.'

Maria couldn't think of an answer, so she just said, 'OK, Doctor. It won't be too late next week?'

'As I said, it won't be too late. Tell Reception to book you in to see me next Monday.' He stood up. Maria shoved the leaflets and forms into her bag. This wasn't like getting a prescription. Everyone in the waiting-room would know if she came out with the papers in her hand, what she was planning to do. People would peer at the leaflets to see what was wrong with her.

'Thanks, Doctor. I'll see you next Monday then.'

'Bye.'

The flat was very silent when she got back. There was a slight smell of lemon Flash from the bathroom and a hint of garlic from the Chinese meal last night, but Aileen had done all the clearing up before she went to work, so everything in the kitchen was sparkling. She must have inherited the manic need to clean from their mam. Maria felt a little bit guilty about the salsa stain on the green sofa. She had balanced a huge lump on the corner of a triangular tortilla chip and it had fallen off just as she got it to her mouth. Now she scrubbed it with carpet cleaner, and it left a white patch on the fabric which looked even worse.

Maria made a cup of tea, and decided not to read through the information pack yet. She idly flicked on the television.

Getting an abortion was supposed to be easy in England, wasn't it? Girls came over from Ireland all the time to get rid of babies. She bet they weren't put through hoops like this. Doctor Van was probably some idealistic pro-life guy. Trust her to get that one, out of a surgery of five. She peeled an orange, and sneezed as the citrus drops hit her nose. She lay back on the sofa, flicking through the channels on the TV and thinking about Joe. Was he regretting what they had decided? Probably not, especially when he was with his mother all day, every day. That's what he had been most scared about. His mother finding out.

79

Would he call her or would he be too scared that his mother would notice the call on the telephone bill? Which reminded her, she hadn't asked the doctor how much all this would cost. She only had three hundred pounds with her. The post-office savings she had sworn not to use, ever. Well, this was an emergency. They didn't come much bigger than this. Joe hadn't offered her any money, but he probably thought it would be a bit tacky. Paying her off, like in some American B movie.

When she woke up an hour later, she kicked herself. She couldn't keep sleeping at strange times. It wasn't as if she even had jet-lag as an excuse. Maybe bus and ferry-lag was a new phenomenon. The TV was still on, the volume turned down low. The announcer disappeared and a title came up on the screen. *The Miracle of Life*. She turned up the volume. She loved wildlife documentaries.

'*This is the story about the beginning of human life, and the miracle of birth*,' said a deep voice. Maria's heart jumped, but as the programme rolled, she was entranced. She should turn it off. But she had to watch and watch. An embryo changed to a foetus, and grew and grew. The melodious voice of the narrator described each stage of its development.

Maria shouted at the man on the screen, 'No, it's not fair! I know about this stuff! I got a B in biology in the Leaving Cert!'

But still she watched, as a pregnant mother gently stroked her stomach and smiled, feeling the first kicks of her baby at twenty weeks. Maria couldn't get the remote control to work, so she stood up to turn off the television as the screen was filled with an ultrasound-scan picture of the baby moving in the womb, sucking its thumb and kicking. She stopped in front of the screen. It looked so human. It had all its fingers and toes.

The Professor explained that babies sleep and wake inside the womb, and respond to loud noises and even music. Maria looked down at her stomach and pulled up her T-shirt. The baby was already the size of a peach, according to that guy, with eyelids and ears. Finally, as the film showed the slimy, bloodied head of the baby emerging at birth, Maria reached across and turned it off.

She collapsed on the sofa, sobbing. Joe must know all this stuff even better than she did. She couldn't pretend any more that having an abortion was like any other operation. She had never once thought of the little life growing inside her as a separate entity. It had just been a threat to her future and to her relationship with Joe.

Now she suddenly had a surge of protectiveness towards it. That was even more scary, and she wanted desperately to talk to Joe, to tell him what she was feeling.

But he hadn't even called to see if she was all right. Maybe if they talked, he would change his mind too, if she explained how she was feeling. What was she going to do? The fear hit her hard. She ran to the bathroom and retched into the sink. If she kept the baby, her whole life would change. She would have to stay in London. She would probably lose Joe. He wanted to qualify, and he didn't need a family holding him back. Daddy wouldn't have her in the house. Mam would back him up, even if she disagreed with him. They always stuck together. So she would lose nearly everyone who was close to her, if she had this baby.

Chapter Ten

The key rattled in the door and Aileen came in panting, laden with shopping bags.

'Hiya!' she yelled from the hall, and was alarmed at Maria's muffled answer.

'Are you OK?'

She came into the living-room and saw Maria curled up on the sofa, her T-shirt pulled down over her knees. Her pupils were dilated and her eyes looked huge in her tear-stained face.

'Oh, Maria, what's the matter?' She sat on the sofa, and stroked Maria's hair. 'Are you sick?'

'Sick in the head, maybe,' Maria sniffed and tried her brave smile. 'I think I'm going to keep it.'

The tears streamed down her cheeks again. Aileen grabbed a box of tissues from the kitchen and handed them to her.

'Aw, that's great news altogether. You're doing the right thing. I was worried stiff about you.'

Maria sat up and rubbed her face.

'What made you change your mind?' Aileen asked.

'I went to the doctor's today, to get a referral to a clinic.' She balled up the damp tissues in her fist. 'He asked me loads of questions. I suppose he had to, to make me think about it.'

'Which one did you get?'

'Doctor Van, I think his name was.'

'He's gorgeous, isn't he?'

'I wasn't really looking, to be honest,' said Maria, affronted. How could Aileen be so trivial, at a time like this? When she saw Aileen's face fall, she said, 'But yeah, I suppose he was kind of cute.'

They laughed, and Aileen put on the kettle. They sat in the kitchen, hands wrapped around their mugs, and dunked chocolate biscuits in their tea.

'What did he say?'

'He gave me this information pack, and told me I had to think about it some more and come back next week. I didn't even get around to reading the information. I fell asleep on the sofa and when I woke up there was a programme on the telly about babies. Aileen, I couldn't believe it. At twelve weeks old, it has everything formed already, little hands and feet, and eyes and ears.'

A pang of jealousy viciously stabbed at Aileen. Memories of her abortion three years before still haunted her. She could never tell Maria. It happened when she and Paul had just started seeing each other. She took the morning-after pill, but it hadn't worked, and she had been terrified when her breasts had started to hurt and she had been sick every morning for three weeks. But she had the abortion so early that she had been able to tell herself that it wasn't really a baby. Now she banished the thought that Maria, as usual, would beat her to it, and have a child first.

'Are you all right?' Maria asked, when she noticed Aileen's silence.

'Yeah, fine. I was just wondering when you're going to tell them at home?'

'I'd better do it soon, so they get used to the idea of me staying in London.'

'Have you decided that for definite? Just because I said you could get a job here, that's not the only option you know. Joe will be in Galway for another few years, won't he?'

'Yes, but he's made it clear that he's not ready for this. I don't want to rub his face in it by being around Galway. I'm the one who changed my mind about keeping the baby, so I just need to get a job and be independent.'

'What about working in Dublin, or Cork, or somewhere like that?'

Aileen didn't want to be single-handedly responsible for her sister's drop-out from college and emigration all in one go.

'There's much more of a chance of getting decent work over here than there is at home. There's so many graduates and even postgrads in Ireland now, they're getting all the jobs, even the ones they're over-qualified for.'

'Well, you might have to settle for a shop job or something like that to start off with,' said Aileen. 'London is not the proverbial streets-paved-with-gold, you know. There are lots of qualified people here looking for jobs too. '

'Whatever.' Sometimes the big-sister act was very irritating, and Aileen had such a hang-up about not being a graduate. 'More to the point, what am I going to tell them at home?'

Aileen winced. 'Is there any chance you'd get back together with Joe?'

'He hasn't exactly had the phone hopping off the wall to see how I am, has he?' said Maria, munching an apple. She was constantly starving now, and she supposed her body was making up for lost time.

'No, but you've only been here a day, Maria. Give him a break. I was just thinking they might take it easier at home if they thought you might get married . . .'

'Aileen, Joe's mother doesn't even know I exist. He was terrified that she'd find out we were just going out together. There's not a bat's chance in hell that he'll suddenly turn around and want to marry me!'

'OK, OK, sorry I asked. The way I see it, you have two alternatives. Tell them straight away, and get it over with, or wait for a while, and see if Joe and you do get back together.'

'Thanks. Sorry I got ratty. I just feel like I'm backed into a corner with nowhere to go.'

Maria knew she had overreacted because she still secretly hoped that Joe *would* ask her. She constantly pushed the thought to the back of her mind. It hurt too much to bear the light of day.

'I brought you the *Evening Standard*.' Aileen dug around in her huge handbag and took it out, already folded at the job pages. 'You could probably ring a few of these today. Sometimes the jobs get snapped up on the first day the ad goes in.'

Aileen started peeling potatoes and put a bottle of wine in the fridge to chill for dinner.

This was all too quick for Maria. When she woke up this morning, she was an almost carefree student looking for a summer job. By dinner-time she was a single mother looking for a permanent job, emigrating, and probably saying goodbye to her boyfriend and her family all in one go.

She looked at the paper and hesitated.

'Do you want me to help you go through them?' Aileen asked.

'No, thanks.' Maria took the telephone into the other room, so Aileen wouldn't hear her, and after circling five jobs, braced herself and dialled the first number.

She could tell after making three calls that she was being screened out, but she didn't know what she was saying wrong. The last number was answered by a friendly Irish voice, and Maria relaxed, and lost her job-hunting tone of voice.

'How long have you been over here?' the lady asked.

'Only since yesterday.'

'And what do you think of it so far?'

'I haven't really seen many of the sights yet.'

'And have you someone to show them to you?'

'Yes, my sister. I'm staying with her for the moment.'

'Good, I'm sure your mother is glad that you have someone to look after you.'

'She is, yeah.'

There was a lot to be said for the business-like receptionists who had taken her name and address and brightly said, 'Thanks very much, we'll be in touch in a couple of weeks.' Next, the woman would be asking her what she had for breakfast.

'We'll send you an application form, love. You just fill it in and get it back to us as soon as you can, and we'll give you a ring.'

'That last one sounded good,' said Aileen from the kitchen.

'It was like the Spanish Inquisition!' said Maria, 'She was asking me all these questions that had nothing to do with the job.'

'What's it for?'

'A receptionist in a building contractor's.' Then it clicked. She had recognised the voice. It was Ivy Naughtan's. 'Hey, Aileen, I think it must be Daddy's friend Paddy Naughtan's business. Isn't that what he does?'

'It is. Over in West London somewhere – did you ask where it's based?'

'It says Acton on the ad.'

'It's got to be him, Maria. Excellent!'

'How long would it take me to get there?'

'About an hour. Once you get used to the idea that it takes that long to get anywhere in London, it doesn't bother you.'

Maria grunted. The job started at eight in the morning. She'd have to get up really early.

'I'll have to tell Dad first that I'm going for it. Paddy's bound to ring him, isn't he?'

'Good point. You might as well get it over with tonight then.' Aileen hugged her. 'Have a little glass of wine – it will calm you down.'

When Paul came in from work he could smell grilling lamb chops and hear giggles from the kitchen. He kissed Aileen and said, 'Is there any wine left for me? It looks like you two have been at it for a while.'

'I only had one glass,' said Maria, pointing accusingly at Aileen. 'She drank the rest of it!'

'We're celebrating,' said Aileen, waving her glass.

'Are we?' Paul was surprised, after what Aileen had told him in bed last night. She had cried inconsolably and said that having the abortion was the worst decision she had ever made in her life. For the first time, last night as he held her tight, he wished that they had gone ahead and had the baby. He definitely knew that Aileen was the one for him. But how were they to know that three years ago? And maybe it would have been too much pressure too early.

'She's keeping it.' Aileen smiled.

'You told him?' Maria screeched, blushing to the roots of her hair.

'It's OK, Maria, I wouldn't have told anyone, but I'm glad you've decided to keep the baby,' reassured Paul, shooting a disapproving look at Aileen.

Maria let her hair hang down to hide her face. How could Aileen have told him? The biggest secret in the whole world, and Aileen couldn't keep it to herself for even one night. Paul diplomatically went to have a shower.

Aileen sat opposite Maria and leaned across the table, touching her arm. 'Look, I'm sorry if you didn't want me to tell Paul, but I was worried about you, and he knew something was wrong. We tell each other everything. We have no secrets.'

Maria nodded. 'It doesn't matter now that I've changed my mind anyway. It's going to be pretty obvious soon. Thanks for worrying about me.' She smiled.

Chapter Eleven

Maria picked at her lamb chops, mentally rehearsing what she would say. Aileen and Paul exchanged glances and cleared the table.

'I'll wash and you can dry,' Aileen said, and they closed the door to the kitchen, leaving the telephone with Maria. Aileen must have thought she hadn't noticed the dishwasher.

She checked her watch. Nine o'clock. Dad would be back from his parish-council meeting by now. She would wait, and not interrupt the *News*. That gave her another twenty minutes to plan what to say. No, Aileen and Paul would be standing twiddling their thumbs at the draining-board.

'What's the code for home?' she yelled through the hatch to the kitchen.

'00353 and then the number,' said Aileen, running the tap so Maria wouldn't think they were listening.

Now they would know she was dialling. Maria

watched the fish in Aileen's aquarium. They had no idea what an easy life they had. They endlessly visited the stone grotto and nudged the tacky plastic diver searching for treasure. It must be great to be stupid. Or made of plastic. She dialled.

'Hello?' said her mother's voice, surprised that anyone would ring during the *News*.

'Hiya, Mam, it's me.'

'Hello, love, this is a nice surprise. Did you get a job already?'

'No, not really, but I want to go for one, and I just wanted to talk to Daddy about it first.'

'I'll get him in a minute for you. What's the job?' What advice could Sean give her about a summer job, Maureen wondered.

'Receptionist. It's for a building contractor's in Acton, and that's where Aileen says Paddy Naughtan is based.'

'It is too. That would be grand, wouldn't it, love? A job with a friend of the family. Is it for the whole summer?'

Maria swallowed. 'Yes, or even a bit longer.'

'Ah Maria, you wouldn't tell him lies that you're staying over there, would you?'

' No.'

'Good, because Dad wouldn't approve of that at all.'

'Mam, I might be staying here for a while.'

Her mother's voice went shrill. 'And why would you do that, when you have college to come back to in September?'

Sean heard the tone of her voice and came rushing

out of the sitting-room, but left the door open so he could see the sports results.

'What's the matter?' he said.

'It's Maria . . .'

'What's wrong with her? Did she have an accident?'

'No, she's . . .'

Maria sat rigid on the sofa in London, her eyes tightly closed. She could see the pair of them. Mam would be sitting on the third step of the stairs, on the worn bit in the middle. Daddy would be standing by the rickety telephone table. The vein in his temple would be throbbing, and his eyes would be bulging out of their sockets. He had looked the same when he heard that Hugh had failed his Leaving Cert.

'Mam?' she said into the receiver.

'I'm just telling your dad.'

Maureen turned to her husband. 'She wants to stay in London. She's going for a job with Paddy Naughtan.'

He grabbed the telephone.

There must be a mistake. Maureen was always getting the wrong end of the stick.

'Maria, love, are you there?' He was talking in his special voice for giving out to the neighbours when they annoyed him.

'Hi, Dad. I was just saying to Mam I want to go for a job with Paddy and I was wondering if you would give him a ring for me?'

'Of course I will, but what's this about staying in London?'

'I need to stay over here for a while.'

What a pathetic excuse for an explanation. Keep going, she told herself. You're nearly there. Get those words lined up in a row, and spit them out. Like the bullets in a bandolier.

'Why? How long for?' Calmly, he would collect the facts before he blew his top. The other two were a waste of space. Hugh off gallivanting as a waiter in Australia, and Aileen in a clerical job in the bank. Maria was his great hope. She might even follow in his footsteps and become a teacher.

Maria's throat had closed up completely. Her voice wasn't working. She swallowed and took a deep breath.

'I went to the doctor's today.'

'The doctor's?'

Sean's blood pressure went up a notch. She wouldn't do that to him. Not that.

'Is she sick?' asked Maureen anxiously from her perch on the stairs.

It suddenly came to Maria. She could buy some time before she told them.

'I have glandular fever. The doctor said it can last for a long time. Months.' Maybe even nine, she thought. 'He said it was stress-related. He said I should take a year off college instead of trying to keep up with it, and tiring myself out.'

She knew she was gabbling. *'Lies always lead to more lies'* she could hear Mrs O' Malley, her primary school teacher, saying.

'Oh, Maria, that's terrible,' said Sean, but his tone of voice didn't match the words. Thank God she wasn't pregnant.

'Tell me! What is it, Sean?' said Maureen.

'She's not very well. She has glandular fever. That's an awful dose, altogether.' He turned back to the telephone.

'What are you doing getting a job then? Would you not be better coming home, here, where we can mind you?'

'No, Dad, I need to be doing something. I don't want to lose the year completely, sitting around doing nothing.'

'But will Paddy give you a job when you're sick?'

'I'll tell him, Dad, honestly.' Now she had screwed it up. Big hole, big time. 'Maybe I'll wait, and get you to ring him after I've seen him?'

The hole was getting bigger and she'd need a very long ladder to get out, at this rate.

'All right, so, I'll hand you over to your mother. Let us know how you get on with Paddy. Don't be overdoing it. And you can always come home to us anyway. God bless.'

Maureen took the receiver.

'I thought you were looking a bit peaky before you went off to London,' she said.

'I was a bit tired, all right.'

'And what made you suddenly go to the doctor's?'

Maria swallowed. 'Aileen said she was working with someone who had ME who was tired all the time, and I should get it checked out.'

'Mmm. Very sensible.'

Maureen knew her daughter too well. There was something else going on. But on the phone she couldn't look her in the eye, and see if she was telling lies.

'Do you want me to ring the university for you, and find out what the situation is, about taking some time off?'

'I did already. The Registrar is going to write to me, but he said it shouldn't be a problem.'

'Well, you're very well organised, altogether,' said Maureen, and Maria could hear the doubt in her voice. Time to get off the phone before she dug her way through to Australia.

'And did the doctor give you any medicine?'

'No, he didn't. He said I just have to rest. Listen, I'll go now, Mam. It's Pau– Aileen's phone bill. I'll ring you again tomorrow.'

'By the way, Joe rang today, looking for Aileen's number . . .'

Maria's heart leapt.

'He said he's going to ring you tonight. He's another one who'll be disappointed that you're not coming back in the autumn.'

'I know, I'll tell him when he rings. Thanks, Mam. Bye.'

Maria hung up and beads of sweat broke out on her forehead. She tossed her hair forward, and lifted it up in a huge handful, to let the air circulate at the back of her neck.

The anvil on her chest was a bit lighter. Now there was a piano-wire wrapped around her head, slowly slicing off her scalp.

She looked at the fish-tank again. The fish nudged the diver, but he didn't budge. He was locked in his eternal quest for lost treasure.

'How did it go?' Aileen came bursting out of the kitchen as soon as she heard the ping of the telephone.

'Terrible. I told them I had glandular fever.'

'What?'

'I couldn't tell them. I need to talk to Joe, first. Just in case.'

'Maria, it's going to be difficult to blame glandular fever when you turn up with a baby. Could you not have thought of something else?' Aileen said desperately.

'It was the best I could come up with on the spur of the moment. Mam said Joe is going to ring me tonight.'

Paul interjected. 'You're right, Maria. You bought yourself some time to talk to Joe. And if you do get back together with him, your dad might take the news about the baby a bit easier.'

'But she's already –' Aileen started.

Paul shot her a warning glance. 'Come on, let's go out for a walk and let Maria talk to Joe in peace.'

The telephone rang. They all stared at it. Maria knew it would be Joe. She picked up the receiver.

She didn't have time to work out how to play it, so she forgot to be cool with him for waiting so long to ring.

'Hi, Maria.' He sounded tentative.

'Hiya, Joe, how's it going?' She heard the front door quietly closing as Paul and Aileen sneaked out.

'Fine, with me. Are you, I mean, did you . . . how did it go? Or have you booked it yet?'

'No, I haven't booked it yet, as you so diplomatically put it. You have to get referred by a doctor, and get an appointment. It takes a while.'

'Sorry, I –'

'It's OK, Joe. Listen, I need to talk to you. Everything has changed anyway. I think I want to keep the baby.'

Joe was silent for a minute. Then he said, 'You do? But what about all the stuff we talked about?' He sounded panicky, breathless.

For some reason, that made her feel stronger. 'We didn't really talk about any stuff at all, Joe. But I know what you mean. You don't want your mother to find out. Don't worry. I'm going to stay over here for a while and get a job.'

'It's not that. It's just that –'

'You have three years of college left. You can't support a baby.'

'Well, there's that, and –'

'I'm not asking you for anything. I'll look after the baby. I'm the one who decided to keep it. You don't have to do anything. I'm only telling you, because it's yours as well.'

Why was the conversation going this way? She was being really horrible to him when all she wanted was for him to say he would be on the next plane, or even the next bus, to be at her side.

He said, 'Thanks,' in a thanks-but-no-thanks tone of voice. 'So there's nothing to talk about then, is there?' Maria was so strong-minded and independent. He knew he'd have trouble changing her mind. 'Are you telling your mam and dad?'

'Not yet. I told them I have glandular fever, so I've bought myself some time, just in case . . .'

'In case what?'

'Well, I don't know. Just in case.' There. She had left the door open for him, just in case he wanted to come in.

Joe didn't probe any further. He didn't really want to know what she was thinking.

'How long do you think you'll stay over there?'

'I'm not sure. I'll have the baby first, and then decide.' She couldn't keep the bitterness out of her voice. He wasn't going to ask. When the chips were down, he was going to walk away.

'Maria, I love you. I haven't been able to stop thinking about you since you left. Listen, maybe it will all be fine. We can still talk on the phone and email, and stuff, and see how things go?' He just couldn't take it all in. He needed time to think.

'Yeah, no problem. It's worth a try. We can play it by ear.' Maria didn't want the huge hurt that filled her body to get into the little space where her hope was stored, so she was determined to play it cool. Joe was certainly not jumping on his white stallion to be at her side.

'I'll let you go, so,' he said. Maria was acting very distant. She was pushing him away; he could almost feel the palm of her hand flat on his chest. He needed to get his head around the baby thing. There didn't seem to be anything else worth talking about, anyway. She couldn't just spring it on him like that, and expect him to know what to do. They had made a decision together, he thought, and now she was arbitrarily changing it.

She just said, 'Bye, I'll ring you soon.'

Maria was sitting on the sofa, hugging her knees when Aileen and Paul got back.

She didn't even want to cry. She felt a calm emptiness inside that surprised her. The headache was gone. Joe had disappointed her. Again, just like when she first found out about the baby. For some reason, she had entertained the romantic idea that he would drop everything, claim undying love, and come and rescue her from penury and banishment. She must stop thinking she was living in some Celtic legend. It didn't happen like that in the real world. Why would he have changed his mind in the space of two days, just because she had? Was 'talking on the phone and stuff' supposed to be an offer of some kind of continuing relationship, or was he just keeping his options open? It must have come as a shock to him that she didn't want to go ahead with the abortion but if he really, really loved her, wouldn't he have said different things?

She didn't feel inclined to recount the non-event of a conversation to Aileen and Paul, so she went to read in her room, leaving Aileen speculating about what would happen next, and Paul just nodding and listening.

When Pauline rang at eleven, Aileen came to knock on Maria's door. 'Are you still awake?' she asked, poking her head into the room.

'Mmmm,' Maria muttered, and she put down the book which had fallen on her chest when she dozed off.

'It's Pauline – I told her to hang on.'

'I'll be there in a second. I was going to ring her in the morning.'

Maria pulled on a baggy T-shirt and knickers, and went to the phone.

'Sorry to ring you so late' Pauline said. 'I just started thinking about you this evening and I had to call and see if you were all right.'

'Yes, I am, and you'll never guess what I've done!'

'No, tell me!'

'I'm keeping the baby.'

'Oh, Maria, that is fantastic!' screeched Pauline.

'Don't scream the house down, or your mam will be asking questions,' Maria panicked.

'She knows the whole story already,' Pauline teased.

'You didn't tell her?'

'No, your dad told her all about the glandular fever at choir practice earlier on. He's very worried about you.'

'Well, not half as worried as he would have been if I'd told him the truth!'

'What made you come up with glandular fever, anyway?'

'It was totally spur of the moment – stupid, I know. Anyway, the other big news is I'm going for a job at Paddy Naughtan's yard. Do you remember him?'

'I do. What's the job – scaffolding?'

'Pauline, you're absolutely hilarious – you should have a career on the stage. No, seriously, it's for a receptionist – doing the phones, a bit of typing and some admin, I think.'

'What are we going on about – have you told Joe about keeping the baby yet?'

Maria sat down. This was obviously not going to be a quick call. 'Yes. He wasn't too happy and, as usual, he wants to think about it.'

'Understandably,' said Pauline dryly. Maria was her best friend, but she would never want to be her boyfriend. Maria always gave them such a hard time.

'I suppose so. Anyway, I'll be over here for a while, at least until the baby comes, so I can't expect Joe to wait around forever.'

'No, that's true, but he is the father of the child, Maria.' Pauline always did that. She stated the obvious in a really irritating way.

'Only if he wants to be,' said Maria. 'I'm not going to impose anything on him. That wouldn't be fair, when I'm the one who decided to keep the baby.'

Pauline decided it wasn't time to go interfering. Let them figure it out for themselves.

Her mother passed through the hall, checking if she was still on the phone to London. She pointed to her watch.

'Listen, Maria, I hope the glandular fever is all over soon, and that you'll be feeling better. Mam sends her love. Talk to you soon! Bye'.

Chapter Twelve

Joe's mother was out playing bridge. It was the one night of the week that she went out, so he had to make the most of it. If she asked him about the call to London when the phone-bill came in, he would say he had to ring someone about sharing a house next year.

He had to speak to Maria. He had daydreamed about her all day, and then really dreamed about her all night. Sometimes they were making love on the wild swirling colours of the Indian throw on Maria's single bed, trying not to make too much noise so that Orla wouldn't hear them through the partition wall. Other times, he just saw her laughing in the refectory, tossing her shiny hair and smiling seductively across the littered table at him. But there was also the nightmare. Maria was stretched out on a hospital gurney, wrapped in a green surgical gown, her tangled hair spread out on the pillow around her white face. She was screaming in agony as the baby was scraped out with glittering scalpels. Her mouth was twisted in pain, and her eyes seemed to accuse him. Twice last night, Joe had shot awake, pouring with sweat, staring wide-eyed in the darkness of his room, hoping that he hadn't yelled out in his sleep or his mother would come running in.

He found it easy to delude himself that it was all his mother's fault. If she wasn't such a control freak, he could have stuck by Maria, had the child and spent the rest of his life with her. They could have muddled through, and maybe even finished college.

But he couldn't bear the thought of his mother's disappointment . She had spent the last sixteen years of his life grooming him to be like his father. It seemed to be the sole purpose of her existence, and he couldn't destroy her by throwing it all away now.

It must have happened that time when the condom had slipped off; the night of the Med Ball, when they were both pissed. Maria hadn't said anything the next day, so he hadn't, either. How was he supposed to remember where she was in her cycle? He thought they had made a joint decision to terminate the pregnancy, in both of their best interests.

Now, the world had changed completely. He had called to see how Maria was, and to ask if she needed any money for the abortion. The only worries on his mind as he picked up the phone had been how to get the money out of his mother and whether Maria would dump him.

Five minutes and one telephone conversation later, his head was reeling. He was going to be a father. He should be glad. He should be happy that Maria really needed him now, and they could be together. But he wasn't. The prospect of being a father was too scary to even put into words in his head. He stared out of his bedroom window. He watched the stream of cars swish past on the rain-slick tarmac around the bend to the coast road, their headlights briefly illuminating his darkened room, and then moving on.

Did those people ever have to worry about the really big important things in life, or only what the neighbours thought of their new car? Joe disdained their small-town mentality. He had realised soon after starting at university that he had no intention of taking his father's place in the white-tiled surgery downstairs. He couldn't even entertain the thought of staying in Westport as a GP for the rest of his life, listening to the daily grumbles about 'flu and piles and ingrown toenails. He would be a proper consultant; a surgeon in a big teaching hospital, famous for his innovative surgical methods. Even Dublin wasn't big enough. He would have to go further afield, maybe even to America. That's where a lot of the cutting-edge things happened. He would have papers published, and be asked to speak at conferences. His mother thought she had him tied to her apron-strings forever, but there was plenty of time yet before he had to break the news to her. A few years at least. Or there had been. The baby changed everything. Now all his thoughts were circular. They all came back around to the baby.

Maria had been very cool and distant again. She was really freaking him out. Did she want to be with him, or not? Maria didn't have to say much, to make it hurt. She was usually so warm and loving that her withdrawal was enough to cut him into shreds. Then he had a flash of anger. She was sitting over there in London, making him feel bad, when she had made the decision to keep the baby by herself. He had no choice in the matter, whether to be a father or not. She had no right to impose that on him. His mother would kill him. She would despise him, for being stupid and throwing away his dream career. She would say she had warned him about getting involved with girls. They were nothing but trouble.

The telephone rang. Joe leapt downstairs two steps at a time. His heart was pounding as he picked it up.

'Hello, Maria?' he said breathlessly. She had the power to make him drop everything. He knew in that moment that he would go to her.

'No, em, that's Joe, isn't it? It's Sergeant Duffy here, down at the Garda station,' came a strong Mayo accent.

'Oh,' said Joe, slowly sinking onto the blue chintz-upholstered chair with gold braid that stood proudly beside the mahogany telephone table. 'Is it my mother?'

'It is, I'm afraid. She had an accident on the Castlebar road. She's above in Castlebar Hospital now.'

'Is it bad?'

107

'They're not sure how bad, Joe. But she's unconscious at the moment.'

The sergeant paused. 'Can I give you a lift over there?'

Joe stood up. 'Please. I'll be at the station in ten minutes.'

'Grand. I'll be waiting here for you.'

Sergeant Duffy was relieved that the first part was over. The rest of it could wait until they were face to face.

Joe pulled on a jacket and stumbled around the house, locking the back door and switching off lights.

He couldn't lose his mother. She drove him mad, but didn't all mothers do that? It was probably in the job description when God put them on the planet.

Joe slammed the heavy blue front door and ran to the Garda station. Every minute might count if she was in a coma. Back in the house, the telephone rang and rang on the shiny mahogany table. After six rings, his mother's voice on the answering machine crisply told the caller to leave a message.

Joe's mind raced as he sat beside Sergeant Duffy on the drive to Castlebar, trying not to inhale the sickly smell of the forest-pine air freshener in the shape of a pine tree, dangling from the mirror.

What was his mother doing on the Castlebar road? They played bridge in Moran's Hotel, in town. She didn't need to be out on the Castlebar road at all. Maybe she was giving someone a lift home? But that was a long way out of her way. He looked at his watch.

Eleven thirty. Usually the chat after the game of bridge would only be just finishing now.

'How did you get the news about the accident?' Joe asked the silent frowning Sergeant.

'We got a call to come to the scene because there were injuries involved,' he said quietly.

'Were there other people hurt as well?'

'Yes.' The Sergeant stared fixedly at the road ahead. 'A ten-year-old girl and her mother were cycling out the road and they got hit. They were badly hurt. The girl probably won't survive the night.'

He was glad he wasn't telling her family the news. Castlebar station was handling that.

'No other car?' Joe asked, incredulous.

'No, apparently not.'

'So how did it happen, then?'

Surely someone must have driven on the wrong side of the road, and crashed into his mother's car or something?

'We think your mother was going a bit fast around the bend and she braked when she saw the cyclists and skidded on the wet road. She hit them, and then skidded across the road into a wall.'

Sergeant Duffy didn't point out where it had happened – the car had already been towed away. Joe had his eyes tightly closed so he didn't see the slivers of glass glittering in the headlights as they passed.

Joe wanted to throw up. His mother was obsessively careful. Sometimes she drove so slowly that he wanted to reach across and press the accelerator-pedal himself. What was she doing, racing home from Castlebar at that hour of the night? She should have been in the smoke-filled function room, with the other ladies in their silk blouses and high heels, and the henpecked husbands in their freshly ironed shirts and rubber-soled shoes.

Sergeant Duffy looked at the pale face of his passenger as he dropped him outside the hospital. Poor lad, with his dad dead and him an only child.

Maria's resolve weakened after talking to Pauline. It was easier said than done to push Joe away. She had reread the same page of her book about ten times. The television might be a bit more distracting, so she came back out of her bedroom, flopped down on the beanbag in the living-room, and tuned into *Never Mind the Buzzcocks*.

Aileen and Paul sat entwined on the sofa for a while, talking and giggling in low voices, and then went to have a bath together. Maria couldn't stand it any more.

She had to speak to Joe. She ached for him. He was just as scared as she was. She shouldn't be so horrible to him. Maybe if they talked, things could really work out, like Joe said, eventually. What if the mother answered the phone? Maria could just be a friend from college. The mother wouldn't suspect a thing. The telephone rang six times and Maria was just about to hang up, embarrassed that she might have woken them up, when the answering machine clicked on.

What now? If she left a message, the mother would hear it. But if she didn't, Joe would think she hadn't called back.

She summoned a bright and breezy tone. 'Hi, Joe, it's Maria from college. Hope you're enjoying your holidays. Give me a buzz when you get a chance. Talk to you soon. Bye!'

The mother would never guess that her darling Joe's pregnant maybe-ex-girlfriend had called to talk about how they could maybe stay together and be a family.

She sighed. The adrenaline rush subsided and settled as an acidic weight on the muscles of her arms and legs. It was over to Joe again. She would not chase him. If he was going to suggest that they keep up some kind of long-distance relationship, it was probably worth a try, but she would go it alone if she had to. She had to adjust to the idea that London was her home for now, and try to make the most of it. She wanted to brush her teeth and go to bed, but the splashes and giggles from the bathroom sounded as if they could go on all night. She went to bed anyway, with a taste of bile in her mouth.

Chapter Thirteen

Maureen and Sean got undressed for bed. Sean was very quiet, and Maureen wondered if he had the same suspicion as she did about Maria. Usually with a family crisis, they talked endlessly, around and around, until they figured out together what to do. It had always worked before, even though sometimes it drove her mad, that Sean had to look at all the angles of a situation before deciding what was for the best. But this time, they kept their unspoken worries to themselves. Maureen knew there hadn't been time for Maria to get the results of a blood test to confirm glandular fever, even if she had walked straight into a doctor's surgery the minute she landed in England.

She wondered if that had occurred to Sean, too. She was desperate to talk to someone, but if she didn't say it out loud, it might not be true. Her sisters would sympathise, but they would be secretly feeling smug, glad it wasn't one of their daughters. Not that they were saints either. Wasn't Sinead living in a weird commune in California, sleeping with all the men in it and telling the whole world about it? And Aisling had a brazen look about her that would make you think she was up to something all the time. And she usually was.

Sean knelt down beside the bed, something he hadn't done for years, since he got rheumatism in his knees. He stretched his arms out in front of him across the quilted green eiderdown, with his hands firmly clenched in prayer. His tightly closed eyes didn't hide the pain in his face, and Maureen was overwhelmed with love for him. Still Sean didn't speak as he climbed into bed and lay on his back, staring at the ceiling.

Maureen touched his arm and whispered,' She'll be grand, love, really. She will.'

He didn't answer. He just rolled away when she lowered her hand to stroke his thigh, their little signal that it was the safe time of the month. Not that she was in the mood herself, but sometimes she liked to offer, so that Sean didn't have to feel like he was always the one to make the first move.

The next day, Sean wished that he hadn't accepted the invitation to the university reunion. He wasn't a great man for reminiscing, and he felt stupid when he didn't recognise people as they came up and shook his hand, saying, 'Sean, how are you? You're looking well. Are you still out in Carraroe?'. Everyone else seemed to have travelled to exotic places, worked for big multi-nationals or made loads of money. They took one look at him and they knew that he was 'still out in Carraroe'. He felt them sneering at his vocation as a teacher, and he knew they had no idea what it took to be a headmaster. They didn't ask, so they didn't know that his school had an excellent track record for Junior Cert and Leaving Cert results. But they weren't quoted on the stock exchange, and the school didn't feature in the business pages of the *Irish Times*. Every time he tried to steer Maureen towards another group of people, hoping to find a new topic of conversation, they were all busy networking and mutually back-scratching. Or speculating about how much the PR would be worth if their company contributed to the fund for the new Arts faculty building. Maureen saw him gradually wilting before her eyes. She had had his best navy suit pressed, and she was wearing her mauve outfit from Doctor Moran's daughter's wedding. This morning, as they had left the house, Sean had dipped his finger in the holy-water font beside the front door and blessed himself. He straightened his tie in the hall mirror, saying, 'Well, we won't let the side down, anyway.' She knew he had felt good, and he was very chatty in the car on the way into Galway. But now, he was shrinking. No one was interested in talking about the value of teaching life and work skills to teenagers, and the problems of keeping discipline.

They were only worried about what useful connections they were making, and looking successful in front of their peers. She went to the loo, leaving Sean standing on his own at the mullioned windows looking out at the sun-dappled quadrangle.

Sean was wondering how long the meal would take and how soon they could respectably escape, when someone tapped him on the shoulder. He turned around with a fixed smile on his face, ready to be polite, and saw Martin O'Shaughnessy, his best friend from university. His skin was leathery and slightly yellowing, and he was very thin, but Sean would recognise the deep-set blue eyes and the wide smiling mouth anywhere. They embraced.

'Sean, how are you? Bored stiff yet with all these corporate types?' Martin clapped him on the back.

'Thank God for a sane and sensible man to talk to!' said Sean, grinning. 'Are you home for long?' His frustration and sense of inadequacy instantly lifted, and he felt a surge of elation. Then he registered Martin's bloodshot eyes and the yellow pallor of his skin, and just as he was deciding whether to ask the question, Martin said, 'Yes, I'm home from the missions for good, I'm afraid.'

Sean's smile faded. 'Are you sick?' He knew that Martin wouldn't come home by choice. He had found his vocation in the missions in South America and for the last twenty years he had worked with refugees in Nicaragua, homeless children in Mexico City and earthquake victims in Bolivia. His Christmas cards were always full of peaceful blessings for Sean and his family, but his annual letters were full of the strife and violence and sadness with which he worked every day.

'They're not sure what it is. Some kind of a virus. I can only stay awake for about five hours a day, and I'm a bit weak and breathless all the time. I'm not much good to the mission any more.' Martin's voice was still strong and vibrant, but Sean could hear the catch of regret.

'It's good to see you, though, Martin – are you in Galway for long?' He wondered how much he would see of his friend. Sean found himself thinking that if Martin was going to die, he wanted to see a lot of him, to make up for all the lost years.

'I'm not sure. They might let me do a bit of work for the college, up in Dublin.'

'Knowing you, you won't be happy unless you're working,' said Sean, steering his friend towards a chair when he saw him wavering on his feet.

Martin had been the most diligent of students, burning the midnight oil in their room long after Sean was asleep, and up again at dawn, determined to get a first class honours degree, and read about every other subject under the sun. He knew by his third year that he wanted to study for the priesthood and go on the missions.

Sean and he had shared a grotty room in their digs, gone to dances at the Seapoint ballroom together, and usually they liked the same girls. They developed a funny double act to chat them up, each giving in gracefully to the other when the girl made her choice.

'Is Maureen here?' Martin asked, grinning as he lowered his creaking bones onto the seat.

'She is. As lovely as ever,' said Sean, smiling.

Maureen had chosen Martin first, and only after three dates had she changed her mind and agreed to go out with Sean instead. Maybe Martin's life would have turned out completely differently if he had continued dating her. He could be married and have a family and wouldn't have some foreign virus circulating in his blood, draining away his life.

Sean hadn't even reached the end of his train of thought when Martin looked up at him and said, 'No regrets, Sean. I've had a great life and I'm glad that I made the choices I did.'

'You always knew what I was thinking, didn't you?' said Sean fondly. It was quite spooky, but it had been like that, since the first day they met in the queue to sign up for college. Sean hadn't realised how much he missed this man until he was there in front of him. He should have written more often, stayed in touch better. They were real soul mates. Not in any kind of weird sexual way like they would portray it in a film these days, but just close, good friends who could talk about anything.

'I remember when you went looking for your real mother, that time,' said Martin. 'I felt like I was inside your skin, I could feel the pain so badly.'

Martin said it softly, not sure how Sean would take it after all these years.

Sean's face went grey. The memory flooded back and he blinked, as he felt a black sheet billowing in his brain.

'I'm sorry, Sean. I shouldn't have said anything.' Martin gripped his arm.

Sean could feel the tight hold on his arm, and he could hear the babble of voices and the tinkling of glasses. He knew he was sitting down, and that his feet were on the floor, but he felt as if he was floating and the sounds came over him in waves.

When Maureen came back into the room and glanced around to find Sean, she was confronted by a strange, stilted tableau. She recognised Martin sitting silently facing Sean, the two men awkwardly perched on the spindly mock-gold plastic chairs. As she crossed the room, edging her way around the groups of chattering people, she could see that Martin was a very sick man. He was so thin.

When she had dated him, part of the attraction had been his height and his broad chest and shoulders. A wizened, jaundiced man was sitting there now, and he must have just told Sean something terrible, because his face was screwed up with pain and he was holding tightly onto Sean's arm. He looked so old – at least twenty years older than Sean. She fixed a smile on her face just as Martin looked up.

'Maureen, how are you?' he said warmly, releasing Sean and standing up to kiss her cheek. Sean seemed to snap out of some kind of reverie, and stood up as well.

'Isn't it great to see him?' he said, and she knew by the tone of Sean's voice that things weren't good.

She kissed Martin and said brightly, 'So, they finally let you come home and see us?' She couldn't bring herself to say the automatic phrase, 'You're looking well,' so there was a tiny silence before Sean interjected, 'He might only be in Galway for a little while, so we have to make the most of him.' Sean looked a bit pale himself, Maureen thought.

'Don't be standing up for me,' she said briskly, sitting down so the men would follow.

'I was just saying to Sean, there's a chance I might get some work with the brothers in the college up in Dublin,' said Martin.

'That's grand,' said Maureen. 'So, are you home for good then?' It was the most diplomatic way she could think of asking the question.

'I am. Sean will tell you. But I'm delighted to see you. How are the kids?'

'Grand. Maria is in London at the moment. Unfortunately, she got glandular fever, so she'll have to take a year off college. Aileen is over in London all the time, working. And Hugh is off having adventures in Australia.'

'So you have an empty house.'

'Yes, they're all grown up on us now,' said Sean sadly. 'What do they call us, the marketing people? "Empty-nesters", isn't it?' He was really missing Maria.

'Making their own decisions and making you feel

old,' said Martin intuitively. The parents he spent most of his time with didn't have such abstract worries about their children. Survival was the only driver in their lives, and if their children just lived to adulthood, they had fulfilled their role as parents.

'Still, you can look forward to grandchildren next.'

Martin's smile was only half returned by Maureen, but Sean said brightly, 'Yes, it will be a while though. None of them are in serious relationships yet. Late developers, the lot of them!'

The sound of a gong stilled all the conversations in the room and the Master of Ceremonies called everyone to lunch. They moved towards the dining-room. Sean scanned the seating plan, oblivious to the tiny shake of Maureen's head and the look of sympathy that Martin gave her behind his back.

'We're not on the same table. Look, miles apart. Can you see anyone on our table we could ask to swap?'

Martin looked over Sean's shoulder and spotted a name he recognised. 'John Kennedy, there, do you remember him, from Athlone? There's no Mrs. Kennedy on the plan so he must be on his own. Come on, I'll ask him.'

Five minutes later, Martin had finessed the situation, placated the head waiter who was adamant that people couldn't be swapping all over the place, and they were sitting together, catching up on Martin's latest adventures. The men didn't notice that Maureen went quiet when the Registrar stood up to make her speech. Somehow she had known that Maria was lying when she said she had spoken to the Registrar and *he* had given her permission to take a year off.

Chapter Fourteen

Sean only became curious about his real mother when he had to provide a copy of his birth certificate to register at University College Galway. He had always known he was adopted. A rescued orphan. He was special. His mammy and daddy had picked him to be their only son. As he curled up with a hot-water bottle in his cosy bed, the memories of rows of beds in the dormitory with their hard sheets and grey scratchy blankets faded into dimness. Now, his mammy washed him gently with soap and a sponge in the tin bath in front of the fire on a Saturday night. He gradually forgot the nun's crabbed hands scrubbing his genitals with a nail-brush, and Sister Rose throwing a bucket of cold water over him as he stood shivering in the communal washrooms, his little penis shrinking from its morning erection and his heart pounding with fear. The family mealtimes, with his sisters chatting about school and his daddy talking about the farm helped him to forget the silent meals at long trestle tables. The only sound would be of cutlery scraping against plates and the spluttering coughs of the children with TB trying not to make a noise, so they wouldn't be smacked by the nuns for bad table manners. Sean had so successfully blocked out his life at the orphanage that he didn't ask the usual teenage questions about his real mother and why he was adopted. When he had his first lesson about genes in biology at secondary school, he was mildly curious, but that evening, as he sat at the dinner table, he had such a surge of love for his parents that he didn't want to hurt their feelings by asking any questions.

Then when he got the application form for the scholarship to UCG, the notes requested an original birth certificate to be submitted. Sean had to ask if he had one. His mam said she had been waiting for a long time for him to ask, and she went into the front parlour and took out her red-leather folder where she kept all the family documents.

Before she handed him the folded certificate, she said, 'We don't know who your real father was, but you must understand that your mother couldn't keep you. She was only a girl herself, really, and she had no choice but to give you up.'

Sean opened the certificate and stared at it. 'She was the same age as me,' he said.

'Yes. Can you imagine having a child yourself, now,

123

at seventeen? You wouldn't know what to do, but you'd want the best for it, wouldn't you?' his mam said softly.

'I suppose so.' Sean didn't want her to see the tears in his eyes, so he went outside, and climbed on the stone wall behind the house so that he could see the sea. He stared at the waves for a long time. Then he went back into the kitchen and hugged his mother from behind, where she stood at the stove.

'You'll always be my real mam,' he said.

This time, she had to wipe away her tears.

Chapter Fifteen

Joe thanked Sergeant Duffy for the lift. At the reception desk he got directions to the intensive-care unit. The night nurse looked sympathetically at him. The bluish night-lights created an eerie glow as he squeaked down miles of shiny hushed corridors. The daytime hospital bustle was gone, leaving a subdued and watchful silence on the wards. The red ICU sign gleamed at him like a beacon. Through a glass screen, he saw his mother, as white as a sheet, hooked up to monitors and drips. A nurse was tucking her in. She looked so frail. The folds of skin on her neck were almost translucent and her eyelids seemed paper-thin. For the first time in his life, Joe saw his mother as a person. An old person. She was so dynamic and forceful for every waking moment that in Joe's mind she was eternally middle-aged; forty something. But she must be sixty. He took her limp hand, and noticed the brown freckles of age on her skin.

She was breathing shallowly, tied to a respirator. Joe kissed her cheek and went to find someone to tell him the prognosis.

The duty nurse bleeped the doctor, who arrived ten minutes later, haggard and pale, looking as if he needed to have a rest on one of the hospital beds himself.

'Are you Frank?' he asked, ushering Joe into a visitors' waiting-room.

'No, who's Frank?'

'We don't know, but she did regain consciousness for a few moments, and was asking for Frank.'

'My father is dead, but his name was Derek. Could she have been asking for Derek?'

'No, it was definitely Frank.'

'Well, I've no idea who he is. I'm sure we'll get to the bottom of it when she comes around.'

The doctor's face tightened.

Joe swallowed. 'Is there any danger she wouldn't?'

'We, em, we're not sure. We're still waiting for some test results to come back. Your mother has had severe spinal damage, so she may have partial or complete paralysis, even if she does regain consciousness.'

Joe sat down heavily. His head was spinning.

'When will we know?'

'In the next few days.' The doctor reached out and touched Joe's shoulder. 'We're doing our best for her.'

When the telephone rang the next morning, Maria pounced on it. It wasn't Joe.

'Hello, is that Maria?' The jolly voice sounded half familiar. 'Hi, it's Paddy Naughtan here.'

Maria smiled, imagining his big round face, red-skinned from working outside and drinking too much, and his twinkling blue eyes.

'Paddy, how are you?' she said delightedly.

'Very well. So it is you! I was talking to Ivy yesterday about all the people who rang up for the job, and we thought it must be you.'

Maria laughed. 'It's a small world. I should have known Ivy's voice on the phone. It was only after I hung up that I thought it might be her.'

'So you decided to give up the college, did you? You know this is a permanent job?'

'Can I tell you about it when I see you?' She didn't want to mess it up if Dad had already said something to Paddy about the glandular fever. This would need some finessing.

'Grand. Can you come over to see me this afternoon?'

'That would be fine. Is three o'clock all right with you?'

'No problem. Acton Town is the nearest tube station. We're only a two-minute walk from there. Have you an A to Z map?'

'Yes, I can use Aileen's. I'll see you later then. Bye.'

This could be her first break.

She put on her black trousers and white blouse, and left Aileen's place in plenty of time. The yard was easy to find once she got the knack of turning the A-Z upside down and reading the maps that way. She was fifteen minutes early, but there wasn't anywhere around where she could have a cup of tea, so she decided to go straight in.

Paddy was just like Maria remembered. He and Ivy used to come back to Carraroe every summer for their holidays. Paddy would spend long nights drinking whiskey with her father. As a child, Maria thought Paddy was a real uncle and used to sit on his knee to hear his great adventure stories. Now, he was sitting behind a scarred oak desk, piled high with papers and tile samples, and a box of bathroom fittings. He was a bit fatter and a bit redder in the face, but he was the same Paddy.

'Hello, it's me,' she said, smiling as she knocked and came in the door of his office.

'Come in, come in,' he said, standing up. 'I'll shake your hand, since it's a business meeting we're having.' He took both her hands in his, and said warmly, 'How are you, love?'

'Very well, thanks, Paddy.' She flushed under his admiring gaze.

Paddy was struck by how beautiful Maria looked. As a small girl she was pretty, but as a teenager she had gone through a gawky phase. Now she was glowing; beautiful soft skin, full black hair, and a smile that would knock you down.

'Sit down here. Will you have a cup of tea?'

He cleared the visitor's chair in front of his desk,

making a wobbly pile of folders, crumpled invoices and brochures on the floor. It promptly fell over, and he shuffled the mess with his foot, looking slightly embarrassed.

'No, thanks, I'm grand,' Maria said, even though her throat was dry.

She perched on the edge of the chair. She couldn't decide whether to tell him the truth.

'You can see why we need someone,' Paddy said, waving his hand expansively to include the other random piles of paper around the office. 'So how's your Mam and Dad, then?'

'Very well. In good form,' she said. 'And how's Ivy?

'She's fine. She might be in soon, so you can say hello. And what does your Daddy think of you leaving college and coming over here to work?'

'Well, he's . . .'

'I was a bit surprised he didn't ring me to tell me you were coming to London.' He smiled. 'But I suppose you have Aileen to keep an eye on you!' If the truth were known, Paddy was hurt. What were friends for, if it wasn't to look out for each other? He could have told Sean about the job, and not bothered advertising it. It was pure chance that Maria had seen it. But Sean was sometimes a bit funny about asking favours – he never wanted to be 'under a compliment' to anyone.

'So Daddy hasn't rung you this morning, then?' she asked.

'No, why, should he have?'

'I wasn't sure if he would. I only decided yesterday to stay in London after the summer,' she said nervously.

'Surely the job doesn't look that exciting!' Paddy laughed.

'I'm having a baby, and I know that Daddy won't want me back in the house,' she blurted out.

Paddy blanched. 'Does he know?'

'I told them I have glandular fever.'

'Ohmygod!' How could he not give her the job now? He had practically promised it to her on the phone. She would never get one anywhere else in that condition. 'Well, that explains a lot,' he said, sitting back in the big leather chair that made him feel like an emperor.

'Don't feel obliged to give me the job, Paddy. I would completely understand if you didn't want to,' Maria said earnestly.

'Can you type?'

'Forty words a minute.'

'Can you use a fax machine?'

'I can.'

'And our little switchboard?'

'I'm sure I could learn it really quickly.'

'When are you due?'

'Christmas time.'

'So we'd get a good few months of work out of you?'

'You would.' Maria smiled.

'When can you start?'

'Tomorrow?'

'Fine. Be here at about nine so Ivy can show you

everything. After that you start at eight and finish at five. Will that suit you?'

'That would be great. Thanks. I'll work really hard for you.'

'Will your dad kill me, when he finds out?' he said under his breath. 'Or will he be glad you're under someone's wing?'

Maria thought it politic not to answer that one. 'I'll see you tomorrow, then.'

They shook hands. Maria caught him surreptitiously glancing at her tummy, still flat in the tight black trousers. Then his eyes moved up and lingered on her breasts, just for a fraction of a second. She shivered. Their eyes met.

'Bye.' Her smile was a little bit forced. You couldn't blame him for being curious.

As she left, Paddy had to shift his trousers slightly before he could sit down. What was he thinking? She was like a niece to him. Only a slip of a girl. But a girl who managed to get herself in the family way couldn't be as innocent as she looked. That didn't happen from kissing behind the bike sheds. Paddy shook his head. Sean would be devastated. His mind would be running at ninety miles an hour worrying about what everyone in the parish would think of him. Apart from all the memories of his early childhood that it would bring back. Sean had really gone off the rails that time, in college, when he found out about his mother. Paddy felt a bit disloyal, keeping Maria's secret from Sean. But she'd have to tell her mam and dad herself, soon. It wasn't the kind of thing you could hide for long, and it wasn't his business to be getting involved in.

Maria was exuberant when Aileen and Paul came in from work. She had bought all the ingredients and made spaghetti bolognese, and they opened a bottle of Chianti to celebrate. Aileen said Maria could wear her navy suit for the rest of the week, and they could go shopping for work-clothes on Saturday.

Chapter Sixteen

When the alarm rang at half past six the next morning, Maria thought it was a mistake, and snuggled down into the duvet again. Then she shot awake, remembering what day it was. She moved so fast she had showered and dressed in half an hour, and got to Acton by eight fifteen.

The tube was a lot busier in the mornings, she thought, as she was swept along with the other commuters. She almost expected to be pushed onto the train by one of those white-gloved platform attendants they have on the Japanese metro. When she arrived, Paddy and Ivy had been at work for two hours already. They had just sent off the last van with the men working on a local job in Shepherd's Bush. There was a lovely smell of bacon rolls as Maria came in.

'There she is!' Ivy saw Paddy's face light up as Maria passed the window.

She smiled at Maria. 'You're nice and early.'

Ivy handed her a cup of strong working-man's tea. An hour later, even though she was gasping for a drink, Maria poured it discreetly into the rubber-plant pot by the reception desk. She hated scummy brown tea. She would have to make her own from now on.

The week flew, with learning the new switchboard, trying to remember all the men's names, figuring out the worksheets and, most of all, tackling the huge piles of random bits of paper. She created a new alphabetical filing system, and bought three trays to organise Paddy's desk. She had a feeling he would soon slip back into his old ways, but when she opened his post, she put it in the in-tray, and reminded him every day to use the out-tray for things he wanted done. Eventually he would understand that it was not the place to put brass fittings and bits of rubber hose, so she took them and stored them in labelled plastic boxes. By the end of the week she was starting to see some order emerging from the chaos.

At lunch-time on Friday, Paddy came out of his office to talk to her.

'Well, your dad and I were chatting last night,' he said. He stood with his back to her, looking out the window at two men unloading a pile of bathroom fittings. 'He's worried about you.'

'You didn't say anything to him, did you?' Maria fiddled with the pens on her desk, lining them up at the edge of the blotting pad.

'Of course not. He thinks you shouldn't be working

though, with glandular fever, and he asked me to take it easy with you.' Paddy turned around. 'Having a baby is not a big deal, these days. You should tell them soon.'

Maria nodded. 'I know. I keep putting it off. I just don't want to hear him telling me never to come home again.' Her voice broke, and her eyes filled up. A tear rolled down her cheek.

He stepped towards the desk and tenderly brushed away the tear. 'Don't worry, love. It will be fine.'

The door opened, and Ivy came in. She saw Maria's big tear-filled eyes, and heard Paddy's words. *Please, God, don't let him be at it again,'* she sent a prayer heavenwards. She shot a fierce, sharp look at Paddy, and said, 'Come on, Maria. I'll introduce you to the lads out here that you haven't already met.'

She hugged Maria to her sideways, as they went out, and Maria could feel Ivy's plump breast against her bare arm. She was enveloped in the scent of Anaïs Anaïs, which she hadn't worn herself since she was fourteen. She couldn't understand why Ivy had suddenly taken on this maternal role with her. They walked through the yard to a big storeroom, which Ivy opened with a key on her brown leather belt.

'Come in here, until I tell you something,' said Ivy conspiratorially, as she ushered Maria inside.

The fluorescent overhead light flickered on. They were surrounded by metal racking full of fittings, and lengths of timber. At their feet was a pile of cement bags. Ivy stood square, put her two hands on Maria's shoulders, and looked into her eyes. Maria felt like she was back at school.

'Did he touch you?'

'Who?' It was the same question her father had asked when he saw her kissing the lad from Cork after walking home from one of the summer ceilis.

'Paddy of course. Who else?' said Ivy impatiently.

Of course he had touched her. He was always hugging her when she was small. They shook hands on Tuesday. And just now, Paddy had touched her face. There was no harm in it.

'No . . .' she hesitated. 'Yes, but he was just being nice.' Suddenly Maria thought she understood the look of scorn that Ivy had flashed at Paddy a minute ago.

'Good. Because I have to tell you something. We haven't been able to keep a receptionist for longer than three months, and it's only fair that you should know.'

Know what? That Ivy was possessive of her husband? Maria couldn't think of anything more revolting than a physical involvement with Paddy. Ivy need have no worries on that score. Maria was silent.

'You're a very attractive girl, Maria. I can see by the way he's looking at you, that he is having Impure Thoughts.'

Maria shivered. She hadn't heard that expression since the nuns used it at school.

'But he wouldn't dream of doing anything,' Ivy went on. 'So don't worry about it. I just wanted you to be aware, so you don't get upset. That's all.'

The girl looked a bit shell-shocked. Surely to God she must be a bit worldly wise, a girl in her condition?

'Thanks. Are we finished?' Maria asked, looking towards the door, desperate to escape.

'Yes. I'm glad we had the chance to have this little chat.' Ivy locked up the store, and said jovially, 'Here's the lads.'

She beckoned them over, and introduced Maria to the two men, who wiped their hands on their trousers and shook her hand.

She had been the subject of their ribald jokes since the beginning of the week, and there was a slate running on how long she would last under Paddy's ogling eyes and roving hands.

That evening, Joe was woken by the night nurse gently shaking him.

'You should really go home, Joe, and try and get a decent night's sleep.'

She looked at his haggard unshaven face and bloodshot eyes. 'You're not doing your mother any good, sitting here. We can ring you if there's any change in the night.'

Joe gave in and nodded. He really wanted to lie down. The nurse called him a taxi and by eleven o'clock he was fast asleep in his own bed. The old house creaked around him as it settled for the night, and downstairs on the mahogany telephone table, a little red light blinked twice.

On Saturday morning, he showered and shaved, packed a few changes of clothes and some things for his mother, and ran to catch the bus to Castlebar. He sat by the bed, resigned to a weekend vigil without any news from the consultant. He had brought three text books from home to study, having exhausted the magazines in the hospital shop. He couldn't concentrate for more than twenty minutes at a time, but something might eventually sink in. When the nurse realised that he was studying medicine, she showed him his mother's chart, and explained everything they were doing for her. According to the nurse, Noreen's vital signs were satisfactory, although she hadn't moved for three days. His mother was usually so full of vitality. How could this motionless, shallowly breathing body be the same person? If only he could share this with someone. He had thought about Maria in the last few days, but only in an abstract way. Although he had sat for hours doing nothing beside his mother's bed, it was like as if his brain could only cope with one worry at a time.

He had no spare emotional capacity to think about Maria or the baby. He had a theory that if he focussed totally on his mother, holding her hand, and willing her to get better, that he could somehow transfer some energy into her, and she would turn and look at him, and smile. That was all that mattered. Medical science didn't explain everything. There were apparently hopeless cases all the time, where a close family member or partner made the difference, and the patient came around. He idly wondered if Maria had returned his call. He went down the corridor and dialled in to hear the messages on the answering machine. Her chirpy voice surprised him. She sounded very well. Quite cheerful and upbeat. He didn't have the London number with him, so Maria would have to wait. She would understand why, as soon as she heard about his mother. The second message really surprised him.

'Hello, Nonie, it's Frank. I hope you're well. Just checking to see if you're still OK for Sunday afternoon. Give me a ring when you get a minute. Bye.'

The voice sounded oldish, quite deep, with only a hint of a Mayo accent. A very distinguished voice. So this was the mysterious Frank. Joe had completely forgotten about him, assuming that the doctor had misheard the name. He called her Nonie? Only his father had ever been allowed to call her that. His mother insisted on being called Noreen. So maybe they were having a relationship. Maybe she had been on her way back from seeing him? Looking at her now, so frail and wrinkled, it was hard to imagine her in the role of girlfriend – what a bizarre idea! He wondered idly what you called old people, when they go out together? How long had her secret life been going on? Did her friends know where she was going on a Monday night, instead of to bridge? Suddenly Joe realised that he hadn't told any of them about the accident. He could ring Mrs Duffy, and she would pass on the word. He didn't really want them all clucking around, but he felt better to be doing something.

Joe was sitting holding his mother's hand when Rita Duffy arrived, laden with grapes and magazines. She was shocked to see Noreen so still and pale on the pillow. She tossed the grapes and magazines onto the bedside locker.

'Joe, how are you holding up, pet?' she asked, patting his shoulder.

'I'm all right, Mrs Duffy. I just wish I knew how long she'll be like this.'

It was quite nice after all, to have someone to talk to, even if he could hardly get a word in edgeways.

'Do they know how it happened?'

'She was driving along the Castlebar road on Monday night, and she skidded into a wall, trying to avoid two cyclists,' Joe said concisely.

Rita gasped. 'Monday night? And were the others hurt as well?'

'There's a young girl down the corridor still in intensive care. The mother has a broken arm.'

'Poor things. Hopefully they'll be all right.'

She tucked in the sheet around Noreen. 'Have you managed to get hold of everyone you need to?' she said coyly. Noreen must have been on her way back from seeing the mysterious Frank when she had the accident. She wondered if Joe knew about him.

'Just you. I was hoping you'd know better than me, who to ring.'

'Oh, don't worry. I rang all the regular friends straight away. We've worked out a rota. Anne Murphy will be in tomorrow, and Kay Green on Tuesday. But is there anyone else?'

'There was a message on the answering machine from someone called Frank,' said Joe cautiously. 'I don't know his number, so I couldn't call him back.'

He didn't want to give away his mother's big secret.

Rita's eyes lit up. 'That'll be Frank Delaney. He's a solicitor here in Castlebar.' She stopped. She didn't want to give away Noreen's big secret. But she didn't know anything else about him. Maybe Joe did.

'I wondered,' said Joe.

'Do you want me to ring him for you?' Rita offered eagerly, thinking she could get the solicitor's number in the telephone book.

'That would be great, if you didn't mind,' said Joe. Rita obviously knew him, and it would be easier for her to break the news.

Rita came back triumphant from her telephone call. 'I managed to track him down,' she said. 'He'll be in to see her as soon as he can. He sounds like a very nice man.'

'Good,' said Joe distractedly. Surely she knew whether he was a nice man or not, since she was his mother's best friend?

It was quite a relief when Mrs Duffy finally left. She hung on until the last minute of visiting time, just in case Frank turned up.

'I'll be in again tomorrow,' she reassured Joe, as he walked her to the front doors.

'And by the way, would you ever call me Rita? You're a bit too grown-up to be calling me Mrs Duffy. Don't worry, love. Your mammy will be fine.'

She breezed out through the doors with the supreme confidence of someone who knows nothing about medicine, but everything about human nature. Noreen was a fighter. She would come around soon.

The blue nightlights reminded Joe of his first journey along these corridors. It seemed like weeks ago. He had spent one hundred and twelve hours by his mother's bedside. He had seen her being washed and changed, her drips being replaced, her temperature being taken. Not once had she moved a muscle. That was not his real mother on the bed. She would be fighting back. She would be sitting up reading her chart and demanding to know when she could go home.

Chapter Seventeen

Maria stood staring up at the coloured strobe lights splitting the dark sky, and then lowered her gaze to the fairy-lit trees, and the people strolling in Leicester Square. Improvised jazz swirled from one corner, and a dinner-jacketed tenor sang an aria from another. She inhaled deeply and smelt hot, greasy chips, caramel-coated chou-chou nuts and Chinese spices. She wished she had come to London before, when Aileen had invited her.

'Do you know what famous square this is?' asked Paul.

'Trafalgar Square?' she hazarded when she couldn't think of any others.

Paul laughed. 'No, that one has Nelson's Column! You have heard of him in Ireland?'

'Of course I've heard of him,' she said indignantly. Paul could be a bit of a smart-ass sometimes. 'Actually we used to have a Nelson's Column in Dublin too – on O'Connell Street. Before the IRA blew it up.' She knew she sounded like a petulant child, and decided she wouldn't rise to the bait again.

'Trafalgar Square is only just around the corner from here though,' said Aileen to placate her, and to avoid further discussion about the sensitive topic of Nelson's Column. 'Come on. We'll be late for the movie.'

Maria was having a really good time. She had really enjoyed the bus journey over Lambeth Bridge and past the softly lit Houses of Parliament and Big Ben floating on the edge of the river. Beautiful strings of white lights were strung all along the Embankment, around the bend in the river, promising more. Aileen said you could walk all the way to Tower Bridge along the South Bank.

Now they were in the Empire cinema. The screen was huge, and it seemed like you could fit the entire population of Carraroe in it, with room to spare. After the film they were going on to a thirtieth birthday party in Covent Garden. This definitely beat the grotty nightclubs of Salthill and a bag of curried chips afterwards.

She did miss having Joe to share it with, and had a little twinge of loneliness. He hadn't called her for three days now. But she had given him a lot to think about. She couldn't push it.

Covent Garden was Maria's favourite place so far, with the buskers and the trendy little arcades of shops.

Cafe Havana was brilliant. Tapas food was delicious. Latino music was cool. Aileen and Paul's friends were a great laugh. They were throwing back tequila slammers and cocktails like there was no tomorrow. Andy, who was having the party, was a really nice guy. Everyone in the group listened to him when he was telling stories, and it wasn't just because it was his birthday. He was funny and entertaining, and he had a wicked twinkle in his eye. At the end of the night he just took out his credit card to pay for all the drinks and no one seemed surprised. He had dark wavy hair and tanned skin, and the most amazing white teeth when he laughed. His baggy yellow shirt showed off his tan, recently acquired in Barbados, and he had DKNY sunglasses hanging casually from the top pocket.

'He didn't look thirty at all,' Maria said to Aileen in the cab on the way home.

'He'll probably look the same when he's forty.' Aileen said with an edge to her voice that Maria missed.

Earlier, Andy had pulled Aileen to one side as she went to the loo, his pupils huge, and grinning like a madman. 'Hey, Aileen, your sister is gorgeous. Is she, you know, with anyone?'

Aileen could practically see him drooling. She looked across at Maria, who was laughing, her head thrown back, stretching her slender white neck, her red sleeveless top showing every curve. The way she had her legs crossed, with her black skirt tight against her thighs, did look very sexy.

'Listen, Andy. She's not available, right?' Aileen said fiercely.

Andy was notorious for his 'Wham, bam, you should thank me, Mam,' attitude. Somehow, he had managed to sleep with most of the girls around the table, but still keep them as friends afterwards. Some irresistible charm that Aileen could never fathom.

He put his hands up, as if shielding himself from Aileen's glare. 'OK, OK, big Sis. I won't touch her,' he said, still grinning.

Aileen told Paul, and he promised to get Andy to back off. But for the rest of the evening, Andy didn't even glance at Maria, so Aileen relaxed.

In the morning, Maria felt sick for the first time in a week, and as she hovered over the toilet bowl, she felt stupid as well. How could she have even thought of fancying Andy last night? What guy was going to be interested in her when they found out she was pregnant? Even Joe didn't want to be with her, and it was his baby. No fella wanted to go to Mothercare with his girlfriend on a Saturday afternoon. Or sit in with a screaming baby on a Saturday night. For a few hours last night she had managed to forget that she was pregnant. She had drunk too much, and she had enjoyed the rebellious feeling of doing what she wanted, flirting with Andy across the table, and having a laugh for the first time in months.

Back in bed with a cup of tea, she remembered the

appointment with the doctor for Monday morning. Look at how much could happen in a week. It wasn't even seven days since she had been to the doctor's. She had contracted glandular fever, got a job, been sexually harassed (at least in Ivy's mind), spent £200 she didn't have on work-clothes, and biggest of all, decided to keep the baby.

Glandular fever. What was she thinking? How soon did she have to tell them at home? Joe still hadn't bothered to call her back. Even in her drunken state last night, she had gone straight to the answering machine when they got home to see if there were any messages. She would give him 24 more hours. He probably had to wait until his mother went out, to use the phone. But that wasn't an excuse.

He had to decide if he wanted a relationship or not. Being a father didn't come in half measures. It would be hard enough to keep the relationship going, long distance, even if he was totally committed to her. He would have to tell his mother eventually, just like she would.

Last night, Maria had looked around at all of Aileen's friends and realised that she could make a new life over here, and survive without Joe. If she had to. In the sober light of morning, it didn't seem quite so easy, especially when she took out the picture and stared at Joe's face, imagining life without him.

She rang home, knowing that her dad would be doing the collection at ten o'clock Mass. Her mother went to a later Mass, so she could put the Sunday roast in the oven first. Maria apologised for not ringing sooner. Maureen asked her how she was feeling.

'Fine,' she said.

'So you haven't been sick or anything?'

Oh, she meant that kind of feeling. Was that one of the symptoms of glandular fever?

'A little bit, not too bad,' she said shortly, changing the subject. 'I hear Paddy spoke to Dad during the week?'

'Yes, I think they're both a bit worried about you.'

'I'm fine, honestly, Mam. I agreed with Paddy that we'll have a trial period, and see how it goes.'

'And how is it going?'

'Fine. It's grand.'

'How much is he paying you? It's expensive to live in London, you know.'

'I don't know yet,' Maria confessed. 'I have to work a week in hand, so I don't get paid until next Friday.'

It sounded kind of naïve, even to herself. Aileen said she could expect about ten thousand a year. That was nearly a thousand pounds a month. She'd be able to save for a deposit on her own flat, and be out of Aileen's place well before the baby came. She tuned back in to her mother's voice, which was probably lecturing her about minding her money.

'. . . so don't let him take advantage of you,' said Maureen.

'Yes, Mam, don't worry. Say hi to Dad for me. I must go. I'll ring again during the week.'

Maybe she would tell them next week. That would give Joe another few days to make up his mind. And give her a few days to work out how to tell them. Maria remembered when she was small, coming home from school and asking her mother what the worst sin was. She said it was telling lies, and ever since then, Maria had blushed furiously every time she told her mother a lie. Thank God for telephones.

Maria made a tray with a cafetière of coffee, orange juice and cinnamon rolls to bring to Aileen and Paul in bed. She knocked on their bedroom door and walked in. All she saw was Aileen's slender white back as she sat astride Paul, the duvet thrown on the floor. All she heard was the little animal panting sounds of Aileen having an orgasm.

She quietly backed out, and left the tray outside the door.

Now she wanted Joe. It was easy to forget about him when she was rushing around, but the thought of Joe's firm lips pressed against her teeth, his tight bum and his hard thighs made her tingle all over. Being pregnant seemed to make her more horny, and thinking about Joe all the time certainly didn't help. She got into the shower, and under the hot water, in the slippery soap suds, she slowly brought herself to a climax, weak-kneed against the dripping yellow tiles. The telephone rang, and she ran trembling, wrapped in a towel, to answer it.

'Hello?' said a male voice. Not Joe.

'Hello. Aileen and Paul are – still in bed. Can I get one of them to ring you back?'

'Is that Maria?' said the voice. Smooth, with a slight cockney edge.

'Yes, who's that?'

'It's Andy, you know, from the party last night.'

'Oh yeah. It was a great party. Thanks for letting me come.'

Let you come? thought Andy. I want to make you come, again and again. She heard it in his voice when he said, 'It was my pleasure.'

Maria could see his smile, and she imagined the rasp of dark morning stubble on his cheeks.

'Will I get Paul to ring you?'

'Actually, I was calling him to get your number. But now that I've found you, I don't need to speak to Paul.'

His slightly gravelly voice sounded so strong and male and just downright sexy.

'Oh.' Just as well he couldn't see her now, hair dripping and fat red cheeks.

'Do you want to go out for a drink sometime?'

'That would be lovely.' How could he not be attached, and him so gorgeous? She could find out from Aileen. What about Joe? Just a drink with Andy wouldn't be any harm. As a friend.

'Wednesday?'

'Yes. I work in Acton until 5 o' clock, but I could meet you in town,' she said.

'*in town.*' What a quaint expression, he thought. 'I'll

meet you at Hammersmith tube station, by the flower stall, at six o' clock, and I'll take you down by the river,' he said.

'Great. See you then.' Maria was relieved. She wouldn't have to wander around trying to find some cool venue in the West End.

Chapter Eighteen

The tall, well-dressed man who came into his mother's room on Sunday morning took Joe by surprise. He had silver-grey hair and looked as if he spent a lot of time on a golf course. He smiled with perfectly capped white teeth, and put out his hand to shake Joe's.

'You must be Joe, the faithful son,' he said jovially.

Over-familiar, in Joe's opinion.

'And you must be Frank.' Joe looked him in the eye and shook his hand firmly.

Frank's face fell when he saw the pale form stretched on the bed, her mouth hanging open. Joe gently wiped a dribble of saliva from the edge of her mouth.

'I'm sorry I didn't come sooner,' said Frank, 'but I was up in Dublin all week, and I only heard last night.'

'I would have rung you, but I didn't know your number,' said Joe pointedly.

'Yes, well, obviously,' Frank muttered. He was

looking aghast at the shell of the woman he had started to feel very fond of. She was so dynamic and full of life, and eager to try new things. After five years of caring for an ailing wife who had died of cancer only two years ago, Frank was filled with horror at the thought of going through it again.

He looked distraught.

This guy won't be back, thought Joe. He's far too smooth. He was just looking for a nice time. One of those fellas who always has everything easy.

In Joe's look, Frank could see that he was off the hook. There were no expectations here. After all, they had only just met.

'Can I take you out for lunch?' he asked. 'You must be sick of hospital food at this stage.'

Joe was curious. What kind of a man would his mother have fallen for? No harm in having lunch, even if they never saw each other again.

They went to Flanagan's Hotel, where there was a very good carvery for Sunday lunch.

All around them, families out for a special treat were chatting. An old couple at the next table clinked glasses. 'To the next forty years together,' they said, and smiled at each other. Joe could hear the woman's false teeth clicking as she chewed.

Both men thought the roast wasn't as good as Noreen's but neither of them said it.

'So you're doing medicine, aren't you? Taking after your father?' Frank said.

'Yes, I have another three years to go, including the internship,' said Joe, his mouth full.

'And what then? Your mother says you want to have a surgery in the house, like your father?'

Joe swallowed and hesitated. How much should he say?

'I don't know. Anyway, it depends on Mum's progress. I might have to change my plans.'

'So, what's the prognosis on Nonie? I mean, your mother?'

'I'm hoping to see a consultant tomorrow and get some news, but she hasn't moved a muscle all week.'

Frank looked down at his plate. 'What a shame. She's such a lovely woman. So energetic. To be struck down like that seems wrong. She was on her way home from seeing me, you know.'

'I guessed, when I heard your message.'

'Did she tell you about me, at all?'

'No, she didn't,' said Joe. 'But she seemed very happy, recently.' Frank seemed to need that reassurance.

Frank smiled. 'You'll make a good doctor, with those diplomacy skills.'

'Thanks. I think I must have got them from my father.' Joe realised how that must sound. 'I mean, Mum says I did.'

'It's all right to be honest, Joe. Your mother is a very direct woman. It's one of the things I liked about her. You always knew where you stood with her.'

Joe noticed the past tense.

'We used to have dinner every Monday night, at my house. We took turns to cook it and we tried to outperform each other.' Frank laughed.

He must have learned to cook, being a bachelor for that long, thought Joe.

'My first wife, I mean, my wife, was sick for a long time, so I had to get domesticated. It did me no harm at all.'

Frank was flustered at his *faux pas* and nodded to the waitress, who came over to the table. 'Will you have dessert?' he asked Joe.

They sat for another hour over dessert and coffee, with Frank reminiscing about his student days in Galway. Joe couldn't believe how fast the time went.

'I decided to set up a practice in Castlebar, because that's where our roots were. For my wife and me, it was more important for us to have a good home life, than for me to be a rich lawyer up in Dublin.'

Was there supposed to be an element of fatherly advice in this conversation? Joe was surprised that he didn't resent it. He found himself liking Frank.

'Have you got a girlfriend?' asked Frank, conscious that he had dominated the conversation so far.

'Sort of.' Joe squirmed. 'She's gone to London . . . for the summer.'

'Just for the summer? Sure you can get back together afterwards. Is she at college?'

'Yes. Doing history and politics.'

'Oh, an idealist, not like us hard-nosed professional types.'

He was pushing this bonding thing a bit too far. Joe just nodded and sipped his coffee.

'Does she know what she wants to do when she graduates?'

Joe didn't want to be rude, but it was a bit weird to be talking about Maria like this.

'She's only just finished first year, so she has a while to go yet,' he said, his tone non-committal. She probably would never get to finish her degree now.

Frank was looking intently at Joe. Nonie had said he wasn't interested in girls. Too busy studying. But this was a serious one.

'Will you keep in touch with her, during the summer?'

'It's not very easy to have a long-distance relationship.'

'Will you not just get together again, in the autumn?' It was a strange way to describe a temporary summer separation.

Joe looked up. It was fine. Frank wouldn't be hanging around. He was desperate to talk to someone about it.

'She's having a baby over there.'

'Yours?'

'Yes.' It seemed so bizarre to be having this conversation. Maria didn't sleep around. There was no question that it was his. He felt like he was reading from a script.

'Don't tell my mother.'

Frank just looked at him scornfully. 'Hardly.' Then his face softened. 'What are you going to do about it?'

'I don't think she wants me to be involved.'

'Why not?' Frank could hear the defensiveness in Joe's tone. Classic male evasion tactics.

Joe leaned across the table and whispered, conscious that ears might be flapping at the other tables. Although that old couple looked more like candidates for hearing aids.

'We decided together that she should have an abortion, and she went off to England. Now, she's decided to keep the baby, without even asking me what I thought.'

'Maybe if she's over there by herself, she thinks she has to make all the decisions on her own?'

'But she's blocking me out. When I spoke to her on the phone, she was really offhand with me and I feel like she's pushing me away.' That cheerful answering machine message said it all. She was acting like they were just friends. Letting him off the hook, so he didn't even have to feel guilty.

'Well, if it's meant to be, it will all work out,' said Frank. 'But remember, if she really is the right one, she's worth fighting for. Maybe all this has come too soon for you, but you can't dictate what life throws at you, and when. Sometimes you just have to go for it.'

Joe avoided looking at him, and sat with his shoulders slumped.

'Sorry. That was a bit of a lecture. You don't need that from me. Come on, I'll drop you back to the hospital.'

157

He stood up and pushed back his chair, indicating to the waitress that he had left the money on the table. Joe was relieved that the interrogation was over. They drove back in an awkward silence. As he dropped Joe off outside the hospital, Frank promised to come and visit, but as they shook hands, Joe had a feeling that they wouldn't meet again.

Chapter Nineteen

'He's not right for you!' Aileen shouted at Maria.

'It's none of your business, Aileen. Joe obviously doesn't want to be with me any more, so why shouldn't I go out with other fellas?'

Aileen wished that Paul hadn't gone to play cricket. He might be able to persuade Maria that even though Andy was his best friend, he was bad news when it came to women. 'It is my business, because I know what Andy is like, and I'm worried about you. It will end in tears.' She stood up and started clearing the table.

'Now you sound like Mam,' said Maria, who couldn't help laughing. Aileen got so uptight sometimes.

'Seriously, Maria, he's gone through more women than you've had hot dinners.'

'So? I'm not planning to marry him. I just want to go out for a drink with him. I'm not going to do anything stupid.'

It's a bit late for that, thought Aileen. 'What about Joe? You haven't even spoken properly to him yet.'

'He's the one who hasn't rung me back. And if he rings now, Aileen, I don't want to speak to him. Tell him I've moved out, or something.' Maria fiddled with the saltcellar. She wouldn't admit to Aileen how much it hurt that Joe hadn't been in touch. She knew deep down that going out with Andy was just her way of reassuring herself that life could go on without Joe.

'Maria, you should at least talk to him about his baby. You owe him that.'

'I don't owe him anything. He's made it very clear that he wants nothing to do with this child. It was *my* decision to keep *my* baby.'

Aileen sighed. Talk about melodrama. Maria couldn't stay in the flat much longer. She was already driving Paul mad, leaving things all over the place, and spending ages in the bathroom. He didn't want Aileen to say anything to Maria about the mess, because he felt sorry for her. But Aileen was stuck in the middle, and she still had to listen to him complaining every night when they went to bed. It was his flat, after all.

'Promise me you'll only have a drink with Andy?' she pleaded with Maria.

'I promise.' Maria smiled. 'You're such a mother hen. I can look after myself. I've gone out with lots of guys too, you know.' She flicked the switch on the kettle. 'Do you want a cup of tea?'

On Wednesday, Maria wore her favourite new work outfit, a tailored red suit and strappy black sandals.

Totally inappropriate for a builder's yard, but perfect
for a date. She couldn't wait for the day to be over, and
looked at her watch every ten minutes. At five o' clock,
she went into the unisex toilet to put on fresh make-up
and take her hair out of its ponytail. As she came out,
Paddy was on his way in. His arm brushed her breast,
just slightly, in passing her.

'Hot date tonight?'

'Yes, actually,' she said, her eyes sparkling.

'Have a good one, then,' he said, his eyes travelling
down her body as he pushed open the door. She still
had a great figure.

Maria flounced out as best she could in her high
heels. To think she had sat on that man's knee! But it
was quite funny, really. She didn't feel at all threatened
by Paddy. If that was how he got his kicks, then let him
get on with it.

She arrived really early at Hammersmith station,
and bought a *Marie Claire* magazine to read nonchalantly
while she waited. Andy saw her from the entrance. She
stood out among the drab navy and grey commuters
shuffling home on the tube.

He felt the familiar rush of adrenalin. He loved the
beginning of the chase. He sauntered up to her and
although Maria sensed he was there, she didn't look up
until he flicked her magazine.

'Oh, you sneaked up on me!' She smiled.

Andy smiled back, and she felt a thrill inside. She
looked down. That was her 'Joe' feeling. He was still

there inside her, with the power to make her heart flip, just like that.

'Shall we go, madame?' Andy said, gallantly sweeping his arm towards the exit.

The sun was glimmering on the river as they sat on the wall outside the 'Old Ship'. To their left, Hammersmith Bridge spanned the river, its Victorian ironwork glowing in the evening light. A team of oarsmen laboured past, the diminutive cox yelling instructions.

Andy kicked his heels against the stone wall and threw crisps to the ducks. 'I love ducks,' he said. 'My mum used to take me to the park to feed them when I was a kid. She said 'uck' was my first word.'

Maria laughed. He was very easy to talk to. 'This is lovely,' she said aloud.

He wasn't the predator Aileen made out, at all. He was charming and interesting. And gorgeous. He had the darkest brown eyes. They were like mysterious deep pools in the bog, with hidden secrets. When he squinted into the sun, he looked like a hero from a spaghetti western. He was only missing the poncho.

When Maria said she was starving, Andy suggested a Mexican restaurant on King Street. She had never had Mexican food before, so Andy recommended fajitas. They laughed when she dropped the filling all over the place.

'Fajitas should be on the list of things not to order on a – first date,' Maria said as she wiped her mouth after the first successful bite. Delicious. She licked her lips. It was a first date, really, she admitted to herself.

'Like corn on the cob, and tagliatelli,' said Andy, deftly swallowing half a chimichanga in one bite.

Maria was intriguing. She was very sexy, but she had this air of naïvety about her, like she was discovering the world for the first time. He wondered if she was a virgin. Irish girl from a small village. Maybe. But no, she was too sexy to be a virgin. He had a strange urge to protect her, but he also wanted to shag her senseless. Her voice was soft and musical, much more Irish-sounding than Aileen's. English girls were much more upfront. You knew where you stood, and when to make the next move. This particular conquest would probably take a bit more time. But that was fine. He had a feeling that Maria would be worth it.

Maria looked up from rolling her next fajita and caught him staring at her.

'What?' she said, looking down to see if she had dropped food all down her front.

'Nothing,' he said, reaching for the hot sauce. He had a hard-on all evening under the table.

'So, are you going to see him again?' Aileen demanded when Maria got home at eleven o'clock.

'I might,' said Maria coyly. Andy hadn't asked her out again. He was playing it cool. He would ring her by Friday at the latest, she reckoned. 'As you can see, I'm home, and I didn't do anything silly.' She was raiding the fridge for orange juice. 'Mexican food makes you really thirsty, doesn't it?'

Aileen shook her head in exasperation. She told Maria that Joe had called again. 'He sounded kind of desperate to talk to you. He said he was sorry that he hadn't called sooner but something had come up with his mother and he won't be able to call again until the weekend. He wanted to tell you about it himself.'

Maria's heart sank and she sighed. 'I've never known a guy so much under his mother's thumb. I don't know what to do. One minute I think I should just forget him, and try to get on with my life, and the next minute I'm wishing I was with him. What would you do?'

'I honestly don't know, Maria. I suppose he must be confused now, with you deciding to keep the baby and stay over here. Maybe he thinks that you don't need him any more. You probably should ring him and see what he has to say.'

'I don't think I can face another conversation about how he can't tell his mother about the baby. I can't ring the house in case the mother picks up the phone, and he's obviously got to wait until she's out before he can ring me. What kind of a way is that to carry on a relationship?'

'Well, to be fair, you haven't told Mam and Dad yet, either. It can't be any easier for him.'

'But at least Mam and Dad know about Joe. He

hasn't even told his mam that we've been going together for the last year.'

'Mmm. I see what you mean. You have to do whatever you think is right. But don't let Andy confuse the issue. He's not good news.'

Maria decided a change of subject was appropriate. 'I was thinking I'd start looking for a flat next week, when I get paid. I have three hundred for a deposit.'

'You might only be able to afford a house share, rather than a flat, but it's a good idea to start looking around.'

'I'll find something,' Maria said confidently. There were hundreds of places advertised in the paper every day. She only needed one of them.

Andy didn't wait until Friday. On Thursday morning an Interflora van delivered a huge bouquet of flowers, to the great amusement of the men working in the yard.

While Maria was reading the card, Ivy came in. 'Oh, aren't they lovely! Is Joe finally pulling out all the stops?'

Maria shook her head. 'No, they're from a *new* man,' she said, grinning.

'That was quick,' said Ivy. Maria certainly had a twinkle in her eye that wasn't there before.

'We only went out for a drink last night.'

'He's a bit of a catch, sending you flowers after your first date.' Ivy fingered the petals of a soft pink rose.

'I think he is, you know!' said Maria, burying her nose in the bouquet, full of the promise of things to come.

Joe sat by his mother's bedside and wrote his first love letter. Maria obviously didn't want to speak to him. He had heard the slight embarrassment in Aileen's voice the last time he had called. She was obviously pretending that Maria was out. He wanted to tell Maria how he felt. He might have lost her, but at least she wouldn't think he was a complete bastard. A letter was best. He could hardly talk to her properly on the hospital telephone, with all the fat dressing-gowned women on the ward queuing up behind him.

As he came back from the postbox, he wondered if his mother had lost Frank as well. He had called a few times to say he was too busy to come in, but how was Noreen? And always, the news was the same. No change.

Joe looked down at her. He blinked and stared. Her fingers were moving. He rang the nurses' call bell, and held his mother's hand. There was a very faint gripping response in her fingers.

'She's moving!' he shouted exuberantly as the nurse came running in.

Chapter Twenty

'So, what's the new flat like?' asked Paul as they sat down to dinner. He successfully hid the delight in his voice at the thought of Maria the Untidy moving out, and order being restored.

'It's more of a studio than a flat,' said Maria. 'Aileen was right. I couldn't afford a flat – they were incredibly expensive.'

'Where is it?' asked Aileen.

'It's in Ealing Common, so it's dead easy to get to work on the bus. I have to share a kitchen and a bathroom with four other studios.'

'So it's a room, really, is it?' Aileen couldn't resist saying. 'Would you like us to go and check it out, before you commit yourself?'

'No, I know I'm happy with it, thanks. I paid the deposit in case it went to someone else. I have my own basin in the room, and loads of storage space, and my own cupboard in the kitchen.'

'It'll be just like being back at university, then,' said Aileen.

Maria didn't mention that the state of the bathroom and kitchen would send their mother into paroxysms, and that there had been a distinct smell of dope lingering in the hall when she went back to pay her deposit. It was unlikely that Paul and Aileen would ever see the place, so the less said the better. She didn't think she would be entertaining them to dinner in the grotty kitchen.

'I'll move next Saturday, I think,' she said.

'Sounds good,' said Paul. 'Do you want us to drive you over there with your stuff?'

'No, thanks. I'll be fine. You're going out on Saturday, aren't you?'

'Yes, one of our bands is playing support to The Chemical Brothers at the Milton Keynes Bowl. But I could easily drop you off on the way.'

'Not at all – it's miles out of your way.' Whatever about showing them the room when it was cleaned, she would be mortified if they saw it now.

'Suit yourself,' said Paul, and smiled at her.

He was such a nice guy, Maria thought as they sat on the sofa to watch a James Bond movie. Aileen was besotted with him, Maria could see. Her face lit up when Paul came home from work, and when she talked about him, she was animated and happy. They never seemed to have rows.

It used to be like that for her and Joe. He was such good fun to be with, and they talked about loads of things. He made her think, and have opinions, but most of all the way he looked at her made her feel so special. He was the kind of guy that you imagine spending the rest of your life with – if he wanted to spend it with you. She pushed away the hurt, and tried to ignore the pangs of guilt. She had told Aileen on Sunday night as she went to bed that she didn't want to speak to Joe if he rang. It was easier this way. He hadn't called last weekend, so he was obviously cooling off her. His mother couldn't possibly be around the house every minute of every day, watching the phone. After a miserable two days of sitting around waiting for him to ring, she had finally seen sense. She didn't want to hear him say out loud that the relationship wouldn't work out with a baby on the scene. It was easier to just let it drift away and keep the good memories.

Then she thought about Andy. It seemed to have sneaked up on her, but she really liked him a lot. The butterflies in her stomach did loop the loops when she thought about him. He was so gorgeous. He was much taller than Joe, so when he held her in his arms, he made her feel small and feminine and delicate. He told her she was sexy and he had a way of stroking her skin that made her tingle all over. He just had to touch her and she got goose bumps. Andy said he liked her to wear short skirts and her hair up, and she didn't mind.

It made her feel sophisticated. Less like a student and more like a woman.

'Are you seeing Andy this weekend?' Aileen asked when the ads came on during the movie. She usually avoided the topic, because they always argued when she raised it. Maria knew she was only trying to be protective, but she resented Aileen telling her to steer clear of Andy.

'Probably. He said we might do something on Sunday,' Maria muttered. She wasn't in the mood for another lecture.

'Have you told him yet?'

'No, I will soon.'

'I'm not being horrible, but you need to –'

'I know, Aileen. I need to be prepared for him to dump me when he finds out that I'm having someone else's baby.'

Maria fought back tears of frustration and self-pity. She knew Andy could have his pick of girls. Why would he go out with a big fat pregnant girl? And where would it lead? He wouldn't want to be involved with a baby. She just wanted to capture and enjoy the short time she had before her life changed completely. No one would want to take her on with a baby.

'Sorry, Maria. I'm only trying to help,' Aileen said softly.

'I know.'

Aileen was feeling guilty. She knew that Andy had got a girl pregnant in Australia, when he was travelling, and he had left her behind because he couldn't face the responsibility. She wouldn't tell Maria, but the sooner Maria found out what he was really like, the better.

007 came back on and, as he swung off a cliff, Maria escaped with relief into the bathroom.

Aileen snuggled up to Paul with a packet of Revels and they played their silly game of guessing what flavour each one was, as they fed them to each other.

Maria lay in the bath, surrounded by a Hollywood-movie amount of bubbles so that she wouldn't have to see the slightly rounded stomach that would soon give her away to Andy. The peach-scented candle glowing on the edge of the bath did nothing to soothe her. She didn't want to lose Andy as well as Joe.

She hadn't slept with him yet, but she wanted to, and so did he, very soon. Should she tell him before, or after? Should she just break it off now, like Aileen said, before it went any further? Why did life have to be so complicated? She looked around the bathroom, with the colour co-ordinated towels, potpourri and fish mobile hanging off the ceiling, and thought about the damp smelly bathroom in her new place.

She couldn't imagine spending hours soaking in there. Somehow she didn't think that a candle would last long without being nicked. Imagine queuing up with your own toilet roll, towel, washbag and candle. At least in college, when she shared with Pauline and Orla, the loo-roll and shower gel were bought out of the kitty. She suddenly felt lonely. At this moment, she would even swap Miss Pious Knickers with her blue silk pyjamas for the dodgy-looking dopehead who might steal her shampoo if she left it in the bathroom. She closed her eyes and sank right down under the water and the bubbles, for once not caring that her hair would be sticky and frizzy in the morning.

Chapter Twenty-one

Her bags seemed a lot heavier than they had been only a few weeks before, and Maria was exhausted by the time she had carried them downstairs to the front lobby. Paul was in the hall when she staggered back upstairs to pick up her handbag.

'Maria, please let me take you in the car – you'll never manage all that stuff on the tube. Aileen's got a hair appointment and won't be back until two, so I'll have plenty of time to take you and get back.'

Maria hesitated. It was tempting. She had been contemplating spending £20 on a taxi, but she couldn't afford to throw money away.

'All right,' she said, already planning how she could get him to just drop her off without seeing the room. 'Thanks, Paul, I really appreciate it.'

'No problem. Come on, let's go,' he said, grabbing

his leather jacket off the curved stainless-steel coatstand in the hall. He patted his pockets, checking for keys.

Maria took one last look in her room to make sure she had picked everything up. The sun was shining into the room, making it bright and warm, and she shivered in anticipation of the dark, chilly room she would be sleeping in that night.

She followed Paul downstairs and he had already loaded the boot of the car by the time she caught up with him. Capital Radio burbled in the background as Paul deftly negotiated one-way streets and triple lanes of traffic. Maria's mental map of London was in the regular, rectangular shape of the tube map, so she always enjoyed a journey above ground, to put architectural faces on the names she knew from her journey to work.

She loved the dark red-brick of the Georgian mansions on Clapham Common, and the majestic, prow-shaped glass and steel apartment block on Vauxhall Bridge. Paul pointed out the M15 building on the other side of the bridge, and she said, 'Isn't that supposed to be secret?' remembering her George Smiley cloak-and-dagger plots.

'Everybody knows that's where they are,' Paul said, enjoying, as he always did, imparting his knowledge to Maria, who was so easily impressed.

She was a funny girl, so sassy and switched on in lots of ways, and then so young and naïve in others. He felt sorry for her, because she would have to grow up so quickly when the baby arrived. She was completely underestimating how difficult it would be to raise a child on her own in London. He was determined that he and Aileen would be there for her, whenever she needed them. But he was still relieved that she was moving out, before familiarity bred contempt.

Paul glanced across at her, when they stopped at a set of traffic-lights outside Earl's Court Exhibition Centre. She was staring at posters advertising the Ideal Home Exhibition. He looked down. Her hands had instinctively settled in the classic pose of the pregnant woman, nursing the slight bump under her jumper. A stab of regret jolted him. Aileen could have had their baby three years ago, but they had been too scared that it would change their relationship. He could only admire Maria for her courage, not pity her or patronise her, as he realised now he had been doing. She was younger than Aileen, and was going to keep this baby, even without Joe. Paul patted her on the shoulder, with a sudden urge to say something to convey his admiration. The lights changed to green and the car behind beeped before he had the chance to say anything. The moment was lost, and Maria was singing along with some poppy song on the radio.

'It's great to see all this above ground,' Maria said, as they crossed the A4 and accelerated into the fast lane.

'Yes, it took me ages to get used to driving,' said Paul, 'after five years of using the Tube when I came to London first.'

Shepherd's Bush roundabout was congested, and

Maria admired the tall blue water-sculpture in the middle of it, fascinated, as always, with the strange places that monuments get put.

'You won't have too much time to get back,' she said, ' so you can just drop me outside if you like.'

'I'll carry the bags in for you,' said Paul. 'I promise I won't tell Aileen how horrible it is.' He softened his tone so she wouldn't think he was being patronising.

Maria looked at him. 'What makes you think it's horrible?' she asked, defensively.

'For three hundred pounds a month, in West London, it has to be pretty bad,' he said. 'But everyone has to start somewhere. I think you're being really brave.' He couldn't look at her because he was concentrating on changing lanes, avoiding an erratically driven white transit van.

Suddenly, Maria was choked with the tears she had been fighting for the last three months. 'Don't be nice to me,' she said, as he heard her gulping, and quickly glanced across. She was staring out the passenger window at the huge white BBC buildings, bristling with satellites and a sense of their own importance.

'I just want you to know that Aileen and I will always be here for you, if you need us,' he said, and she nodded, still not able to look at him.

'It's a bit scary,' she said in a very small voice.

'I know.'

They pulled up outside the big red-brick mansion block, with its seven doorbells, and suddenly Maria didn't care what Paul thought. It didn't look too bad on the outside, and with a good clean, her room would be fine.

Paul carried all the bags in and put them in the corner of her tiny room. He managed not to show his horror. The room was even worse than he had imagined, and his glimpse of the kitchen as he passed didn't give him any reason to alter his view.

'I must dash,' he said, 'or Aileen will be pacing up and down, waiting for me.'

He gave her a quick hug, and said, 'See you soon, yeah?' as he closed the door behind him.

Maria took a deep breath and started unpacking her bags. If she sat down and thought about things, she would fall apart. Cleaning was the thing to do. She rolled up her sleeves and unpacked the Tesco's bag full of cleaning materials that Aileen had donated.

When she woke up on Sunday morning, it took a moment to remember where she was. The single bed seemed narrow and the room was much darker than Aileen's spare room. Her heart sank. This was supposed to be exciting. Her first independent step away from home. All she felt was a suffocating pressure on her chest and a churning in her stomach. She knew why. Telling Andy about the baby was the least of her problems. She had promised herself that as soon as she got her own place, she would tell her mam and dad as well. It was something to do with being on her own territory, showing them that she was grown-up, and not dependent on them or Aileen for support. Sunday was her day for ringing home, so she couldn't put it off any longer. The glandular fever story now seemed so stupid. Why could she not just have told them straight away, and they might be used to the idea by now. No, her dad would never get used to it. He was so judgmental. When Annie Kelly in Maria's class at secondary school got pregnant, he had gone to pieces completely. Annie was a star pupil, all set for a scholarship to Cornell University in the States, and Maria's dad was so proud that one of his pupils had done so well. He was in really bad form for a week after he found out she was pregnant. And when she did badly in the Leaving Cert, he got upset all over again and said she had thrown her life away.

Maria sighed and threw back the duvet. She slipped on her dressing-gown. Today was the day. No escaping it any longer. After breakfast, which she ate at the tiny table in her room, looking out at the overgrown back garden, she went to the newsagent's to get change for the pay phone. Only when she was standing in the hall with a handful of coins warm in her fist, did she wish that she'd called from Aileen's place before she left. People kept coming out of their rooms and going to the bathroom, and someone had a radio on really loud in the kitchen while they fried eggs and burnt their toast. A blue haze of smoke wafted out the door and made Maria cough.

She dialled the number and gulped several times as the ringing tone started.

She said, 'Hello, Mam?' as the ringing stopped, and her heart plummeted when she heard her dad's voice. She panicked. He should be at Mass. She wanted to tell her Mam first and let her pass on the news.

'No, it's me. Is that Maria?'

'Yes, hi, Daddy.' She hadn't called him that for years. She felt like a kid again, and she jammed her knees together to stop them from trembling. 'How come you're at home?'

'That's a nice greeting! I swapped with Joe Murphy on the collections today, because I wanted to play golf this morning, so I'm doing the twelve o' clock Mass instead.'

'Oh, right.'

'Are you all right, love? You sound a bit funny. And what's all that noise in the background?'

'I'm in a new flat. I moved in yesterday. That's someone in the kitchen with the radio on.'

'Oh, I didn't even know you were looking. Honestly, your mother doesn't tell me anything these days.'

'She didn't know either, I wanted it to be a surprise.'

'Well, it is. A nice surprise. Very grown-up. Is it handy for getting to work?'

'Yes, it's great. That's one of the reasons I wanted to move. I was cramping Aileen and Paul's style a bit as well, and –'

'I'm sure Paul was glad that you were there to keep

179

Aileen company, with him over on the other side of London.'

'Yes, you're right, of course, yes,' said Maria. She had lost count of how many times she had nearly given the game away. Just as well her dad was so obtuse. Mam had probably guessed by now. She felt a surge of irrational irritation. Why couldn't Aileen just tell them, for God's sake?'

'And how are you feeling, these days? Any developments?' He had been reading about the symptoms of glandular fever, and giving her tips about how to look after herself.

'Well, Daddy, I have something to tell you about that.'

'Oh? Is it getting better, then?'

She took a deep breath.

'It's not glandular fever at all. I'm having a baby.'

'What?' he roared.

'Dad, Daddy . . .' Maria's tiny voice came down the line to the receiver he was holding away from his ear, as if to stop the message reaching his brain.

This time it was Maureen's turn to come rushing out into the hall. She was wiping her hands on a tea towel as Sean turned to her, his face red and blotchy.

'She's having a baby.' His voice cracked. He saw Maureen's face slowly register the news.

'A baby? Who? But how?'

Sean leaned against the spindly table and it creaked ominously. He handed over the receiver.

'You talk to her.'

He stood up and shuffled into the sitting-room like a man twice his age and closed the door.

Maureen spoke quietly. 'Is it true?' Her suspicions had been allayed when Maria had kept up the glandular-fever story for so many weeks.

'Yes, Mammy.'

Maria had expected the weight to lift off her chest when she told them, but it was even heavier.

'And why didn't you tell us here at home, to our faces?' Maureen's voice was chilly.

'Because I was going to –' Maria stopped.

'Going to what?'

Maureen was on automatic pilot. The questions just came, and she was just asking them.

'Get some advice from Aileen first. I wanted to talk to her about it,' gasped Maria.

'What does she know about anything?' asked Maureen disdainfully. Maria should have confided in her, first. That's what mothers were for.

Maria was shocked at the harshness of her mother's tone. 'Aileen's been great, Mam. Very supportive.'

'Unlike you,' hung unsaid at the end of the sentence, but Maureen heard.

'How far gone are you?'

'Eighteen weeks.'

'Oh, my God. Is it Joe's?'

'Yes.'

'Does he know?'

'Yes.'

'And I thought he was such a nice lad. I can't believe he did this to you.'

'He didn't do anything to me, Mam.'

'So how did you get in your condition then, if he did nothing to you?' Maria had never heard her being so nasty. 'He's a medical student. He should know better. And as for you . . . you weren't brought up to be sleeping around.'

'Mam . . . it was an accident.' She had expected to get the speeches from Dad, and support from Mam, the peacemaker. 'So that's why I'm staying over here.'

'No glandular fever?'

'No.'

Suddenly Maureen couldn't take any more. Her head was full. 'Listen, I'm going away now. I need to let this sink in. I will discuss it with your father and ring you tomorrow.'

Maria heard a tiny hint of conciliation in her mother's tone. Maybe there was some hope.

'OK, Mam. Sorry.'

'It's a bit late for sorries.'

'I'm in a new place now – let me give you the number.'

She read out the number, and her mother took it in silence, and didn't even ask her what the place was like, or where it was, or if she was happy in it.

Chapter Twenty-two

'Bless me, Father, for I have sinned,' said Sean, kneeling in the darkness of the confessional on Saturday evening before Benediction. The smell of furniture polish filled his nostrils and he could feel his pupils dilating, seeking out the familiar shape of the crucifix on the wall above the grille. The side of Father Duggan's face, lit in the glow of his little red confessional light, leaned towards him.

'Yes, my son.' The expression came naturally, even though Sean Hardy was the same age as himself.

'Father, I have a problem, and I need some advice.' Sean leaned forward.

'Yes.' That particular inflection would coax the details of the most horrible sins out of his parishioners.

'My daughter is having a baby, and she's not married,' whispered Sean.

He was pressing his hands together so tightly that

he could see his knuckles glowing white in the darkness.

So the rumours were true. The priest just nodded, waiting.

'I can't find it in me to forgive her, Father.'

'Is it your place to forgive people's sins, Sean?' the priest said sternly.

'I brought her up as a good Catholic. She knows it's a sin to have a baby like that. I told her and her sister that often enough. Sure I tell the girls in the school the same thing as well. You have to drum it into them.'

'Sean, is it your forgiveness she needs now, or God's?'

'She's let me down, Father, and she has broken away from her family.'

That wasn't how Father Duggan had heard it. According to Emer Kennedy in the Post Office, Sean had told her not to come back.

'Sean, tell me, is it a sin for a girl to let her father down?' he said softly.

'No, I suppose not, technically, Father, but –'

'Wouldn't it be worse to have the sin of pride, and cast off your daughter when she made a mistake? You'd be excluding the grandchild from the love of her family.'

Sean gulped and nodded.

'And don't forget, if she's off in England, she had choices over there that she wouldn't have here. We should be glad that she made the right choice, Sean.'

Sean shook his head fiercely. Words escaped him. He hadn't thought of that.

'Is it advice you're looking for, Sean, or someone to confirm your judgement?'

The priest knew he wasn't giving Sean what he wanted, but the man was being unreasonable.

'I suppose I want advice about how to be a good father, and make her understand that what she has done is wrong,' Sean said.

'I think you have probably let her know that already, Sean. Think about your own relationship with God the Father. How does he treat you when you do something wrong? If you come to him with genuine contrition, and promise to try harder, he always forgives you.'

'Yes.'

'Remember, Sean, absolution depends on forgiveness. Now, have you anything else to tell me about?' asked the priest, and he heard the rest of Sean's confession.

Sean stood up and the air puffed out of the red vinyl cushion on the creaking kneeler. As he put out his hand to push the door open, he realised that he hadn't heard the sound of the grille-cover sliding across as Father Duggan turned to the other side of the confessional. He looked sideways. The face was still there, glowing in the dark.

'Sean,' the priest whispered, 'for your own peace of mind, you need to think about why you are pushing Maria away, just when she needs you the most.'

'Yes, Father,' Sean said gruffly, and stepped out into

the side aisle of the church. He knelt in one of the pews to thank God for forgiving his sins, and to say the prayers for his penance.

That night, the dream came back to Sean. He hadn't had it for years. It was Sean's turn to wheel the soiled bed linen in the big blue trolley from the dormitory over to the laundry.

He would come back with the clean sheets, and the older girls in the orphanage would put them on the hard narrow beds. His heart was beating fast. It was scary going across the yard to the tall spiky gates of the laundry, especially in the winter, when it was dark and wet.

A big fat nun would be standing there. She would rattle her keys and open the gates, and he would pass through to the other side. The nuns said that the women on the other side were mad and evil, and you should never speak to them. They were sinners, destined for hell, and if you looked them in the eye you had to tell it in confession or you'd go to hell yourself.

So Sean pushed the trolley with his arms at full stretch, looking down at the ground, not daring to raise his eyes. He heard the keys rattling. The big gates swung open, and he lifted his head to see where he was going. Suddenly, one of the bad women came running out from behind the nun.

She grabbed him, sobbing, 'Seanin, Seanin, look at me, for the love of God!'

Sean screamed. He looked into her eyes. He couldn't

help it. He saw the madness that the nuns talked about. He also saw the love, shining in her brown tear-filled eyes, before she was dragged away screaming by the big nun. Sean was left standing alone in the yard with the trolley. He knew in that moment that he had seen his mother. She wasn't dead of TB, like the nuns said. She was one of the bad women, and that was worse. He ran back through the gates, crying. That night, he wet his bed, and the nuns made him lie in it all the next day. He would never forget the pungent smell of urine and the scratchy wet pyjamas chafing against his skin.

He had to change the bed himself and put the sheets into the blue trolley. The bad woman's face loomed in every corner, and he was afraid to sleep, in case she came to haunt his dreams.

Sean shot awake, sweating. The image of her face hung over him for a second, in the darkness. He heard her whisper: 'Seanin.' He threw off the blankets to relieve the huge weight on his chest. He crept downstairs so that he wouldn't wake Maureen, and stirred up the embers of the fire. He had never seen the woman again. A few months later, a farmer and his wife, who had five daughters, took him away to Carraroe to be their son. His new mammy doted on him and he tried to forget about the bad woman. He was always a good boy and he worked hard so they wouldn't send him back to the orphanage. The parish priest said his altar boy's surplice was the cleanest and the best pressed, and the teacher said he was the star in his class. At secondary school, he won a scholarship to go to university in Galway. When he met and married Maureen, he fulfilled his dream to come back to Carraroe as a teacher and raise his own family there.

So what had he done wrong? None of his children had lacked for anything. They had a stable home life, and good Catholic parents. Why did Maria need to go off sleeping around and getting pregnant? She was so brazen about it, that was the worst thing – as if she had nothing to be ashamed of.

They had told everyone that Maria was taking a year off college to get some work experience in London. But Paddy Naughtan would soon be back home for his holidays, and you couldn't trust him not to blather it all over the place, when he had a few drinks on him. So it was only a matter of time before everyone knew. You couldn't keep it a secret these days, like you could in his mother's day. Most people didn't seem to think there was anything wrong with it. He went back to bed and lay wide awake.

Maureen pretended to be asleep but she knew that Sean was lying there, thinking. He was busy deluding himself that everyone in the village believed the story about Maria taking a year off. Of course they knew what was going on – they weren't stupid. And it wasn't the worst thing in the world that could happen. Poor Evelyn Duggan just had her son back from New York after three years, a drug-addict with so many debts they had to sell their two top fields to pay them off. You only had to look at him to know he had a problem. He might even have AIDS, someone said. But no one would think the worse of Evelyn and Padraig because of their son. Apart from Sean. He was a terrible man for judging others, and because of that, he didn't want anyone else to look down their noses at him. She turned her back to him, thinking about poor Maria. A tear slid down her cheek onto the pillow.

Chapter Twenty-three

Maria regretted bringing Andy back to her room as soon as she opened the front door, but she had put him off for a month, saying his place was much nicer, and he was getting curious. Andy wasn't impressed. He wrinkled his nose at the smell of damp in the hall, and looked around her room as if expecting to see at least three doors leading to more space. His flat was huge, by comparison, and he had a cleaner once a week and a lady who did his ironing. He looked with distaste at the clothes-horse draped with damp wrinkled clothes, and sat on the bed. Maria had discovered that Andy was really fastidious, with his CDs arranged in alphabetical order by category and the towels in his bathroom folded edge to edge and piled neatly on the shelf above the door.

Andy took his eyes away from the surroundings and looked Maria up and down. 'You look great, darling,' he said, pulling her down on to his knee and kissing her. Maria had taken special care to look good, because she was going to tell him tonight. She was wearing a short soft purple jumper-dress that showed off her slim legs and hid the bump that seemed to suddenly have emerged in the last week. Andy slid his hand along her thigh and tugged at the waistband of her sheer opaque black tights.

'We've got time, before the movie, haven't we?' he said, nuzzling her hair.

Maria sighed. Sometimes they didn't even have a proper conversation before Andy wanted to have sex. He had told her once that he used to fantasise about her being a virgin, when they first met, and she wished she had told him then about the baby. But they had been lying arm in arm exchanging butterfly kisses, and she didn't want to break the spell.

Now, she wriggled off his knee and stood up. 'Listen, Andy, I have something to tell you,' she said, her voice taut.

'Don't act so serious. It can't be that bad.' He took her hands and pulled her towards him. The semi-sweet smell of Saturday afternoon beer lingered on his breath.

'I'm pregnant.'

His laugh sounded like a short bark. 'No way. Don't joke about stuff like that,' he said, suddenly gruff.

'I'm not joking. I was pregnant before we met. It's due in December.' She was blushing now, and could feel the prickly heat on her neck, under the collar of her woollen dress.

'Fucking hell!' Andy rubbed his hands through his hair. 'This is like some weird fucking karma thing.'

Maria didn't register the meaning of that, but launched into her pre-prepared speech. She would understand if he didn't want to see her again – he shouldn't feel under pressure and she was sorry she hadn't told him before. He stood up and looked out the window for a full minute in silence, while she nibbled her nails.

He turned around and said, 'Look, I'm going. But I'll give you a bell in a couple of days, when I've got my head around this, all right?'

Maria nodded dumbly. At least he wasn't angry. She had only seen him lose his temper once, but it wasn't a pleasant sight. A friend had told him that he couldn't afford to repay a loan of £1,000 until September. Andy had lost it completely, throwing the phone at the wall and sweeping the Sunday newspapers and magazines onto the floor along with a mug of coffee that splashed the wall like a dried bloodstain. Then in a flash, it was gone, and he muttered an apology to Maria and started cleaning up the mess, saying he wasn't usually like this.

Now, he kissed her in a businesslike way on the cheek and let himself out the door without looking back. Maria burst into tears and lay on the bed, staring at a damp patch on the wall that looked like a map of Australia. This baby had driven away everyone she cared about, and it wasn't even born yet.

Her dad hadn't spoken to her for six weeks, after

banishing her from the house. She could only talk to her mam in secret when he was out, or sometimes she had whispered conversations on the phone so that he wouldn't overhear. Joe was, no doubt, at home being pampered by his mother, conveniently forgetting all about Maria and her 'little problem'. And now Andy, the only good thing that had happened to her lately, was out the door and gone running a mile, never to be seen again.

Men were all the same. They just wanted you to live up to some image created inside their heads. Dad wanted an intelligent charming daughter, unsullied by the hand of man, or even the angel Gabriel, she suspected. Joe wanted a girlfriend, not a wife, and certainly not another mother. He had enough with one in his life. Andy wanted a sex object with no strings attached, except the ones that he pulled himself. Even Paddy wanted a pretty receptionist to brighten up his office and give him the occasional thrill with a glimpse of a stocking-top. She felt empty. Who was she, now? She had failed them all, without figuring out who she really was. She wanted desperately to talk to her mother. But not standing in the cold hall, feeding pound coins into the telephone. She wanted to sit in the kitchen with the warm Aga at her back, dipping biscuits in her tea and watching her mother stirring marmalade in the big pot. Most of all, she wanted a hug from someone who loved her for herself, not her body or her looks, or even her brains. Aileen was always there for her, but now she felt stupid, and couldn't go running over there for comfort. Aileen had warned her about this happening with Andy, and she had ignored the advice. Maria rolled over and curled up with her back to the wall, closing her eyes to relieve the burning sensation in her eyeballs, and escaped into sleep.

Chapter Twenty-four

Once she was able to speak, one of the first things Joe's mother asked him was:

'Has Frank been in?'

Joe could honestly say that he had, and that he seemed like a very nice man. She smiled and stroked the bedclothes.

'He's a lovely man,' she said softly. 'I'm sure you'll like him even more when you get to know him.'

'I'm sure I will, Mam,' Joe said, pasting on the fixed grin he had perfected over the last few months.

Gradually, as she gained a sense of the weeks and months passing, Noreen realised that Frank wasn't coming back. She didn't say anything. Joe saw it in her eyes. First the expectant smile and the furtive glances towards the door at visiting time, and then the hurt. She slipped into a state of quiet resignation that sapped all her energy. The physiotherapist said she was making slow progress. By the time October came and Joe had to go back to college, she still needed constant care.

For the last few months, Joe had worked into a routine of studying really hard during the week, sometimes staying up until 2 am to get all his reading done. He caught the bus to Westport on Friday evenings and took his mother home from the nursing home in a taxi. Joe had put a bed in the living-room so she didn't have to climb the stairs, and she seemed to be a bit more lively at home with her own things around her.

She was gradually recovering her movement. Her speech was almost back to normal, but she still wasn't the same person. She was lethargic and uninterested. Even Rita Duffy said so when she came to visit on Sunday afternoons to give Joe a break.

'I suppose it takes a long time to get over these things,' said Rita, making tea in the kitchen one afternoon in November. 'She was in a coma for how long? Six or seven weeks, wasn't it? You can't expect the body to just go back to normal straight away.'

Joe nodded. He was standing at the kitchen sink looking out at the sleety rain sweeping across the garden. Mrs Duffy didn't have a clue. It had nothing to do with the body. His mother's spirit had flown away. He was so lonely. He had lost Maria, and he felt like he had lost his mother too.

When he had gone back to college in October, everyone was gossiping about Maria for a while. They all knew she was having his baby, and at first he wondered if they judged him, thinking he wasn't standing by her. But, after a while, he stopped caring what they thought, exhausted by the regime of looking after his mother and trying to keep up with his study.

Mike, tanned and muscular after a summer of working on the kibbutz, took him to the Union bar and got him drunk on their first evening back, and asked him what he was going to do.

'She threw me completely, Mike, when she decided to keep the baby. If Mum hadn't had her accident, I would have just gone straight over there and talked to her. Maybe I would have even stayed for the summer, to see how things worked out.'

'But she does know about your mother, doesn't she?' asked Mike, struck with the thought that there had been some massive breakdown in communication.

'I tried to tell her on the phone, but she wouldn't ring me back, so I wrote a letter to Aileen's address and I never heard anything back.'

'And you left it at that?' Mike asked incredulously. 'Things get lost in the post all the time. Did you not ask Aileen if the letter arrived?'

'No, I didn't, Mike, because believe it or not I had other things on my mind too. My mother nearly died.'

Joe hadn't had a beer all summer, and the drink had gone to his head. He had an urge to burst into tears, but managed to hold it together.

Mike said, 'Sorry, Joe, It's none of my business. You have to do what's right for you. It was only that I was surprised Maria wouldn't send a card or something, for your mother, you know?'

'I know,' Joe said. 'But you know what else? I always thought she would leave me for someone else eventually. She could have her pick of men. I bet she's found someone in England already.'

Mike couldn't stand it when Joe got maudlin. 'Maybe it is for the best then, but just be sure it's what you want as well.' He stood up to get another round, and from then on they had a tacit agreement not to discuss the subject.

Mike didn't want to let it go, so he decided to talk to Maria's friend Pauline. He waited outside one of her lectures, on a frosty November morning, rubbing his hands together to warm them up. The heating had broken down again, and all the students who came piling out of the lecture hall had coats and scarves on, and a cloud of steamy breath followed the stampede to the refectory. Pauline was almost last out, and she was surprised to hear her name being called.

'Oh, hi, Mike,' she said, blushing a bit. He was still as gorgeous as ever.

'Hi, Pauline. Listen, can I get you a coffee to warm you up?' He nodded in the direction that everyone was going.

'Yeah, great,' she said, intrigued. Her heart was pounding. He could not, in a million years, fancy you, she sternly told herself as they walked along.

'How's it going, this year?' Mike asked, as they joined the long coffee queue.

'Great. I'm getting more into the legal subjects this year, so I'm really enjoying it,' she said enthusiastically.

He hadn't noticed her lovely smile before. She looked a bit thinner than he remembered, as well.

'What about you?' she asked.

'It's tough, but it has been from day one, so that's no change,' he said, ' but we start doing clinical stuff after Christmas, so I'm looking forward to that.'

'Across in the hospital?'

'Yes, we get to follow the consultants around the wards, intimidating the patients in their beds, and reading their notes with very serious faces on us,' he laughed.

They sat at a busy table, and he finally got to the point.

'I'm worried about Joe,' he said, and Pauline nodded, wondering what that had to do with her. 'He says that Maria just won't communicate with him, and he thinks she's just dumped him, and gone off with someone else.' His tone was meant to convey disbelief that such a thing could be true.

He looked at her and she wouldn't catch his eye.

'It's true,' he said.

'Only after Joe dumped her!' Pauline said, leaping to Maria's defence.

'He never dumped her – he wrote her a long letter declaring his undying love, and that he would stand by her and the baby. She never even acknowledged it,' he said, equally indignant on Joe's behalf.

'Shit, what do we do now?' Pauline asked, and Mike

shrugged. The tears in her eyes made them look even bigger and brighter.

'When is the baby due?' he asked, wondering how much time they had to wreak a miracle.

'About six weeks' time. Just around Christmas. Maria is a bit vague about the dates.'

'Not much time, then. How long has she been seeing this other guy – what's his name?'

'Andy'. It was only later that Mike realised Pauline hadn't answered the other question.

'I don't think it's up to us,' said Pauline. 'If they're ever going to work things out, they have to figure it out for themselves.'

'I know, but what if it's just one big misunderstanding? We don't want to be responsible for knowing, and not telling them.'

'Let's have a think about it for a couple of days,' said Pauline, desperately trying to think what Maria's reaction would be. She seemed to be quite taken with this Andy, although Aileen had said he was bad news.

Just before the Christmas holidays, Joe bumped into Pauline in the queue for the bank. She looked a bit embarrassed, he thought.

'How's it going?' she asked, as she always did. She knew about his mother, but never liked to ask directly, not wanting to pry.

'Fine. I'm heading home the day after tomorrow. Any news about Maria? She must be due soon.'

'She's probably in labour now. Her mam rang me last night to say that her waters had broken. She's two weeks early.'

Joe's heart jumped. That's why Pauline had looked a bit sheepish. 'Oh my God!' The surge of emotion that swept through him took him by surprise. It was really happening. Right now. 'I'm going over there. I want to be with her.' He turned out of the queue, deciding to head for the student travel desk to book a flight.

Pauline tugged his arm and then looked down. 'Joe, she's with somebody else, now.' It was the hardest news she had ever had to break. She was wishing that Mike could be there. She watched as desolation washed over Joe. He went pale, and looked like he needed to sit down.

Pauline said quietly, 'Maria said she'll send me some photos of the baby. Do you want to see them?'

Joe was torn. Maria had found someone else, as he had suspected all along. She hadn't even bothered to tell him, just left him hanging all that time. She was completely excluding him. But he would love to know what the baby looked like. It was still his child. No one could take that away from him, even if they pretended to be the father.

He mumbled, 'I don't know. I'll see you after Christmas anyway,' and turned away so she couldn't see the tears in his eyes.

That evening, he remembered an incident from his hospital training day on the labour ward. A huge beefy farmer was standing awkwardly by his wife's bed, holding her hand and urging her on when the midwife told her to push. He looked as if he would be more comfortable delivering a calf onto a bed of straw, than standing there in the pristine whiteness of the delivery room. When the baby finally emerged, and was placed on her mother's chest, the woman looked up at her husband and said, 'She's arrived. Our little girl is here, at last.' He bent and put his huge red hand on the baby's head, and tenderly kissed his wife, his eyes full of tears, and he just nodded at her, speechless.

Joe knew what he had to do.

The postnatal ward was unusually quiet, with no babies crying, trolleys clanging or excited visitors' voices disturbing the peace. The duty midwife was surprised to see a sandy-haired man sitting by Maria's bed, having an intense whispered conversation with her. She checked the watch hanging from her uniform pocket. Only fathers were allowed to visit after eight o'clock at night.

At first, she had thought that Maria didn't have a partner, because her sister was with her during the labour. Then a tall, handsome dark-haired man had turned up with an orchid in a plastic box and a pink heart-shaped helium balloon saying '*It's a girl!*'. He had only arrived after Maria was stitched and the baby and she were cleaned up and settled on the ward. The dad must have been working away somewhere, unable to make it back in time for the delivery. Maria had looked very excited when he came in and kissed her, but the midwife noticed that he didn't bother to look at the baby for a few minutes.

Now there was this other chap and Maria seemed to be having a very heated exchange with him. She didn't like to interrupt but it wasn't fair on the other girls, and rules were rules, so she rustled the curtain and poked her head into the cubicle. 'Excuse me, it's after eight o'clock – I'm afraid only fathers are allowed . . .'

Maria looked up and begged with her eyes for them to be left alone. 'Just one more minute, please?'

The midwife nodded and backed out. She would leave them for ten minutes. No harm in that.

Joe was pleading as he took Maria's hand. 'Maria, it's not too late. I'll give up college. I'll do anything. She's more important than anything else.'

He looked down at the tiny baby girl, wrapped in a white cellular blanket, only her little face and dark hair showing. He couldn't believe the surge of feeling he had for the tiny mite, even though he hadn't felt her kicking during the pregnancy, or seen her delivered, or even held her in his arms.

Maria's face was ashen. 'It is too late, Joe. I'm with Andy now. I'm happy with him. I really am.' She kept looking around nervously, waiting for the curtain to swish back and Andy to come back in. What if he turned up now? She couldn't possibly explain why Joe was here. She had nearly died when she heard Joe's voice coming down the ward, talking to one of the nurses, his Irish accent out of place among the English voices of her ward companions. She looked back at Joe.

'I suppose he's got loads of money, and you think he can look after you, like I can't.' said Joe a bit resentfully.

Maria took a deep breath. Joe hadn't been in touch for months. How could he expect to just walk back into her life now, and claim rights over Molly? 'Yes, as it happens, he looks after me very well, and he's prepared to take on . . . someone else's baby.' There was no nice way to say it.

'But he's still not her father.' Joe finally let the tears come. They had been building up for six months, and now they flooded out. He sobbed like he hadn't done since his own father died.

Maria just stared at him. It was a bit late for tears now. Joe was acting like a spoiled child who couldn't have his way. She wanted a strong, decisive man who would provide a good home for her and baby Molly. Andy was all of those things. Joe was offering her too little, too late. Andy had been there for her when Joe wasn't.

She would never forget the loneliness and desperation she had felt when Andy had walked out of her bedsit after hearing that she was pregnant. She had sat in her tiny room, just crying and sleeping for three days. Then she answered the door one Saturday morning, and Andy was standing there, smiling. He asked her how she was feeling, and held out a bunch of flowers. He took her in his arms and said he wanted to look after her; he couldn't live without her. He asked her to move into his flat, and said the baby could have the spare room. Maria was ecstatic. They would be a real family. Joe had opted out of that.

'Joe, how can you expect to just pick up where we left off? We were supposed to be having a relationship, but you didn't even bother to call me after the first few weeks.'

'I did try. Aileen told me you didn't want to speak to me. I had other things going on at home as well . . .'

'I know, your mother probably kept you very busy.' Maria couldn't resist the jibe. Joe looked really hurt, but what did he expect? He needed to grow up and find his own two feet. If he wasn't prepared to stand up to his mother, what kind of relationship could they hope to have?

Joe couldn't believe that Maria could be so cruel and unforgiving. OK, maybe he should have come over to London instead of writing to her, but surely she understood that his mother needed him? She had nearly died, for God's sake.

'I'm sorry I didn't live up to your expectations, Maria,' he said bitterly. 'I can see that you won't change your mind, but I had to try one more time.' He leaned over and kissed Molly on the forehead and stroked her little wrinkled cheek. He didn't say another word to Maria. He picked up his leather jacket off the bed and pushed the curtain aside, not looking back as he walked down the ward.

Maria sat back against her pillows, exhaling all the air in her lungs. Her heart was pounding. She hadn't expected to feel confused, but Joe had touched something inside her again that she thought was gone forever. She shook her head. She had definitely picked the right man. Admittedly, Andy hadn't come into the labour ward to be with her during the delivery. He was squeamish about blood and things. But she didn't want him there anyway, to see her in that state, with all her bits hanging out, and screaming her head off. It was much better that Aileen was there to hold her hand and time the contractions, and hold the paper bowler hat to catch her vomit. She couldn't imagine Andy doing that. But he had come in afterwards, smelling of her favourite aftershave, and one of the girls across the ward said later that he was a real hunk.

'You're very good to me, Joe,' Noreen said as he wheeled her out of the nursing home on Christmas Eve. They went through the lobby, hung with tattered decorations that had seen many years of service, and passed the squat Christmas tree in the porch.

'What else would I be doing, Mum? We're going to have a lovely quiet Christmas together. There's lots of cards waiting for you.'

The late afternoon sunlight shone in the puddles in the carpark. Busy people scurried past with steaming breaths, doing their last-minute jobs in town and collecting their relations for the holidays.

When they got home, Joe lit a fire in the living-room and made a pot of tea. He gave his mother the stack of Christmas cards that had been piling up on the hall floor.

She savoured opening each one, and Joe put them on the mantelpiece after she had read them out.

'It's quite nice getting them all together,' she smiled at him. 'Will you make me a list, so I can write back to people?'

It was the first time that she had expressed an interest in anything for a long time.

Then she opened a big gold-embossed envelope, addressed in careful block capitals. Her face fell when she read it. 'It's from Frank,' she said, slipping it down the side of the sofa cushion where she sat wrapped in a blanket. 'I'll keep that one. We won't put it up.'

Joe heard a trace of the old determination in her voice.

He knew how she felt. That kind of hurt took a long time to heal. Joe sat with his mother on the sofa and sadness washed over him again. He hugged her and they both stared into the flames and blinked away their tears.

Chapter Twenty-five

Sean came in from playing golf, soaking wet. Maureen didn't know what possessed him, playing golf in the Christmas holidays with the weather so terrible. He and Doctor Moran were as bad as each other. She took a deep breath and told him that Maria's baby had arrived early.

'What kind of a name is Molly for a child?' he said, when she told him their granddaughter's name. 'No self-respecting priest will pour water over that child's head.'

He tugged off his wet anorak and hung it near the stove. Steam rose from the seat of his trousers as he warmed himself.

Maureen wondered would Sean ever cop on? Maria probably hadn't been to Mass since she went away to college, never mind worrying about christening the child.

'I think it's a nice name,' she said. 'It probably doesn't sound so funny over in England. They go in for more modern names over there. Anyway, it's a derivative of Mary.'

She put a rack of mince-pies on the table to cool. 'Aileen said on the phone that she's really cute. She looks just like Maria, apparently.'

Sean forgot himself. 'Wasn't she a lovely baby? Do you remember, she had that big head of dark hair on her when she was born?'

Maureen looked across at him. If he wasn't so damn stubborn, Maria could come home with the child. But after twenty-seven years of marriage, she knew that now wasn't the time to be arguing with him. She would bide her time and wait until everything calmed down, and then she would come at it sideways. She often had to do that with Sean.

'Yes, and her hair never fell out. I wonder if Molly is the same? Aileen said she'll bring home some photos.'

Sean didn't say anything. He knew what Maureen was thinking. But he wasn't having an unmarried mother under his roof, daughter or not. She had let him down. He couldn't bear to be hurt any more. It was better that she was away, out of his sight.

Maureen put some more turf on the stove. 'Christmas will be very quiet this year,' she said for the umpteenth time. 'Usually I'd be rushing around getting organised. But with only Aileen coming home, it's not the same.'

Sean puffed on his pipe, justifying things to himself. Maria wouldn't be fit to travel, after just giving birth. If Hugh got himself a decent job, he'd be able to afford to come home from Australia. But Maureen was right. It did feel strange. There was none of the bustle of Maria arriving back from college with a load of books she would never read during the holidays. Neither of the girls begging for a lift into Galway on Christmas Eve to finish their shopping. No long drive like last year to pick up Hugh from Shannon Airport, looking like some kind of Aboriginal dropout with his big rucksack and his greasy ponytail. What would Maria be doing on Christmas day? You could hardly celebrate Christmas on your own with a tiny baby, away from home. But she had brought it on herself. All she had to do was admit that she was in the wrong, and ask for forgiveness. She had to see that, surely?

Aileen had a second gin and tonic on the plane. She was dreading Christmas at home. She had a big argument with Paul before she left, because he wanted to spend the holiday with her. He said she didn't have to go home just because no one else in the family was going. He made her promise that at least she would tell her mam and dad about them living together. Somehow, when she was home in August, there hadn't been a right moment to break the news. They were still getting over the shock of Maria. She couldn't do a double whammy on them.

Any day now, Maria would be telling them she had moved in with Andy, so Aileen had to get to them first. She knew that Paul couldn't see what all the fuss was about. He had outrageously liberal parents and no religion. He didn't even know any of the stories from the Bible. He said that her dad was living in a fifty-year-old, pre-War time warp, and he was right. But that didn't make it any easier. She made a decision. She would tell Mam first, and let her break it to Dad. He would find it easier that way.

In the choir loft on Christmas Day, Sean looked down during the Hallelujah Chorus and saw Maureen and Aileen beneath him in the pew, clapping in the traditional thank-you to the choir. He felt a stab of sadness as he scanned all the seats, full of returned emigrants. He recognised lots of his past pupils. Some of them had families of their own now. They nodded to each other as they filed up to receive Communion. They only saw each other once a year at Christmas, when they came home from the far-flung corners of the earth. The children wore trendy American-looking clothes and the boys had very short haircuts. Some of them didn't keep up with the kneeling and sitting and standing, and you could tell that they weren't taken to Mass every week. The irony was, his own first grandchild would be brought up as a heathen with an English accent and no father. Maria had thrown away the best years of her life. She should be getting her education and making her way in the world. And as for the boy, Joe? He should be ashamed of himself. Any decent, well-brought-up fella would have seen the writing on the wall, and done the honourable thing. It seemed he had just disappeared off the scene altogether and left Maria high and dry.

Christmas dinner was quiet. The table seemed empty. The large box of silver and gold crackers sat on the sideboard with nine left in it. Only Maureen wore her paper hat.

'I got a chicken instead of a turkey, since there's only the three of us,' she said apologetically, trying to fill one of the long silences. 'We'd be eating turkey for weeks, and I'd be driven mad with the carcass in the fridge, getting in the way.'

Aileen nodded. She only had two more days left to tell them. She was pretending she had to go back early because it was her turn to work in the bank between Christmas and New Year. That way, she and Paul could have a few days off together.

'Did you bring any pictures home?' asked Maureen as they sat with coffee and Baileys after dinner. She looked doubtfully at Sean, but any conversation would be better than this silence. She was dying to see what Molly looked like, and Aileen had been home for twenty-four hours already, without showing her any pictures.

'I did. I'll go and get them.' Aileen ran upstairs.

Maureen and Sean sat in silence until she came back

212

with the pictures. Despite himself, Sean couldn't resist leaning across to see the pictures in Maureen's hand. He couldn't help smiling at Molly's tiny fingers and toes. The funny oriental expression of a newborn baby was emphasised by the long dark hair on her head.

'I forgot how small they are,' he said, holding up a picture of Molly in Maria's arms.

'Maria is looking very well in these pictures,' said Maureen proudly.

'She was only in labour for six hours, so she wasn't too exhausted,' said Aileen.

'That's quick, for a first one. Hugh had me screaming and pushing for sixteen hours. Look, she has the hair, Sean, just like Maria.'

Maureen handed Sean a close-up photograph of Molly, wrapped in a white blanket on the hospital bed. He smiled but he didn't say anything. He wiped away a tear with the corner of his napkin but nobody saw it.

The photographs at the end of the film had been taken in the flat. Aileen didn't think anything of them, until her father said, 'Paul is looking very at home in your flat,' holding up a photograph of Paul in a dressing-gown, his hair awry, very obviously eating cornflakes.

Aileen's stomach lurched. 'Actually, it's his place.'

'That picture on the wall behind him is in your flat, isn't it?' Sean persisted, pointing. 'I remember admiring it when we were there. Has he got the same one as you?'

'No, that's what I'm saying, Dad. It's his flat. But I live there.'

'And where does he live?'

God, he could be so stupid.

'He lives there as well.'

'Sean, isn't it obvious what she's telling us,' said Maureen, sighing. 'They're living together.'

She scrunched up her holly-patterned napkin. She really could have done without this, on Christmas Day. Her paper hat fell off, a wrinkled remnant of Christmas cheer. She was secretly delighted. Paul was a lovely man, and they might be having a wedding soon, at this rate. But God help them all when it finally sank in with Mr Dark Ages Hardy.

Sean looked wide-eyed at Aileen. 'Do you mean to tell me that all this time you've been living together in that flat?'

'Yes, Dad. I didn't want to upset you before, but it's time for you to know.'

The next day, Aileen got up early, with a huge feeling of liberation, and went for a walk down to the sea. She called Paul from her mobile phone.

'It didn't go down too badly,' she said. 'Dad was fine with me this morning. Resigned to it, I think.'

Paul resisted the urge to tell her that he had suspected all along that would be the case. Aileen and Maria both had an exaggerated perception of Sean's reaction to things. They'd be much better off standing up to him a few times, and showing him they were adults capable of making their own decisions.

'How was Christmas Day?' he asked.

'A bit quiet. I really missed Maria, and so did Mam. I kept on thinking how nice it would have been to have the baby here, to make a fuss of.'

'There's no way they would have been ready to travel, even if things were different,' said Paul, 'and you just have to hope that next year everything will have settled down, and Molly will be much more aware of everything that's going on.'

'You're right. Listen, Paul, thanks for being so patient with me. I know it's difficult to understand, but we got there in the end, didn't we?'

Paul laughed. 'This call will cost you a fortune, from Ireland. I love you lots, and I'll be at the airport tomorrow, all right?'

'Love you. Bye,' said Aileen, turning away from the sea and walking back up the lane, looking forward to a cup of tea with her mother in the kitchen.

As she passed Pauline's house, she saw her come out, all wrapped up in a scarf and gloves.

'Did you have the same idea as me?' Pauline asked. 'I desperately need to work off all the food and sweets I ate yesterday!'

'Yes, Happy Christmas, or do you say Happy New Year now?' said Aileen, giving her a hug. 'You're looking very well. The hair suits you.'

It wasn't just the new hairstyle. Pauline had lost

weight since the summer, and looked like a new woman.

'Thanks.' Pauline's grin lit up her face.

Aileen knew what it was.

'You have a man, haven't you!' she said.

'Yeah, only for a few weeks, but it's going really well.'

'Anyone we know?' Aileen asked, grinning and leaning against the garden wall in a theatrical gesture of 'tell me all'.

'I'm not sure if you know him, but Maria would. He's a good friend of Joe's. He's in the same year of medicine. Mike is his name.'

'And is he gorgeous?' Aileen teased.

'Yes, I still can't believe he asked me out. It was funny, because it was talking about Maria and Joe that started it. So maybe something good might come out of a horrible situation.'

Aileen looked down. 'Maria can be so stubborn. Did you know that Joe came over to see her and the baby?'

'I thought he would. You should have seen his face, when I was talking to him in college just before Christmas – it was like it had suddenly sunk in that he was a father.'

'There's a pair of them in it. Andy was the worst thing that could have happened to Maria. He swept her off her feet while Joe was dilly-dallying around, and by the time Joe came to his senses, it was too late.'

'So what's this Andy like, then?' asked Pauline, her curiosity overcoming her need to defend Joe.

'I have to say, he has proven me wrong, in some ways. I thought he'd run a mile when he heard about the baby, because he has a bit of a track record.'

'What, sowing his wild oats all over the place? '

'There's at least one girl I know of, in Australia, who got pregnant by him and hasn't seen hide nor hair of him since.'

'Does Maria know about it?' asked Pauline. She hadn't had a good gossip in ages.

'Well, if she doesn't, I'm not going to be the one to tell her. That's up to Andy. He's a changed man though. He did up a room in his flat for the baby, to surprise Maria when she moved in, and he's certainly looking after her well since she came out of hospital.'

'Maybe he's trying to make up for past mistakes,' said Pauline, softening her view of Andy as the wicked usurper.

'I shouldn't say it, Pauline, because he might be the one for her, but I think Maria could do better. From what I heard about Joe, I can't believe she dumped him.'

'Me neither,' said Pauline. 'But even Mike said that Joe didn't handle the whole thing very well. The problem with Joe is that he always thought Maria was too good for him, so he gave up a bit too easily, because he thought he didn't deserve her.'

'I don't think he got very far when he came over, either. Maria was upset when I went to see her on the way to the airport, but she couldn't really tell me much because Andy was around, so she was whispering bits and pieces.'

'I spoke to Mike on the phone yesterday and he said Joe rang him when he got back, and he was devastated. He saw the baby, and finally realised how much he's lost. Maria was horrible to him, too.'

'That doesn't surprise me. She's really confused, but she gets very defensive when she's in the wrong and she can be very cold. I've been on the receiving end of it, and it's not nice.'

'Poor thing, you can't blame her. In fact, you have to admire her for going through with it. I was with her when she did the pregnancy test and she was terrified.'

'I know. It seems like such a long time ago now, that she told me. It's weird how things work out, and you could never predict them.'

'Anyway, it's freezing out here. I must go and do my constitutional, or I'll be tempted to just go straight back inside and have tea and Christmas cake!' said Pauline. 'Give my love to Maria when you get back, and give her a big hug for me.'

'I will', said Aileen. 'Enjoy the rest of the holidays. I'm going back tomorrow, so I probably won't see you again. Say hi to your mam for me.' She waved back as she continued up the hill.

Chapter Twenty-six

When Molly woke up crying at 4 o'clock on Christmas morning, Maria slipped quietly out of bed so that she wouldn't disturb Andy. He slept spread-eagled across most of the bed, snoring after quite a few beers to celebrate Christmas.

He said he usually went out with the lads on Christmas Eve, but this year he would stay in and keep Maria company. She was delighted, knowing how much he liked a drink with the lads, so she could hardly say anything when he laid out the line of cocaine on the coffee table. He always made her laugh when he did coke. He got so hyper. And happy. And horny. Sex with him was so wild – she loved it. He knew all her secret little places, and he took his time, keeping her hanging on the ecstatic brink before plunging into the depths of the most incredible orgasms.

Andy said coke was to ordinary dope like

champagne was to beer. So if you couldn't have it at Christmas, when could you have it? Maria wasn't tempted. She said it would be wasted on her, and Andy was happy to have it all for himself.

Maria crept into the back bedroom and picked up the baby. Molly immediately nuzzled at her mother's breast for milk.

Right from the start, Andy said he didn't want Molly in the same room as them. He said she should learn to be independent, and not get picked up every time she opened her mouth. Maria had hardly slept since she got home from hospital, constantly straining her ears for the tiniest sound from the other room, and obsessed with the advice in the leaflets on cot death that said you should have the baby near you for the first six months. No wonder Andy said she was looking tired. She only got a couple of hours' sleep every night. He was getting a bit impatient that she didn't feel ready to have sex yet. One girl at the Health Clinic said she didn't make love with her husband for four months after her first baby, but Maria hadn't told Andy that. She would be all right in a couple of weeks, when the stitches had healed up.

She opened the curtains and sat in the rocking-chair, nursing the baby. She looked out at the frost-covered garden, glittering in the moonlight.

Andy wasn't a traditional Dad in any way, but she could hardly expect that. He still worked long hours and then went out drinking. Molly never woke him during the night. He snored through it all. Maria didn't really understand how the city-trading thing worked, but Andy said he needed to keep up his contacts, so he socialised a lot, especially coming up to Christmas. He had to 'keep people sweet'. To get the deals. He certainly earned a lot of money, and he was very generous to her and to Molly. She had the best of everything.

Maria looked around the moonlit bedroom. Andy had surprised her when she moved in, holding his hands over her eyes as he steered her into the room. His friend was a painter and decorator, and he had it done up with Winnie the Pooh wallpaper and curtains. Maria had screeched with delight, and hugged him tightly.

'You're so good to me.' Her eyes filled with tears. Not many men would be interested in someone with a baby, and then ask them to move in, and decorate a room specially – Andy was one in a million.

'You're so gorgeous, I can't help it,' he said, kissing her eyelids. 'Come on, let's get your stuff moved in, before you drop that baby early with all this screaming.

Molly stopped sucking, and Maria held her over her shoulder, rubbing her back. Such a tiny thing, Maria thought. She has no idea that she was an accident, and that the man in the other room isn't her real father. She's not even able to see properly, just nuzzle for milk and sleep, like a little kitten.

She tucked Molly back into her Moses basket and stared at the still, silvery garden, thinking about home. It was probably lashing rain there, and Mam and Dad would be snuggled up in bed after midnight Mass. She should ring them early in the morning to wish them a Happy Christmas. She hadn't given them her new telephone number yet. Time enough for all that. They didn't even know she was going out with Andy, never mind living with him. She fleetingly thought about Joe. She hadn't been very nice to him in the hospital, but he was being so needy. She wanted someone to look after her and be strong for her. He would be at home now, for the Christmas holidays. To be with his clingy mother. She had never met Andy's mother, but he never even talked about her. She lived down in Devon somewhere, and there didn't seem to be any contact between her and her son. You couldn't get much different from Joe, the mammy's boy.

She pulled the curtains and crept back to bed. For the first time in her life, she wasn't sleeping in her own bed in Carraroe on Christmas Day.

Chapter Twenty-seven

Joe couldn't get Maria out of his head. When Pauline had shown him the photographs after Christmas, he had been fascinated by Molly's tiny form, but he was drawn by the look on Maria's face. She looked different. Like a beautiful, unattainable woman in a painting, smiling at someone else. That smile twisted his heart every time he looked at the photograph. Was it Andy behind the camera? He knew it was unhealthy to keep the picture in his wallet.

He hoped that Maria had thrown away his letter. It would be too embarrassing if anyone else ever read that. She had never replied to it, and she hadn't even acknowledged it when he went to see her. He had made promises in it that he didn't even know if he could keep, but she had pushed him away again, and now he really should try to forget her, and move on. She seemed harder than the Maria he knew, stronger in herself than she had been when she went off to England.

Mike told Joe one day in the refectory that he was going to Greece for the summer to get a bartending job. He asked Joe if he wanted to come.

'You could leave your mother in the nursing home for the summer. It wouldn't do her any harm at all,' he said, when Joe shook his head. 'Listen, Joe. You're either studying or looking after her the whole time. You'll go mental if you don't take a break.'

Joe remembered the time in the hospital six months ago, when his only worry was how long his mother would take to recover. Now he knew that she would always be dependent on him.

'She'd die if she thought that she was holding you back,' said Mike, gulping down his coffee. Joe gave him a scathing look.

'Sorry, but you know what I mean,' said Mike, embarrassed into silence.

Joe smiled at him. 'You get yourself sorted out, and we'll see how it goes.' He did deserve a break, he thought, chewing his thumbnail. And he had sworn last year that he wouldn't spend another summer in Westport. But everything was different now.

For the next few weeks, Mike kept asking him if he was going, because the closing date for the cheap flights was the end of March. When he finally said yes, Mike was delighted. 'You're doing the right thing,' he said.

'You'll be much better off next year, if you have a good break and a bit of sun.'

That weekend when he went to collect his mother, Joe started noticing things about the nursing home that he had never registered before.

There was a smell of old people as he came in the front door: the stale smell of fading flesh, overlaid with the tang of 'little accidents' that was never quite disguised by the floral air freshener. The walls and floors of the corridors had been scuffed by the legs of walking-frames and the rubber tyres of wheelchairs. He passed the TV room, and glanced in. Three old people sat in there with vacant stares on their faces, and the volume was turned to the maximum for University Challenge. A stack of board games on the scratched mahogany sideboard looked as if it hadn't been moved for years. The little folding card-tables were piled up with old curling magazines, probably donated by a hairdresser or a doctor's surgery. Joe walked along the hall to his mother's room, trying to choose the words to banish her to this place for three months, with no weekend escapes.

Her face lit up as he came into the room. 'Hello, Joe, it's lovely to see you. I really look forward to Fridays, you know.' She finished brushing her hair.

'All ready?' He took the handles of the wheelchair.

A nurse waved from the end of the corridor. 'Bye, Mrs Shaw, have a lovely weekend, and we'll see you on Sunday!'

Joe's feet felt leaden as he pushed his mother past the TV room.

'God love them, they sit in front of that thing all day long, no matter what's on it. I never go in there,' she said.

'We should get you a little portable for your room.'

'Ah no, it wouldn't be worth it. I only watch TV at the weekends really.'

The usual taxi was waiting in the forecourt. Seamus the driver lifted Mrs Shaw into the back seat while Joe folded the wheelchair.

'Well, have you a nice weekend planned?' boomed Seamus as they drove along the canal.

Joe smiled at his mother. This was their private joke. Seamus's father was as deaf as a post, and he shouted at all disabled people and foreigners alike.

'A quiet one, I think, Seamus,' was Joe's standard response.

They were hardly going gallivanting around the town with the wheelchair.

The woman who came in to clean the house was just leaving as they arrived, and she held the front door open for them.

'You're doing a great job on the house, these days, Mary,' said Mrs. Shaw. Mary felt a bit guilty because she didn't pay much attention upstairs now, knowing that Mrs. Shaw couldn't get up there, and Joe wouldn't know the difference. She resolved to do a good spring-clean next week as she waved goodbye.

Joe waited until Sunday afternoon to tell his mother, when they were having their last cup of tea before the taxi came. Her face fell.

'I must admit, I was looking forward to the whole summer, here with you,' she said, sipping her tea to hide her trembling lip. Joe felt so bad he nearly changed his mind.

He was just about to speak when she said, 'You're right though, love. You have to get on and live your life. I can't be always depending on you being around.'

Joe had expected a bit of emotional blackmail, even tears.

'It's just that I wanted to go away this summer anyway,' he said. 'You know, even before this happened.' He touched the arm of her wheelchair.

'I know, you were very twitchy last year, weren't you, with all your friends away in foreign places?'

So she had noticed. He nodded.

'Well, we'd better be getting back,' she said briskly.

As he kissed his mother goodbye in her room, he looked around. The walls were a pale institutional beige, and the brown velvet curtains were dusty. They were never pulled because she had Venetian blinds for privacy. She had a few of her own bits and pieces, a framed photograph of his father, and a little porcelain vase with daffodils in it. He would buy her a portable TV and maybe a print or something, to brighten the place up a bit.

She summoned up a smile and waved him off, saying, 'See you next week. Bye'.

Back in Galway, Mike was exuberant. 'I had a feeling you might back out, when you had to tell her,' he said. 'Fair dues to you. Now we can really start looking forward to it!'

His enthusiasm was infectious, and they took out his map of the Greek Islands to decide where to go first

Chapter Twenty-eight

Maureen always felt a bit low in February. The rain never stopped, and the cold Atlantic winds whistled through the house, even with one of Sean's old socks stuck in the letterbox, and the new double-glazing out the front. She couldn't stop worrying about Maria, in a poky little room on her own, trying to cope with a new baby. Maureen remembered struggling herself, after Hugh was born. And that was even with her mother around the corner, and Sean racing home from school every afternoon to admire his son. She remembered the guilt when she dropped Hugh head first on the hearth when he was only three weeks old. She was still crying herself long after he had stopped, thinking she had given him brain damage and afraid to tell anyone, especially Sean. She heard Sean sighing, and looked at the display on the clock radio. Another two hours before it was time to get up. She rolled over and tried to go back to sleep.

At seven o'clock, the alarm went off. It was still dark outside, and the rain was belting against the bedroom window. Sean and Maureen were both wide awake, and got up, relieved to start a new day and not to be trapped in the bed with their thoughts. They didn't say much at breakfast-time any more. Maureen only wanted to talk about the baby, and that was the only thing Sean didn't want to talk about. So they sat in silence, except for passing the brown bread and offering a hot drop of tea.

This morning, Sean was distracted from the size of the telephone bill by a postcard from Hugh. He was on his way home via Thailand and Hong Kong.

'He'll be home by Easter, so,' said Sean, smiling for the first time in weeks.

'That's great timing. You'll be on your Easter holidays and we can make a real fuss of him,' said Maureen, already planning to paint the back bedroom. It got a bit damp in there in the winter with no one in it.

'And that's a good time to be looking for a job, before the new graduates come out in June and July,' said Sean, optimistic that his son might finally settle down.

'Ah, Sean, don't put pressure on him too soon, or he'll go off to Dublin before we even see him.'

'He's twenty-six this year, and he should be settling down to something if he wants to make his way in the world,' said Sean as he pulled on his coat to go to work. 'I'll see you later.'

Over her second cup of tea, Maureen made the decision that she had been mulling over during the night. She would go and visit Maria. If the mountain couldn't go to Mohammed and all that, she thought, making a list of things to do.

She had her own savings from the housekeeping. Sean had always said to her that if she economised and saved a few pounds, she could keep it for herself. She never kept a track of it, but there should be a tidy little sum in the post office by now.

She could catch the eleven o' clock bus into Galway and go to Ryan's travel agents and enquire about flights.

She gulped down her tea and washed up the breakfast things in record time. She hadn't had so much energy for ages. If she updated her savings book in the village post office, Emer Kennedy would only be wondering why, and it was none of her business, so she'd do it this morning in the main post office in Galway.

She searched through all the drawers in the dressing-table, and found her lost gold earring and the out-of-date TV licence, but no post-office book.

She tugged out the drawers. Sometimes, if they were too full, things fell down the back. It wasn't one of those flimsy modern dressing-tables where things would just land on the floor. It was a solid frame, built by her father. When all the drawers were out on the carpet, she reached in and immediately her fingers touched the crumpled post-office book.

Then she noticed something else. A folded piece of yellowing paper was stuck to the back of the drawer where Sean kept his tax and insurance papers. She unfolded it, never thinking that it might have been hidden there on purpose.

It was an old-fashioned long-form birth certificate, from the Galway register of births and deaths, dated 15th July 1948. Sean's birthday. She was about to tuck it into Sean's drawer, when she noticed something wrong.

It had the child's full name: Sean Seosamh Kelly.

Kelly? Not Hardy?

The mother's name, Aine ni Ceallaigh, was there, in Irish. She was described as Spinster, of Salthill, Galway. Nothing was written in the long box for the father's name and occupation.

Maureen stared at it for a long time, and then she delicately folded it and stuck the paper behind the drawer when she slid it back into place. She looked at her watch, and quickly put on some lipstick and combed her hair before running for the bus.

Joseph the driver was a great man for knowing everyone's business. He always asked, 'What are you off into town for?' as they bought their tickets.

When Maureen just said, 'A bit of shopping,' he knew with his infallible instinct that she was up to something.

Maureen was relieved to get a window seat on her own. She took out her *Reader's Digest* to discourage any friendly advances. Joseph noticed in his mirror that she spent the whole journey along the coast road into town staring at the sea.

The rain had stopped for the first time in days, and the

moisture in the air magnified the hills of Clare, looming across the bay. They looked close enough to touch. They said it was a sign that it was going to rain again.

Sean came home early to an empty house. Maureen must have gone into town. She would be back on the five o'clock bus, in time to make the dinner. He marked some copybooks and read a bit of the paper. It was very quiet without her in the house. At ten to five, he walked down the hill to meet the bus. It was nice to get a bit of fresh air, after all the rain. Maureen was surprised to see him.

'Hello, I thought I'd come down and carry the bags up the hill for you,' he said.

She didn't have any bags, as Joseph had already noticed. 'I'm fine, thanks.'

They walked in silence, until Sean asked, ' Did you have a nice time in town?'

'I did.'

'Did you meet anyone nice?'

'No.'

'You didn't say you were going into town?' he ventured.

'I just decided at the last minute.'

When they got home, Maureen went to peel the potatoes. She didn't feel like eating. Her stomach had shrivelled into an acidic lump. Her head was banging. She didn't even want to look at him. He had been living a lie for twenty-seven years. Longer: it was thirty since they started courting.

'What's wrong, love?' Sean finally asked after the silent meal.

Maureen hadn't eaten anything. Maybe she was sickening for something.

'I'm going to London to see Maria and the baby,' she said defiantly.

Sean was shocked. They were supposed to be showing a united front on this thing.

He and Maureen always stuck together on things. It was the only way to raise children, so they knew what was what.

'But Maureen, you don't condone what she's done, do you?' he pleaded.

'No, indeed I don't, Sean, but it's tearing me apart. I feel like I've lost her. We've driven her away.' Maureen looked at him directly, and he couldn't hold her gaze.

'Do you think I don't miss her, every minute of every day?' he said.

'But the difference is, Sean, that you're too proud to forgive her, and I'm not.'

The words hit him like body blows and winded him. Maureen didn't seem to understand that Maria was the one who was in the wrong, and she should be coming to say sorry, before everyone could forgive and forget, and move on. He went upstairs to bed, because it was raining again and there was nowhere else to escape to.

Chapter Twenty-nine

'Aileen, help!' said Maria frantically down the telephone.

'What? Tell me!'

Several colleagues were looking curiously at Aileen, hearing the panic in her voice.

'Mam's coming over!'

'Oh my God, when?'

They still didn't know about Maria living with Andy.

'The week after next.'

'There's time. Don't worry. We'll think of something.'

'Can me and Molly stay with you while she's over?'

'She knows you're not living with us though, Maria,' Aileen whispered, looking around.

'I know, but we could say I'm staying with you to make it easier for her. That way, she can see us all together without going forward and back across London.'

'What about Andy?'

'I don't want her to meet him – she's not ready for that, yet.'

Aileen's boss was frowning at her, and nodding towards a customer who was waiting for service.

'I have to go, Maria. I'll ring you tonight at home.'

'No, I'll ring you.'

'Talk to you later, bye.'

Aileen's boss came over to her desk. 'Is everything all right?' he asked as she hung up.

Aileen blushed. 'Yes, sorry. My sister had an emergency.'

She turned to the customer, smiling. 'How can I help you?'

Maureen was busy making dinners to put in the freezer for the week she would be away. She felt a huge sense of liberation. Of course a married couple had to be united, especially on the really big things in the family. Sean was usually so logical and reasonable that over the years she had got into the habit of just agreeing with him. But, for the last nine months, she had felt that Maria was gradually slipping away from her. Soon, she would lose her completely.

It was so nice of Aileen to have them all staying with her. And Paul, of course.

What would it be like, with them sleeping in a double bed in the room next door?

She sighed. It seemed to be the way young people did it these days. There was something to be said for living together first. She and Sean had had lots of niggly little arguments in the first few months of marriage. Even about deciding which side of the bed to sleep on. Of course, sex was new to them as well. She couldn't see what all the fuss was about. Except when she sometimes had an orgasm.

Maureen blushed and looked around guiltily, even though she was on her own in the kitchen. She rolled out a circle of pastry on the floury board.

With the natural rhythm method, you could only have sex when the wife didn't really feel like it. Other times, Sean just had to keep himself to himself. She wondered if contraceptives made it different. She shook her head. Condoms hadn't kept Maria out of trouble, either.

She put the pastry crust on a steak and kidney pie, labelled it 'Thursday' and added it to the pile of aluminium trays on the table.

Sean would be sick of reheated dinners. Mind you, Marian Finucane on the women's programme said it did the men no harm to fend for themselves for a few days. It made them appreciate you more when you came back.

That wouldn't be any harm. Sean had really gone into his shell. The latest was, should he give up the Parish Council, in case people thought he was a hypocrite? Sure, the world was full of hypocrites. No-one was perfect. He would be better off remembering the parable of the prodigal son.

Maureen slammed the freezer door and went upstairs to make the bed and do some dusting. She wouldn't let Maria go. She wanted to see Molly. If Sean couldn't handle that on his home ground, she would go to them.

Maria couldn't take the risk of ringing Aileen tonight. Andy had promised to be home early for a change. It wasn't really something she wanted to talk about on the phone, either. She needed some advice. Aileen didn't seem to mind that Paul stayed out late a lot, but he didn't come in roaring drunk every night either, like Andy. Maria suspected that Andy was taking even more drugs than he let on about, but she didn't know what to do. She wanted to ask Paul if Andy was always like this, or if he had changed. They had known each other since school, and Paul always said Andy was a good mate.

Maria had cooked shepherd's pie, Andy's favourite dinner. Molly had gone down to sleep and she wouldn't wake now for a feed until the early hours of the morning.

'It's nice to have you home.' Maria smiled at him across the table when they sat down.

Andy looked at her suspiciously, and his pupils seemed to grow huge in his narrowed eyes. 'Are you saying that I go out too much?'

'Not at all! I was only saying it's nice to have you in,' said Maria, a bit taken aback.

'Because it's *my* flat, and *my* life, and I don't need you nagging me when I get in.'

Maria blinked back the tears which still came so easily. Her hormones were up the creek. He hated when she cried, so she turned away. 'I'm not nagging you, Andy.'

'No, you're so fucking goody-goody that you wouldn't stoop to nagging, would you?' he said, throwing his cutlery down on the empty plate. 'But you still manage to make me feel like I've done something wrong.' He gulped down the last of the beer in his can. 'I'm going out. I don't need this.'

He grabbed his jacket and stormed out the door, slamming it behind him.

Maria stood in the kitchen, with her arms in the sink full of washing-up, and let the tears come. She felt like some middle-aged married woman, stuck in a rut.

On her birthday, only two weeks ago, she had been so happy. Andy had completely spoiled her. He took her out for dinner at Mezzo, while Aileen baby-sat. It was her first night out in ages. He ordered champagne and insisted that she have lobster, the most expensive thing on the menu. Efficient waiters glided around their table, changing the ashtray and topping up their champagne. The place was full of cool, sophisticated Londoners, and the buzz of conversations on the tables around them filled her with euphoria. She could forget that she was a mother, and that she had given up college and would soon have to go back to work. In the taxi home, Andy had stroked her thigh, and fondled her nipples. When they got home, she quickly got rid of Aileen, and Andy jumped on her, ripping off her knickers on the sofa. She had never had sex like that with gentle, considerate Joe. Andy was such a good lover, and so much more romantic than Joe. He often gave her flowers on a Friday night, and he made her feel like a real woman.

By the time she finished clearing up, Maria had forgiven him for tonight's outburst. He must be under pressure at work. She never really asked him anything about it. She should make more of an effort to understand what he did, and be more supportive. They didn't really talk about stuff like that. Most week-nights they watched TV or a video if he was home early enough, and at weekends he read the papers a lot, watched Sky sports, and they talked about anything but work. The red devil on her left shoulder told her she was just acting out the submissive wifey stereotype, but the green one on the other side shrugged and said, 'This is life'.

Maria was reading in bed when Andy came in at closing time from the pub, reeking of beer and smoke.

'Get that off,' he said, roughly tugging at her T-shirt. He bit her nipple and stuck his hand roughly down between her legs. 'You're gorgeous,' he said, kissing her eyelids and stroking her hair. He smiled down at her.

Maria loved him best when he was assertive like this. Her hips thrust up to meet him, eager to have him inside her, claiming her.

Chapter Thirty

Metallic announcements about carousels and oversized baggage echoed around the Arrivals hall at Heathrow. Maureen felt a bit intimidated, but she finally found the right place to wait for her bags. Last year, when they came over, Sean had done everything, and told her to just mind her handbag from pickpockets. She quite liked the feeling of independence, as she patiently waited. It was a great place for people-watching. She could tell who the smokers were, dying to light up, but having to wait another few minutes to get out of the terminal building. There was one poor harassed-looking woman with a baby and two toddlers, struggling with loads of bags and a pushchair. Maureen gave her a hand to load her trolley, wondering what her story was and where was the husband? She didn't like to push, so she stood waiting behind the yellow line until the conveyor belt was nearly clear, before reaching in to pull off her own small suitcase. No one challenged her in the blue Customs channel, and she relaxed when she saw Maria leaning over the railings, waving like mad.

The baby was in one of those sling things. That didn't look very secure, and it couldn't be good for the child's back, thought Maureen, as she smiled and waved back. They hugged awkwardly, and Maureen put down her bag and made Maria turn around so she could see the baby.

'Ah, she's gorgeous, isn't she?'

Maureen was rewarded with a smile. 'And she's smiling already, little dote!'

On the escalator down to the Underground station, Maureen stood on the step above her daughter, and stroked Molly's hair and soft baby cheeks.

People kept pushing past with their bags, elbowing Maureen in the ribs. What was the hurry – wasn't the escalator moving already? She remembered from last time how manic everyone was in London, always in a hurry.

'So I won't see your place at all, while I'm over?' she said, when Maria explained they were going straight to Aileen's flat.

'No, we'll be much more comfortable at Aileen's.' Maria was glad she didn't have to look her mother in the eye as they sat side by side on the tube.

'I suppose your flatmates don't like mothers descending on them anyway, cramping their style.' Maureen had visions of them panicking, thinking they had to clean up and have special food in for her. She understood.

'You could say that, yeah,' Maria said, smiling. If only her mother knew.

Molly dozed on the tube, soothed by the rumbling of the train and the heat of Maria's body.

'Is she good with meeting new people?' asked Maureen, cocking her head sideways to look at Molly's sleeping face.

'Yes, she's great. She just smiles at everyone. She's a real flirt. I brought her in to see Paddy and Ivy last week and they thought she was a gem.'

'You must be going back to work soon, are you?'

Maria was in two minds. Andy said she should take another couple of months off. He would keep supporting her, but she didn't like depending on him. Although he was very generous, she still felt funny when he handed over money to buy things for the flat or for Molly.

'I haven't talked to Paddy about going back yet, and he has a great temp in there, so there's no pressure,' she said. 'Mind you, Ivy didn't look too well. I think she's trying to do too much. The doctor said she should slow down and lose some weight.'

Maureen wouldn't be distracted from her theme. 'The state benefits over here for single mothers must be much better than they are at home?' she asked. 'Do they pay your rent and all that, when you're not working?'

'Yes, it's very good.' Maria tried to sound convincing. She didn't have a clue whether they did or not. Andy said he had plenty of money and he didn't want his girlfriend signing on for benefits, so she had never found out.

'That's great. I suppose they have to, over here. It's not like at home, where people would have their families to look after them,' said Maureen.

Maria didn't say anything. Her mother could start a career in diplomacy at this rate.

Aileen got home early from work to find her mother sitting on the sofa drinking tea.

'You made great time from the airport,' she said, surprised they had got there before her.

She swooped down on Molly. 'She's getting so big, Maria! I can't believe it!'

Maria smiled, 'Yeah, she's five and a half kilos now, just under average for her age.'

Maureen looked at her two daughters and felt old. Maria seemed so grown-up and self-possessed all of a sudden. Maureen could hear the envy in Aileen's tone, and she felt a twinge of sympathy. Aileen always seemed to be overshadowed by her younger sister. Later, she rang Sean to tell him she had arrived safely. He sounded a bit lonely.

'Paul cooked us a nice dinner, some kind of a casserole. I'm not sure what was in it, but it was lovely,' said Maureen. She had never cooked with garlic, wine, or coriander, preferring to stick to her rule of producing wholesome, simple food. Now she thought she might get a few recipes off Paul, and learn a few new dishes.

'Well, I had my dinner out of the freezer and that was very tasty,' said Sean.

It was nice to hear her voice. She sounded very excited. 'How are the girls?'

'They're grand. Molly is a dote, and our two are looking well.' She lowered her voice. 'Maria has put on a bit of weight, but it should fall off her again in no time, with the breast-feeding.'

Sean was disgusted at the thought. Such a primitive activity. And the child was three months old – what was she doing still feeding it herself? He went suddenly quiet. His awkwardness reverberated down the line, and Maureen gave up after a while and said goodbye. Sean could be so narrow-minded sometimes. She had watched a documentary the previous week about cultural differences in child-rearing, and they said that Ireland was the worst for being embarrassed about breast-feeding. Ridiculous thought, when for generations they produced so many children they would need a dairy herd to keep up with the milk.

Paul was absently appraising Maureen as a potential mother-in-law as they all settled down on the rug for a game of Scrabble.

'This is lovely. It nearly makes up for not seeing you at Christmas,' she said to Maria.

He couldn't believe it. Maureen had an incredible knack for putting her foot in it, in the nicest possible way. Poor Maria had been told in no uncertain terms that she wasn't allowed home for Christmas. She didn't have much choice now but to smile and say, 'Thanks, Mam,' in a gritted-teeth sort of way. She really had a lot to put up with. But she seemed to have worked wonders on Andy. He was a new man – more relaxed and less hungry to move onto the next new thing in his life. Paul reckoned that if Andy could settle down to domestic bliss, anyone could. He looked across at Aileen, sitting cross-legged on a Turkish cushion, concentrating intently on her letters, a small grin making her look even more elfin. Maybe he would propose to her on top of a mountain when they went skiing in a few weeks' time.

'Your turn, Paul,' Maria nudged him.

'Oh, sorry, I was miles away,' he said.

Maureen saw the way he was looking at Aileen, and how his whole face softened when he spoke to her. They seemed very happy together. Maybe they'd soon be having a day out.

Maureen laid out her tiles and scored twelve points, her highest ever. Aileen clapped.

Maria saw the look on Paul's face as well. Joe used to look at her like that, and she loved it. It was a gentle, caressing look that made you feel all gooey inside. Andy wasn't soppy in that way. More macho and sexy. She liked it when his eyes filled with lust as he undressed her. Especially when she was pregnant. He was really turned on by her heavy breasts and her smooth, round white tummy.

Now it was Aileen's turn to nudge her.

'Sorry,' she said, and put down an 'r' on 'love', scoring only eight points.

'Speaking of lovers,' said Aileen, suddenly, to Maria, 'I completely forgot to tell you that Pauline and Mike have got it together – she said you would know him, he's one of Joe's friends.'

'No way!' said Maria excitedly. 'God, Mike wouldn't usually go for the brainy ones – I wouldn't have thought Pauline was his type at all, but she's fancied him for ages. That's brilliant!'

'Pauline has lost a load of weight, and got her hair cut – she's looking very well on it,' said Aileen.

'I thought that when I saw her at Mass over the Christmas,' said Maureen. 'And you never told me she had a man!'

'I don't know how I forgot – she was so excited about it. I bumped into her on my last day at home. Maria, she loved the photos of Molly.'

'I must send her some more over. Molly has changed so much in only two months,' said Maria, looking over at her baby, blissfully sleeping in her Moses basket through all the noise.

'I'll take loads of pictures while I'm here, and give her some copies, if you like,' suggested Maureen, reminded to rummage in her handbag for the new camera she had got for Christmas.

Aileen won the game of Scrabble because she was the only one who was concentrating. At bedtime, Maria reassured her mother that she was happy to sleep in the living-room. She would have a broken night anyway, with feeding Molly.

'Is she not sleeping through the night yet? I'm sure you did, when you were that size. But anyway, you're the young mother,' Maureen said. 'We'll swap over tomorrow night and you can have the proper bed.'

Maria didn't want to argue. The streetlight shone directly into the room, defying the flimsy muslin curtains. Molly slept soundly, occasionally grunting and rubbing her head from side to side. Maria lay on the rubber airbed, feeling every ridge under her back. She couldn't sleep. Her eyes went round and around, tracing the pattern of the Victorian plaster fresco on the ceiling. Andy had been really annoyed that she would be away for three nights. She hadn't had the nerve to tell him that her mother was over for a week. She'd have to break it to him later. She knew he had no desire to meet her mother; he just didn't want to be left on his own. He liked to have his dinner cooked for him, and his little woman waiting for him. Maria had reminded him that he would be out every night anyway, so what difference did it make? He said that wasn't the point and she was turning into a right nag. They hadn't parted on very good terms that morning, when Andy went off to work, sulking. She probably should have called him tonight, but he would be out drinking. He had become very irritable and irrational lately, and she should probably leave him to stew for a couple of days. It wouldn't do him any harm.

Maria missed his arms around her, and the warmth of his body curled around her, but she did enjoy stretching out full-length across the bed. Eventually, she fell asleep, her hair spread across the pillow in the pale-grey city night-light.

Chapter Thirty-one

The ticking of the clock had never seemed so loud, thought Sean, when he turned the television off at eleven o'clock. He had sat in front of it all evening, even watching the soaps he usually scorned, just to block out the silence in the house.

It wasn't that Maureen usually made a lot of noise, but she would always be pottering around, or sitting in the other armchair, reading or knitting.

When he got in from work, it took only twenty minutes to heat up his dinner and eat it. Then the long dark evening stretched in front of him. The house had creaks he had never noticed before. The stove kept the kitchen warm, and the cat did his usual ritual weaving in and out between Sean's legs looking for food and company, but it wasn't the same without Maureen.

This is what it must be like for a bachelor, he thought. Unless you made a hectic social life for yourself, or you went out to the pub every night. You'd have to have hobbies. You would probably go to bed earlier if you had no one to talk to about your day. Mind you, Maureen had stopped asking him about his day at work lately. Before, when things happened, he would be thinking in the back of his mind 'I must remember to tell Maureen that'. If one of the girls was sent to his office for talking in the class, he would be giving out to them, and at the same time saving it up to tell Maureen later. But since that day she bought the ticket to fly to London, she hadn't been the same. It was as if she had changed sides, to go against him. They always stuck together on things, and the single-handed battle was really wearing him down.

He opened the newspaper, looking for distraction. He didn't want to go to bed and stare at the crack in the ceiling for another night. He really should stick a bit of Polyfilla in it, instead of getting irritated by it. He saw the article on the third page and folded the paper over to read it. The headline wasn't big, but it stood out.

'*Last Magdalen Laundry Knocked Down.*'

He started reading, mildly curious.

He had been following a series of articles exposing scandals in religious institutions. Most of them were in England, and a lot of them were about orphanages, and the disastrous statistics of crime levels among people who had been put into care as children. But here was one a lot closer to home. And this wasn't just the scandal of the children in the orphanage – it was the treatment of their young mothers. The Galway laundry was to be knocked down to make way for a new development of town houses in Foster Court. He wasn't surprised. Every time he went into Galway, they were knocking something down for new buildings to go up.

The Magdalen Laundry had been a well-established institution in the town. A euphemism for a place where poor unfortunate single mothers were sent to do hard labour. Literally. He read about the ordeals suffered by girls who were sent to the nuns in the 'forties and 'fifties for 'rehabilitation' when they had an illegitimate baby. Their families would put them in, hoping to avoid a scandal. The nuns took in the washing from the hotels and big houses in Galway, and used the girls as slave labour to run the laundry operation. The nuns told the girls, especially the pretty ones, that they had the devil in them, luring men into evil ways. They were sinners, being punished by God. They were virtual prisoners, forbidden to leave, and never being visited by their families. So much for the forgiveness that Jesus gave to Mary Magdalen for her sins. The nuns made it their business to punish the girls in this world, in case Jesus forgave them in the next.

Sean's eyes widened as he read the interviews with three ex-inmates, now in their fifties, who had escaped years ago, but only now had the courage to tell their stories. Their heads were shaved if they broke the rules. The nuns made them wear shapeless pinafores, telling them it was displaying their bodies that got them into trouble in the first place. They worked from seven o'clock in the morning to seven o'clock at night, getting only bread and milk for breakfast and potatoes and milk for dinner. The temperature in the laundry often reached ninety degrees, and if a girl fainted, she was made to work an extra hour at the end of the day, cleaning out the mangles.

They were forbidden from seeing their babies, who were kept across in the orphanage. The babies were breast-fed to save money on milk, but when they were weaned, their mothers had to hand them over, never to see them again. Their only consolation was that their children might go to nice homes, and have better lives than they could ever hope for with a single mother. Some of the girls were put working in the nursery looking after the babies, but only if their own children had already found homes. They watched and memorised the babies' gestures and gurgles and secretly whispered their progress to their anxious mothers.

Even as an adult, Sean had never tried to imagine what his mother must have gone through in that place. The nightmares only reminded him of how he felt as a six-year-old, terrified when she grabbed him that time. She had big brown eyes, he remembered that. And black curly hair.

It was short, but he could imagine it long and flowing down her back, and her tossing it in the wind as she walked along the shore in Salthill. Maybe she climbed in the rockpools, collecting mussels for the tea. Maybe she fell in love with one of the lads doing mackerel-fishing from the big black rocks. She would have walked hand-in-hand with him, laughing when he sent the flat stones flying across the waves and got five skips out of them. They might have stood there on the beach and kissed, tasting the sea salt on each other's lips. He would have taken her to dances at the Seapoint Ballroom, and walked her home to her gate, and kissed her quick before her mother could see out through the net curtains. Maybe he persuaded her that she wouldn't get pregnant if they were careful, and he loved her, and they were going to get married anyway, so it was just a matter of time. Sean had never thought about her like this before. The nuns had done a very good brainwashing job, and each child was told that their mother was dead, or that they had been given to the nuns because their own mother couldn't look after them.

Mothers were the ones who washed you in the tin bath on Saturday night, and put plasters on your knee, and made you do your homework. That's what his mammy had done. That's what Maureen did for their own kids. He remembered from the birth certificate that his mother was only seventeen when she had him. Even younger than Maria. Did she pick his name? Maybe after the father? She probably had her hair shaved off for trying to see her son, and clinging to him for just a moment, six years after he was born. That might have been the last straw.

In their second year at university, Martin had encouraged him to find out about her. He said it couldn't do any harm. Sean didn't even have to get in touch with her. Just knowing where she was now, he said, might banish the 'bad woman' from Sean's dreams. Every night, he heard Sean screaming in his sleep. He reckoned, from reading his first year of psychology, that the only remedy was for Sean to face up to her, and to see her as a real person instead of a mad ghost. She probably had another family by now. She wouldn't want to be reminded of her teenage mistake. But maybe if Sean saw her going to Mass with her family, or doing some weeding in her front garden, he could make her human, and banish the crazy, tearful young woman of his imagination once and for all.

They planned the investigation together, and Sean felt like a detective as he rang the doorbell of the convent. A corpulent nun wearing a voluminous white apron over her uniform answered the door. She wore a short veil, and her dress only went to her knees, but her chubby cheeks and wire-rimmed glasses reminded him of the gate-keeping nun of his childhood, and he looked down, expecting to see a ring of keys hanging from her belt.

'Yes?' she barked, after he had stood there for a moment, not saying anything.

'Hello, sister,' he stammered. 'I'm at UCG at the moment, and I'm looking for –'

'We don't have any work for students.' She started to close the door.

'No. I'm looking for –'

'Yes?' she said again, in an 'I have better things to do with my time' tone of voice.

'My mother.'

'Well, you won't find her here. We only have sisters and lay nuns here,' she sniffed.

'Not really looking for her here, but –'

'If you're not looking for her here, then why are you here, looking for her?' Sister Marie-Therese was renowned for her sharp wit and she regularly had to confess the transgressions of her sharp tongue.

'I'm trying to trace her. She was here about twelve years ago, I know that for sure.'

The nun's face tightened. Another one.

'We didn't keep records of the girls who were in our care,' she said abruptly and slammed the door before Sean had time to draw breath. He stood staring at the distorted reflection of his face in the shiny brass door-knocker.

He was tempted to just give up then. He was obviously not meant to find her. He told Martin, who insisted that they keep going.

'It's unfinished business, now, Sean. You'll never get over it unless you face up to it.'

Sean decided to skip the nuns and check the register

of births, marriages and deaths, to see if she had got married in Galway. The chances were pretty good that she would have married locally. Maybe even to her boyfriend, after she got out. Martin didn't like to dampen his zeal with logic, by mentioning that the boyfriend, having abandoned her in the first place, would hardly have waited six years for her to get out.

Sean made an appointment with the Registrar, and had the system explained to him. He was left alone in a green-painted room with fat radiators and peeling window-frames to look through a stack of black-bound record books. He started with 1954, the year he went to his new family. Maybe she would have got out as soon as he was placed in a home? He patiently went through the records for each district and parish, looking for Anne Kelly. His heart jumped a few times, as various Kellys were married off, but she wasn't one of them.

He got a headache in the stuffy room, and paced up and down outside for a few minutes to clear it. The muggy weather didn't help, and he felt a bit disheartened at his lack of progress. He couldn't think of any other avenues to check. Apart from the death register. It seemed a bit morbid. She would only be thirty-seven now, but you never know. Maybe she did really have TB, like the nuns had told him when he was a boy.

Inside, he tentatively tapped on the frosted glass hatch, and asked the clerk for the register of deaths. She stopped typing and sighed. She slid across the doors of a metal filing cabinet and extracted more black-bound books. She passed them over the counter and gave him a tight little smile. 'Are you finished with the other ones? I don't want a big load of filing to do at the end of the day. Give them back here to me, please.'

Sean cleared the table and put the new pile of books in front of him. This time he started with 1968 and worked backwards. He found himself reading lots of the records, fascinated with the causes of death. It was almost like the game he used to play as a child, looking up a word in the dictionary, and finding other, much more interesting ones on the same page. In the records, there were poisonings, drownings and blows to the head, and even one decapitation. He speculated about farming and fishing accidents and suspected that one might even have been a murder. At ten to five, the clerk loudly cleared her throat, and tip-tapped past the door of his room, emanating closing-time signals.

Sean was on the last book and flipped the wide pages over to see the index of names at the back. He ran his finger down the list, almost missing her name because he no longer expected to find it. There it was, in Irish, Aine ni Ceallaigh, written in neat, round calligraphy. A page number was pencilled beside it. It couldn't be her, but he'd better check, just in case. The pages suddenly seemed to wilfully stick together, charged with the electricity in his tingling fingers. He separated them, and laid them flat, looking down the names in the left-hand column. Then his eyes were scanning horizontally across the columns even before his brain had registered the name. Under the 'cause of death' column, three words were inked with a black fountain pen. His eyes jittered. Wrong row. He went back and ran his finger across from the name to guide his eyes. The words were still there. *Asphyxiation by hanging.* He looked at the date; 12th July 1954. He looked at the place; Hospice of Mary Magdalen, Galway.

The clerk was standing in the doorway now, tapping her pen against the doorframe with an expert flick of finger and thumb. 'Finished?' she asked, showing a fleck of fresh lipstick on her front tooth. Her beehive hairdo was teased to fullness for her evening date. The heavy scent of her freshly applied perfume made Sean want to throw up.

'Yes.' He stood up in a daze, leaving the big black book lying open on the table. He walked past the clerk.

She sighed loudly, saying, 'You're welcome', in her special martyred tone, and slapped the book shut.

When Sean got back to their room, Martin was full of questions. 'Did you find her? Is she married?'

Then he noticed Sean's pale face and the glassy look in his eyes. Maybe the shock of having loads of brothers and sisters was worse than they had expected. 'You don't have to get in touch with her, Sean, if it doesn't feel right,' he said consolingly.

'She's dead. She hung herself the day after she saw me.'

'No way! How do you know?'

'I found it in the register. Asphyxiation by hanging.

Three days before my birthday. I never want to talk about it again. I have a mother already. I don't know why I wanted another one.' Sean sat on the bed and put his head in his hands. 'She's dead, because of me.'

Martin tried everything to get him to talk to a doctor or a priest, or someone, to get it off his chest. Sean refused to discuss it further. But the nightmares stopped.

Sean folded the newspaper on his knee and stared into embers of the fire. Now he could see that of course he wasn't responsible for her suicide. Her life must have been hell, and seeing him might have been a trigger, but he couldn't blame himself any longer.

Sean's time in the orphanage was locked away in a safe place in his mind. As a child, he had invented a story of his early life with his big sisters. They dressed him up like a doll and pushed him around the village in the big old green pram. They played school, and house, and doctors and nurses. By the time he was twelve, the story was so real that he couldn't remember anything else. The nightmares were the only chink in his armour. When he went to secondary school, everyone had forgotten he was adopted. They even remarked how much he looked like his older sister Eilis. He had never felt the need to tell anyone, not even Maureen, when they started courting. Martin only dragged it out of him because he shared the room with him and heard his screams in the middle of the night. Since the nightmares stopped, Sean hadn't thought about his real mother once.

He wondered how many people were sitting at home with the newspaper tonight, reminded of their early years in the orphanage. They had families of their own now, he supposed, and had put it all behind them, like he had.

Chapter Thirty-two

Maria was relieved that the week was over. She had great fun taking her mother on the open-topped London tour bus, and going to the Aquarium and even on a day trip to Oxford. Molly had loved all the activity, but her routine was so upset that she was getting a bit fractious by the end of the week. The baby was probably picking up her stress vibes, thought Maria, as she remembered her phone call to Andy on Thursday morning, to tell him she wouldn't be back until the weekend. It had been difficult to get five minutes' peace to ring him, with her mother hovering around all the time. Finally, she suggested that Maureen take Molly for a little walk, and she rang Andy at work and told him she wouldn't be back until Sunday. He was raging. Maria told him a little white lie. She said that her mother had extended her trip because she was having such a nice time. What could she do about it?

'You could tell her you haven't seen me for ages and you want to come home in the evenings. You could still see her during the day, when I'm out at work,' he said.

'I'd have to drag Molly forward and back on the Tube every day,' she said feebly.

'Your mother could come and stay here, then,' said Andy, triumphantly. He wasn't going to let her off the hook that easily. Time to call her bluff. She was getting a bit too complacent.

'There's no space, really Andy, and you'll be . . .'

'I'll be what? Pissed as a newt, so you don't want your mother to meet me, is that it?'

'No, it's not that. I just don't think the timing is right.'

'For what, admitting that you're shacked up with another man, when you just had someone else's kid?'

'No, it's not that. You know what I mean . . .'

He lost his temper then. 'You're a selfish cow! You know, sometimes I think you're just using me!'

He slammed the phone down and refused to take her call when she tried to ring back.

She left a message on the answering machine at the flat. 'Andy, it's Maria. We need to talk. I'll be back on Sunday. Maybe we could go for a walk in Richmond, or somewhere, and talk about this? I love you. Bye.' She took a deep breath as she heard her mother coming up the stairs, dragging the pushchair up each step.

She had put on a bright face and told her mother she was just talking to Paddy about when she might go back to work.

263

'I'm surprised he's let you be off this long,' said Maureen, still puffing slightly after her climb up the stairs.

'Sure he was always a lovely man,' said Maria. 'Why wouldn't he keep the job open for me?'

'You shouldn't take it for granted, all the same, Maria. Sometimes you can stretch a friendship too far.'

'It's not like he's paying me a fortune, Mam. I do a good day's work for him, when I'm there.'

'Of course you do, love,' Maureen said, handing her daughter a cup of tea. Maria was getting very edgy about things, and being a bit defensive, when she used to be such a happy, open girl who shared everything. Sean had a lot to answer for.

On one level, she could understand a little bit why he was pushing Maria away. Being illegitimate himself must make him a bit sensitive. But what she couldn't understand was why he would want his own granddaughter to suffer the way he must have.

She looked across at Molly, peacefully sleeping with her chubby cheek pressed against the coloured fabric of the pushchair, her wispy dark hair standing on end, full of electricity from the bobble hat Maria had just gently pulled off. Sean would only have to lay his eyes on her in the flesh, and be on the receiving end of one of her beaming smiles, and he would see things differently.

In theory, of course, she had the same views as him – who would want their daughter to be a single mother in a strange city when they were only nineteen? Or twenty, now. But the reality was different. Maria had given birth to a new little person, who was carrying the family genes, the hair and Maria's own dark eyes and long eyelashes. She had some of Maria's personality too – the mischievous grin said it all.

It broke Maureen's heart to think that Sean was missing out on the joy of this new relationship. Being a grandparent was a whole different ball-game, and for the first time in twenty-eight years, Maureen was experiencing something she wasn't sharing with Sean.

She could feel the tears rising, so she stood up and rinsed out her mug, saying to Maria, 'Can we go to Harrods one of the days? I'd love to buy something just to get the bag so I can carry it around at home!'

Maria laughed. 'I haven't been in it myself yet – we can go this afternoon if you want.'

Maureen was completely speechless as they wandered around the food hall, past the magnificent display of fresh fish, arranged almost like a sculpture, and presided over by a massive statue of Neptune with his trident. She wondered if anyone ever dared to buy one of the fish and disturb the glistening symmetry.

In the handmade chocolate section, they drooled over the samples, trying not to look too much like scroungers. Molly liked the colours in there, and didn't want to leave, so she had to be distracted with a green-jumpered Harrods Bear. Maureen went up to the cashier to pay for it, and was a bit aghast when the plummy-toned assistant asked her for £19.99. She tried to look nonchalant about handing over a twenty-pound note, but said to Maria out of the side of her mouth, 'It's a very expensive way of getting a carrier bag!' Maria was mortified. She couldn't bring her mother anywhere.

They managed to avoid spending any more money, and Maria took her mother into Harvey Nicholls, just so she could say she had been there, but it wasn't as much fun as Harrods, so they called it a day.

At the airport on Sunday, after a tearful hug and a promise to come back again in the summer, Maureen had gone through to the departure lounge, clutching a tissue and putting on a brave face. She was walking backwards, waving madly at Molly, when Maria saw her crash into a group of pink-shirted businessmen having a very serious conversation. After extricating herself, she waved once more, and Maria turned away. She was torn between relief and sadness. 'Come on then, Molly. Let's go home to our house,' she said brightly, and pushed the button for the lift to go down to the Underground station.

Now she was sitting on the Tube on the way home from Heathrow, her stomach churning with anticipation. It could go either way. Andy could just as easily grab her and smother her in kisses, or be all cold and hard, and refuse to speak to her. At least Molly was quiet, she thought as she climbed the stairs to the flat, her bulky bag bumping against her legs. Molly was getting heavy now, especially when she was asleep and she was a dead weight in Maria's arms.

Andy's favourite Radiohead track blared through the walls as Maria turned onto the landing, and she cringed. That would set Molly off, and she'd have to contend with both of them shouting at her. She put the key in the lock, her heart pounding. Andy was dancing in the middle of the living-room floor, eyes closed, singing along with the music. He sensed her in the room and froze, turning to her with such a mean, tight look on his face that she gulped.

'Hiya,' she said, shifting Molly on to her hip and dropping her bag.

Andy sneered, 'Oh, so you've decided to grace me with your presence, have you?'

'What do you mean? I left a message to say I'd be back today,' she said tearfully. He could do that to her. Reduce her to tears just by looking at her.

'Don't start the waterworks, Maria. You have a right nerve, leaving a message like that and just turning up when it suits you.' He was sneering, and for the first time it crossed her mind that he could look quite ugly at times.

'I couldn't help it if my mother decided to stay longer.'

'You could have told her you had other plans. You've got a life over here now, Maria. They kicked you out, remember?'

She looked down at Molly, who was watching Andy, wide-eyed and silent.

'You can't put me in a box, Maria, and just take me

267

out to play with when you feel like it. I've done everything for you, and I've looked after you, haven't I? What else do you expect me to do, fucking marry you?' Andy strode to the CD player and stabbed the stop button. He was working himself into a real frenzy. Maria thought it wise to keep quiet. She stood transfixed, staring at him.

'I thought we had something special together. Even with the kid – I was prepared to put up with her to be with you.' The words echoed around the room, with no blaring music to disguise them.

'What are you saying?' asked Maria, trembling.

'What do you think? I've had enough.' He went into the bedroom and slammed the door.

Molly started to cry and rub her eyes, so Maria took her into the other bedroom to put her down to sleep. She gasped as she pushed open the door. The Winnie the Pooh curtains were in shreds, ripped down and draped across the cot. Molly's toys were thrown around the room, and one teddy bear was armless, with its stuffing spewing out on the carpet. All the drawers were pulled out, and Molly's clothes were thrown around the room. Maria cleared the cot and laid Molly down. She crept into the kitchen, pulled out a bundle of plastic carrier bags from under the sink, and filled them with Molly's things.

The baby was too tired to be disturbed by the rustling noises, and she lay flat on her back, her chest softly rising and falling and a pink flush on her cheeks.

Maria looked down at her, and the swelling love that filled her chest pushed out the anger and the fear of facing Andy again. She stacked the bags in the hall, and opened the bedroom door. Andy was lying on the bed, flicking through a men's fashion magazine. Maria pulled her rucksack down from the top of the wardrobe and started emptying her chest of drawers.

'Haven't you got anything to say?' he muttered in the tone she remembered from childhood when her mother was demanding an apology.

'We're going,' she said defiantly.

'So you don't admit you're in the wrong, then?' He realised that she was serious. 'Fuck it, if you can't get your priorities right, I'm better off without you.'

Maria dragged the rucksack across to the dressing-table and swept her cosmetics and brushes in, on top of her clothes. This was really scary. Was he schizophrenic or something? She hardly recognised him. 'Can I use the phone?' she asked, between gritted teeth. She was afraid they would start chattering if she relaxed her jaw.

'Oh, yes, I think after sponging rent, food and entertainment for the past four months, a phone call won't break the bank, don't you?' He raised his eyebrow. That used to make her laugh, when he did his James Bond impression, but now it was menacing.

Maria ran into the living-room and dialled Aileen's number. No reply.

She left a message on Paul's mobile phone, hoping they would get home before she got there. A mini-cab would cost a fortune, and she dug in the pocket of her jeans to see how much money she had. Only ten pounds. It had been an expensive week, what with eating out and entertaining her mother. She had got used to Andy just handing her money whenever she needed it. She couldn't ask him. She remembered the jar in the kitchen.

Andy hated carrying lots of change around, and he dumped it in there, even pound coins. There might be enough. Maria went into the kitchen and closed the door. She tried to tip the coins out quietly, picking out the pounds. Just as she slipped ten coins into her pocket, the door opened, and Andy stood there.

'What are you doing?' He looked down at her fumbling hands. 'Oh, I see, now you're stealing my money, are you?'

'I need it for the taxi,' she said, stepping back, terrified by the look on his face.

He strode across the room, raising his arm. She screamed, and he froze. His arm fell to his side and he looked a bit scared himself, at what he might have done.

'Just fuck off, Maria. I never want to see you again.' Now he just sounded tired and stressed out.

'I'll send you back the taxi money,' she said, wriggling past him to get out the door.

'Certainly, madam. I'll send you a bill for the rest, shall I?' he shouted after her.

Maria bundled Molly into her coat and picked up

the handles of the six plastic bags in one hand and her rucksack with the other. She struggled out the door and down the stairs with the pushchair and only then remembered the bag she had left on the living-room floor. God knows what would happen, if she went back for it.

She opened the front door, and stumbled onto the road. The net curtains in the ground floor flat twitched as she dragged everything down the street, with Molly screaming now, to the mini-cab office on the corner.

'Are you all right, love?' the plump cab-controller asked her from behind her plastic screen, taking in Maria's gaunt expression and the screaming child.

'Yes, I want to go to Herne Hill, but I only have twenty pounds. Is that enough?'

'We'll make sure it is, love.' She turned to her microphone. 'Five four, five four, job to Herne Hill, twenty quid.'

'It's the white Sierra out the front, love – he'll help you with your bags.'

Maria collapsed on the back seat with Molly, while the driver loaded the boot.

Paul's mobile phone bleeped as soon as he turned it on outside the cinema. He listened to the two messages, and grimaced.

'It's Maria. She's outside our flat – Andy's kicked her out.'

Aileen grabbed the telephone to listen to the

message. They walked quickly through the Sunday strollers on Haymarket to catch the bus home.

'Oh my God, I wonder how long she's been there?' wailed Aileen.

'It can only be since the movie started,' he said, 'or we would have heard the phone ringing.'

Aileen looked at her watch. Seven o'clock. 'The poor things will be freezing. How could Andy do that to her?'

'We don't know the whole story, do we?' said Paul, putting his arm around her as they sat on the front seat of the bus. He had been surprised that Andy put up with Maria being away for a week, and not even being allowed to meet her mother. He wasn't a man who would be happy playing second fiddle.

There was no sign of Maria on the steps as they walked from the bus stop, and Aileen ran the last fifty yards. She opened the front door and saw the stack of Tesco's bags and Maria's rucksack leaning against the wall.

'At least they got inside,' she said, shivering.

Paul led the way upstairs, carrying the bags. They found Maria sitting on the top step, with Molly fast asleep in her arms.

'I didn't want to sit down there like a bag lady,' said Maria. 'The woman from number two let me in.'

'You poor thing!' said Aileen, helping her up. 'Come on in and you can tell us all about it.'

She ushered Maria through the door, and Paul took

the bags to the spare room, where there was still a lingering smell of talcum powder and hairspray after Maureen's recent departure. Maria followed him and laid Molly gently on the bed and covered her with a little pink blanket.

'Are you OK?' he asked, touching her shoulder. He almost expected to see bruises or some other evidence of the fight with Andy.

Maria nodded, and bit her lower lip. They went into the living-room together, and Aileen handed them drinks. Maria flopped onto the sofa, and tipped back the bottle to take a long swig of beer. There was a long silence as they all looked at each other. The fish in the aquarium swam hopefully to the surface, expecting to be fed now that the lights had come on.

'If you don't want to talk about it yet, Maria, we'll understand,' said Paul.

'There's not much to say. He said he never wants to see me again.'

She took another slug of beer.

'Are you hungry?' asked Aileen.

'No, I couldn't eat. My stomach is in a knot.'

Maria rested her head against the soft green cushions of the sofa, and her hair spread out behind her. Like a mermaid, thought Aileen as she looked at her sister's pale, tear-stained face.

'I can't believe what he did. Molly's room was in tatters. He ripped the curtains down, and all her things were thrown around everywhere.'

Paul was shocked. He had known Andy since school. He always had a bad temper, especially when he lost at sports or anything, but this sounded a bit over the top.

'Are you serious?' he said. So he hadn't been far wrong, expecting to see bruises.

'Did he do anything to you?' demanded Aileen, thinking the same thing.

'No, he went to hit me, but I screamed, and he kind of snapped out of it.'

Maria's cheeks were flushed now as she remembered the fear she had felt, looking at Andy's distorted face, his eyes standing out in his head, with huge black pupils.

'He's mad. I reckon he takes drugs, you know,' said Aileen. 'Sometimes he's so manic and spaced out when you talk to him.'

'I was going to tell you that, but now it doesn't matter.' Maria looked down at her hands. The beautiful nails she had grown for work were bitten down to the quick. Living with Andy was like being on the edge all the time, not knowing what would happen next. 'I was really stupid to move in with him.'

'No, you weren't. You thought you loved him, and he loved you. At the time, that was all that mattered,' said Aileen. 'You'll be all right. You can put it down to experience.'

Chapter Thirty-three

'You have a quiet house now, after the invasion,' said Maureen when she rang from Carraroe to say she had arrived home safely.

'Yes, indeed,' said Aileen, waving at Maria to close the kitchen door so that Maureen wouldn't hear Molly. She had just developed tickles, and Maria had her wriggling around on the floor, giggling like a mad thing.

'Well, I had a lovely time, thanks very much to you and Paul for your hospitality.' She felt a bit funny, saying it. She had never commented on Aileen's 'living situation' as she called it in her own mind.

'No problem, Mam, it was great to see you. The next excitement for you will be Hugh coming home.'

'I have the back room painted already, but I think I'll do a spring-clean on the house this week, before your father gets his holidays.'

'Did he survive the week without you?'

'He hasn't lost any weight, anyway.' Aileen heard the rare sarcasm. She had sensed that things weren't quite right between them, but she knew her mother wouldn't talk about it. Too many years of unquestioning loyalty to the man of the house couldn't be thrown away that easily. The metaphorical trousers were still firmly buckled around his well-fed waist.

'Good. Give him my love, and we'll talk to you next week.'

Aileen found herself, as usual, stuck in the middle. She was on Maria's side, but she understood better than Maria that for their father giving in would be a huge sacrifice.

Molly started yelling just as Aileen hung up. She was tired of the tickling game and wanted to be fed.

'So, tell me all about it,' said Sean, sitting back, full and contented after dinner. He wasn't a man who enjoyed solitude. He felt full of the milk of human kindness, now that Maureen was back. His secretary Kate would notice the difference the next day, and silently thank God that Maureen didn't make a habit of going away. He had been like a bear with a sore head for the last week.

Maureen said that the Harrods food hall was her favourite place, and she really enjoyed the bus tour. Sean still sensed her holding back, but he couldn't put his finger on it. The little holiday didn't seem to have dispelled her funny mood. Maybe it was her hormones again. Women had it tough, really.

'Listen, love, I'm glad you went to see them, and put your mind at rest that Maria is all right. Now you can picture her in your mind when you're talking to her on the phone.'

Maybe she would settle down a bit, and they could get into their old routine.

'I never saw her own place, Sean. She didn't want me to see it.'

'I thought she said it was just easier for you all to be staying in comfort in Aileen's place?'

'No, Sean, there was more to it than that. She definitely didn't want me to see where she's staying. Maybe she's ashamed of it, or she's worried that I wouldn't approve of her flatmates? And another thing; I don't know where she's getting her money from. Things are awful expensive in London. I paid three pounds in one place for a cup of tea and a bun.'

'Sure haven't they got millions of single mothers over there, living off the state? Isn't it even worse over there than it is here?'

'Mmm?' Maureen wondered why she had never before noticed Sean's amazing talent for selective self-delusion. She didn't say anything. There was something up with Maria. She had been very flushed and quiet when Maureen came back from walking Molly that time. She must have been talking to someone on the phone. She was definitely preoccupied with something during the week. Maureen had seen her eyes glaze over, and her thoughts wandering, several times.

'I think Aileen and Paul will be giving us a day out soon,' she said, to change the subject.

'Good – he can make a respectable woman out of her, and that will be one of them off our hands.'

'They're going skiing in a few weeks' time.'

'Isn't it well for them? The young ones these days have a great life, altogether.'

Sean opened his paper to read the sports results and Maureen cleared away the dinner dishes.

The ice seemed to be broken, anyway, thought Sean. Maybe she was only tired after the journey. It was good to have her back, and a few of the home comforts. He couldn't make a nice cup of tea for the life of him.

Maureen stood with her arms in the soapy water. For the last week, she had been able to push the birth certificate to the back of her mind. Now that she was at home, it was looming over her again. Would it always be a festering secret, until after the two of them died, and the children were clearing out the dressing-table drawers, in years to come?

Sean looked up from his paper at Maureen, who stood with her back to him.

She was still a fine-looking woman. He looked at her shapely figure and her slim ankles. He felt a stirring. They hadn't slept together for weeks, and the last few days on his own had made it worse.

'We should have an early night tonight, love,' he said. 'I didn't sleep well at all without you in the bed beside me.'

Maureen's back stiffened. She recognised that tone in his voice. She could manage to be civil to him, but she couldn't entertain the thought of him making love to her.

At ten o' clock, she followed him to bed. When he put his hand across to touch her thigh as she put on her flannelette nightie, she said, 'Sean, I'm awful tired after that journey'.

She curled up with her back to him, pretending she hadn't seen the expectant smile on his face. She took deep breaths, but her heart was pounding. This couldn't go on. She'd have to say something, and clear the air.

Sean rolled on to his back, and sighed. Maybe it was the wrong time of the month for her anyway. She didn't always say, and sometimes he lost track.

'I'll have to go back to work soon, and find a childminder for Molly,' said Maria when she had been staying with Aileen and Paul for two weeks. 'I rang Paddy today, and he only needs to give the temp a week's notice.'

'How will you be able to afford a childminder?' asked Aileen. 'I heard from one of the girls at work that she pays about a hundred pounds a week.'

'You're not serious? That's all my wages gone, before I pay rent, or anything!'

'You were spoilt, really, with Andy paying for everything.'

Maria looked at her. This was the first time Aileen

had mentioned Andy since Maria came back. She had her big-sister voice on, as well.

'Do you think I'm a selfish cow?' Maria asked, really feeling like a little sister. 'Andy said I was, and that I just used him.'

'No, I don't think you used him. He was the one who asked you to move in with him, and he knew at the time that you were having Molly.'

'But I took him for granted, is that what you think?'

'Maybe. But from what you said about him drinking every night, and the drugs, it sounds like he got away with murder. Lots of women wouldn't put up with that.'

'I couldn't really complain, could I? Andy was really good to me in lots of ways.'

'You weren't a charity case, Maria. It was supposed to be a relationship.'

'But he was so generous. He paid for everything, and he even decorated the room for Molly.' Maria had convinced herself that she must be doing something seriously wrong, and that it was no wonder neither Joe nor Andy wanted to be with her.

'He destroyed it as well, don't forget.'

'That was just temper, one night after the pub. I did stay away for a week, even though I told him it would only be three days.'

Aileen raised her eyes to heaven. 'Honestly, Maria, you have a lot to learn. He nearly hit you, remember?'

'He only raised his hand. He never would have done

it.' The fear she had felt was all blurred around the edges now, and she just missed him. The loneliness was back, a terrible ache just below her heart that she couldn't chase away.

'Maybe not that time, but he would have hit you another time,' said Aileen, crossing her arms. 'You're much better off without him. It's probably a good idea to just be single for a while, and enjoy it.'

'You're probably right,' said Maria miserably. She was beginning to wonder if Andy had just been an antidote for the loneliness after she lost Joe. She had been postponing everything, and now it felt like she had a double dose of pain coming to her.

So Andy was right. She had used him. But not on purpose. She wanted to ring him. Every night, she stood in front of the telephone after Aileen and Paul had gone to bed. Once she even dialled the number. It rang and rang. He was probably still in the pub. She was glad in a way, because she didn't know what she would have said.

'Anyway,' she took a deep breath and picked up the *Evening Standard*, 'I have to find another room.'

'Listen, we're going skiing the week after next, and it would be great if you were here to look after the flat while we're away,' said Aileen.

Paul had agreed to Aileen's little plan, as long as Maria found her own place when they came back. Paul couldn't have a shower without stepping around Molly's plastic toys in the bath and her smelly disposable nappies seemed to fill the bin. There were limits, even for family, Paul said.

'Great!' Maria was delighted. That was another three weeks without paying rent. 'I'll tell Paddy that I'll be back to work on the first of April then.'

'Fine,' said Aileen. 'Maria, in the meantime, could you try and keep Molly's things a bit tidier? Maybe in a basket, or something, rather than all over the place? I'm afraid one of us will fall over them one of these days.'

'Of course, sorry,' she said, picking up a teddy bear and a squeaky ball from the living-room floor. Paul must have said something to Aileen, she thought, blushing.

'Will I make us a cup of tea?' She must remember to put the mugs in the dishwasher afterwards as well.

They sat on the sofa with their tea and Aileen asked, 'Do you think Mam will get Dad to change his mind, now that she's been over here to see you and Molly?'

'Not at all. You know what he's like, Aileen. Have you ever known him to change his mind about anything?'

'He took the news about me and Paul living together very well, considering.'

'That's only because you're not under his nose. The neighbours don't need to know. Anyway, isn't it obvious that you and Paul will be getting married soon?'

Aileen laughed. 'Where did you get that idea from?'

Chapter Thirty-four

The flat was very quiet in the afternoon when Molly went for a sleep. There was no air of expectation that Aileen or Paul would be home from work soon. Maria sat on the sofa, restless. The only things that would break the monotony of the evening ahead were Molly's tea-time and bath-time. The other two had gone off skiing the day before, with enough bags to keep them going for months. Aileen had gone mad buying co-ordinated skiing accessories. One night she came into the living-room, dressed up in her ski suit, gloves, scarf, woolly socks and even her sunglasses, with a matching sporty string to hold them on. She didn't even know if she would like skiing, but they were going to Canada with a very trendy crowd, and she wanted to have all the right bits and pieces.

Maria sighed. Aileen and Paul were so happy. Sometimes, when they were just sitting watching telly together, Maria would look at them and wonder, is this it? No huge ups and downs, the occasional night out, and two holidays a year. A bit of a cliché and on the surface, very boring. But they seemed so complete, like the two halves of the Disney characters that she made from moulds when she was ten. She painted them and baked them in the oven. Sometimes they exploded, and Maureen would be cleaning out bits of painted clay for weeks afterwards. Sometimes when she put them on her bedroom windowsill, the two halves would just fall over backwards with a clunk like something out of a cartoon. Aileen and Paul were like the model of Mickey and Minnie Mouse dancing together. It was really hard to make, but it had lasted the longest.

It was still in a box up in the attic at home. If they got engaged, she would give it to them as a present, for a laugh.

Then she realised she couldn't just go home and pop up into the attic any more. It wasn't her home now. What about all her other stuff in the attic? The little red five-year diary, and the poems she wrote when she was fourteen and in love with that boy from Dublin, what was his name? Ronan, that was it. The romance had started on his second day in the Gaeltacht. Pauline spotted him first, getting off the coach on the Sunday, and she bagsed him. The next day, he came up and asked Maria if she wanted to go to the beach with him. His Irish was terrible but he was a good kisser. Later, Maria told Pauline what French kissing was like.

Pauline said it sounded disgusting, but Maria said you had to do it. That week, she wrote three poems about love, but she never showed them to Ronan. He was sixteen and far too cool for poetry. She went to the beach with him, and snogged him behind the sheds when there was no one smoking there already. At the ceili on his last night, he took her outside behind the hall, and in the dark, he touched her boobs. Her nipples stood out under her blouse, but she thought it was just the cold. She wouldn't let him touch her *down there*. The kissing was much nicer, anyway.

She opened the newspaper in the 'Rooms to Let' section, but there was nothing interesting. She heard Molly stir, and held her breath, but the expected cry didn't come. Often, when Maria went in to check on her, she would be lying there quite happily, staring at her mobile on the ceiling, or sucking her thumb. She would turn her head and smile at Maria, as if seeing her mother made her little world complete.

It was so depressing, dragging Molly around to view different rented rooms, with manky carpets and damp bathrooms full of other people's pubes. Molly needed a proper home and a proper cot, rather than a travel-cot stuck in the corner of a studio room. Later, when she was older and she had little friends, she could invite them round to play and Maria would make buns for tea with white icing and Smarties on the top. Maria just kept thinking back to that bedsit in Ealing. If Andy hadn't rescued her, that's where she would have taken

Molly home from hospital. How would she have given her a bath, or even had the space for a cot once she grew out of the Moses basket? Now Maria was back to square one, but it wasn't about proving her independence any more – it was about providing a safe and secure home for Molly. She had never understood until now, how having a child would change her as a person. She was a mother now, and whichever way she looked at it, she had better start behaving like one.

It wasn't healthy to sit around sighing, so she went to the bookshelf to get something to read. Paul had such an amazing collection of books, it was like being in a library. She speedily passed over the Shakespeare and Dickens and Thomas Hardy books. She skipped the 1997 guide to the 100 best albums, and a coffee-table book on Feng Shui. The next title rang a bell. *A Handmaid's Tale*, by Margaret Atwood. Aileen had said that was really good. She pulled it out.

Maria listened again at the bedroom door. Only the gentle sound of breathing. She loved the delicate baby smell that emanated from the room. It was like the shade of pink you find inside a conch shell, that you never see anywhere else.

She sank on to the sofa and bit into an apple as she opened the first page, looking forward to another half an hour of peace.

An envelope fell out and landed upside down on her lap.

She turned it over. It was addressed to her, care of

Aileen, and Maria recognised Joe's black spidery handwriting. She swallowed the lump of green apple without chewing, and it jammed in her chest. Aileen must have kept the letter, when Maria told her she didn't want to hear from Joe. Trust Aileen to take that literally. To be fair to Aileen, though, Maria hadn't really given her any choice. She had been such a cow to everyone, and had latched on to Andy as the answer to everything. It would have been easy for Aileen to deal with Joe's phone calls. Telephone words disappear as soon as you hang up. But that letter must have sat on the hall table, daring her to read it or throw it away.

Aileen hadn't done either. Had she told Maria that the book was brilliant, so she would find the letter one day? Or had she just tucked it into the first book that came to hand?

Maria squinted at the stamp. It was postmarked in August last year. A long time ago.

She picked up Paul's fancy letter-opener from the coffee table. The letter had waited this long to be opened; it deserved a bit of ceremony.

Joe must have completely given up on her by now, so she had nothing to worry about. Why were her hands sweating? Why could she feel a flush spreading up her neck to her face? She swallowed convulsively to dislodge the apple. It slid slowly down her oesophagus as she pulled out two flimsy pages and unfolded them.

Castlebar Hospital was printed at the top. Maria sat up straight.

He hadn't said anything about being in hospital. What had happened to him?

'*I'm sitting at my mother's bed,*' he wrote, and Maria slid back into the soft cushions, suddenly nervous.

'*She had a car crash and she's in a coma. She hasn't moved for three weeks.*'

Shock surged through her. Poor Joe! He must have gone through hell. God, that was why he hadn't been calling her every day . . .

'*But I'm not writing about her, I'm writing because I want you to know how I feel about you. I've had plenty of time to think about everything since I let you go off to England.*'

Maria summoned some indignation to counteract the alarm and confusion building in her chest. The cheek of him! Let her go off to England. He had practically packed her bags.

'*I realise now, looking at my mother lying here on the bed, like an old person who hasn't got long to live, that you only get to live your life once.*

I was really scared when you first told me about the baby. I agreed with you about getting rid of it because it seemed like the easy way out for both of us.

Then I started thinking about why I am doing medicine, and what kind of person I want to be, and I realised I was wrong. So I should have been happy when you said you were keeping it, but I was even more scared. Not about telling my mum, which is what you think, I know, but because of the responsibility, and how it would change everything.

I tried to talk to you on the phone, but Aileen said you didn't want to hear from me. I hope this letter won't be too late.

I want to spend the rest of my life with you, Maria, and the baby. I love you so much, and I think about you every day for hours, sitting here, wondering what is happening to you.

If I have to give up college to work and support you and the baby, that's what I'll do. This is more important than my career, or what my mother will think of me.

I only realise that when I see how close I am to losing her. I don't want to lose you as well. Having said all that, I might have blown it already, and I wouldn't blame you if you didn't love me any more. I haven't done much to deserve it, so I won't hassle you if you decide you don't want to have anything more to do with me.

If you do want to get in touch, a letter would be the best, because I only go home to sleep and change my clothes. Otherwise, I'm here at the hospital all the time and I can't have a mobile phone switched on in here.

I will love you always

Joe XXXX

Maria sat frozen on the sofa, in the same place where she had decided not to have the abortion. Angry heat flooded her face. Her head was suddenly full of swirling questions. Why had no one told her what had happened? The poor fella was sitting there, for God knows how long, not hearing from her, and not knowing if his mother would die on him. Was the mother dead by now? Pauline must have known; how could she have kept quiet? Aileen had known there was a letter sitting there on the shelf all the time, and never said anything. And then her thoughts moved on. How could Joe just send a letter, and leave it at that? If he wanted to be with her and the baby that much, he could have made more of an effort. It was far too late, waiting until the baby was born to come over and sit on the edge of her bed in the hospital and think they could try again. Did he think her whole life would be on hold? She stopped herself. Joe had been stuck at his mother's bedside while she was busy fancying Andy. And she had been so horrible to Joe in the hospital when Molly was born, sneering about how busy his mother must be keeping him. Shame washed over her now.

Maria went to the telephone and punched out Pauline's number. She couldn't separate all the emotions that were welling up, but as soon as she heard Pauline's voice, she burst into tears. 'Oh, Pauline, you won't believe it!'

Pauline couldn't make herself heard through the sobbing for at least five minutes. 'Maria, what's wrong? Is it Molly? Tell me! Are you all right?'

Finally, Maria drew a deep breath and said,' Why didn't you tell me about Joe's mother?'

'What about her?'

'She was in hospital, in a coma!'

'What, you mean last year?

'Yes – did she recover?'

'She's in a wheelchair.'

'Why didn't you tell me?'

'Maria, it was in the summer, when you said you never wanted to hear anything about Joe ever again, remember?'

'Yes, but . . .'

'Anyway, why are you so upset about it now?' Pauline was feeling a bit guilty. Maybe she should have said something. But Maria could be stubborn, and she had been very clear on the subject.

'I just read a letter from Joe that he wrote from Castlebar Hospital, last August,' Maria sobbed.

' He said he tried ringing you quite a few times, too.'

'Aileen must have hidden the letter, Pauline. I just found it inside a book. I never knew he sent it.'

Maria wasn't getting the full dose of sympathy she had been expecting. This was a major crisis, and Pauline sounded like she was on Joe's side.

'He did mention it to Mike I think, and he was upset that you didn't acknowledge it.'

'So you talked to him about it, did you?'

'He's my friend as well, you know. He and Mike are sharing a house, so I see him nearly every day. I could hardly avoid him, could I?'

'You never told me he was trying so hard to get in touch.'

'You specifically said to me and to Aileen that you didn't want to hear anything about him.' Pauline was getting exasperated now.

'Does he ever talk about me?' Maria asked tentatively.

'Sometimes. He asks about Molly. He's always asking if I have any new pictures of her.'

'Pauline, you should hear what he says in the letter. I can't believe it. He said he'd give up medicine to support us.'

'But you knew that. Didn't he say that to you when he came to see you in the hospital?'

'Yes, but I told him I was with Andy. And anyway, I thought he was just saying it because he should. Not because he meant it.'

'Well, it is a bit late now, with Andy around, isn't it?'

'I've left Andy,' said Maria bluntly.

'Left him, why?' Pauline sighed. She couldn't keep up with Maria.

'He kind of kicked me out, really. He said I was a selfish cow because I spent a week with Mam when she was over.'

'He kicked you out for that? So where are you now?'

'Back at Aileen's. We have to move out next week when they come back from skiing. We're looking after the flat.'

'You and Molly?' Pauline wasn't sure if 'we' would suddenly include another man, acquired in the last two weeks.

'Yes. It's really hard to get a place where they'll accept a small baby. I can only afford to do a flat-share, or get a Council place. I put myself on the Council list, even before I moved in with Andy, but I don't know how long it will take to move up the list. You get certain points, and then you have to wait until something comes up.'

'That sounds very long term. Are you definitely staying in London, then, even if it's finished with Andy?' It sounded like Andy had lived up to Aileen's expectations rather than Maria's.

'I was planning to, until I read this letter. I don't know if it changes anything though. What do you think I should do?'

'Do you love Joe?'

'I don't know, Pauline. I thought he was being such a wimp about the whole thing, and not even telling his mother. I had no idea she was sick. He must think I'm such a cow.'

'I don't know what you should do, Maria, but whatever you do, don't do it in a hurry. Don't forget that Joe wrote that letter last summer, and when he came over to see you, you told him you were with Andy. Lots of things could have changed by now.' Pauline had always been the level-headed one.

'Is he going with anyone?' Maria asked. Was Pauline trying to break it to her gently?

'Not that I know of. He wouldn't have the time. He races off to Westport every Friday to get his mother out of the nursing home for the weekend, and he doesn't come back to Galway until Sunday.'

'The poor thing. He never even mentioned his mother when he was over here. I was too busy telling him to go away to listen to anything he had to say. I was terrified that Andy would turn up at the hospital and see him. What happened to her, anyway?'

'A car crash. She knocked down a girl on a bike, and then hit a wall herself. She's paralysed from the waist down now, but she was in a coma for nearly two months.'

'My God, poor Joe! How does he cope?'

'He doesn't talk much about it really. He just gets on with it.'

'The accident must have happened just after I came to London, did it?'

'It was – the same week I think,' said Pauline.

'And no one told me. That's why it took him so long to get in touch.' It was so obvious now that she couldn't believe she had been so stupid.

That was the last straw for Pauline. She took a deep breath, and tried not to yell down the phone.

'Maria, you can't go around laying down the law about what you want people to tell you, or not, and then complain when they don't.'

'Pauline, don't be mad with me. It's all a shock. I just wanted someone to talk to.'

Pauline heard the catch in her voice. 'All right. Sorry for shouting at you.'

'It's OK. I'll talk to you at the weekend. Bye.'

Maria sat on the tall kitchen stool with her arms hanging down by her sides, like a rag doll. She didn't have the energy to move. She had totally screwed up her life. When her Dad had told her not to come back home, she thought she was so tough and independent, she could deal with it, especially when her mam was still on her side.

Maria was so busy proving that she could make her own way in life, working for Paddy, satisfying Andy, looking after Molly, hiding things from her mother, that she had lost Joe, who was still in love with her and had tried desperately to get her back, even when he knew Andy was on the scene. She had been so self-centred, it hadn't even entered her head to wonder why Joe had taken so many months to come and see her. Maybe she should get in touch, even if it was only to apologise. She couldn't expect anything from him now, but she owed him an explanation.

Molly woke up, looking for a feed, and Maria took her out of her cot and sat in the same spot on the sofa, enjoying the feeling of being needed. She looked down at the top of Molly's head as she nuzzled at her breast, and almost choked with the surge of emotion that rose in her chest. She knew in that moment that Molly's happiness was more important than hers. No more selfish behaviour.

Deep down, her reasons for moving in with Andy had been selfish. She needed him, not just for a roof over her head, but to reassure herself that even with a baby, she was still attractive.

Ever since she was twelve, when she realized that boys fancied her more than Aileen, or Pauline, or any of the girls in her class, she had taken it for granted that they would always come to her. And they had. In every relationship, long or short, she was in control, and she was the one to finish it. Maria never had to think too much about how she treated her boyfriends, because they always came back for more. Even poor Joe came back, after she had been so horrible to him. Andy was the first one to turn the tables on her, and it was a shock to the system.

Maybe she should leave Joe alone now, rather than stir things up again. She would ask Aileen's advice when she came back. Her anger had completely disappeared and she just felt drained. As Pauline said, she had no right to be angry with Aileen for hiding the letter. Aileen had tried loads of times to get her to ring Joe, and Maria had just told her to mind her own business.

The phone rang, and she gently pulled Molly's puckered lips from her breast, and stood up to answer it

'Could I speak to Maria Hardy, please?' asked a bored-sounding voice.

'Speaking.'

'Hello, Maria. It's Jocelyn here, from Lambeth Housing Department. I'm ringing to let you know that we have transferred your file to Hammersmith and Fulham, as you requested, and they will be in touch with you shortly.'

'Oh, great. Thanks very much. Do you know how long it might take for me to get a place?' Maria asked, excitedly.

'No, not really. They're not quite as badly off as we are for housing stock, so you might get something a bit quicker. They'll probably offer you Bed and Breakfast accommodation first.'

Maria's heart sank. Those places were often on the news, and she had seen a fly-on-the-wall documentary about a B&B in Hackney. It looked awful.

'OK, thanks anyway. What should I do now?'

'Just wait for them to contact you. It should be in the next week or so, to let you know what happens next.'

'Thanks for your help.'

'No problem. Goodbye.'

Maria had the very strong feeling that she was just another tick on the list of 'things to do' for Jocelyn, and she went back to Molly, who was lying placidly on the sofa, waiting for her source of food to come back. She smiled as Maria leaned over her to pick her up.

'You're so good, I don't deserve you,' said Maria, and she could feel the tears rising as she put Molly back to her breast.

Chapter Thirty-five

'How's Ivy these days?' Maria asked Paddy when he came into the office late again, after a visit to the physiotherapist with Ivy.

'Making slow progress,' he said, wiping his sweaty forehead with a wrinkled hanky from his pocket, and flicking the switch on the kettle to make tea. He was a changed man, pale and quiet since Ivy had the stroke in May.

'She really misses coming in here,' he said, 'but she's glad that you're holding the fort so well.' He smiled. 'Did you ever think you'd be doing all the job-scheduling and the bookkeeping, when you came in to be a receptionist?'

'No, I still can't believe it.' She found it difficult to talk to Paddy about it. She loved the bigger job, and the money, but she felt bad that Ivy's illness was the cause of her good fortune.

'We were planning to go home to Carraroe in

August, if Ivy was a bit more mobile, but I think we'll have to give it a miss again this year,' said Paddy sadly.

'That'll be two years in a row, won't it?' said Maria sympathetically.

She knew how he must feel. Three weeks ago Aileen had tried to celebrate Maria's being in London for a year. She opened a bottle of champagne and Paul proposed a toast to new beginnings. They were full of excitement, planning their wedding, and she was really happy for them, but it didn't help the homesickness.

That was kind of why she had the urge to ring Joe last night. He had been very quiet while she was talking. She couldn't tell if he was glad to hear from her or not. She wasn't looking for anything. She just thought it was time to give him an update on Molly's progress, and see how he was doing. As a friend. It was so good to hear his voice, even if he was a bit distant. It must have been a surprise to hear from her after so long. She had said 'sorry', too. It had really been playing on her mind over the last few months, even though Aileen had said to leave well enough alone.

'Penny for them,' said Paddy, when Maria had been standing motionless with the kettle in her hand for at least a minute.

She whirled around.

'Sorry, Paddy, I was miles away,' she said, fumbling with the tea caddy.

'Were you thinking about home?'

'Sort of.'

'If it's any consolation, I didn't go home for the first fifteen years after I came over here. My mother didn't want me to come to London at all. She thought I'd end up a drunken navvy like my father. She wouldn't speak to me when I left home.'

'Really? So what happened?'

'She died,' he said, looking down at his feet. 'That's my biggest regret; that I was so pig-headed I never made my peace with her.'

'But she was the one who wasn't speaking to you.'

The spoon clinked against the side of the mug as she squeezed hard at the tea bag.

'Ah yes, but after they're gone, that's no consolation. The guilt lies on you like a wet sack, and you wonder what you could have done differently.'

He sank wearily into his emperor's chair with his mug of dark tea. He had shrunk in the last few months, thought Maria, looking at him.

'It would be good if you and Ivy had a little holiday,' she said, touching his arm.

He was only half the man without Ivy around, as if she was the source of his energy. 'Maybe in another month or so, she'll be well enough to travel.'

'Maybe, love, maybe.' He shuffled some papers around and tried to sound brisk. 'Well, we have lots of work to do, haven't we?'

Maria took the hint and left him to it.

Joe inhaled the hot salty air and grasped the rail of the

boat, stretching his arms out and imagining the freckles popping to the surface of his skin. His feet were bare on the wooden deck, which had only just cooled down enough to stand on. He watched the white diagonal line of the wash streaking across the dark blue sea, and the hopeful seagulls cruising behind the boat.

Mike came up from below and handed him a can of Coke.

'This is the life, isn't it?' he said, grinning, his dark skin tanned after only three days in the sun.

'You look like a Greek fella already,' said Joe, gasping as the cold sweet bubbles hit the back of his throat. He could feel the heat of the sun penetrating his bones and radiating through his bloodstream.

'You were right, Mike. This is what I need. A complete break from everything.'

'Yeah, that phone call from Maria didn't help the stress levels, did it?'

'God, I got so drunk that night. It was such a shock, hearing from her after so long.'

'Anyone would have done the same,' Mike said.

Maria had somehow got Joe's number in Galway and rung him on the night before his last exam. She said she hadn't called before because she didn't know what to say. Joe had sat stunned on the sitting-room floor for about an hour after he hung up and then went to the pub.

The exam the next day had been written in a hungover haze and he had no idea if he would pass.

'You didn't tell me what she said on the phone,' said Mike, after waiting a minute to see if Joe would volunteer any information.

'She read the letter I sent her last summer. '

'What?'

'She only found it in April. I sent it care of her sister, but Aileen didn't give it to her because Maria said she didn't want to have anything to do with me any more.'

Joe stared out over the sea, his eyes squinting in the sun.

'She admitted all that, and now suddenly she wants to get in touch?' asked Mike cynically. 'What happened to the English boyfriend?'

'They split up ages ago. She's got a Council flat over there now, and she's working for some old friend of her Dad's. She's fine for money – she just got promoted because the owner's wife had a stroke.'

'So what did she want?' Mike didn't want to see Maria hurting Joe again, when he was just getting over her.

'Just to say sorry for being horrible to me when I went over to see her in December, and to tell me that she's doing all right and the baby is well.'

'That's a bit strange, isn't it, after all this time?' said Mike. There must be more to this than met the eye.

Joe looked at him. 'Maybe she wanted to know if I was still interested. If she came home, she might need me, I suppose.'

Mike's eyes widened. 'Would you still do it? Give up everything for her, after what she did to you?'

'I would. I told her that when I saw her in the hospital, but of course she was with the English guy by then.'

'So he dumped her, and now she's decided you're good enough, after all.'

Joe sat down heavily on the slatted wooden seat and propped his head on his hands.

'I don't know what to think, really. I do still love her, but there's so much water under the bridge, and anyway, I don't think she loves me, so it's irrelevant what I think.'

Then he sat up. It wasn't fair to inflict all this on Mike. 'It's good to be over here, away from it all for a few months so I can get my head around it.'

'You're right. Take it easy and just chill out for a while.'

Mike couldn't believe how little Joe thought of himself. He was one in a million. Not many guys would do what he had done for his mother, and here he was, saying he would still give up everything for the girl who had broken his heart, just because she picked up the phone and said sorry after six months of silence.

He reached across to chink Coke cans, and Joe grinned at him as they toasted their temporary freedom.

Chapter Thirty-six

Sean sat in the Fair Green carpark, waiting for Aileen to meet him after her Saturday afternoon shopping. He was always amazed that she wanted to go into Galway whenever she came home on holidays, even though she lived in the shopping metropolis of the world. Across the road, the old laundry was finally being demolished. The place was hardly recognisable, with a digger and a demolition crane trundling across the dusty rose-beds, and half of the blue main building already collapsed in a pile of rubble. Through the haze of dust, he looked across at the orphanage building, still standing stark in its concrete yard, the windows blanked out with panels of wood.

He couldn't resist crossing the road, and pressing his face in between the rusty black uprights of the gate so that he could see into the corner of the yard where he had so fleetingly met his mother, over forty years ago.

He closed his eyes and he was back, looking into her tear-stained face as she was dragged away.

Suddenly, he could understand the frenzied look in her eyes. It wasn't insanity, but frustration, and fear. She was being torn away from her son again. And she knew that any punishment the nuns would inflict would be nothing compared to that pain of separation. No wonder she had taken her own life. It was worthless to her if she couldn't be with her son.

'Dad, are you all right?' Aileen tugged his arm and he turned around.

He didn't know how long he had been standing there.

'My God, you have rust marks all over your face,' she said, taking out a tissue and gently rubbing his cheeks. A tear splashed onto the back of her hand, and she looked up at him. 'Come on,' she said, taking his hand and leading him away.

They walked silently down Merchant's Road, and when they reached the Spanish Arch, she took him to a bench facing the river and sat him down.

She snuggled up to him like a trusting child, but her voice was like a mother's as she coaxed him, 'Do you want to tell me about it?'

As he talked, they watched the swans sailing down the river to the estuary, past the rotting hulls of the old boats pulled up on the shingle. Seagulls cruised on the thermals where the river met the sea. They could hear the rumble of traffic and the shouts of children playing, but father and daughter were alone there on the bench.

Aileen let him talk, uninterrupted. When he stopped, she said, 'Does Mam know?'

He shook his head. 'I don't know how to tell her, after lying to her all these years.'

'You'll tell her now, won't you?' she said gently.

'I will. It doesn't seem so bad, now that I've said it out loud.'

'It's not bad at all, Daddy, just very sad.' Aileen's eyes were shining with tears as she took his hand. 'How could they do that to the little children? It seems more horrifying in a way than some of the stories of abuse you read about the priests, doesn't it? You would think that women would have more compassion.'

Sean just shook his head again.

'They were doing what they thought was best, I suppose,' he said. 'I read in one article that the nuns thought they were fulfilling a very important purpose, by rehabilitating fallen women and prostitutes.'

'But your mother wasn't a prostitute. She was probably an innocent young one who made a mistake, and she was treated like a criminal.' Aileen was indignant. This was her real grandmother they were talking about, she realised with a jolt.

'She took her own life, Aileen.'

It took a while for Aileen's brain to register the meaning of the euphemism.

'Oh, my God,' she said. So the white-haired old woman she had just conjured up, sitting in a cottage somewhere, waiting for her real family to appear one day, had never grown old.

'In there?' she asked, gulping.

Sean nodded. 'Let's go home. Don't tell anyone else, will you, love? I need to deal with it in my own way. It's taken me all my adult life to face up to it, and it's not easy.'

Aileen tucked her hand into his arm, and they walked back to the car.

In his head, Sean knew that the nuns' childhood indoctrination must have influenced his attitude to his real mother. And his one encounter with her as a six-year-old had reinforced that fear of her as a strange outcast. Intellectually, he could see that it was wrong. But emotionally, he couldn't help how he felt about it.

All his life, following the rules had been very important to him. It was the way to survive, and the way to get on. Following the rules of the Church was an integral part of how he lived his everyday life, and followed his faith.

The Church was only a human institution, but it was also his conduit to God. If he didn't go to Mass, and confess his sins, and receive Holy Communion, he might as well be a pagan, and pray to the sea, or the sun. And although everyone these days seemed to think you could pick and choose which bits of your religion appealed to you, and ignore the rest, that was not the way it worked. If you wanted to be a Catholic, you had to follow all the rules, or try to, anyway. But the word 'compassion' kept going around in his head as they drove home.

The drive seemed to take forever, and Aileen looked out the passenger window all the way. The sea was fresh and blue, and the dark hills of Clare seemed miles away. Windsurfers zigzagged across the bay at Silver Strand, their brightly coloured sails like children's toys. She thought about Maria, and felt a bit guilty about this special time she was sharing with her father. Maria had always been his favourite. For the first time in her life, Aileen felt really close to her father, and imagined the hurt that Maria must be feeling, having been pushed away by him.

After driving in silence almost all the way to Carraroe, Sean said, 'I'll tell your mother tonight – I can't keep it in any longer.'

'I'll call over to see Pauline after dinner and stay out of your way.'

'Thanks, love.'

He smiled wanly at her. She didn't quite have the courage to ask him why he was doing to Maria almost exactly what had been done to his own mother. He seemed so vulnerable. She had never seen him like that before.

After the *News*, Aileen went out, and Sean started fidgeting. Maureen had a feeling that he was going to suggest an early night. Last week, he had asked her how long the menopause lasted. She had told him months ago that they couldn't risk any sex at all while her cycle was disrupted, but he wouldn't put up with it for much longer.

'Maureen, can I talk to you about something?' he ventured, shifting the cushions on his chair.

'Mmm?' She pretended to be engrossed in the list of things to do for Aileen's wedding.

'I have something to tell you.'

'That sounds a bit serious.' She looked up over the top of her bifocals.

'Will you take your glasses off a second?' He couldn't talk to her when she was only giving him half of her attention.

She took them off and picked up her mug of tea, cradling it in her hands. If he dared to say anything, anything, about not having sex, she would go for him.

'I just wanted to talk. We haven't talked properly for a long time.'

'About what, Sean?' She wasn't going to make it easy for him. She could feel her heart-rate increasing.

'About something that I didn't think was important to us, but now I think it is.'

He always said to her that sex was only one small part of marriage – he would never force it on her. But they hadn't done it for nearly six months. A man has his needs, she knew, but she couldn't do it. 'Sean, I know what you're going to say.'

'No, love, you don't.' He had that patient teacher's voice on him.

'Sean, don't patronise me, for God's sake!' She put down her tea, in case she might be tempted to throw it at him.

Sean blinked.

Maureen leaned forward in the armchair, and said in a low, hissing voice, 'I will not let you touch me *that way*, Sean, while I'm feeling the way I do about you. It wouldn't be right.' She sat back, and stared into the fire with her arms folded.

'What do you mean, love?' he asked, startled. He wasn't talking about sex. He hadn't even asked her about sex for months. It was the last thing on his mind.

'You are not the man I married.' She threw the challenge at his feet, not raising her eyes from the fire.

'Maureen, where did this come out of?'

'You've lied to me all these years, Sean Seosamh Kelly,' she spat at him.

His eyes widened in shock. 'Maureen, you won't believe it, but that's what I was just going to tell you about.'

'Oh, yes, tell me another one. You suddenly got the urge, after thirty years, to tell me, did you?'

'I did, today in town. I was looking at the orphanage and –'

'So it has nothing to do with me turning my back on you in bed these last six months?'

Sean gasped. 'What? You told me that was – the what do you call it, the *change* thing.'

Maureen raised her smouldering eyes from the fire.

'Sean, you are living in cloud-cuckoo land. I don't want you touching me and saying that you love me, when you've split up our family.'

'What do you mean?' Sean felt dizzy now. This was not how he planned it. Maureen was supposed to feel sorry for him, comfort him. But here she was, like a she-wolf, going for his throat.

'You have such a nerve. The hypocrisy of it, telling Maria that she can't come home with little Molly, when you know well that you're a – that you're illegitimate yourself.'

'Maureen, listen to me. I was going to tell you tonight, honestly, I was –'

'Sean, I don't care tuppence if your mother had you when she wasn't married. I don't even care that I'm married to Sean Kelly and not Sean Hardy.'

'What is it then? What else?' They said that women's hormones went haywire at this time of life. She was like a madwoman.

He had that voice on him again. Maureen went on. She couldn't stop herself, now that the plug had been pulled. '. . . but I do mind that you are driving our daughter away.'

'You don't understand, Maureen.'

'You're right, I don't. You of all people should be tolerant, when you know that your own mother got herself into trouble. It's not like the old days any more, Sean. People don't judge so much.'

'I'm not worried about that,' he said, sullenly, totally

deflated. She wasn't even going to listen to what he had to say. He changed tack. 'I'm letting Maria get on with her own life. Didn't I let you go and see her?'

Maureen was speechless. He let her go and see Maria, did he? As if she had no free will of her own. Honestly, that man could be so infuriating, at times.

'It's still wrong, Maureen. It might be over fifty years on from when my mother had me, and we've had Vatican Two, but it's still a sin . . .' Although perilous, the moral high ground seemed the safest refuge at the moment, with Maureen acting so irrationally.

'Which particular sin are we talking about, Sean? Is lying not a sin any more? Is pride not a sin? And hypocrisy?' she spat at him.

'I've talked to Father Duggan about it in confession.' He looked away. This conversation was supposed to be about him, not about Maria.

'That's all right then, Sean,' she said bitterly. 'As long as you think you've made your peace with God, the rest of us can just suffer. Don't forget that you won't have absolution yourself unless you can find forgiveness in yourself for others.'

She stood up and reached across for his empty mug, avoiding his eyes. If he could preach what was right and wrong, then so could she. Why did everything have to be so black and white for him?

She closed the door quietly on the way out, put the mugs on the draining-board in the kitchen, and went to bed.

Sean sat up for a while. Maureen hadn't given him a chance to explain. He had spent all his adult life blaming himself for his mother's death. No matter what he had read about the laundries over the years, and the demands for apologies and the stories the various inmates told, he had never really put himself in his mother's shoes. She had hanged herself the day after she saw him, so it must be his fault. He had never revisited his naïve, eighteen-year-old logic.

Seeing the orphanage being knocked down had helped, but talking to Aileen had clarified his thoughts. It wasn't his fault. His mother was a victim, and so was he. But how could he explain that to Maureen, without her turning it back on him, and telling him he was only making history repeat itself with Maria?

It was very quiet when Aileen came home at eleven o' clock. No one was sitting up, and the only sound in the living-room was the ticking of the clock.

The next day, Sean went off early to play golf, and Aileen had Maureen to herself.

She wondered whether to ask about last night. Her mother was very subdued. Aileen decided to distract her and talk about the wedding.

'We were thinking of getting married in January, if we can,' she said as they sat with their tea on the patio after breakfast.

Maureen brightened up a bit. 'Oh, that's great, love, but you might have a problem getting a nice hotel at such short notice. Even if you could get a Saturday in the church, you might not get a hotel.'

'Well, we could always have it in London,' said Aileen tentatively. Paul said he didn't mind where it was. Bless him, he had even said he would do it in a church for her. But Aileen wasn't getting married without Maria there.

'I suppose most of your friends are over there, and Paul's family,' said Maureen diplomatically, thinking Sean would have a fit. 'But wouldn't it be nice to show off the place where you come from?' Sean would want to marry off his daughter in his home place. She stopped herself. What was she doing, thinking about what Sean would want? Force of habit, after so many years.

Aileen saw the emotions playing across her mother's face. 'To be honest, Mam, I do really want to have it here at home, but . . .'

'But what?'

'I want Maria to be there.'

'Of course you do,' said Maureen. She looked down the garden, and after a moment, she smiled and said, 'Everything will be grand by January.' She felt very confident. A plan was formulating in her mind. She would get Martin to help, and maybe even Paddy.

'What do you mean?' Her mother sounded very sure of herself. Daddy must have told her everything last night, and maybe he was finally coming around to the idea that Maria wasn't such a pariah.

'Your dad will soon see that he can't keep Maria away for ever.'

'But there's no guarantee that he will have changed his mind by then, is there?'

'I'll sound him out, but in the meantime, you can ring up some places and see what dates are available. Isn't January an awful cold old month to be getting married in?'

She was torn between an early wedding that would bring Maria home sooner, or a later one where there might be a bit of sunshine. 'Easter would be nice. You could have daffodils and freesias, and –'

'The longer we leave it, the more planning we'll do, and the more stressed out we'll get. We want to keep it very small and simple.'

'You're right. I've never been a great one for these big, flashy weddings. So, who are we going to invite?' She sat with pen poised, mentally going through all the neighbours' weddings they had been to.

Aileen and her mother launched into the thorny subject of keeping it to close family and friends and their gentle bickering was what Sean heard drifting over the hedge as he came back from playing golf. He was looking forward to joining in with the wedding plans.

When Aileen was married off, that would be two of the offspring sorted out. Hugh had come back at Easter, freckled and healthy, and more mature than when he went away.

It didn't take him long to get a good job up in Dublin, managing the catering in the Exhibition Centre. He had done well for himself in Australia. They didn't see much of him now, because he had to work at weekends, but he was well set up in his own flat.

That only left Maria, who was supposed to be the bright spark out of the three of them. He wondered how she was getting on with Paddy Naughtan. Paddy wouldn't be home any time soon, after poor Ivy's stroke. Not that they were on the best of terms anyway. He was still angry with Paddy for keeping Maria's secret from him. Sean hadn't spoken to him since he found out.

Maureen shot Aileen a warning look as she heard Sean coming through the kitchen to the back garden where they were sitting on canvas deckchairs. 'I'm going to say that you're having the wedding in London,' she said in an urgent whisper. 'Just you stay quiet for the moment.'

Sean was delighted when Maureen looked up and smiled at him, without that tight look on her face that he had got used to seeing for the last few months. It was good to clear the air, every so often. Maybe it was best that he hadn't told her the whole story about his mother. Maybe everything would be all right. Some things were best left unsaid, and they had got this far without upsetting the apple-cart.

'So, tell me how far you've got,' he said, unfolding another deckchair for himself, and putting it down on the patio beside Aileen's.

'I invited Doctor Moran today anyway, but who else have you got on the list?'

Aileen sighed.

Chapter Thirty-seven

Maria ran through the gate, panting. She was late again. Work was so busy that she sometimes didn't notice the time. The childminder would give her a hard time again. Her husband came in at six-thirty and she wanted Molly to be gone by then. Twice in the last week, Maria had turned up just before seven. The sullen husband was eating his dinner in the kitchen, and Molly was in the sitting-room, tied into her pushchair with her jacket on, her little cheeks flushed with the heat. Maria was mortified. She was going to give Amanda an extra tenner this week to make up for twice being late. But she was going to say that she wasn't happy with Molly being stuck in a room by herself with her coat on, either.

She gasped, 'Sorry!' as the front door opened, expecting to see Amanda standing there. It was the husband. He pointed at Molly who was bundled up in the pushchair again, sitting in front of a *Teletubbies* video.

'Is Amanda in?' asked Maria.

'No, she's gone out,' he said gruffly, holding the door rigidly.

Maria didn't have the nerve to say anything to him. Molly smiled when she saw her mother, and reached out her arms to be picked up. Maria kissed her on the forehead and wheeled her into the hall, blushing under the stare of the man, whose pungent aftershave filled her nostrils. She shuddered as the front door banged behind them, and Molly jerked in her seat and whimpered.

Forget an extra tenner; tomorrow she would give Amanda such a hard time. How dare she leave Molly with that creepy guy? Maria had never heard him utter a complete sentence before this evening. God knows what would have happened if Molly had cried. He would probably have thrown something at her. Maria's heart was pounding as she reached the bus stop.

She unstrapped the baby so she could cuddle her while they waited for the bus. Molly's smile just melted her. She was such a good baby, never complaining when she was woken up early in the mornings and dressed in a hurry. Usually she was very placid in the evenings, sitting contentedly playing on the floor while Maria changed out of her work-clothes and made the dinner. Then they would have a little while playing together before Maria pulled the cord of the lullaby mobile and lay Molly down to sleep after her bath. Often, Maria would sit on the big old chair in Molly's room and just watch her sleeping. The intense love she felt for her was something she never could have imagined. She realised that she had always taken her own parents' love for granted, because it was such an integral part of her life. Since she was fourteen, she had thought that being *in* love was her mission in life, the thrill of attraction, the flirting, the novelty of a new relationship seemed to be enough. But there was always an element of choice – how involved she wanted to become, what compromises she was prepared to make, how much of herself she gave away. That, she could see now, was just a selfish love, as much about receiving as giving. Her love for Molly went miles beyond those limits – it was totally unconditional.

The Indian summer was hanging on, and they were hot and sticky by the time they got home. Molly's cheeks were still bright pink and she was a bit crotchety. Maria ran a cool bath and piled all the plastic toys into it before undressing the baby. As Molly's dress was slipped off, she winced. Maria took off her vest and was just laying her down to take off her nappy when she noticed slight red marks across Molly's chest.

She must be growing out of that dress. Maria picked it up again and stretched the elastic in the bodice. It didn't seem too tight. Maybe it was just a bit of heat rash. They splashed and played in the bath, and Molly giggled when they poured water into her plastic dolphin and made it spurt water onto her little round tummy.

Maria looked down on her daughter's dark hair, just beginning to curl at the nape of her plump neck, and she felt such a surge of love and tenderness that she hugged her tightly. Molly squealed, and her face crumpled up. This was very strange. Maybe she was coming down with something.

Maria sat her on a big fluffy white towel to dry while she pulled on her own clothes, and wondered if she should take her temperature. Then she remembered the thermometer was broken.

'Never mind, love,' she said as she tucked her into bed. 'If you're still feeling funny in the morning, I'll bring you to the doctor's.'

Bright white sunlight was streaming across the bed when Joe woke up. He checked his watch and then looked across at Mike's bed. No surprises. It was ten past ten and Mike's bed had not been slept in. Joe yawned and stretched. It had become almost a routine now. He had the apartment to himself most of the time. Mike was either at work, on the opposite shifts to Joe, or staying with one of the numerous girls he had shagged since they got here. He was really living up to the stereotype of a serial holiday romancer, waving one girl off on the flight to London or Birmingham or Dublin, and practically picking up another one coming down the hot metal steps from the next plane. He wondered how Mike had left things with Pauline. They seemed so right together – but it was none of his business.

Every night, the bar was packed with girls in halter-neck tops, glowing and giggling after a day on the beach and an evening downing jugs of sangria. Joe could have had his pick. Being a barman seemed to have some kind of cachet all of its own. But he found himself scanning the crowds for a particular toss of the head, and Maria's long dark hair and slim legs. He had this bizarre fantasy that she would just turn up one day and sit at the bar and order a drink. Needless to say, in his fantasy she wasn't carrying a baby around on her hip.

He sighed and swung his legs out of bed, wincing as the soles of his feet touched the cold ceramic tiles. He padded over to the fridge and took out a huge wedge of watermelon. He had time for breakfast and a swim before his shift started at noon. He sat on the balcony overlooking the dusty white carpark, and savoured the cool breeze. The juice of the melon dribbled down his chin and he sucked it harder, enjoying the freedom of sitting in just his boxer shorts, dripping juice everywhere. He really would have to snap out of this obsession with Maria.

He had screwed up and lost her, and there was no point in dwelling on it any longer. She wasn't interested. Life must go on. Tonight he might meet someone and if he could just chill out he might even enjoy being with another girl. He grabbed his towel and the shorts and T-shirt with the club logo that he wore behind the bar and headed for the beach.

The sun dried the seawater from his tingling skin as he wrote a postcard to his mother. It was a weekly duty that saved him having to call from a public box and wait while a nurse ran down the corridor to get his mother to the telephone. While he was queuing for stamps in the post office, he heard his name being called, and he looked up to see a postal clerk waving a white envelope at a tall fair-skinned English guy at the counter. 'Joseph Shaw?'

The guy shook his head.

Joe stepped forward and flipped open his wallet to show his driver's licence. 'I'm Joe Shaw,' he said, and took the envelope. It was just addressed to him at the Aghios Nickolaious post office. The poor clerk behind the counter must have waved it at every vaguely Northern European-looking man who came in.

Joe recognised his mother's newly spindly handwriting. It was different to the strong, bold print she had used before the accident, but it was still quite legible. He went and sat on the stone pier of the harbour with his legs dangling down, and opened the envelope.

Dear Joe,

I hope this reaches you. I lost the address of the apartment, so I had no other way to get it to you. Thank you for the lovely postcards. I have them stuck up on the wall in my room and they certainly brighten the place up a bit. I am much happier here, since I decided to make a few friends instead of just waiting for Friday to come for you to take me out.

I have been very selfish, asking you to give up all that time to look after me, so when you come back, I won't expect to see you every weekend. You have to live your life as well. I hope you're having a great time, and don't work too hard. Be careful in the sun. I'm looking forward to seeing you next month.

Lots of love
Mum

He sighed. She was definitely on the road to recovery. This was much more like her than the needy, tearful woman he had seen over the last year. In some ways, it was easier to love her when her guard was down, and she wasn't constantly going on at him to do well, or to live up to her expectations. But he had missed his strong, tough decisive mother, and maybe now she was coming back. He tucked the letter in his pocket and went to work, whistling.

Chapter Thirty-eight

Maria was looking forward to seeing Aileen and Paul. It had been a hectic week.

Amanda had looked a bit sheepish when Maria handed her the extra money this morning. But she got very defensive as soon as Maria said she wasn't happy about Molly being left with the husband.

'He's very good with kids. Anyway, if you turn up late, I can't hang around, can I? I've got other things to do.'

'I'm sure he is very good with children, but you're the one I'm paying to look after Molly, not him,' said Maria.

'He wouldn't touch a hair on her head.'

Maria held her ground. 'Amanda, I will give you a commitment not to be late, but if I pay you to look after Molly until six-thirty, I expect you to be there, not someone else.'

Amanda said defiantly, 'Well, you'll just have to make sure you're on time then, won't you?' She tucked the money into her purse, and picked Molly up. 'Come on, sweetheart. We're going to a play group this morning.'

Maria mulled over the conversation as she watched the Friday-evening commuters cramming themselves, sweating, into the Underground carriage. It was amazing how people always made room for the pushchair, so that Maria and Molly had their own bubble of clear space among the hot and bothered passengers.

Molly was smiling at people and waving, and getting a great response. She loved an audience, especially when she could make them smile back at her.

Maria had a niggling worry about the arrangement with Amanda, but she couldn't afford to pay for a registered childminder. It was already a struggle. There was no point in changing when Molly loved Amanda, just because the husband was a bit creepy. Maria would just have to make sure she picked her up on time in the evenings from now on. She would have a word with Paddy, to see if there was any way of getting some extra help in the office to get through all the work.

They got off the tube at Brixton, and Maria remembered that first morning she had arrived here with Aileen, overwhelmed by the noises and the bustle. She felt a lift of exuberance as they got to the top of the steps just as a number three bus pulled in. A black teenager with headphones blaring reached down and helped her to lift Molly on to the bus, without even making eye contact. Maria said 'Thanks', but there was no chance he could have heard her, and he swung up the stairs without breaking his step, rocking his head in time to the music.

She looked out the window of the bus as they passed the Ritzy Cinema, and glanced at the film listings. She hadn't been to see a film in ages. The last one had been with Andy; some Quentin Tarantino one with loads of violence and his kind of black humour.

She wondered how Andy was. If they bumped into each other now, would they pretend to be friends, or just ignore each other? It would depend on Andy's mood. That unpredictability was something she didn't miss. The apprehension she felt when she heard his key in the door. Would he make her laugh with stories about work and then snuggle up on the couch, or would he be mean and horrible, and go off to the pub after his dinner? At least now, she could control her little world with Molly. She didn't wish for a man at all. Joe and Andy hadn't exactly inspired her with confidence.

Paul opened the door, grinning. 'Hello, strangers! We haven't seen you for ages.'

He kissed them both. A delicious smell of roasting peppers and stir-fried chicken wafted from the kitchen. Aileen came out of the bathroom with fresh make-up on, smelling of Hugo perfume.

'Hiya!' she said, hugging Maria. She picked Molly

up. 'She's the spitting image of you, isn't she?' She tickled her and Molly giggled. 'You're going to be a little heartbreaker, aren't you?'

'So, who else is coming?' asked Maria, admiring Aileen's new top. Aileen never used to get dressed up for her before.

'No one else, why?'

'I was just wondering,' said Maria as she handed over the Oddbins bag to Paul. It was nice to be a proper guest, she thought, as Paul made approving noises about her choice of wine. She was delighted she had asked the man in the shop for his advice. Paul handed her a gin and tonic and she nibbled on mesquite-flavoured Kettle chips. She had a lovely Friday-night winding-down feeling.

Molly entertained them for half an hour, rolling over and trying to pull herself up to see the fish in the aquarium. Paul held her over the water and let her trail her fingers in it, and she was delighted. Maria told them all about the new job, and Aileen asked about Ivy.

'It's really sad. She hasn't been making good progress with the physio, and Paddy says the prognosis isn't great,' said Maria. 'I feel sorry for Paddy, because he's torn between wanting to stay with her, and having to come into the office and keep the business going. That's why I'm ending up working really long hours.'

'Maybe he could get some more help in?' suggested Aileen.

'That's what I'm going to ask him for next week. I

327

decided on the way over here,' said Maria. 'I'd better get this girl ready for bed before she gets cranky.' She swooped down and picked Molly up off the floor.

Aileen kissed Molly on the cheek. 'Night night, sweetheart. See you in the morning,'

After she had put Molly down to sleep, Maria went back to the others.

'So, how are the wedding plans going?' she asked.

'All right,' said Aileen. 'Great,' said Paul, simultaneously.

'Do I detect a note of disagreement here?' asked Maria, grinning.

'It's OK for him. He doesn't have to ring up Father Duggan and lie through his teeth about going to Mass over here all the time,' said Aileen, throwing Paul a mock dirty look.

'Do they mind that you're not a Catholic?'

'Apparently not. We both have to go to these pre-marriage courses though – three months of it, can you believe that?' said Paul. 'It's a load of nonsense, as far as I'm concerned.'

'Have you set a date, yet?'

'The twentieth of February was the soonest we could get. It's a Friday, but otherwise we'd have to wait even longer,' said Aileen. 'Guess what? We're having the meal at Ballinahinch Castle.'

'Wow, Aileen, that is such a brilliant place!' said Maria. 'It'll cost you a fortune though, won't it?'

'We're keeping it very small.'

'Small but special,' said Paul. 'No aunties, uncles,

second cousins twice removed, and only really good friends.'

'How did that go down at home?' asked Maria, looking sympathetically at Aileen.

'Not great. Daddy was just back from inviting Doctor Moran when I told him, so he wasn't too happy.'

'Well, Mam and Dad have been to two weddings in that family,' said Maria.

'That's what he said. But he shouldn't have invited anyone,' said Aileen indignantly. 'We're paying for most of it, so it's our wedding.'

'You're dead right,' said Maria. 'But I don't envy you.'

'I think Daddy was afraid we'd do a registry-office one over here, if he pushed it too far, so he shut up after a while,' said Aileen, grinning wickedly.

'And would you?'

'Not really, but it was no harm to have the threat up our sleeves,' said Aileen, standing up to change the CD.

'I don't know why we couldn't,' said Paul, winking at Maria. 'Aileen, you haven't been to Mass for, what, seven years?'

'Except for when I go home.'

'That doesn't count. You only do that to keep the peace.'

'I know, but I hate registry-office weddings. They're so impersonal. In and out in twenty minutes. Do you remember Ken and Sandy's? We were in a queue, and as we were coming out, the next lot were going in. It was like a conveyor belt.'

'Really?' said Maria.

'Oh, yeah. They just do the legal stuff, sign the book, and that's it. No messing about with candles and hymns and all that,' said Paul. 'That's what I like about it.'

'But you don't mind having it in the church, either, do you?' said Aileen in a little girl voice, pretending to need reassurance.

'Not if that's what you want,' he said, kissing her on the forehead on the way into the kitchen.

'He's lovely,' said Maria, forgetting all her earlier thoughts about how good life was without a man.

'Isn't he?' said Aileen, hugging herself. 'Listen, Maria. I said to Mam that I want you at the wedding. She thinks she can get Daddy to come around to the idea.'

'But you didn't say anything to him?'

'No, Mam wants to do it her way.' Aileen looked away. She couldn't stop thinking about her dad's secret. It was burning a hole inside her. Maria had a right to know about her grandmother too. She might be tempted to tell Maria except that it would only make Sean look even worse in Maria's eyes, and that wouldn't be fair. She told herself she wasn't being a coward.

Maria couldn't help feeling a surge of resentment, but she hid it. Aileen was so excited, she didn't want to spoil it. Daddy's word was law, no matter how much Aileen wanted her at the wedding.

'So we'll just have to wait and see, then?' she said, trying to sound optimistic.

'It's only five months away!' said Aileen, her eyes bright.

'That's so exciting! Does Paul know what Ballinahinch Castle looks like?'

'I got Daddy to drive me out there when I was home and I took loads of photos. Paul thinks it's great.'

'So, how many people are you having?' For the first time, Maria felt like the big sister, and it was a nice feeling.

'It works out about fifty, I think, but if all the English people can't travel, it might be less.'

'That will still cost you a fortune, won't it?'

'It's not the money. I want to have a day out with the people we really like, in a really special place. At least this way we don't have to work out which cousins to invite without offending anyone.'

'Offend the lot of them!' said Paul, coming back into the room flourishing a tea towel. 'Ladies, dinner is served.'

'I'm a bit worried about Molly,' said Maria as they finished eating and Paul offered to make coffee.

'Why, is she not well?' asked Aileen.

'No, she's not sick. I don't think so anyway. But sometimes when I pick her up in the evenings, she's very quiet, and a bit jittery.'

'Is she still at Amanda's?' Aileen asked as she plunged the cafetière. The aroma of rich-roast coffee overlaid the perfume from the vanilla-scented candle in the centre of the table.

'Yes. The husband really gives me the creeps. He's so rude. The problem is, if Molly isn't happy there, should I move her, or would she be the same anywhere?'

'Does she cry when you leave her in the mornings?' asked Aileen.

'Only sometimes. Amanda is so good with her, she calms her down straight away. They have loads of toys there, as well, from Amanda's own kids. Bouncers and cars and walkers and everything.'

'So what's the problem?' asked Paul.

'There's been a couple of times when I'm late that Amanda has gone out. I think she does an evening cleaning job or something. And the husband is there, minding Molly.'

'That's not right,' said Aileen.

'I know, but what can I do?'

'You should say to Amanda that you're not happy with it.'

'I did, but she said her husband was great with kids, and he wouldn't lay a finger on her.'

'That's a funny thing to say,' said Paul.

'I know. I think that's what's worrying me. This could be really paranoid, but the other evening I saw red marks on Molly's chest, and I thought it was the elastic on her dress. But what if it was something else?'

Aileen's voice was highpitched as she said, 'Maria, are you thinking he might do something to her?'

332

Maria blushed. She hadn't meant to say anything. It sounded a bit melodramatic now. It was only a tiny doubt in her mind, not even a suspicion really.

'I don't know. It's a terrible thing to say about anyone.'

'It's a lot more terrible if he is doing something,' said Paul. 'You read so much stuff in the papers about childminders shaking children, never mind their dodgy husbands.'

'I'm not sure if I'm overreacting,' said Maria, looking at Aileen who had gone very quiet.

'I'd take Molly out of there altogether and put her with someone else,' said Aileen.

'You don't want to take any risks, do you?' said Paul.

'No, but what will I say to Amanda?'

'Just tell her you've found somewhere closer to home,' said Aileen. 'You'll never have to see her again, so you can say whatever you like.'

'You're right. But it's not very easy to find someone else as handy.'

'It's worth it, seriously, Maria, to know that Molly is safe when you leave her for eight hours at a time.'

'I know it is. You're right. Now that I've said it out loud, it sounds worse than it is, but I'll get off work early this week and see if I can organise a place in a nursery or something.'

Paul suggested a game of Jenga, and they sat cross-legged on the floor with their coffee and the After Eight mints that Maria had brought. The Verve blasted from the stereo, and Aileen tried to convince Paul that the vibrations would make the tower fall down. He said her hysterical squealing was a lot more likely to topple it. The girls were delighted when Paul pulled out a piece with a great flourish and the bricks tumbled down. Molly slept through all the noise.

Chapter Thirty-nine

Maria's plans to ask Paddy for time off were forgotten on Monday morning. When she arrived at the yard, a pall of silence hung over it. There was no clanging of scaffolding poles or revving engines. She ducked and climbed through the small wicket gate, surprised that the big gates weren't open for the vans. Some of the lads were standing in front of the Portakabin, drinking tea. The steam rose silently from their polystyrene cups, and as Maria got closer, she realised that there was none of the usual Monday-morning banter. The lads were shifting from one foot to the other and talking quietly.

'What's the matter? Did all your football teams lose at the weekend?' she asked Tommy, who usually flirted like mad with her.

'No.' Tommy looked down. 'Ivy copped it last night.'

'What do you mean?'

'She died. Another stroke last night, apparently,' he said. 'Paddy's inside.' He nodded towards the office.

Maria gulped. She had a superstitious feeling that she shouldn't have wanted Ivy's job so badly. 'God, I better go in to him – is he all right – what's he doing here, anyway?' she asked, all in one breath.

Tommy shrugged. Maria passed through the silent ranks and went into the office. Paddy sat slumped in his big chair, ashen-faced.

'They told me, outside,' she said.

She went and stood beside his chair, and touched his shoulder. He turned to her, sobbing, and hugged her to him, his head pressed against her breasts. He took huge, heavy gulps of air. Maria stroked his wispy hair. She looked up to the ceiling and her eyes filled with tears.

'Why did God take her away? She was a good woman,' said Paddy. He sat up, and when he saw Maria's wet blouse front, he mumbled, 'Sorry'.

There was a time when she would never have allowed Paddy to touch her, but things had changed. He didn't give her the funny looks any more. Not since Ivy got sick. As if that would be adding insult to her injury. 'It's OK, Paddy. I'll make you a nice cup of tea.'

When Maria came back, he was piling papers up on the desk. 'I don't know why I came in here,' he said, 'but I couldn't think at home.'

Maria gave him the tea. 'Drink that, and we'll work out what needs to be done.'

He winced at the taste.

'I put loads of sugar in it. You'll need the energy.'

Maria sat down and started making a list of things to do. An hour later, she had booked his flight to Galway, and made enquiries about how Ivy's body could be brought home. She tracked down the telephone number for Father Duggan, so that Paddy could speak to him about the funeral. Then she spent half an hour ringing customers to apologise for the delay in their jobs starting. She organised the lads, and by ten o'clock the yard was empty of vans and men. She gave Paddy some papers to sign before he left.

'You're a great help to me,' he said. 'I'll be gone for about a week. Will you be able to manage? I'll have the mobile with me all the time.'

'Of course we'll manage,' said Maria. 'You go home and pack now. Your flight is at seven forty-five, but you have to change in Dublin, so you won't be in Galway until late. Have you somewhere you can stay, in town?'

'Arragh, I'll worry about that when I get there,' he said.

'Don't worry about things here, anyway,' said Maria.

'I won't, with you in charge,' he said, hefting a pile of papers into his battered briefcase.

He stood in the doorway, hesitating to step over the threshold into the yard. Maria pushed him gently in the small of his back. 'Go on now, Paddy. You'll be all right.'

He turned to her. 'Why would I want to go on living, without Ivy?' he asked bleakly.

'She wouldn't tolerate talk like that,' said Maria briskly. 'She's looking down at you now. You have to be brave to get through the next few days.'

'Few days? What about the rest of my life?'

'One step at a time, Paddy. Take it easy.' She hugged him, and kissed his bristly grey cheek.

He squeezed her hand. 'You're right, love.' He turned away. 'I'll ring you from Galway tomorrow.'

'God bless. Drive safely,' said Maria as he climbed into his car.

He waved as he drove out the big gates, and Maria collapsed into her swivel-chair, sending it skittering backwards across the linoleum-covered floor. She sat motionless for a while, staring at the scum on her cup of tea, and then she picked up the telephone to ring her father. She recognised Kate Lally's voice when she answered, '*Scoil Réalt na Mara*,' in her sing-song accent. Star of the Sea school. It sounded more musical in English.

Maria didn't even think before she said in English, 'Hello, Kate. It's Maria here. Is my Dad free?'

'Ah, Maria. *Conas a tá tú? Nach bhfuil focal Gaeilge agat, ar chor ar bith?*'

Maria couldn't conjure up any Irish, sitting in a dusty London builders' yard. Her heart was pounding.

'I'm very well, thanks Kate, and yourself?'

Kate gave up on the Irish. 'Grand, thank God. Divil

a bit to complain about. Your Daddy should be in for his elevenses any minute now. I'll just see if he's coming down the corridor.'

Maria heard the big black old receiver clanging onto the desk as Kate went to the door of the school office. Maria could almost smell the floor polish and see the picture of the Sacred Heart on the office wall with the little red light burning underneath it. When she was small, she used to be frightened of the open heart pumping in Jesus's chest. She thought it would leak blood down the wall, like the blood that dripped from His hands and feet on the crucifix in the church.

'Here he is now, *a ghrá*,' said Kate.

'Hello, Dad?'

'Maria?' Sean felt a pang as he realised he had almost forgotten what his youngest daughter sounded like.

'Hi, Dad, it's me.' Maria had thought about ringing Mam, but that would be taking the easy way out. Now wasn't the time to be worrying about herself.

'Is everything all right?' It must be bad news, for her to be ringing him at the school.

'I'm afraid I have some bad news.'

'Is it the child?' No, he thought, even as he said it. She would have rung her mother about that.

'No, it's Ivy Naughtan. She had another stroke last night, and she passed away.' The old-fashioned words came automatically to her lips.

'May God have mercy on her soul,' said Sean. 'Is Paddy on his way home?'

'He is. He'll be getting into Galway at about half past ten tonight. He has nowhere organised to stay.'

'Do you know when the funeral is?'

'Not yet. He's to ring Father Duggan tonight. Will you get some flowers, from me?' Maria was desperately trying not to cry.

'I will, of course. Thanks for ringing me, love.'

'OK, Dad. *Slán*.' The goodbye in Irish seemed more comforting. She couldn't say any more and she hung up. Finally the tears came. They poured down her cheeks, and she sobbed, gasping for breath. When the switchboard lights flashed, she let her bright answering-machine voice take messages. She used all her tissues and had to raid the toilet-roll cupboard. There was no noise from the yard. No rustling sounds from Paddy's office. No Ivy offering tea or giving out to the lads. Her Dad's voice echoed in her head. She hadn't heard it for so long. He had called her 'love'. Did it just slip out, or did he mean it?

Chapter Forty

Sean drove into Galway after dinner and the bacon and cabbage sat in a lump on his stomach. Maureen offered to come and keep him company, but he needed the time by himself to plan what he would say to Paddy. They hadn't spoken since last summer, he calculated. Not long after Maria had got that job with him. Sean remembered the raging anger he had felt at the time, when Paddy told him he was narrow-minded and judgmental and living in the Dark Ages. Now he couldn't conjure up any anger at all, not even a glowing ember. Sympathy for Paddy and sadness at Ivy's death filled him. Well, it was never too late to make your peace. The traffic-lights changed and he drove out the airport road. He saw the lights of the plane circling overhead before it landed, and he was relieved. He could be standing at the Arrivals door before Paddy came out to get himself a taxi. It was hard on Paddy. He would have to organise everything for the funeral, with Ivy's two sisters in America and the brother in Australia.

The doors swung wide and Paddy was the second person through. Sean hardly recognised the grey-faced man in front of him. He had lost a lot of his hair, and sagging jowls had replaced his happy round face. He was bent over to one side with the weight of his suitcase, and looked as if he had shrunk to half his normal size.

Sean stepped forward hesitantly.

'Paddy, how are you?'

Paddy looked up and summoned a smile for Sean, who clapped him gently on the back, and took his case. 'Come on. I have the car out here – you're staying with us,' he said, leading the way.

Paddy followed. 'It will be good to see Maureen,' he said to Sean's retreating back.

'She offered to come here with me, but I said to stay at home,' said Sean as he opened the boot of the car.

Paddy knew why. But somehow, no words of reconciliation were needed. Sean drove at a steady pace out the coast road, and they talked about Ivy and the stroke, and about when the relations were flying in for the funeral.

When they reached Casla, with only five minutes left to home, Paddy turned and said, 'Maria is a little star, you know. You should have seen her this morning. She had me organised, and the customers sorted out and the lads out on the road before I could blink.'

Sean smiled but he didn't say anything. How much

better she would have done for herself if she had finished college. She was too good to be a glorified dogsbody in a builders' yard. Of course he couldn't say that to Paddy. 'It was she who rang me to tell me you were on your way.' Her voice had sounded so tentative and sad.

Paddy continued, 'And Sean, Molly is only gorgeous. Ivy doted on her. Sweet-natured as anything, and as cute as her mother was, when she was small herself.'

Sean still couldn't think of Maria as a mother. She was only a girl. His little girl.

He turned to Paddy and said, 'I've tried to get used to the idea, Paddy, but I can't.' They pulled into the driveway of the house and he turned off the headlights. In the dark, Paddy reached across and laid his hand on Sean's shoulder.

'What is it you can't get used to, Sean? That Maria is old enough to make her own decisions, and even to be a mother in her own right?'

'That's what Father Duggan said. But Paddy, isn't it obvious? She's no better than my own mother was. She let me down, and ruined her life into the bargain.'

'She hasn't ruined her life, Sean. She's just living a different life to the one you might have planned for her. And you only think she's let you down because she's not doing what you wanted for her. It's a very narrow-minded way of looking at things, Sean. '

'It was strange, talking to her on the phone today. I

really miss her. She was always my favourite you know, even though you're not supposed to favour any of your children.'

'I know. She's always been Daddy's Girl.'

It wasn't the time for Paddy to mention his own theory that Sean seemed to be trying to punish Maria for what his mother had done to him.

Paddy wondered whether he had done the right thing, telling Maureen the full story about the mother's suicide. She had rung him a while back to ask for his advice about how to get around Sean.

On the one hand, telling the secret was a betrayal of his lifelong friendship with Sean, but on the other, he could sense Maureen's frustration with Sean's completely irrational attitude to the situation. For the sake of their marriage, Maureen deserved to know the full picture, and then maybe she would give Sean a bit of time and space to come around.

Maureen heard the car and came and stood at the front door. With the hall light shining behind her head, Paddy thought she looked like an angel. She came forward and hugged him. Only twelve hours before, her daughter had done the same. Sean sat for another second behind the wheel of the car, and then got out and carried the suitcase into the hall.

Maureen wondered if they had made their peace. She ushered Paddy into the kitchen, where she had a pot of soup simmering and a fresh brown-bread loaf steaming on the rack over the stove.

'Did she go quickly?' Maureen asked as Paddy sat at the table.

'She did, thank God, in her sleep. The doctor said she wouldn't have had any pain.'

'If you have to go, that's the way,' said Sean, taking refuge in the platitude.

Paddy looked across at him. 'It is. God love her, she was only sixty-two. But I know she would have been glad to go, instead of hanging on, and gradually losing all her faculties.'

'She was a very active woman,' said Maureen, who had always envied Ivy's involvement in the business.

'She was,' said Paddy. He ate the soup hungrily, although he felt guilty for having an appetite. He didn't feel the need to make conversation with these old friends. There was a real comfort in the few minutes of silence as they each visited their own memories of Ivy.

'I put you into Maria's old room,' said Maureen as they climbed the stairs to bed. Paddy wondered if calling it her old room was a way of saying that Maria didn't live here any more. Maureen didn't even notice that she'd done it. Paddy lay awake most of the night, thinking about his years with Ivy. He saw her smiling face, undistorted by the drooping lip and sagging cheek of her previous stroke. He was dancing with her in the village hall, and walking with her on the coral beach in Carraroe. He finally fell asleep as he remembered kissing her in the tiny kitchen of their first flat in London.

Father Duggan said some nice words about Ivy, a woman he had known since he came to the parish thirty years before. The October wind cut through them as they stood at the edge of the graveyard in the slanting rain. The wreaths had shrivelled in the cold, and the petals of the flowers were bruised and beaten flat in the rain. Paddy's cheeks were red and his eyes were brimming with tears as he threw a handful of sodden earth onto the dark lid of the coffin.

'Goodbye, my love,' he said under his breath.

Loneliness swept over him as he looked across at the bleak grey water of the Atlantic swell beyond the stony fields. Sean stood behind him, and took his arm as he turned.

'I have no one left now, only my friends,' said Paddy, rubbing the rain and tears from his face with the rough sleeve of his coat.

Maureen wiped away her own tears and thought how sad it was that Paddy was a lonely old man before his time, with no children to lean on. She stepped over to Ivy's relations, to invite them back to the house. Their faces were pinched with cold, and they seemed to be in a jet-lagged daze. The sisters hadn't slept for twenty-four hours since leaving America.

One of them said, 'It only finally hit me when I saw Paddy throwing in the clay.'

Maureen stroked her coat sleeve, and Sean overheard her saying, as she led them to the car, 'It's hard to believe that someone is dead, when you're living far away, because you don't see them all the time.'

One of the sisters nodded, unable to speak. 'I wish I'd called her more often. But you get caught up in your own little world, don't you, and you forget about the people who are important.'

'Ivy knew you loved her. She was always talking about you when she came home. She really admired you both, and looked up to you.'

Maureen always knew the right thing to say, thought Sean as he linked arms with Paddy, locked in silence. He couldn't think of any words of comfort as they picked their way across the graveyard.

Maureen had a big fire on in the living-room, and she soon had them all thawing out with tea and sandwiches. Paddy's mobile phone rang stridently over the murmuring voices, intruding into the cosy room like a siren. Paddy fumbled in his coat pocket, surprised that he had forgotten to turn the phone off.

'Hello?' he said, stepping into the hall and standing by the stairs.

'Paddy, it's me,' said Maria. 'I just wanted to see if you were OK. Is it all over?'

'It is. I'm at your mam and dad's house having a cup of tea.'

'Did it go all right?' she asked, thinking that at least

her dad must be on speaking terms with Paddy again, if everyone had gone back to the house.

'As well as could be expected. It's a horrible wet old day, which didn't help.'

'Are you staying with Mam and Dad?'

'I am. They've been very good to me. I'll tell them you rang. I'd better go back inside now. Thanks for ringing, love.'

'Bye, Paddy. I just wanted to let you know I was thinking about you. Will you be coming back tomorrow?'

'I will. I'll come into the yard on Friday, so I'll see you then. God bless. Bye.'

Sean stood rigid on the landing at the top of the stairs, trying not to make the floorboards creak. That must have been Maria. She was ringing Paddy on his mobile phone, in her own house. Paddy went back into the living-room, and Sean heard the quiet chat and the chink of the china teacups before the door closed. He sat down on the third step of the stairs and stared at the telephone on the old wobbly table.

Why didn't she ring on that phone? Did she not even want to talk to her mam? Suddenly Sean wanted to hear her voice again, saying 'Daddy,' and her warm laugh. He slid down one step and reached across to the telephone. He didn't know her number. He didn't even know her address. She had a whole new life, without him. Maureen only told him little snippets of news about her when she thought he was in a good mood. Imagine that. His own daughter. He couldn't ask Paddy for the number. Maureen would think he had lost his head altogether, getting an urge to ring Maria in the middle of a wake. He stood up and went into the living-room. It wasn't too early in the day to offer people whiskey.

Chapter Forty-one

'It's not as bad as last year,' said Joe to the girl from second Med he had met in Ryan's the week before. 'I only go home every third weekend, and she's in a nursing home the rest of the time.'

'There's not many guys who would even do that much,' she said, looking at him doe-eyed. She had seen him in the library at all hours, his hair sticking up on his head from running his fingers through it when he was concentrating. She thought he looked interesting; kind of intense, but attractive in a distracted sort of way. She made sure he noticed her in Ryan's, by standing beside him at the bar, and smiling at him across the room when she caught his eye. Joe liked the look of her. She had a nice smile, and was easy to talk to. He had come back to college this term with a renewed determination to get over Maria. The holiday-romance idea hadn't worked.

He just wanted to meet someone else now. This girl had potential. Mike said she was sexy-looking, but Mike had just had so much sex over the summer, he couldn't think about anything else. He wondered if Mike would just resume as normal with Pauline, or if he would be shamed into telling her he had gone out with other women while he was away. Pauline was besotted with him, but she wouldn't take any crap either, and she had a way of finding things out. Mike shouldn't be too sure of himself on that front.

'Can I get you another drink?' Joe suddenly realised that he hadn't said anything for a while.

'I'll have a glass of Guinness, thanks.' She was relieved that he had come back to the land of the living. He had been staring glassy-eyed at the table. He must be thinking about his mother, she thought, hoping he wouldn't turn out to be one of those real Mammy's boys. Now he was standing at the bar, looking a bit like an absent-minded professor. He didn't look like a future surgeon. She couldn't see him commanding theatre staff and wielding his scalpel like the consultant she had seen on her visit to the teaching hospital. He was more the cuddly GP with the reassuring bedside manner.

The girl shook her head and drained her glass as Joe turned from the bar. They were only on their second date, she reminded herself. Joe looked at her long white neck as she swallowed, and when she tossed her hair back and smiled at him, something was wrong. It was like he was being haunted.

'So,' he said briskly as he sat down, 'what did you do for the summer?'

Maria heard Molly's wailing as she opened the gate. She ran up the path and rang the bell, hammering on the door with her other fist. There was a pause, an ominous stillness for a second, and then Molly's wailing started again. The door was wrenched open, and Maria was confronted with the huge bulk of a man she had never seen before. His eyes looked big and dark and his face was streaked with red. He seemed to have some kind of red silk shirt on, which looked bizarre on a man so big. Maria registered fleetingly that he looked guilty as she pushed past him, and she heard someone running upstairs.

She followed Molly's cries to the kitchen, and found her hanging listlessly in a door-bouncer, her pale face looking up as Maria came in. Molly was just drawing a deep shuddering breath to cry again when she saw her mother, and stretched out her arms. Maria swooped down on her and lifted her out, holding her tightly. There was no sign of Amanda, but several pairs of her high-heeled shoes were tossed in a corner. Molly's nappy needed to be changed. A hair-curling tongs was lying on the kitchen table, beside a plastic bag full of make-up. Amanda's kitchen was usually immaculate, so Maria was surprised. She looked around, stuffing Molly's things into her bag, and quickly buttoned her into her coat. The husband came into the room as she slung the bag over her shoulder and lifted the folded pushchair. He smelt of that funny aftershave again. A sickly sweet smell.

'Amanda's just stepped out,' he said quietly. His lips looked unnaturally red and his hair was full and curly. He seemed to have physically shrunk. His piggy eyes were narrowed with stress and his face wasn't the normal greasy grey colour, but had a pale pink sheen.

'You're early, aren't you?' he said, looking at the kitchen clock and trying to stuff the make-up into a drawer.

'Just as well, really, isn't it?' Maria said fiercely as she shouldered past him.

'Aren't you going to wait for Amanda?'

'No, tell her we won't be back.'

Maria walked out the front door, leaving it wide open. Molly was shuddering now, taking little sobbing breaths that Maria could feel against her chest. She dragged the pushchair behind them, not wanting to let Molly out of her arms. They went past the bus stop to a mini-cab office. As they settled in the back seat of the car, Maria remembered the last time she had done this. She brushed away her tears, not wanting to upset Molly. She held her baby on her lap, gently stroking her hair.

When they got home, Maria rang Paddy to tell him she would be late in the morning, and then called the nursery to rearrange the meeting. She couldn't face taking Molly there now. If someone looked crooked at her she would burst into tears, and Molly's face was blotchy and red. Molly fell asleep straight away, without even eating. Maria paced up and down. She was trying not to think the worst. That creep could have done anything to Molly. There were no marks on her; Maria had carefully checked. But what did you look for? The poor child was probably just parked in the bouncer for hours to keep her out of the way while the two men got their weird kicks dressing up and putting on make-up.

She should have listened to Aileen weeks ago and moved Molly straight away. But with Ivy dying and Paddy being away, it had been so busy at work. Finally, this week she had found the crèche and organised the meeting for this afternoon. But it was nearly too late. What if she hadn't turned up when she did? They might have used her in some kind of weird ritual. What did transsexuals do for kicks? No, transvestites, that was it. Not that it mattered what they called themselves. They were weird.

Maria turned on the gas fire and huddled in front of it to stop the uncontrollable shivering. She couldn't sit still. She paced up and down the sitting-room floor, and then kept going into the bedroom to check on Molly's breathing.

Molly looked so vulnerable, lying there on the pillow with her tiny hands curled up on either side of her face. The red mark on her chest a few weeks ago must have been from hanging in that bouncy thing for hours. The poor child. No wonder she was jittery. Maria went back to the living-room and tried Aileen's number. No answer. She left a message.

There was no one else to talk to. Mam wouldn't understand. The world of unregistered childminding transvestites was a million miles from Carraroe. Neighbours minded each other's children, and treated them like one of their own. If that included a smack on the back of the legs, they probably deserved it, and smacks and kisses would be doled out in equal measure. Suddenly, Maria felt a horror of Molly growing up in London. Her friends at school would all come from different cultures. But their parents and their extended families would be able to give them a sense of who they were and where they came from. Molly would only be able to say, 'My mum is Irish'. Like Tommy at work. He called himself Irish, but he had a cockney accent, supported West Ham football club and the only Irish thing he ever did was to go and visit his granny in Kerry every summer as a kid. But one of Molly's grannies didn't even know she existed, and her only grandfather didn't want to know her. It was bad enough not having a daddy, but poor little Molly would think she had no family at all. How was Maria going to give her everything she needed, and hold down a job as well?

When Aileen rang back, Maria had made a decision.

'Aileen, if it's OK with you, I'm coming home for the wedding, whatever Daddy says.'

'Is that what the urgent message was about?' Aileen

asked, her heart still pounding after hearing Maria's stricken voice on the answering machine. 'I thought something must have happened to Molly.'

'It did, Aileen. When I went to pick her up, there was no sign of Amanda, and it was only three o'clock.'

'So was Molly with the horrible husband, then?'

'Yes. I thought he had a job, but maybe he lost it. Anyway, Molly was crying when I got there, hanging in one of those bouncy door-things.'

'And what was your man doing?'

'Some other guy answered the door. A huge, big fella. The husband was running upstairs. Aileen, they were dressing up; they had make-up and shoes, and everything.'

'Oh, my God! That is so creepy. Poor Molly! Where was Amanda? Did you find out?'

Maria felt breathless again, as she remembered Molly's wails. 'No. I didn't wait to find out. I couldn't stay a second longer.'

Aileen was speechless for a few seconds. Then she asked, 'So what are you going to do?'

'We're going to see a crèche in the morning. She'll be much better off with other kids anyway, now that she's nearly one. And I'll take her to the doctor for a check-up.'

'What about the police, or the social services, or someone? You should report it really, Maria.'

'Social services won't be interested. Amanda isn't registered anyway. It will only be his word against mine if I tell the police. I'm just glad to have her out of there, before anything worse happened to her.'

'So what has going home for the wedding got to do with all this?' asked Aileen.

'I just started thinking about home, and how Molly deserves better than this.' Maria looked around the tiny flat.

'I just hope Daddy –'

'I know, and I don't want to ruin your wedding day, Aileen, I swear to God. But I'm sick of running away all the time. I need to face up to him, and to everyone. Even Joe. I don't know if I can bring up Molly over here on my own.'

'Don't worry about ruining my wedding. Daddy wouldn't dare do anything on the day, and I really want you to be there, and so does Paul.'

'Does he? That's nice,' said Maria. Sometimes he seemed to like really her. Other times he acted like she was just irritating. Like a real brother, she supposed. Hugh was exactly the same.

'Is Molly all right now?' Aileen asked.

'She's fine. She's been asleep for the last hour,' said Maria, dragging the telephone flex through the hall to peep into the bedroom. 'Yes, she's still out for the count. I'm a nervous wreck. I keep checking her breathing. I'm sure they didn't do anything.'

'Do take her to the doctor's tomorrow, Maria.'

'I will. I'll let you know. Thanks Aileen.'

Chapter Forty-two

'Can I bring Paul home for Christmas?' Aileen asked her mother one Sunday in December.

'Of course you can, love,' said Maureen. 'It would be great to see him before the wedding.'

'I'm very late booking the flights this year,' said Aileen. 'I was a bit distracted with the wedding plans.'

'You are late, love. Have you any more time off for Christmas this year? It was an awful rush for you with only three days at home last year.'

Hugh had to work over Christmas, and Maureen hadn't even broached the subject of Maria with Sean. There would be other Christmases. Her plan was unfolding at its own pace. Martin was keeping his promise to work on Sean, little by little. So was Paddy. Sean was feeling the pressure and he would give in eventually. Hopefully in time for the wedding. 'I need to save my holidays, because we want to take three weeks for our honeymoon,' said Aileen, wincing.

Paul smiled at her from the sofa. She had been dreading this conversation, and had already put it off for two weeks.

'Oh, yes, of course. You'll want to make the most of that,' said Maureen. 'Did you have any luck looking for the dress in town yesterday?'

'Not really. They're all too flouncy in the shops. Like meringues. I want something plain. I might have it made.'

'Do you know anyone over there?' asked Maureen anxiously.

'Not at all. I'll just find someone in the Yellow Pages. There's loads of entries under Wedding Services.'

'If you think so,' said Maureen doubtfully. 'Maybe you could come over a few days early at Christmas and see if you'd find something in Dublin.'

'Mam, I'll find something in time, don't worry,' said Aileen, raising her eyes to heaven.

Paul was laughing now. The conversation was going exactly as Aileen had predicted. Next, Maureen would ask about the cake.

'And the cake? You'd need to be getting that made soon, if you want the fruit to soak up the flavours. It's the same recipe as a Christmas cake, you know.'

Aileen had to put her hand on the receiver so her mother wouldn't hear her snort of laughter. She mouthed 'Cake,' at Paul.

'Yes. I rang up Lydon's in Galway yesterday and ordered that,' she said, managing to keep a straight face.

'Sure I would have done that for you.'

'I know, Mam, but you'll have enough to do. I'll get you to drop in a deposit cheque the next time you're in Galway, if you don't mind.'

'Grand. Listen, I'll let you go. Your phone bill will be huge at this rate. Give my love to Paul, and tell him we're looking forward to seeing him at Christmas.'

'I will. Bye, Mam.'

She snorted with laughter as soon as she put the receiver down.

'Is it nice to have parents who are so totally predictable?' asked Paul as she snuggled up to him on the sofa and kissed the underside of his chin.

'Sometimes,' she said, looking up at him. 'I'd hate the way your parents decide to do things at the last minute, and you never know what they're up to.'

She looked at the clock. 'Mam will be making a pot of tea now, and cutting cake so they can have it in front of the *News* at nine o' clock.'

'That is so boring!' Paul yawned.

'But it's safe, as well,' said Aileen. 'You always know where you stand.'

'I suppose so. Come on, let's go out for a quick drink. I hate this Sunday-night feeling, just waiting for Monday morning and work to start again.'

'OK.' Aileen jumped up, running her fingers through

her hair, and was standing at the front door in her coat by the time Paul had turned off the television and the stereo.

'Just in case you think I'm set in my ways, like them!' she said, laughing.

'You know what they say about your future wife – you should always look at her mother to see how she's going to turn out,' he teased as he locked the door.

They clattered downstairs with Aileen hitting him on the back of his head with her gloves.

'You were very quiet today, love,' said Maureen as Sean climbed into bed.

'I'm feeling old,' said Sean. 'Most families seem to manage to get together at Christmas. But for two years in a row now, we'll only have Aileen.'

'And Paul. He's family now, as well.' Sean must have the thickest skin in Christendom. He still hadn't said anything about whether Maria could come to the wedding. Maureen had given him loads of hints. But she should know him well enough by now to know that he wasn't a man to respond to hints. You had to hit him over the head with things, like a hammer on a nail, if you wanted to make any headway at all. Subtlety was not his strong point, you might say. Maybe she was being optimistic in her hope that Martin and Paddy would be able to move him in the right direction about Maria. It had taken her two years to convince Sean that Aileen had made the right decision about not going to university. 'Paul is a nice lad, isn't he?' said Sean, rolling over. 'Aileen is lucky to have him.'

'He's lucky to have her, too,' said Maureen indignantly. He was always running Aileen down. She changed the subject. 'Maria was saying on the phone this evening that Molly is nearly walking.'

'That's nice.'

He sighed. He couldn't face this now. Maureen probably thought he was in a good mood because he had just started his Christmas holidays. But he was sad. He missed Maria, and hearing about her only made it worse. She was in a Council flat now. He had visions of her in a high-rise block of flats with a smell of pee in the lifts and noises coming from the other flats through the walls and the ceiling. The soundproofing in those places was always terrible. They probably had cockroaches and damp. Like in that documentary on Channel 4 about the sink estates in London. It was always the single mothers and other undesirables who got put in the worst places. Maria would be there now on her own, with a sad little artificial Christmas tree and only the telly to watch for entertainment. She probably wouldn't even cook herself a proper dinner. But she had no one else to blame but herself. She had made her bed and she must lie in it. If she just came out with it and said she was sorry for what she had put everyone through, it would be a lot easier. But even inside his own head, his arguments were starting to flounder.

He grunted, 'Goodnight.'

Maureen gave up and turned over, wondering if Maria was very lonely. Still, all going well she would be home for the wedding, and that wasn't far away. If only she could get Sean over the first hurdle, then maybe she could nudge him along the rest of the way. Maybe Maria could take a few weeks off work in the summer and come over. Molly would be big enough to enjoy the beach, and they could make sandcastles, and show her the rockpools.

Patience, that was the thing.

Chapter Forty-three

Paddy arrived on Christmas morning laden with parcels. Maria helped him in the door, catching one present as it fell off the pile in his arms.

'Paddy, what have you got with you?'

'Only some presents and a few other bits and pieces,' he said. 'Where's the tree?'

'In here. It's only a little one,' said Maria apologetically. She nearly hadn't bothered, but on her way home from work on Christmas Eve, she saw that Marks & Spencer's were doing a clearance of miniature trees with red ribbons on them for only £4.99, so she had bought one. Now a tinfoil star adorned its crown, and a string of tinsel hung across the mantelpiece over the gas fire. Seven Christmas cards were the only other seasonal decorations. Paddy unpacked a red paper tablecloth, balloons, a box of crackers and three slim red candles. He piled presents under the tree.

'Look, Molly, Santa Claus came to see you!' Maria said, holding Molly up to kiss Paddy's cheek.

Molly smiled, showing off her four front teeth, and stroked Paddy's face.

'You're the best girl, aren't you?' he said. He turned to Maria. 'I think it's good for both of us to be having Christmas together.'

Maria put on a Nat King Cole tape of Christmas carols that she would have been too sad to listen to by herself. They pulled all the crackers and picked out the best hats. They had a drink of Buck's Fizz and toasted Christmas.

Paddy said, 'I hope next year will be a bit easier for you, love.'

'And you, Paddy,' she said, smiling and holding up her glass to him, determined not to be maudlin.

She had rung home earlier on to wish them a Happy Christmas. Her father hadn't come to the phone. She had hoped he would, this year. She hadn't told her mam that Paddy was coming over for dinner. She was sometimes a bit funny about Paddy, and a bit suspicious of him for some reason. The stuffed turkey breast was a great success. Paddy said her gravy was nearly as good as Ivy's.

'That's good enough for me,' she said, delighted.

They sat on the floor beside the tree. Maria handed Paddy a big orange cushion to sit on, and he made a valiant effort to sit cross-legged without keeling over.

'This is from Molly, really,' said Maria, handing him a parcel of an unmistakable shape.

He unwrapped it and found a CD of world music.

'Oh great, is this the one with the British Airways advert on it?'

'Yeah,' Maria smiled. He was always humming that tune in the office. Or at least he used to, before Ivy died.

'That's lovely – thanks, Molly.' He leaned across and kissed the baby's smooth round forehead. He held the back of her head gently in the palm of his hand and pressed his lips to her soft pink skin, closing his eyes. She smelt of baby talcum powder. Molly reached up and pulled his hair, disturbing the carefully arranged strands that spanned his bald patch. He opened his eyes and looked over her head at Maria, who was laughing.

'Just as well Santy hasn't got a beard to pull as well,' she said.

Paddy sat up and pulled a comb out of his back pocket. He carefully swept the long strands back into place. 'I've had years of practice at this,' he said, grinning. 'I'll give you a present now.'

He handed her a soft parcel wrapped in crackling gold paper that looked and felt expensive. Maria was nervous. It was a bit strange, sitting on the floor like this with Paddy – almost like they were a little family. But he was old enough to be her father, and he treated her more and more like a daughter, especially since he had lost Ivy. She was feeling a bit panicky. What if she hated his present? She had never been very good at hiding her reactions. She didn't want to hurt his feelings.

'I'm a wee bit nervous,' said Paddy. 'Ivy didn't like surprises, so she used to tell me exactly what she wanted, and she was always happy with her presents. I've never gone out and, you know, bought a present on spec.' He was looking down at the carpet as Maria unwrapped the parcel. The outside layer of tissue paper was stuck with a gold-embossed sticker. She unpicked it and found a soft, cerise mohair jumper nestling among layers of pale pink paper.

She held it up. 'It's beautiful,' she breathed. 'It must have cost a fortune.'

'Do you like it, really?'

'It is really gorgeous but, Paddy, you shouldn't have.' Maria gushed, feeling guilty about the tiny size of the other little present she had for him.

'I thought the colour would suit you.'

'It's my favourite,' she said, getting up. 'I'm going to put it on now. Keep Molly away from the gas fire for a minute, will you?'

She went into the bedroom. The soft folds of the mohair slid down her arms and over her head, and when she looked in the mirror, the rich colour cast a soft glow across her cheeks.

'It's lovely!' she shouted to Paddy.

He was delighted. The lady at DH Evans had been very helpful. He told her the present was for his niece, and she had humoured him, thinking, he knew, that no-one spent that kind of money on his niece. She had reassured him that the jumper hadn't shrunk; three-quarter-length sleeves were in.

She had wrapped it up, thinking that no uncle

described his niece's colouring and size in quite the way that this gentleman did, but if he wanted to pretend, it was none of her business.

'Thanks!' Maria kissed Paddy on the cheek and flopped down on the floor again. Molly stroked her sleeve, enjoying the feel of it. Paddy seemed to like the cufflinks Maria had bought for him in Next, in two minds about whether they were a bit too trendy for him. Molly was delighted with her white teddy bear, and the ABC book with the cardboard pages. She enjoyed chewing them, especially the G for Giraffe page. After Molly went to bed, they played Scrabble and polished off a bottle of champagne.

At midnight, Paddy stretched. 'I should head off, really. I'll ring a cab.'

'Thanks for a lovely Christmas, Paddy,' said Maria as she stood behind him and helped him on with his coat.

'No. Thank you. It would have been very lonely. They say the first Christmas is the worst.' He turned around and they hugged awkwardly.

'See you on the second of January then. Enjoy the rest of the holidays.'

Paddy backed out the door, saying, 'Give Molly a kiss for me!'. He blew a kiss to Maria as he waited for the lift.

He was a very special man, Maria thought as she sat in the silence of the flat, thinking how much had happened in a year. Her first Christmas away from

home would now become her second. She wondered
how many other Christmases stretched before her, with
people feeling sorry for her and Molly, inviting them
over for Christmas dinner because otherwise they
would be on their own. She peeped in at Molly, and
knew that if she never met another man in her life, she
was glad she had kept Molly, and glad that Joe was the
father, even if he took no interest in her.

'She seems like a very nice girl,' said Noreen when Joe
came back into the sitting-room.

'She is. She just rang to wish me a Happy Christmas.'
Typical that his mother would decide to wheel herself
out into the hall to answer the phone the one time when
he was expecting a call.

'How long have you known her, then?'

'Only since I went back to college in October.'

'Is she studying medicine as well?'

'Yes. She's in second year.'

'Oh, she's quite young then? What age is she?'

'I don't know, twenty this year, I suppose.'

'Is it serious? It must be, if she's ringing you on
Christmas Day?'

'No, Mum. Hardly, after only three months. We get
on well. We have a bit of craic. That's all, really.'

'You should get her to come home with you, one
weekend.'

Joe couldn't think of a worse thing to do. The
interrogation would be a nightmare. What did her

father do? Where did she go to school? What were her plans when she graduated? He shuddered.

His mother saw the shiver, and said, 'I suppose she'd be a bit bored. But you could take her out for a drive, or down to the pub. You wouldn't need to be stuck in the house with me all the time.'

'I might, sometime. Let's just see how it goes?'

She heard the plea in his voice. She had done it again. She kicked herself. Old habits die hard, she thought. 'Will we have a game of Scrabble?'

The long evening stretched before them, and she didn't want Joe to turn on the TV to watch some Christmas film re-run. They could chat while they played Scrabble in front of the fire.

'Great idea.' He set up the board on the coffee table, and they sat in companionable silence. She only made the occasional comment, that it was terrible to have a 'Q' without a 'U', or that she had a brilliant word, but all the 'N's were out on the board already.

Joe was seriously wondering if he should bring the girl home the next time he came for a weekend. His mother was trying really hard not to be a control-freak, and he should be a bit more open with her.

Maybe he would bring her home at the end of January. He had lost Maria mostly because he was afraid of what his mother would think of her, and now when he thought about it, what was there for his mother to dislike? He should learn from his mistakes and do it differently this time.

Chapter Forty-four

Aileen didn't know whether to tell Maria or not. It might ruin her New Year's Eve. But Joe must have phoned for a reason. Paul said she should tell Maria, but that was only because he felt sorry for Joe. Aileen couldn't make him see that a few phone calls and one letter over a year ago wasn't really enough. Admittedly, Joe had come over to see the baby when she was born, but he had done nothing since then. Nothing. And now, out of the blue, he was ringing looking for Maria's number, and expecting Aileen to just tell him, like it was the most natural thing in the world. Aileen had put him off, saying that Maria's phone was out of order, and she would pass on the message when she saw her.

Paul looked at his watch. 'She'll be here in less than an hour,' he said. 'Why didn't you tell him that?'

'What if she doesn't want to speak to him? Then

he'd be sitting beside the phone all night, waiting for her to ring back. I'm thinking of him, as well.'

'That's true.' Then he muttered under his breath, 'Women are so perverse.'

'Perverse? Maria is one of the most straightforward people I know. If she doesn't want to speak to him, that's her own business. He hasn't been in touch for ages.'

'Sorry, you're right. Hey, we don't want to have a fight, do we? Let's go and get ready.'

'Ready? I'm dressed.' She smoothed down her top and did a little twirl.

He smirked, and led her through the hall. 'Well, let's go and get undressed, and start again.' He kissed her, and unbuttoned her new silk shirt.

When Aileen answered the door to Maria her face was flushed, with a smudge of mascara under one eye. 'It's funny to see you without Molly,' she said.

'Yeah, it was weird for me, coming over here without her as well.' Maria glimpsed Paul in the bedroom, buttoning up his shirt. She smiled. Those two were like sex maniacs. 'She'll be grand with Ruby, the lady from the crèche. Molly loves her, and she went off to sleep in Ruby's bedroom before I left.'

'The table is booked for nine,' said Aileen. 'So we can have a quick drink here first.'

'Sounds good to me,' said Maria, taking off her coat. Aileen admired her new cerise jumper, but Maria didn't say it came from Paddy. Aileen would only raise her eyebrows and wonder why she was getting that kind of a present from him. It was too special to spoil it like that.

'Mum, I've got something to tell you,' said Joe, looking out the window at the cars slowing down to negotiate the icy curve of the road outside the house.

He could see the faces of the drivers focussed in grim concentration and the happy chatting faces of their families, off for a walk on the windy beach in a seasonal tradition.

Noreen had been nodding off by the fire, wrapped up in memories, but Joe's tone brought her immediately alert. He sounded so like Derek sometimes; so solemn and mature.

'Yes, love?' she said, trying to sound casual. Maybe he was serious about this girl, after all. He was going back to Galway tomorrow, and he obviously had to get something off his chest.

Joe turned away from the frosty window, and his silhouette was framed against the glass. For a second his dark shape almost looked ominous. She couldn't see the expression on his face.

'Pull the curtains, love, while you're standing there. It's getting dark,' she said.

'I don't know if I'm being stupid, telling you this,' he said, tugging the heavy velvet curtains across the cold glass and closing out the January twilight.

'I'm sure it's not stupid.' She fiddled with the blue

and green tartan blanket that was draped across her knees. 'But I won't know until you tell me.'

She was reminded of him as a child, coming home with a story from school, all full of it but not sure how to start. He would fidget around, and start a few different ways before it finally all came tumbling out. Joe sat down on the sofa opposite her, and put his hands on his knees. One of Derek's little habits, she thought absent-mindedly.

'You have a granddaughter.' He had rehearsed this conversation a million times in his head since New Year's Eve and he hadn't planned it to come out that way at all.

'What do you mean?' she shrieked. 'How? When? I thought you only started seeing that girl in October?'

'I did. It's not her.'

'Who, then?'

'Her name is Maria. We went out together all the way through third year.'

'And you made her pregnant?'

'I did.' He was looking down at his hands now. He couldn't look her in the eye.

'Where is she now, for heaven's sake?'

'In London.'

'What is she doing in London?'

'I sent her away. I mean, I didn't try and get her to stay,' he stammered.

'Oh, Joe, how could you do that? Your poor father would turn in his grave.' She reached for the box of tissues on the sideboard. 'And tell me, how old is the child?'

'Just over a year.'

'And has Maria got family of her own to look after her?'

'Her dad threw her out of the house. I think that's really why she stayed in London.'

Joe was confused. His mother was asking all the wrong questions. He had been expecting her to ask, How could you do this to me? What about your studies? Does anybody else know about this? She was crying though. He had expected that, at least.

'Are you in touch with her, at all?'

How could Joe have kept this a secret from her for so long? He was usually very easy to read.

If she was honest, she had always thought he was a bit lacking in gumption. He must have more spine than she had thought, to keep a secret like that.

'Not for ages. But I tried ringing her on New Year's Eve, and she hasn't called back.'

'Is that it? Are you not in touch otherwise?'

'Not really. I wrote to her when you were in the hospital, to say I would look after them, but she didn't get the letter until much later, and by then everything had changed. I even went to see her when the baby was born, last Christmas, but she was living with someone else, so she just told me to go away.'

'What were you planning to say to her on New Year's Eve?'

'I don't know, I just wanted to hear her voice. I have a picture of her. And the baby. Do you want to see it?' He half stood, wanting to escape to his room.

'Later, in a minute.'

She waved her tissue at him, to sit down. He sat on the edge of the sofa. He shuffled his toes into the depths of the yellowing sheepskin hearthrug, a habit from his childhood.

'Joe, did you just want to make yourself feel better, by talking to her?'

'I suppose so. I've tried to forget about her but I can't. I've tried going out with other people, but I just think about Maria all the time. I look at her picture every day.'

'But why are you so busy trying to forget about her, if you love her? Don't you want to be with her, and your baby?'

'Of course I do. But she doesn't want me.'

'I'm not surprised. You haven't exactly gone out of your way to win her heart,' she sniffed. 'Go on, get the picture, so I can have a look at her.'

She had been right. Her son had no gumption. If he put his mind to it, he could win the girl back, Noreen was sure of it, in her bones.

Joe bounded out of the room. He didn't need to go upstairs. The picture was in his wallet. He took it out of his back pocket and sat on the stairs, savouring the last few seconds of being alone with Maria before he shared her with his mother. Just talking to his mother had strengthened his resolve. He wasn't just going to sit back any more and let Maria slip from his grasp. He would fight for her. She might be back with that Andy guy, or someone else, by now. Joe couldn't change the past but he could offer Maria a future together. Even though Molly would be at least five years old before Joe could properly support a family.

'Joe?' his mother's voice summoned him. He pretended to run down the steps. She still had ears like a bat. As he opened the sitting-room door and left the draughty coolness of the hall, the heat of the fire flushed his face. He reached out and handed over the photograph like a precious sacrifice. Noreen slipped on her glasses, which were hanging on a silver chain around her neck, and studied the picture.

'She's beautiful, isn't she?' She looked up at her son, who was leaning over looking at the picture too, as if he had never seen it before.

'Yes. I always wondered why she would go out with me,' he said, half-laughing with nerves.

'I meant the baby. She's tiny in this picture – newborn? What's her name?'

'Molly. It's the only picture I have. I got it last year, just after she was born. I saw her in the hospital. She's even more beautiful in the flesh.'

His mother looked up over her glasses. 'And Maria has a lovely smile. She looks like a nice girl.'

'She is.'

'So what are you going to do about it?'

He felt like he was eight years old again, being sent back with the apples he stole from old Mrs Frith's orchard. 'She had another boyfriend over there. I don't know if she even wants me back.'

'Well, there's only one way to find out, isn't there?' She handed him back the picture. 'I have a lovely little silver frame that would fit in, if you'd like it?'

Joe nodded. Maria and Molly were official. He propped the picture on the mantelpiece, beside the clock. It felt good to see them there. How could he have thought his mother would react any other way?

'Let's have a cup of tea and a bit of Christmas cake to celebrate,' said his mother, wheeling herself to the door. 'I'll make it, for a change.'

She swept out of the room, and left Joe staring at the flickering fire. He felt as if he had hot liquid pumping around the edge of his skull. He was shivering, and when he held them out, his hands were shaking uncontrollably.

Noreen sat in her wheelchair in the kitchen, waiting for the kettle to boil. She looked out the French windows at the glassy surface of the patio. The ice reflected the light from the kitchen, like a mirror on the past.

She had been sure when Joe was conceived that she had a girl growing inside her. Rita had swung her wedding ring over her swelling tummy, and confirmed it. The midwife said that the way the baby was lying, high up, often meant a girl. Noreen had spent nine months imagining her beautiful little girl growing up. She would be Noreen's friend forever, even after she got married herself and had her own family.

Derek said he didn't mind which they had. They were going to have a big family anyway, so he didn't mind whether a boy or a girl came first.

Joe had struggled to come into the world, lying breech, and then gasping for breath when he finally did come out. In those days, husbands didn't come into the delivery room, so she was on her own when she heard, 'You have a boy, Mrs Shaw.'

It took a while to sink in. She knew she should be grateful that he had even survived, after the difficult birth. They didn't whip them out with emergency Caesareans like they do now.

When Derek came in and said, 'He's lovely; fine and healthy,' she couldn't return his smile. He thought she was just exhausted after the labour. It had been so easy when people asked, pointing at her bump, 'What are you hoping for?' to say, 'I don't mind, as long as it's healthy'. What else could she say? But she didn't mean it. She had picked the name Josephine for her daughter, and it was only a small consolation to call the boy Joseph, and tell herself that the next one would be a girl. But then she had two miscarriages, and Derek died when he was only forty-six, leaving her with an only son.

She used to burst into tears whenever the baby cried, not knowing what she was doing wrong. Joe didn't take to breast-feeding. She felt guilty when she was heating bottles in the middle of the night, her feet cold on the tiled kitchen floor, trying to keep him quiet so that Derek could get a night's sleep. She thought she didn't love him enough, this poor little mite whose head was so soft and vulnerable. He couldn't help being a boy, she told herself, but it didn't make her feel any better. She couldn't look at other people's babies, in case she felt a pang of jealousy to see a pink-clad smiling girl in someone else's pram. Derek was supportive, but in those days doctors didn't have a name for postnatal depression. You just had to get on with it; run the house, make the dinners, feed the baby, until you worked yourself through it, and out the other side.

Joe was a very loveable baby. He was always smiling, and was as bright as a button. At least he never had to suffer being relegated to second best when the next child came along. She had seen it so often with her friends; pushing a pram with two toddlers trotting alongside, hanging off the handle when they crossed the road. Joe got lots of individual attention, and when she lost Derek, Noreen gave him even more, determined that he should have the best possible start in life.

The kettle came furiously to the boil, steaming up the window. Noreen turned away, wondering if Derek was looking down on her now, smiling because they had a beautiful granddaughter. Molly was a nice name.

She wheeled herself back to the fireside, a tray of tea and cake balanced across the arms of her wheelchair.

Joe turned around from staring into the fire. 'Mam, I do not ever want to see you doing that again!' he shouted, lifting the tray as she manoeuvred the wheelchair into her usual spot.

'Don't be ridiculous, Joe. It was perfectly safe,' his mother snorted at him, reaching across to the table to pour their tea.

'It was not, and if you insist on taking such ridiculous risks, I will have to arrange for someone to be with you all the time, to keep an eye on you,' he said sternly.

His mother looked up with a twinkle in her eye. 'Speaking of which, I have some news for you, too.'

'Oh?'

'Frank has been in touch a few times, and he's coming over for lunch tomorrow.'

Joe was dismayed. 'Don't get your hopes up too much, will you?' Joe couldn't believe the guy would have so much front. They hadn't seen hide nor hair of him for almost a year, and now he was going to just waltz back in when his mother was showing the first signs of getting back to normal.

'Hopes of what, love? There's not much chance of anything happening with me in this, is there?' She smacked the arm of her wheelchair.

'Why is he suddenly back on the scene now?'

'He fully admits that he couldn't cope with the idea of me being sick, and his wife died after a prolonged illness, so he couldn't face the idea of it happening to him again.'

'And now that you're out of danger, he'll consider seeing you again, is that it?'

'Joe, you don't need to be so protective – I've managed thus far in my life, without getting myself into too much trouble, so I think I can handle Frank.'

Joe didn't like the humorous tone she was trying to take. Frank had hurt her badly, just when she needed him most, and he wouldn't forgive that lightly.

'What time is he coming?' he asked, wondering if his mother had contrived it so that he would be gone back to Galway already before Frank showed his face.

'I thought if he came late morning, we could all have a cup of coffee together before you get your train?' She was being more conciliatory now, realising that from Joe's point of view, Frank probably wasn't too popular.

'Fine. To be fair to him, I thought he was a nice guy when I met him. I just don't want him to hurt you again, that's all.' Joe swallowed another mouthful of tea, and stood up to offer her the cake before his mother was tempted to do another wheelchair feat.

Chapter Forty-five

'Who's Joc, then?' Pauline's brother asked at the dinner-table, and her mother's ears pricked up.

'A friend of Maria's,' she said tersely.

'So why was he ringing you, then?' he teased.

'To get Maria's address in London.' She blushed, feeling guilty for giving out the address.

Her brother gave up after a few more attempts, and her mother sighed. Would that girl ever meet someone and relax a bit, and settle down? She looked at Pauline, who obviously had something on her mind. Last year, when she was doing a line with Mike, Pauline had been a different girl. She paid a bit more attention to herself, and was a lot more confident. But seemingly when Mike came back after the summer holidays in Greece, she didn't want to have any more to do with him. He seemed like a nice lad, and doing medicine, so he had a brain in his head. But Pauline had gone off him for some reason, and if she knew her daughter, that would be that. Such a shame. She didn't seem to have taken a shine to anyone else since. Still, plenty of time for all that.

Joe had begged Pauline for Maria's address, and against her better judgement, she had given it to him. He said he wanted to send Maria a card, and after the letter fiasco, he thought that Aileen wouldn't pass it on. She hoped that Maria wouldn't kill her. Joe said he had tried to ring Maria on New Year's Eve, but they hadn't spoken. It was a bit mean of Maria not to ring him back. She was the one who said they should stay friends, for Molly's sake.

Joe had a right to know how Molly was, even if he hadn't been much of a father so far. Should she ring and warn Maria? No, it might not come to anything. Joe might let her down again.

Stansted Airport was like a space-station, Joe thought as he climbed out of the driverless shuttle-train that had taken him to the Arrivals Hall. Gleaming stainless-steel pillars towered above him. You could park a plane in the terminal building. He felt like an explorer landing on a moon settlement as he followed the signs to the baggage reclaim. There were hardly any other people around. Or there might be thousands, but the place was so cavernous they could all be somewhere else in the building. It was eerily quiet compared to Knock Airport, which was always full of people sitting around waiting for fog-delayed flights.

He grabbed his rucksack off the conveyor belt, impressed that it had arrived there before him. He already had his ticket to Liverpool Street station. The travel agent had told him it would take about forty minutes on the train. Other travellers rushed past him on the escalator, elbowing him out of the way until he realised he was supposed to stand on the left. He ripped the luggage-tags off his rucksack. He didn't need labels on his bag declaring that he was a hick from the west of Ireland. Mum had said to take it easy with Maria, not to go barging in there, expecting her to drop everything. He was hardly the barging type. It had taken him nearly two years to get this far. He still hadn't figured out how he would get to talk to her, away from the boyfriend, if there was one on the scene. Aileen and Pauline had both refused to give him Maria's phone number. He felt a bit guilty for tricking Pauline into giving him the address. Still, all is fair in love and war, he thought. This was going to be both.

He successfully navigated the Central Line to Notting Hill Gate, and was delighted to see he was only two stops from Shepherd's Bush, where Maria was living.

Mike's brother Aidan had said he could use his flat in Ladbroke Grove for a few days. He was due back from Ireland on Wednesday and had lent Joe his keys. Joe couldn't work out the buses, so he walked, following Aidan's scribbled directions.

The tall gracious houses and droning black cabs

reminded him of the movie set for *Four Weddings and a Funeral*. No, it was *Notting Hill*, he thought. Of course it was. He grinned. He was in Notting Hill. He almost expected to see Hugh Grant opening one of the big black doors, with Julia Roberts pouting on the doorstep. Andie MacDowell would have been much better, he thought.

He unlocked the door of the basement flat and the stench of sour milk and damp hit his nostrils. The flat was gloomy, and he went to open the curtains, and then realised that they were open already. He turned on the lights and the gas heater, and threw away the solidified milk, scalding the drain with water he had boiled in the kettle.With a mug of black tea to warm his hands, he sat down. What next?

'Intrepid explorer grinds to a halt,' he muttered under his breath.

He spotted a telephone directory. She might be in there. He noticed 1996 on the curling cover. A smell of damp exuded from it as he put it back on the shelf. He dialled 100. An operator told him to ring 192.

'Maria Hardy, please, of Flat 46, Bessemer House, Shepherd's Bush,' he said, trying to sound English.

'What town?' said a Scottish accent.

'London.'

Surely she had heard of Shepherd's Bush? Even he had heard of Shepherd's Bush.

A computerised voice said, 'The number you require is 0208 746 9638.'

He didn't have a pen ready. He hung up. There she was. She existed in London. She was a person with a telephone number. Unlike him. If a red bus knocked him down, no one would know who he was. He would be a John Doe. Depressing thought.

He got a stub of a pencil from the kitchen drawer and dialled 192 again, his hand shaking as he wrote down the number.

Now he'd have to ring it. Maybe he should go and find the address. Just to see the place. He might see Maria coming or going with Molly, and they could talk. He might even see the fella with her, and get an idea what he was up against.

He gulped down the scalding tea. No time like the present. He girded his Levi'd loins and stuffed the number into his pocket. He might ring her from a phone box across the road if the coast looked clear. He had to tug the front door really hard to lock it. The damp had swollen the wood. Aidan had told him to always double-lock it. Not that there was much in the flat to steal, as far as Joe could see.

A double-decker bus pulled in to the stop just as he reached it, and he jumped on the back. The driver said, 'Hold tight,' and the bus jolted away while Joe was still hanging on to the pole, trying to get his money out.

'Seventy pence,' the driver said disdainfully, the ticket machine whirring.

Joe fumbled with his change. When he finally realised that the ten-pence pieces were much smaller than the ones at home, he managed to count out the money.

He plonked himself down beside a fat old lady with lots of bags, the half-smile freezing on his face as he caught the stench of her unwashed body and matted hair.

She grinned toothlessly at him. 'New to London?'

Was it that obvious? It would be rude to change seats now, he thought, inhaling through his mouth. He had no idea where this bus was going, he realised as it stopped at a set of traffic-lights.

'Where are you going, love?' she asked him, her breath smelling like old catfood.

He swallowed. 'Shepherd's Bush?'

'You want to be on the other side, love,' she said, pointing at a number 12 bus going the other way, displaying Acton Town as its destination on the front.

'Thanks.'

He stood up and nearly landed in her lap as they jolted off again. He rang the bell.

The driver shouted, 'Oy! Make your mind up, mate! Are you getting off?'

'Yes. Yes, please.' He jumped off the bus, and a cyclist screeched on his brakes, skidding to a stop only inches away.

'For Christ's sake, watch where you're going, mate,' he yelled, easing his way back into the traffic, not even making eye contact. As if it was a routine event.

Joe crossed the road, trembling. He felt like a five-year-old doing it for the first time by himself. Another bus passed, and he ran to the stop. This time there was a queue.

He remembered that English people like to queue properly, so he stood at the end of the line. Only two people got on the number 12 bus, and no one else moved. He didn't dare to nudge ahead. The doors were just about to close, and he had to grab at the pole, pulling himself on as they folded shut, beeping. He looked back. People were still queuing patiently. The others must have been waiting for different buses. How were you supposed to know? He had the right change for the driver this time, and sat down on his own. He asked how many stops he had to go, and counted off five, swinging casually off at the right one.

He could get the hang of this. How big was Shepherd's Bush? It should be easy to find a big block of flats. A tall grey block loomed over the shopping centre. That might be it. Twenty minutes later, he hadn't found it.

'Sorry, do you know where Bessemer House is?' he asked a glamorous black lady pushing a baby in a buggy. She looked kind of cool but friendly, with loads of beads in her hair and a Reebok tracksuit and trainers. She ignored him completely, turning her head away.

'Excuse me, I'm trying to find Bessemer House?' he said to an old man in a long filthy trenchcoat, who was shuffling along with a walking-stick.

'Eh?' he said, craning his neck up to see Joe's face.

'Bessemer House. Do you know where that is?' Joe said slowly and clearly.

'No need to shout, son, I can hear you. It's over there, down a bit, on the left. You can't miss it.' He pointed down the main street, indicating vaguely to the left.

'Thanks.' Joe tried to saunter, but his bowels had gone funny. Maria could be out shopping, and he might bump into her. He might have already passed the boyfriend, on his way home from work, or out to buy a newspaper. Joe turned into another busy road. The old man was right. You couldn't miss it. Bessemer House wasn't a high- rise, but a solid redbrick block, with little balconies outside the windows. Washing-lines hung on some of them, with children's clothes hanging stiff in the cold evening air. A large sign banned ball-games on the scrubby hard grass. There was not a soul in sight. Joe looked at his watch. Six o'clock. The kids would be inside having their tea. He suddenly realised that he had mentally accelerated Molly's growth and imagined her running around in a little woolly red cap and gloves. She would barely be able to walk, he remembered. She was only just over a year old. He sighed. Some father he was. Somewhere in there was number 46. Should he get closer? He stood at the bottom of the concrete steps at the corner of the block, trying to get out of the cold wind that was whipping around the building. Almost as if it had its own force field, to put off strangers. The acidic smell on the stairs reminded him of the nursing home. He coughed, and a hail of barking came from the ground-floor flat beside him. A heavy dog hurled itself at the door, making it shudder. A sticker above the keyhole depicted the silhouetted head of a Rottweiler. A brass plate screwed under the letterbox warned, *Beware of the Dog*. The dog was getting frenzied now, unused to being ignored. Most people scurried straight up the steps or went away. Joe went away.

If Maria agreed to meet him, she would probably want to do it on neutral territory. He wasn't being a coward. Just to prove it, he would ring her as soon as he got back to the flat.

He bought fish and chips. They tasted delicious and kept his hands warm as well. This time the bus journey went without incident, and as he walked from Notting Hill, he looked in the windows of the flats and houses. People over here didn't pull their curtains. Maybe they wanted to show off their fancy Christmas trees, with the gold baubles and the little white lights. They all seemed to be in couples, snuggled up on trendy burnt-ochre sofas, or making dinner in stainless-steel basement kitchens with their cats sitting on the windowsills watching the feet passing by. Not a net curtain in sight. He remembered the blank, netted windows of Bessemer House, concealing all its inner life. The houses became a bit seedier as he got closer to Aidan's flat. They had more of a rented air about them. Striped blankets and odd curtains were strung across the peeling window frames.

This time when he went in he was ready for the

smell of damp and it wasn't so unwelcoming, after the cold air outside. He wouldn't let himself take off his coat, but went straight to the telephone. He dialled. She answered. His heart flipped.

'Maria?'

'Yes?' She didn't recognise his voice. 'Who's speaking?'

She sounded very English. 'It's me, Joe. Can you talk?' he almost whispered, as if he could stop the boyfriend overhearing the conversation by keeping his own voice down.

'How did you get my number?'

Curiously? Crossly? Conspiratorially? He couldn't tell. 'Never mind that, Maria. I really need to talk to you. Can we meet?'

'Where are you?'

'In, eh, Lad Broke Grove.'

She laughed. 'Lad-*brook*, you say it like brook. What are you doing there?'

She was laughing at him. That was good. 'I came over to see you.'

'Oh, did you now?' She was teasing him. Even better.

'And – and Molly as well,' he stammered.

She paused. 'Why?' she asked.

He could hear the guarded tone that had crept in. She was probably wondering if he wanted to claim rights over Molly or something.

'Look, can we meet, and talk about it? Will you be able to get away?'

'Away?'

'You know, to meet me.' The boyfriend might be one of those possessive types, wanting to know her every move.

She looked at her watch. 'It's too late, now.'

'But, Maria . . .'

'It's Molly's bedtime.'

Too late this evening. Relief. God, he was sweating in his coat. He shrugged it off his shoulders, still holding the receiver. 'Tomorrow? In the morning?' He didn't want to waste a minute.

'Where?'

'I don't know. You tell me a good place, and I'll find it.'

'You could come here, I suppose. That would be the easiest thing for me. Molly has a bit of a cold – it's better not to take her out in this weather.'

'Are you sure that will be all right?'

'Yes. Ten o'clock. I'll give you the address. It's 46 –'

'I have it,' he said and then bit his tongue. Now he would get Pauline in trouble.

'Can you find your way here?'

'I'm sure I can. Thanks, I'll see you in the morning.'

His coat landed in a heap on the floor as he stood up and punched the air in a victory salute. 'Yes!'

Chapter Forty-six

Maria plumped up the green and red Indian embroidered cushions on the sagging sofa, tidied away Molly's toys into her basket and put three drops of refresher oil in the dark-green glass bowl of potpourri that Aileen had given her for Christmas. She ran the carpet-sweeper over the living-room and hall, picking up the trail of digestive crumbs that Molly had left after trying unsuccessfully to stuff the biscuits into the video recorder. Molly looked adorable in the red corduroy pinafore and woolly tights that Maureen had sent over for Christmas. She was in great form, and her teeth didn't seem to be bothering her, for the first time in weeks. Her cold was nearly gone. Maria didn't want Joe's first impression to be of a snotty-nosed, irritable child. She couldn't decide what to wear, herself. She didn't want to look like she had made an effort but at the same time, she wanted to look cool, in control. In the end, she wore black Gap trousers and Paddy's cerise jumper.

The doorbell rang at ten o' clock on the dot. Joe had always been hot on timekeeping. She buzzed him onto the landing, and then opened the flat door so she could direct him. He came down the corridor, his trainers squeaking on the floor, and Maria fought the surge of nervous nausea that swirled in her stomach.

'Come in.' She smiled at him, and looked into his eyes to see if he had changed. He seemed even more nervous than her, and he wasn't smiling. He looked older. He would be one of those guys who gets better-looking with age, she thought. He looked more like a doctor now. Molly was sitting in the middle of the floor, her legs spread-eagled, shoving plastic bricks into a little red bucket with shaped holes in the lid. She looked up as her mother came back into the room, and offered her a square yellow brick, saying, 'Ta-ta'.

Maria knelt beside Molly and said, 'Say hello to – Joe, Molly.'

Molly looked at him and, with a tiny replica of her mother's smile, showed her four teeth. She offered him a red circular brick.

'Thank you,' he said. 'You're very clever, aren't you?' He looked up at Maria. 'She's so big!'

He sank down onto the floor beside Molly. She tipped the bucket upside down on the Indian rag-rug and laughed. Together, she and Joe put all the bricks back in. He held her hand to guide her to the right holes. He clapped when they were finished, and she copied him, giggling. Maria watched in silence. Joe looked up and caught her absent gaze.

'Sorry,' she shook her head. 'I was miles away. Can I get you a coffee, and take your coat?'

He stood up and shrugged off his coat. 'Great, thanks. Black with no sugar.'

'I know,' she said, going into the kitchen, and then thought it would have been cooler to have forgotten. Then she kicked herself. Why was she still worrying about being cool? The father of her baby had just stepped back into her life. He couldn't take Molly away from her, so she had no reason to resent him. She should listen to what he had to say – be open-minded.

Molly sang, '*Ma, ma, ma, ma,*' as she tipped out the bricks again, and looked at him, waiting for him to start the game again.

Joe was surprised. She was a little person, not a baby. He hadn't expected to be so intrigued by her.

Maria came back and handed Joe a mug of coffee. He sat up on the sofa, taking in the colour scheme for the first time. 'You have this decorated really nicely. You'd never know it was –'

'A Council place?'

'Sorry, I didn't mean it like that.'

'Don't worry. I used to think the same.' She remembered her nightmares about the Rahoon flats in Galway. A long time ago.

Joe noticed the prints of sailing boats in Galway Bay,

and line-sketches of men carrying currachs and mending fishing-nets.

'They're nice.'

'Aileen gave them to me last year, to remind me of home.'

'I like the colours in here.' The walls were painted a dark red that cast a warm glow and seemed to make the drab grey carpet dramatically stylish. The cushions brightened the dull beige fabric of the second-hand sofa, and beaded curtains softened the rusting metal-framed windows.

'So . . .' she said.

'I just wanted to see you, to talk to you.'

He seemed a bit distracted, and he was still looking around.

'About what?' she asked.

'About us, I suppose, and Molly.' No sign of a man's coat on the rack in the hall, no shoes lying around, no sports pages open on the coffee table. No 'feel' of a man around the place, but he couldn't be sure.

'Us?' she said quizzically, as if to say, 'What's an 'us'?' It seemed like such a long time ago since they had been together.

Joe couldn't take his eyes off Molly. She was balancing on her toes, holding tightly on to the edge of the coffee table, her lower lip clenched under her two top teeth in total concentration as she edged around the table towards him. He smiled at her. She stopped, and plonked onto her bottom.

'Come on, Molly. You can do it!' he said, holding out his hands towards her.

She looked around at Maria, grabbed the table, and balanced herself again.

'Come on!' he said.

She launched herself towards him, took three steps, and fell into his arms. He hugged her. 'Very good! You're the best, aren't you, Molly?'

He looked at Maria. 'How long has she been walking?'

'That's the first time by herself.' Maria had tears in her eyes. She blinked them away.

Molly's warm body leaned against Joe's legs. She started playing with his laces.

'What do you want, Joe?' Maria was feeling nervous again. Joe seemed to be more interested in Molly than in her. He couldn't take her away, could he?

'Is that . . . I mean, are you still . . . I mean, are you with somebody at the moment?'

'Why do you want to know?' she said quietly.

'It makes a difference. If you're with somebody, and you're happy, that's a different ball-game altogether, than if you're not.'

'Ball-game? What kind of ball-game are we talking about here?' Could he claim that she wasn't providing a family environment for his child?

'I want you back. I want us to be together. I want to look after Molly.'

Her heart thudded in her chest. So that was why he

had come. 'And does what Molly and I want come into the equation, at all?'

'Of course, Maria. I just wanted you to know that's how I feel.'

'What, suddenly, out of the blue, made you come over here?' Maria didn't want to be lured into another situation where she would get hurt. She was better off on her own, with Molly. They were fine. Molly was happy in her new nursery, and had some little friends. Maria's job was going well. They had a nice little life.

'I've missed you the whole time. I know it doesn't seem like that – I didn't show it very much, but that was because I thought you didn't want me.'

'And why do you think I want to be with you now?' If she was hard, he couldn't breach her shell. She felt mean and a bit detached, like another person acting out a script. It was easier that way. She could feel her heart pounding. Joe was so serious and intense. She could see that he meant everything he said. He seemed stronger, more determined this time, like he was really going to fight to get her back. She was scared.

'I know how it must look. Mum said she wouldn't be surprised if –'

'Your mam knows about me? Us?' She looked down at Molly.

'I told her last week.'

'She told you to come over here.' Maria sighed. Those apron-strings were very long and very elastic. Maybe he hadn't come on his own account at all.

She could feel the disappointment welling up inside her.

'No! It wasn't like that. I told her because I had already decided. I want to look after you and Molly.'

'Look after us? You're still in college, aren't you? You must have another three years to go?'

'Two, and then specialising.'

'So, how would you look after us? You're the one who's still living at home with his mother.'

'I don't know. I'll find a way. I'd give up college if I had to, but . . .'

'But what?'

'I have to know whether there's any chance for us, first.'

This was all moving a bit fast. Could Joe really expect to walk back into their lives after all this time and just say "Don't worry. Everything will be fine?". She had fought too hard to create the little safe world in which she and Molly lived, to just let someone take it over so easily.

She shook her head. 'We hardly know each other now, Joe. There's a lot of water under the bridge.'

'I know, and I don't expect you to drop everything now. I just need to know if there's a chance for me to win you back.'

Maria's cheeks were flushed and her eyes were glassy with tears that she wouldn't let fall. She was tougher than the old Maria, but Joe thought he could see through her hard act. He thought he could see some hope. He stretched out his hand, but he couldn't reach hers without standing up and leaning over Molly.

Maria couldn't hold back the tears for much longer. She stood up. 'Well, thanks for coming around. It was nice to see you. When are you flying back?' She put on her polite tea-party voice.

'Tomorrow.' He looked up hopefully, a question in the word. Could he see them again?

'That's a shame. I go back to work tomorrow. Busy day. It always is after the Christmas break.' She didn't catch his eye. Her heart was in her throat.

Joe bent down to Molly and picked her up, holding her at arm's length so he could talk to her. Maria thought how strong his arms must be. She couldn't hold Molly up like that any more.

'Bye, Molly,' Joe said, nuzzling her neck.

Molly giggled and lifted her hand and waved, her fat fingers curling delicately. 'Bye, bye,' she said.

Joe kissed her soft forehead and handed her over to Maria, who was holding out her arms. The colours of the bright red corduroy and the soft pink mohair clashed as Maria hugged her daughter close. They walked to the door. Joe wanted to kiss Maria, just on the cheek, but she turned away to open the door. Butterflies were rocking and rolling inside her.

'Can I ring you?' he asked.

She nodded. 'That would be nice. Thanks, Joe, really, for coming over.'

He walked down the corridor. When he turned, they were both waving at him, but he heard the door closing before the squeaking lift arrived.

Chapter Forty-seven

'How did it go?' Joe's mother asked as soon as he put his head around the door of her room. He hadn't seen her so animated since he came back from Greece.

'All right, I think,' he said. 'She only saw me the once. In her flat. I don't think there's anyone else on the scene.' He smiled.

'Did you ask her?'

'She was a bit evasive, and she wouldn't say. I suppose he could be living somewhere else, though.' That hadn't occurred to him before. His tentative little bubble of happiness burst with a soggy pop.

'What was Molly like? Was she very cute?' Noreen was really excited.

He sat down heavily on the bed. 'Gorgeous. You would have loved her. She took her first steps when I was there.'

'Really? Did you feel as if she was yours?' Noreen

wanted to know everything. She felt like a teenager again.

'Sort of. Especially when she smiled at me. She's the image of Maria. The same smile.' He sighed. 'We played with these little coloured bricks, and she copied me when I clapped my hands. She's really lovely.'

'Did she listen to what you had to say? Maria, I mean.'

'Yeah, but it came out a bit funny. I was really nervous and I just blurted it out. She didn't believe me when I said that I could support them. She has a job and everything already. She doesn't need me.'

'But Molly hasn't got a father, Joe. That must count for something. Support doesn't just mean giving them money. But would you be prepared to give up college, and work, if you had to?'

'I would. I knew it as soon as I saw them. I'd do anything. Maybe she'd believe me then?' He paced up and down the room. 'I have to show her what I'm made of.' It sounded a bit melodramatic, even to him. Like he should twirl a six-shooter on his index finger and hit six targets in a row and then lasso a rogue buffalo in full charge. He felt trapped in the tiny room.

Noreen let the brake off her wheelchair and opened the door. 'Come on. Let's get some fresh air. It gets awful stuffy in here when they have the heating on all the time.'

She led the way down the corridor, wheeling herself. Her palms were calloused and hard, and her upper arms were better toned than they had been for years. Joe stepped ahead to open the double doors and they went out into the bare garden. No one else was out. Through the TV room window, Joe could see them all huddled in front of a black and white matinee with Fred Astaire and Ginger Rogers.

He pushed his mother along the gravel path and she pointed to the green tips of snowdrops just pushing their way out of the dark soil.

'Spring will be here before we know it,' she said.

The smell of damp soil and moss filled Joe's nostrils. A blackbird flitted across the path, chattering its alarm.

'Park me over there,' she said, pointing to the cedar tree that dominated the garden.

Joe sat on the rain-swollen wooden bench.

'How did it go with Frank, after I left?' Joe asked. It was strange that they were both on the brink of change, and he felt a stronger bond between them than there had ever been before. His mother was finally treating him like an adult, with a mind of his own, and opinions that might be different from hers.

'It was lovely. He ended up doing the cooking, and told me I should have a bigger variety of herbs!'

'We haven't exactly been doing gourmet cooking for a while, have we?' said Joe wryly.

'No, but it's my turn next week, and I'm determined to do better than him.'

'Just like old times then?'

His mother laughed. 'It's no fun without a challenge!

I've got Rita Duffy taking me to Quinnsworth on Thursday to get all the ingredients. I'm going to try something new from my Delia book.'

They were silent for a while.

'What do you think I should do?' Joe asked.

For the first time in his life, his mother resisted the temptation to tell him. 'What do you think, yourself?'

'She said I could ring her.'

'And what then?' Sometimes he needed a good kick, but Noreen held her tongue. Joe had to figure this one out for himself.

'We need to get to know each other all over again. Maybe I should just go to London and get a job too.'

'Your dad and I courted for two years while he was studying up in Dublin, and we only saw each other about once a month.'

'But that was in the fifties.'

'What difference does that make? We weren't jumping into bed together every five minutes, granted, but you can chat on the phone, and write letters, and maybe you could see each other every so often, as well.'

'That's what we were supposed to be doing when Maria went to London first, and it didn't work. She met someone else while I was over here, not able to do a thing about it.' He felt defeated already.

'But you were distracted because of me. Now you can focus all your spare energy on them. You've got some ground to make up, but I don't think that going to London is the answer. You shouldn't rush her, before she has got used to the idea that you want to be back in her life. '

'I'm scared of really losing her this time.' He had never been competitive at sports or games, for that very reason. The fear of losing. But he had never had so much to lose before.

'I'd say you have to play it nice and slowly in the beginning anyway, so being apart is probably a good thing.' She wasn't going to spell it out for him. She looked up at the grey looming sky. 'I think we're in for a shower.'

She turned the wheelchair and headed towards the house. Joe stayed for tea even though he hated the urn-stewed taste of the tea and the processed cheese sandwiches with stale edges from having the crusts cut off hours ago. He wouldn't see his mother for two weeks now, until after the January exams.

'Good luck, love. I'll be thinking of you,' she said, as she waved him off.

He wasn't sure if she meant in the exams, or what.

'Will we go for a drive out to Ballinahinch?' suggested Sean, who was always restless on a Sunday afternoon if Doctor Moran didn't want to play golf.

'Grand,' said Maureen, putting away the last of the dishes after the lunch. She hated being cooped up when it was raining. 'We can check the wine list for Aileen and Paul. That's one of the jobs we still have left to do.' She put on some lipstick and patted her hair.

They drove off. There wasn't much of a view through the slanting rain, so they listened to a radio quiz show and Sean tried to beat the contestants to the answers. He was delighted when he beat the winner by one point. He had played this game for years, whenever they went for a Sunday drive with the kids. Usually he lost, claiming that he couldn't concentrate properly on the questions while he was driving.

The hotel looked cosy, with the porch-lights glowing as they drove up the slick black tarmac drive through the dripping trees.

'It's a pity in a way that Aileen didn't wait until later in the year, when the rhododendrons would be out,' said Maureen. 'It would be nicer for the photos.'

'It's still a lovely place, even in the rain,' said Sean, pulling into a parking space. They sat in the car for a minute, taking in the view down to the river, and admiring the smooth green circular lawn in front of the house.

They ducked through the rain and went into the stone-flagged hall. A receptionist ushered them into the bar to wait for the duty manager. A fire roared in the huge open hearth and the mahogany tables gleamed in the firelight. They ordered tea and smoked salmon sandwiches.

'It's funny. It was Maria who said she'd like to get married here, when we came here years ago,' said Maureen wistfully. 'She was only about fourteen at the time.'

Sean knew what she was doing. He was tired of

fighting the battle with himself in his head, and hearing the voices of Maureen and Father Duggan and Paddy and Martin, all telling him he was in the wrong.

'Well, it's the next best thing that she'll be here for Aileen's wedding then, isn't it?' he said, smiling.

Maureen's face lit up, but she didn't have time to say anything before the manager arrived with the maroon leather-bound wine list.

'I believe you wanted to discuss the wine list, sir?'

'Yes, we're having our daughter's wedding reception here.'

'Oh, lovely. When is the big day?'

'20th February,' said Maureen.

'Ah, yes, the Thornton party,' he said.

Sean looked confused.

'That's Paul's name,' whispered Maureen behind her hand.

The manager smiled indulgently. 'I'll leave you with the list, and come back in a few minutes.' He had heard of people being bad with names, but you'd think he would know his own son-in-law's name.

'Are you serious?' said Maureen as soon as he was gone.

'About what?'

'About Maria. I'm delighted!'

She patted his knee under the table. Little did he know that Maria was coming anyway, with or without his blessing. But her plan had worked. That was all that mattered.

'Yes, well, it would be a bit harsh to stop her coming to her sister's wedding, wouldn't it?' He was pretending to concentrate on the wines, consulting the list of options that Paul had sent.

Maureen was exuberant. She would ring Martin and Paddy and thank them. Father Duggan would be delighted too. Next thing, Sean would fall in love with Molly. He wouldn't be able to resist her. Maria said she walked for the first time last weekend. They were so cute at that stage. They did something new nearly every day. She felt a swelling of emotion inside her chest.

Sean could sense Maureen's excitement, but he decided that the casual approach was best. There was giving in gracefully and there was falling over backwards. He was never a man for the latter.

'Will we go for this, number sixteen, with the starter, and then a choice of red or white house wine for the main course?' he said, pointing at the unpronounceable name of a chateau in the Loire valley. Then he stage-whispered, 'The prices are astronomical, but they are the ones that Paul asked for.'

'That sounds nice.' She couldn't care less, not being a great wine-drinker anyway.

She couldn't wait to get home and ring Maria. She wandered into the dining-room while Sean made the arrangements with the manager, and she stood at the big picture window, looking down at the black, swollen river. It slowed down as it curved around the bend and then raced off across the smooth round stones where the trout and salmon would be jumping later in the season. There was a lovely little wooden bridge that would be great for romantic pictures. All they needed was the weather. It would be a shame if they couldn't have photos outside. It would be a good place to impress the English visitors. Four swans came gliding through the dark sky over the woods and landed gracefully on the water. Like the children of Lir. Maria had always loved that story as a child, even though it had a sad ending. Molly would probably love the swans. Maureen could imagine her pointing at them with her little chubby finger and smiling. She would have changed a lot since Maureen saw her as a tiny baby. She'd have a real little personality now.

Sean came and stood beside her, with his arm on her shoulder. 'All fixed. Do you want to head for home, or will we have another cup of tea?'

'Let's go home,' she said, smiling at him. And this time, when she looked into his eyes, she wasn't pretending.

Chapter Forty-eight

Aileen emerged from the changing-room looking like a princess. The heavy brocaded bodice cinched her waist, and the flowing satin skirt had just enough train to add elegance as she swept across the carpet to the mirrors.

'That's gorgeous,' said Maria, amazed that her sister could be so transformed. Aileen had never been into clothes, and had very different taste to Maria. Now, she glided rather than walked, with her head held high, and a smile that completely lit up her face.

'I love it – oh, Maria, have you ever seen anything like it?'

'It's stunning.'

'Is it a bit over the top? Paul and I agreed a budget, and this goes way over it,' she said, fingering the rich fabric.

'You only get married once,' said Maria firmly.

'I know, and you only wear the dress for one day,'

said Aileen pragmatically. She had never wanted a possession more in her life. 'I didn't think I was into all the frills and stuff, but when you put on a dress like this,' she looked in the mirror, ' you feel different, really like a bride.'

'Do you think you could persuade Paul?' asked Maria.

'If I told him I really, really wanted it.'

She swept across the carpet again, looking over her shoulder to see how the soft train moved behind her. The shop assistant had been keeping a low profile, waiting for the right moment. She stepped forward. 'This style is very popular,' she simpered. 'It's very complimentary to the figure. And it shows off your lovely shoulders.'

Aileen smiled. 'You're preaching to the converted, believe me. I just need to have a battle with my conscience now.'

'I think you should go for it,' said Maria, bouncing Molly, who was getting restless, on her knee. Molly wanted to have her feet on the ground all the time now that she had tasted walking.

'I'll have to think about it,' said Aileen decisively, pulling the heavy curtain across her cubicle.

The assistant smiled at Maria. 'Are you going to be the bridesmaid?'

'Yes.'

'We have some lovely dresses over here,' she waved at a rack of puffy-sleeved taffeta, and took two steps towards it, trying to lead the way.

'I have mine already, thank you,' Maria said firmly, not even tempted to browse. She knew what she wanted to wear, and Aileen liked the idea too.

'Oh, that's good.' The assistant pretended indifference and started to rearrange a shoe display to Maria's right.

Aileen came out, her cheeks and neck flushed with heat and excitement. 'I left it hanging in there, is that all right?'

'Fine, madam. There's about a five-to-six-week order period on those dresses, just so you can bear it in mind.'

'Thanks.'

Aileen took her coat and bag from Maria and suggested a coffee. They made their way through the racks of exotic lingerie, with Molly trying to grab everything in sight.

Maria found them a table in the cafeteria and settled down with Molly, surrounded by the smells of soup and lasagne. This department store hadn't gone for the trendy minimalist look yet, with stainless-steel tables and black floor tiles. A plump, sweating, Saturday waitress clattered past with a tray of clean cutlery, and then Aileen arrived with Danish pastries and mugs of cappuccino.

'I thought we deserved a little nibble as well,' she said. 'It's hard work getting in and out of all those dresses.'

Maria broke off a piece of pastry for Molly, not caring that most of it would end up all over her clothes. 'Yummy.'

Aileen shrugged off her coat. 'Now, tell me the latest on Joe,' she said, leaning across the table.

Maria smiled, dreamy-eyed. 'He rang again last night.'

'That's the third time in a week.'

'I know. Aileen it's so nice. He's so easy to talk to. It's like we never split up. We're on the same wavelength, and I tell him stuff about Molly, and we laugh, and I can tell he's really proud of her as well.'

'That's great. You haven't had a daddy to share all that stuff with. No one can stand in for that.'

'I'm really scared though. I can't let go completely, because I don't want to get hurt. I can't see how we can be together, but I don't want to be apart.'

'So what kind of things does he talk about?'

'Nothing too heavy. Just college, and his mother, and he asks about Molly.'

'Does he ask about getting back together?'

'We agreed we would take it a step at a time, for now. I couldn't handle it. I can't sleep at night as it is, thinking about him.'

Aileen licked the froth on her cappuccino and appraised her sister. 'For now?'

'I'm trying to be sensible, and not rush into anything. Paddy said that Joe might be just doing it to alleviate his conscience, and I should be careful not to get my hopes up.'

Aileen looked at her sister. 'You talked to Paddy about it?'

'I talk to Paddy about everything. He's great.'

Aileen gave her a strange look. 'I thought you said . . .'

Maria blushed. She wished she had never told Aileen about her conversation with Ivy – at the time it had just seemed funny. Now she felt like she had betrayed Paddy. He obviously had a bit of a problem with being attracted to much younger women, and she knew from the lads that he had got into trouble over it more than once. There was a sexual harassment claim a couple of years ago from one receptionist, which was only stopped by a settlement out of court.

Aileen saw the blush. 'Maria?'

'We're friends, good friends. He's been like another dad to me for the last year.'

'So he doesn't do any of that . . .?'

'No! Aileen, that was just in Ivy's imagination. Paddy is a sweet, nice man.'

'But he's jealous of Joe?'

'No, of course not! He's Daddy's age, for heaven's sake. He's just being protective.'

Maria swept the crumbs from the Danish pastry into her paper napkin, folded it precisely and laid it on her plate.

She wasn't sure how she felt about Joe. She wouldn't let herself love him again until she was sure. He was certainly making up for lost time. A postcard had arrived this morning. It had a picture of a faint rainbow in a grey cloudy sky over a lake in Connemara. It made her homesick, but she put it up over the gas heater anyway. Joe's message written on the back had brought tears to her eyes.

'It's nice to have a ray of hope again. Love, Joe'

Did she have a ray of hope? Was that why she wasn't able to sleep, or was she just worrying about going home at last?

'What are you thinking?' asked Aileen, spooning out the last of the foam from her mug. She always saved a bit for the end.

'About going home.'

'Well, at least you don't have Daddy to worry about.'

'I wouldn't quite say that, Aileen. He won't throw us out. That's a start, I suppose, but we have a long way to go.'

'Mam was so pleased with herself, that her plan worked,' said Aileen.

More like a game of 'wait and see' than a plan, thought Maria, but she should give credit where it was due, even though the supposed plan had taken nearly nine months to come to fruition.

'We'll have to rename her the Mo Mowlam of Carraroe,' she said. 'Come on, we have jobs to do. It's only six weeks to the wedding!' She pushed her chair back. 'Thanks for the coffee.'

'How's the courting going?' asked Noreen when she saw her son after the exams.

'I rang her three times this week,' he said. 'We talked about loads of things. We said we wouldn't talk about getting back together yet. It's too soon.'

'That's right. Don't rush the girl.'

She was at the cooker, checking on the progress of the boiled potatoes and cabbage. 'I thought we'd have a bit of gammon tonight,' she said, pulling out the grill.

Joe was amazed. She seemed to have been galvanised into action, making pots of tea, weeding the path out the back, and now, making dinner.

'You're full of beans these days, Mum. Are you seeing a lot of Frank?

'Still just once a week. We old fogies need to take things gently. I want to get a bit more independent, if I ever want to get out of that home. It's an awful drain on the finances.'

Joe felt himself going cold in the steamy kitchen. 'Mum, you're not going to tire yourself out to save money, are you? We have enough.'

'Of course I am. Needs must, and the devil take the hindmost. You'll need every penny soon.' She rattled the grillpan. 'Pass that gammon over. Do you want pineapple on yours?'

'Yes, please.'

'Set the table there, love, and open that tin.' He didn't mind her bossiness any more. It was kind of nice to have it back.

He got the tin-opener out of the drawer. She obviously had it all worked out.

'This is lovely,' he said as they sat down at the table. 'The first dinner you've cooked in how long?'

'Don't remind me! Eighteen months, apart from my

culinary masterpiece last week for Frank. I can't believe I sat around for so long feeling sorry for myself. Your father must have been looking down, wondering what had happened to me.'

'Mum, you were in a coma for two months!'

'I know, but I didn't fight back as hard as I should have. There's no stopping me now, though!' She stabbed a new potato with her fork, mopped up the juices on her plate and savoured each buttery bite.

Chapter Forty-nine

'How long now, to the big day?' Father Duggan asked Sean as he shook his hand in the porch after Mass, his surplice billowing in the chilly wind.

'Only three weeks,' said Sean, rubbing his hands together and blowing on them. He looked around for Maureen and saw her standing chatting to Eileen Folan. Most of the congregation was already gone, eager to get into their cars or the newsagent's across the road, to get out of the wind.

'I suppose you'll have a full house, with everyone home?' said the priest.

'Yes, even Hugh has managed to book the weekend off work,' said Sean.

'Will Maria be able to make it from England?' he couldn't resist asking. She hadn't appeared with the child yet, and Sean might still be holding out, but he had heard a rumour.

'She will.' Sean looked across the carpark as if there was something interesting to see.

'You haven't seen her for a while.' Father Duggan affected a casual tone, as if 'a while' was a few weeks or a few months.

'No, indeed. Listen, I must rescue Maureen there, before she gets roped into helping Eileen with the book fair. She has enough on her plate. Bye, Father. See you during the week.' He touched his forehead and strode over to the women. He had changed his mind, in his own time. He didn't need a homily now from the priest, or even a word of praise. That would mean admitting that he had been wrong all this time.

Maureen was blue with the cold, but she had escaped the book-fair trap. They turned and waved to Father Duggan as they went out the gate, fighting the blustery wind. The priest turned back into his church. He loved the special peace that settled in there after the last Mass on Sunday. He had the familiar sense of ease, having given a good sermon and had a nice chat with a few of the parishioners on their way out. The last altar boy scurried past him whispering, 'Goodbye, Father. See you next Sunday.'

He nodded at the boy. The smell of just-extinguished candles reached his nostrils as he sat in the front row, looking up at the altar. He sighed. It looked as if Sean had finally given in, thank God. His prayers had been answered. That child must be over a year old, by now. Mothers have a terrible time, he thought, looking across at the Lady Altar, with its statue of the Madonna and child. Poor Maureen must be tormented, missing all the things a granny should see, like a first tooth coming through, and the first step. And Maria was over there in England, a young girl trying to cope with everything by herself, without her own mother's advice. He sent up a fervent little prayer that everything would work out all right for them.

Noreen hadn't felt so good for ages. Seamus helped her into the car and folded her wheelchair. He wondered what she was up to, visiting a solicitor in the middle of the week, without Joe around. Mr Delaney the solicitor stood in the doorway of the converted Georgian house on the square, waiting to make sure she got safely installed in the taxi. He was known to be a gentleman. As far as Seamus could remember, he had lost his wife a few years back to cancer and had gone into his shell a bit ever since. He waved a brief salute as they drove off, and then turned and closed the big black door.

'Back to the home, is it?' Seamus shouted.

'Yes, Seamus, I think I've had enough excitement for one day,' she said, catching his eye in the rear-view mirror.

'Getting your affairs organised?' he bellowed.

'Yes, Seamus, and I feel a lot better for it.'

She wouldn't rise to the bait. Seamus was a notorious gossip. The news would be out all over the town and people would be looking at the house before she got a chance to tell Joe.

Seamus smiled at her in the mirror as he pulled into the nursing-home carpark.

'There you are, Mrs Shaw. Back before you even knew you were gone.'

He jumped out to help her.

'I don't know what to write in this speech,' said Sean, sighing and putting down his pen for the umpteenth time.

He reminded Maureen of Hugh doing his maths homework, years ago. She looked up from the seating plan that Aileen had sent her to look at. The smell of fresh gloss paint on the skirting-boards in the living-room had driven them to sit in the kitchen by the stove, and Maureen was savouring its cosy comfort. Sean was huffing and puffing over the speech, and had even volunteered to make a pot of tea, he was so distracted.

'What have you got, so far?' she asked.

'Nothing, really. I want it to be funny, but I can't think of any funny stories about Aileen.'

'Why does it have to be funny? Can you not just say nice things about her, without being funny?'

'But there's nothing very interesting, is there? She's always worked hard in school, she was a good girl, and now she's doing well for herself in England.'

'I'm sure you can make it sound a bit more inspiring than that.' Maureen knew better than to make any suggestions. He was just thinking out loud.

Sean nibbled the top of his pen, scribbled out a few

422

lines and settled down again. Maureen didn't know why she was checking the seating plan. She didn't know half of Aileen and Paul's friends. She noticed there were only nine names instead of ten on one of the round tables, and wondered if someone had dropped out. Maybe they couldn't travel, or something. She made a note for Aileen in case it was a mistake.

Aileen came home on the Sunday before the wedding and her excitement was contagious. Every evening that week, when Sean got home from work he found Maureen and Aileen plotting at the kitchen table, discussing the minutiae of flowers, confetti and brown and white bread rolls.

Aileen was radiant. Compared to Maria, she had always seemed a bit dull. Like a brown female bird, blending into the background. She just went quietly about her life, not rocking any boats. But now, as the day of the wedding approached, she seemed to have an inner glow that made Sean look at her differently. He felt a bit excluded from all the female bustle. They told him he wouldn't be interested, when he asked what on earth they could still be talking about. He escaped to the sitting-room. It was a haven of normality, with the nine o'clock news telling him that the real world continued about its business as usual.

Maureen couldn't sleep on Wednesday night, tossing and turning and trying to calm the flutters in her stomach. Maria and Molly were due to fly in to Knock Airport with Paul on Thursday morning. She wasn't sure how Sean would handle things, and she didn't want anything to spoil Aileen's big day on Friday.

Aileen was up at seven on Thursday, making tea for her father when he came down for breakfast.

'You're up early, love. Could you not sleep?'

'No. Only one more day to go, and I can't wait to see Paul!' She jiggled up and down in front of the stove as the first wisps of steam escaped the kettle. 'Dad?' She turned to him, frowning anxiously.

'Yes, love?'

'It'll be all right, won't it?'

'It'll be grand. Paul is a great fella, and you'll be happy with him. Enjoy yourself tomorrow. You're only a bride once.'

Aileen shook her head. 'I didn't mean that, but it doesn't matter.'

She wet the tea and slipped the cosy onto the teapot. He liked his tea very stewed.

'Thanks, love.' He went to the cupboard under the sink to get a shoe-brush and briskly polished his shoes while he was waiting for the tea to draw. With one foot balanced on a kitchen chair, he said, 'It's normal to have nerves, you know. It's a sign of how seriously you're taking the whole thing. It's good, really.'

'I know.'

'I'm glad you're having the wedding here. It wouldn't have been the same over in England.'

424

He poured the tea and buttered two slices of Maureen's crumbly brown soda bread, and coated them with thick home-made marmalade.

Aileen looked at him. He would be like a fish out of water over there. In London there would be too many variables outside of his control. Here in Carraroe, he was a big man; Headmaster, Choir Leader and Pillar of the Community. He could stay in control, ignoring the things he didn't like. She had a momentary flicker of pity for him but then, as she sipped her mug of coffee, she dispelled it. He had made his own choices.

'Your mother must be having a lie-in,' he said, looking at his watch. 'She had a restless night.' He stood up and brushed the crumbs off his navy blazer. 'Well, enjoy your last day as a single girl! Give my regards to Paul, and I'll be home at about half four.' He kissed her on the cheek as she half rose from her chair.

'Bye, Dad. See you later.' The back door slammed shut. Tears stung her eyes as she watched him passing the kitchen window. He waved at her. She forced a smile and waved back. Maureen came downstairs in her dressing-gown and found Aileen sobbing at the sink.

'What's the matter, love?'

She hugged her and Aileen inhaled the scent of talcum powder and freshly showered skin like a tonic. She clung to her mother, who stood with her feet firmly planted on the kitchen floor in her sheepskin slippers, and Aileen's head nestled under her chin. They stood like that for a while. The tap dripped on to the pile of washing-up suds, in the sink, making a hole like a volcano, and the birds outside started twittering as the dull winter daylight crept into the sky.

When Aileen came up for air, her cheeks were pink, and her hair was still in a night-time tangle.

'Sorry, Mam. It's just that he didn't say anything about Maria coming home today, and I –'

'He knows well that Maria is coming home today. This is just his way of dealing with it. Don't worry, everything will be fine.'

'But why does it always have to be his way of dealing with it that matters? What about the rest of us?' Aileen had pushed the kettle back on to the stove and was cutting bread with agitated strokes.

Maureen sighed and sat down. 'Maybe some of it is my fault. For our generation, the man's word was law, so I'm not a great one for challenging him. Give him a bit of leeway. He's coping with this as well as he can.'

'Coping with what?'

'You all growing up on him.'

Aileen snorted. 'What's so hard about that?'

'It makes him feel old, I suppose.'

'And does it not make you feel old?'

'Sometimes. But mothers are different. I can look at the next generation, like Molly, and please God, your children, and take pleasure in it.'

'So why can't he?' Aileen made another pot of tea.

'Because he has to lose something first.'

'What do you mean?'

'He has to let his little girls go, and accept that you've turned into women.'

'Well, as long as he doesn't upset Maria. It's taken a lot for her to come back, and I don't want him to spoil it.'

'He won't. I promise. Now, what time do we need to leave for the airport to collect them all? Will you be all right driving on those windy roads? I wonder if Molly will remember me?'

Aileen ate her breakfast, and while she chatted to her mother, something was gradually sinking in. Her father had already let her go a long time ago, when she moved to London. She wondered if he would ever be able to let go of Maria.

Chapter Fifty

'How are you feeling?' Joe's mother asked him on Friday morning.

'Incredibly nervous. I wish she knew I was going to be there.'

'Her sister would never have invited you to the wedding if she thought it would upset Maria.'

'But still. I don't know what to say to her.'

'Just talk to her the same as you do on the phone. The only difference is that you'll be face to face.' She resisted the temptation to straighten the knot on Joe's tie. He looked good in his new navy suit. Like a young doctor, nearly.

'Do you not think I should ring Maria, and see if she minds?'

'No. If Aileen wants it to be a surprise, you should go along with it. She knows Maria even better than you do.'

'So I'll just turn up at the church?'

'You could go a bit early, and get the lie of the land. If Maria is a bridesmaid, though, she won't arrive until just before the bride, so you probably won't get a chance to talk to her before the Mass.'

Joe took one last look in the hall mirror and straightened his tie. Outside, he climbed into his new blue Nissan Micra and waved to his mother as she watched him from the front door. He beeped the horn as he turned the corner in the road.

It shouldn't take more than an hour and a half to get to Carraroe, he calculated. He had plenty of time. He was hungry, but he couldn't eat anything. His mouth was so dry he had only been able to sip a coffee. For once, his mother hadn't nagged him to eat a good breakfast.

He was almost relieved when a tractor pulled out in front of him on the Leenane road. He had to slow down to thirty miles an hour, and no one would expect him to overtake on this narrow winding road. He could just concentrate on driving slowly and still have room in his brain to think. He still couldn't believe his mother had sold the house. When he got home one Friday a few weeks ago, he had two big shocks.

The first had come in the post; a gilded, hallmarked envelope with an invitation to the wedding, and a handwritten note from Aileen.

'I really hope you can be there, Joe. It would mean a lot to Maria, and to me. I feel a bit responsible for keeping you two apart when I hid your letter, but maybe now there's a chance

for things to work out. It's a surprise, so please don't mention it to her.

Hope to see you there, Aileen Hardy.'

His mother had clapped her hands. 'That's great, Joe!'

He couldn't see how it could be so great. 'But Maria doesn't know about it.'

'No, but Aileen knows. Trust me, it's a good sign! Come and have your tea. I have other news for you.'

Joe sat with her at the kitchen table and she told him her plan. She had already accepted an offer on the house, for more than she was expecting, and the sale would go through in a few weeks.

'But where will we live?'

'I've bought a bungalow out on the Castlebar road. I'll never be able to cope with stairs again. I have some chance of independence with a bungalow, and I can get some alterations done.'

'Already? You've bought a place already?'

'Well, I've put an offer in, and it's accepted. I'll show you. It's lovely. Three bedrooms and a little garden that I can manage.'

'Are you not upset about losing this place?' He waved around the high-ceilinged kitchen. The house had been in her family for generations.

'Of course I am. And I'm sorry about losing the surgery for you. But we have to be practical. This way, we can free up some money for you and Maria and Molly, and I can live in the bungalow, and have someone coming in every day to help me with cleaning and things.'

'You did it to free up money for me?'

'Partly. It's better to give it to you now, rather than in twenty years' time when I pop my clogs and you have loads of your own money. Now is when you need it, while you're a student.'

Joe looked down at the table and gulped. 'So I can stay in college and still ask Maria to come back from England?'

'That's the idea,' she said briskly. He had absolutely no excuse now. Let him get on with it. She wouldn't interfere any more. The rest was up to him.

His old mother was most definitely back. But this time it was different. Joe smiled at her. 'What would I do without you?'

Joe rehearsed a little speech as he got closer to Carraroe. The tractor pulled into a gateway and he found himself accelerating to seventy miles an hour, eager now to get there. On one corner, he nearly lost his grip on the road, and slowed down, remembering his mother's accident. The sun came out as he crossed the mountains at Maam, and a rainbow curved across the skyline, reminding him of the card he had sent to Maria.

The coffee he had gulped down before he left was burning a hole in the lining of his stomach as he drove into the village, looking for the church.

Hugh drove Maria and Molly to the church early, so that Pauline could take charge of the little girl. Molly was delighted with her new red dress, and all the attention from her grandparents. She happily went off for a walk with Pauline, waving back at Maria, who stayed outside the church. Hugh started his ushering duties, and went to direct the other early arrivals into the carpark at the back of the church to leave room at the front for the family cars. Maria stood by herself on the front steps of the church, adjusting the bodice of her deep-red velvet dress. Everyone would be giving her an extra look over. Had she put on weight? Did she look different, or depressed, or destitute?

There were photographs of her in her white Communion dress and veil on these steps, and five years later, her as a twelve-year-old, squirming in a horrible aubergine-coloured Confirmation outfit. Now here she was, about to be a bridesmaid. Maybe one day she might even get married here.

Inside, Father Duggan came sweeping down the central aisle, his eyes swivelling from side to side, doing a last-minute check on everything. He really enjoyed celebrating weddings. It was his favourite ceremony. He smiled benignly at the unfamiliar faces in the pews – friends over from England, obviously. Not many locals, he noticed. He wondered how many of them were Catholics. He saw Maria standing in the porch. 'Maria, I'm delighted to see you back.' He grasped her two cold white hands in his big warm ones.

'Thanks, Father,' she said, smiling nervously.

'Where's the little one? Did you not bring her?' He

was looking around, as if Molly might be perched on the holy-water font, or hiding behind Maria's dress.

'Pauline took her for a walk. She'd never sit still for an hour, so we're trying to tire her out beforehand.'

'Good idea. You don't want her crying at the moment of the vows, do you? I must go and get organised. We can have a nice chat later.'

Maria turned to watch people arriving, and gasped as she saw Pauline and Joe coming in the gate, each holding one of Molly's hands. They walked her along, chanting, *'One, two, three, wheee!'* and lifting her up, giggling, into the air.

Her cheeks were red with cold, but she was laughing and saying, 'Again! Again!' each time her feet touched the ground.

Joe looked really comfortable, holding Molly's mittened hand, and he was grinning like mad at Pauline as they approached. What was he doing here? Did everyone but she know that he was coming? She would kill Aileen. She just had time to fix a smile on her face before Joe glanced up.

She had never seen him blush before. He looked back down at Molly, and let go of her hand.

Pauline lifted Molly onto her hip, not caring that she was creasing her new Paul Costello suit. 'Come on, Molly. Let's go inside to the nice warm church,' she said, pulling off Molly's mittens. She winked at Maria as she passed through the door.

Joe just stood there in his navy suit.

'You're looking very smart,' said Maria. She felt suddenly shy.

His Adam's-apple bobbed up and down. 'You look gorgeous. I love that colour on you.'

'Well, I thought I'd go for the whole 'scarlet woman' look, while I'm at it!' She laughed.

'Aileen invited me. I hope you don't mind?'

'Not at all. I was going to ring you, while I'm home. I wasn't sure if I'd see you though. I thought you might be busy, studying or looking after your mother, or something.' Why did she always have to gabble when she was nervous?

'Molly is getting big.'

'Yes. She likes you, doesn't she?' Maria smiled. It seemed such a ridiculous thing to say to the child's father.

Hugh came bursting into the porch, his breath steaming. 'They're coming, Maria! Are you ready?' he asked excitedly. He had abandoned all pretence of mature, brotherly indifference to the proceedings. Maria nodded, giving her dress a final tweak.

Joe pushed open the door of the church, saying over his shoulder, 'I'll see you later, then. Is it all right if I sit with Pauline and Molly?' He didn't want to take any liberties. Not now, when he was so close.

'Of course it is, Joe. She's your daughter as well.'

Maria smiled at him. He blinked as if to photograph the moment. He carried the smile imprinted on the inside of his eyelids. That smile. It looked to him like a mammy to daddy smile. A forever smile.

Hugh made a rapid exit to open the car door for his mother, and escort her up the church steps.

Sean stood up and looked over the sea of expectant faces. Not a very big sea, but a bit intimidating, none the less. He recognised only about half of the guests. He had just briefly met the best man outside the church before the ceremony. During the meal, he had warmed to the confident young merchant banker, Paul's best friend. Now in the silence that this young man had commanded, with the clink of a teaspoon on his crystal wineglass, everyone was waiting for Sean's words of wisdom.

He cleared his throat and looked across the top table at Aileen, who was looking expectantly at him, and then at Maria, who was half-turned towards him with a fixed, nervous smile. He wished for the tenth time that he had rehearsed the speech with Maureen. He sipped his water. Paul was giving him a sympathetic eye, waiting for his own turn to stand up.

'I was having terrible problems with this speech last week, wasn't I, Maureen?' he said, glancing over at her.

She nodded vehemently, raising her eyes to heaven, playing to the crowd. A low wave of sympathetic laughter flowed around the room.

'I was really stuck, trying to think of funny stories about Aileen. Because that's what fathers of the bride are supposed to do. Tell little anecdotes about her running around in her nappies, having teenage tantrums and bringing home her ugly first boyfriend.'

He stopped and sipped his water again. 'But I soon realised that there aren't any stories like that about Aileen. She was always a good girl, and now she's grown up into such a nice person, that there's nothing even a little bit disreputable that you could pin on her!'

'Hear, hear,' said Paul, kissing Aileen.

'Aww,' said the best man, grimacing for the audience.

Laughter filled the cosy hotel dining-room.

'Aileen worked hard all the way through school. She didn't even go through a rebellious phase when she was a teenager. Then she made the big leap, and went off to London to get a job. She's doing very well for herself at the bank. She has lots of friends, whom I'm glad to have the opportunity to meet.' He waved around the room.

'She met Paul five years ago, and they got married today, after a *respectable* courtship.' He coughed, and there were a few discreet giggles around the room. 'Nothing striking about that, you might say.'

Paul held Aileen's trembling hand under the white linen tablecloth. Surely Sean could have come up with a few more imaginative things to say? He had managed to make Aileen sound completely dull.

Sean took a deep breath. 'But I have to tell you that the most courageous thing that Aileen ever did, was to teach her old dad the biggest lesson of his life.'

He stopped and looked over at Aileen. She looked at Maureen. Silence filled the room. No one even moved to fill a glass or stir their coffee.

'Aileen was the only one in our family who really

stuck by Maria, when she went over to London to have Molly.'

Maria flushed the same colour as her dress. The tears that stood in the corners of Aileen's eyes rolled down her cheeks. She didn't wipe them away, but reached across Paul to squeeze Maria's hand. Sean cleared his throat. Joe was staring at him, ashen-faced, with Molly sitting on his knee.

Then Molly clapped her hands and broke the spell. Everyone laughed, and she looked around, grinning, not used to quite such a big and responsive audience. Chairs shunted on the wooden floor. Flushed faces gulped at wine. Smiling eyes connected across the round tables.

'So,' said Sean coughing loudly, to get their attention again.

A respectful silence descended again.

'After being a teacher all my life, I would like to thank Aileen for being my teacher. She is responsible today, not only for starting her own family by marrying Paul, but for reuniting our family, after too long apart.'

He sat down suddenly. The room erupted with clapping and cheering. The best man had the presence of mind to propose a toast to the bride and groom, and Sean didn't even notice his own omission. As they all stood, Sean's eyes met Maria's, and amidst the noise they raised their glasses to each other in a silent toast.

THE END